Dark Lord

FALCONFAR

BOOK ONE

Dark Lord

ED GREENWOOD

SOLARIS

First published in 2007.
Mass Market edition published 2008 by Solaris
an imprint of BL Publishing
Games Workshop Ltd
Willow Road
Nottingham
NG7 2WS
UK

www.solarisbooks.com

ISBN-13: 978 1 84416 617 6
ISBN-10: 1 84416 617 1

Cover illustration by Jon Sullivan

10 9 8 7 6 5 4 3 2 1

A CIP catalogue record for this book is available from the
British Library.

Designed & typeset by BL Publishing
Printed and bound in the UK.

Chapter One

SHE WAS CRYING as she swung the sword. Tears of pain and rage and desperation, as the knights in black armor crowded close around her, their black blades hacking ruthlessly. Sparks flew from her armor as she reeled, driven by one sword blow back into another. They were killing her, she was going to—

No! Don't! I won't watch, I—

But he could not look away as laughter echoed inside closed black helms, and long white feathers swirled in a swiftly spreading cloud.

They're hacking off her wings!

The Aumrarr fought on, her shattered armor clanging, as blood stained the snow-white curves above her shoulders. It was hopeless; she was doomed, whether he shouted or cowered. The Dark Helms were too many and too vicious.

She shrieked as a black blade thrust through one wing, and twisted wildly away to meet the biting black steel of another Dark Helm, a cut that tore away an armor plate, lacings and tatters of torn underjerkin spinning with it.

Rod had a glimpse of bare, sweat-slick hip as the winged woman threw herself around at the foe that had wounded her, stabbing upwards with her silver sword.

The Dark Helm stumbled back, hissing in pain, and the Aumrarr's war-steel came out of him dark with blood, to swing—

Too late. Rod winced back into shuddering darkness as two Dark Helms shouted in glee as they brought their blades down and sliced off a wing in a welter of blood that sent the sobbing Aumrarr to her knees.

In half a breath they were all over her, kicking and stabbing, battering her remaining wing down into bloody ruin. Armor shrieked and clanged in protest as it was hacked from her, her vainly defending sword broke in a whirl of bright spell-sparks against seven black blades, shards flashing… and then it was over. She lay huddled and still, severed armor straps strewn about her, snow-white belly slit open and lifeblood steaming. The Dark Helms spat on her, laughed a farewell, and strolled away.

Leaving Rod staring into her agonized, pleading eyes.

Emerald green eyes, wet with tears, yet not yet dimmed in death, and somehow seeing him, *really* seeing him…

And Rod Everlar came awake screaming, clawing sweat-soaked sheets as he sat up to stare wide-eyed across the familiar darkness of his bedroom.

* * *

HIS THROAT WAS raw. Panting, Rod shook his head, trying to swallow and hoping the silvery chaos dancing in front of his eyes would clear. That had been a bad one.

Hooh.

His dreams of Falconfar were always vivid—he glanced toward the notebook, ready beside the bed—and sometimes held huge dark snakes and other menacing monsters, but this…

"This takes the…"

His voice was a thick croak, and the silver mists wouldn't clear. He shook his head again, and—

Something large, dark and heavy slammed down onto the bed from above. Rod's heart leaped and froze, all at once.

It was on his *legs*…

Frantically he kicked out, trying to scramble up and back at the same time. There was nothing but bare plaster ceiling overhead, nothing up there that could fall so heavily without half the house falling down. This couldn't be hap—

"Mercy!" the voice sobbed out of the darkness, from very close by. On the bed. "Mercy, Dark Lord!"

The weight on his legs was moving, and panting as hard as he was, and there was something warm and wet…

Rod got his legs out from under the heavy weight at last and grabbed for the flashlight he kept on the floor beside the bed, swinging himself away and up to his feet just as fast as he could.

Light snapped into brilliant being. He whirled, snatching his Olde Excalibur letter opener out of the book he'd left it in and brandishing it as if he were some sort of armored knight instead of a hairy, skinny man wearing only boxer shorts.

The light gleamed off the point of his letter opener, and Rod found himself staring over it and into the pleading emerald eyes and pain-twisted face of the woman from his dream, the blood-drenched stumps of her severed wings jutting up from her shoulders.

She was on her hands and knees on the end of his bed, trembling violently, amid a dark red sea of soaked sheets and dripping, hanging-down innards. Skin whiter than his sheets where it wasn't dark with gore, long black hair tangled and matted… and those eyes.

Her jaw quivered in pain as she gasped, "Dark Lord! Help me!"

Rod stared at her in disbelief, shaking his head without really noticing. This couldn't be happening, this… He must still be dreaming, this must all be part of it…

Dark Lord?

"I—I'll—"

I'll what? What the hell would I do, if I were awake?

"I'll get an ambulance," Rod snapped, striding across the room to the phone. Letter opener down, receiver up; an old, ugly rotary, heavy and solid and black, reassuring to hold on to in this crazy drea—

Something silver flashed bright moonlight as it spun past his cheek to *thunk* solidly into the wall. Something that left severed coils of phone cord dancing in Rod's face, and the dial tone of the heavy receiver in his hand suddenly silent. He whirled to face whatever it was in the direction it had come from, aiming his flashlight like a gun.

Rod found himself looking at the blood-slicked, clenched and trembling hands of the woman on his bed, who promptly cried, "No! No one here must know, or your power will be ended, and with it all our hope! Dark Lord, you must undo the evil you have wrought on us!"

Rod Everlar stared at her, dazedly wondering why he'd never bought a gun, and then wondering what he'd do with one right now, if he had it. She was dying, she should be dead already, and… and women didn't have wings and snow-white skin, and didn't swing swords while wearing armor. Or hurl daggers, either.

Except in Falconfar. In his dreams.

He was going mad, he must be. If he'd drunk anything stronger than soda this week, he'd be blaming this on booze right now. This just couldn't be happening.

Not even in his books did… did women with wings who'd just been gutted and left to die fall onto the beds of lonely thriller writers in the middle of the night. Any night, drunken or otherwise.

Transfixed in the beam of his flashlight, the shuddering Aumrarr sank belly-down on the bed, her strength plainly failing.

"Please," she whispered, eyes desperate, her voice strangely purring. "Please…"

Rod shone his flashlight up at the ceiling—whole and unmarked—and wildly around the room to make sure there was no one else lurking anywhere. Not that it sounded like it. He lived alone, and the creaks and small moans of the old house were familiar things.

This... *visitor*... was not.

The flashlight showed him a wicked-looking dagger buried in the wall beside his head. Its hilt was dark and wet with blood, but he flung the phone down and seized it unhesitatingly. Grateful to have some sort of weapon, Rod wrenched it out of his wood paneling with some effort; it had bitten deep.

"Dark Lord," the Aumrarr moaned, her voice fainter. She tried to say something else, but it came out as wet, choking sounds.

Rod took a step closer to the bed, waving the dagger. The room smelled of blood, and sweat... and fear.

"Get out," he snarled suddenly, as something wild rose inside him, sharp and sudden. Fear. His own fear. "Get out of my house!"

He lived alone by choice. He didn't want the world thrusting itself into his dreams, didn't...

The woman on the bed moved, but only to sag forward, shards of shoulder-armor clattering briefly. She wasn't going anywhere, she was dying on his bed for chrissakes.

When was this nightmare going to end?

The floor was cold under his bare feet. The moonlight faded as he left the ruined phone behind and strode back to his bed. This was enough!

He was going to wake up, somehow; he was going to leave his imaginary world of Falconfar behind and go watch a... No, no, he was going to read a good book. A book written by someone else, one that had nothing at all to do with wizards and dragons and Dark Helms and the soaring castles of Falconfar. He was...

Coming to a stop, disgusted. Staring up at him, she reeked of blood and urine and… Hell, look at all the blood!

Must wake up, must jolt myself out of this somehow.

Rod reached out an angry hand. "Come on, get up and out of here! Get—"

Matted black hair lashed his fingers. Beyond it her shoulder felt solid. Hard and real… and quivering under his fingers.

He snatched his hand back. "Get out, damn you!"

Her head sank down, night-black hair hiding that pleading face, and she collapsed into sobs.

Rod waved the dagger wildly in the air, feeling very far indeed from being a hero of Falconfar or anywhere else, and wished—God, how he wished—he'd wake up, and leave all this behind.

The Aumrarr weren't real; they were something he'd invented for Falconfar, a race of warrior-women who did good, flying over the forests of the dream-realm with their long, snow-white wings, taking messages from one hold to another, and fighting wolves and worse.

Hmmph. Since Holdoncorp's game designers had gotten their grubby hands on Falconfar, much worse. The Dark Helms, for one, and…

The dying Aumrarr slid sideways off his bed, dragging his sheets with her. They were now more red than white, and there was a puddle of blood on his mattress.

"Out!" he roared again, waving the dagger as if it were some sort of magic wand that could banish her and her mess, and take him into comforting wakefulness in his favorite chair three rooms away, all at once.

She was now arching and shaking in agony, her sobs as faint and strangled as the mewings of a kitten, but those long, trembling fingers were... were reaching out to clutch him around the ankles!

Rod jerked back. Too late. Her grip was surprisingly strong, and he had to slam his hand down onto the bed, dagger and all, to keep from falling. His knuckles burned, and with a snarl he bent over and grabbed at her shoulders, trying to pluck her away—

Pain. Sharp, stabbing... Finger sliced open on jagged metal. He'd cut himself on her effing armor!

Rod Everlar flung up his hand and stared at the blood and the throbbing wound.

Oh, Jesus Christ. I *am* awake.

HE SWAYED, SHAKING his hand as if he could wave his cut away, and shaking his head even harder. This couldn't be happening; this wasn't happening! Dreams just didn't become *real* like this.

And then the woman at his feet clawed at his leg and curled her shoulder up against him. He flinched away from the sharpness of her torn armor, reeling and almost falling.

And then he *was* falling, hands waving wildly. Flashlight gone, dagger bouncing onto the bed, sitting down helplessly hard against it as blazing emerald eyes and desperate fingers clutched at him like talons... Her breath was warm and smelled spicy, almost like cinnamon, as her softness glided up his own hairy skin. Rod fumbled to get his feet under himself, to be able to—and then stiffened. Warm, wet lips were sucking at his injured hand!

He tried to yank it away, but her cool, trembling fingers were surprisingly strong as she held him, and where her mouth and tongue touched, there was… icy relief. Pain ebbing swiftly.

There was a sort of glow down there, around her cheeks, as if her mouth was full of dancing blue moonlight that he'd be able to see when she lifted her head.

She did that, eyes very large and dark, and her mouth was briefly full of blue fire.

And Rod's hand tingled. The pain was gone. Gone with the cut and the blood. His fingers were bare, clean, and… whole.

She held them up for him to see better as he curled and flexed them in astonishment.

"Please aid us, Dark Lord," she murmured, the purr stronger and the sobbing sound almost gone. There was still pain in her face, but she seemed stronger, somehow.

She'd been strong enough to overbalance and pounce on him, that much was certain.

"Please. You are Falconfar's only hope, and my only hope, too."

Rod Everlar stared into those anxious, beautiful emerald eyes, and took a deep breath. He managed to sound fairly calm, he thought, as he asked, "Who are you? And what did you just do to me?"

"Lord Archwizard, I am Taeauna, Taeauna of the Aumrarr. I did nothing, 'twas your blood that healed me. And yourself, for you are of Falconfar as surely as I am."

Tay-awna. Taeauna of the Aumrarr, the winged women he'd thought up. Rod knew he was doing a lot of head shaking, but he just couldn't seem to stop finding reasons to do so. Falconfar?

The world he'd dreamed up. Or rather dreamed about, night after night, until the images had grown so vivid that he could recall them end-to-end upon awakening, and write them down.

Falconfar, that rolling land of vast forests and distant snow-tipped mountains where castles rose up from bare hilltops and warriors rode out to hunt stags. And magic worked. And monsters lurked.

Falconfar: a realm of wizards and dragons and the Aumrarr. Shaped by his imagination, his dreams. A place that wasn't real, couldn't be real, a world he'd copyrighted for God's sake, and written seven books about, and…

"Dark Lord?" Taeauna asked him, her impossibly white face within easy reach of his arm, its sheen of sweat shining in the moonlight. "You seem… angered. Mind-mazed. Please aid us. I-I am desperate."

Dark Lord. There was that phrase again. What was a Dark Lord? He knew what the Dark Helms were: Holdoncorp's creations, sinister villains, ruthless slayers in black armor. The Holdoncorp game designers had thought up many smaller mischiefs, too, but he knew about them. He knew all about Falconfar.

So what was a Dark Lord, and how had he become one?

He stared into the Aumrarr's gravely anxious gaze, and then around his room. The severed phone, the blood-soaked bed sheets, the sliced-off end of an armor strap that was dangling from Taeauna's shoulder to brush his own gut. He could *feel* its caress.

He wasn't dreaming. This was all real.

Or he was losing his mind.

His eyes fell to his wrinkled boxer shorts, covered with its familiar greeting of "Hello, Sexy!" as well as spatters of dark, wet blood that wasn't his own. Blood that shouldn't—couldn't—be there. But was.

"Suppose you tell me," he said carefully, "how I became a 'Dark Lord.' And what this evil is, that I've done. Uh, and who 'us' is, that I've done it to. And what you want of me."

The Aumrarr stared at him. "So it's true. One of the wizards has stolen your memories."

"Stolen my—?"

She flinched back from his shout as if he'd thrust one of those black swords right into her, and Rod swallowed whatever he'd been going to shout, waved an angry hand through the air between them as if to clear something aside, and snapped, "Explain. Please."

"Yes, Lord Archwizard," she agreed hastily, sliding sideways off him with more grace than he'd thought any gravely injured person would be able to manage. On her knees, shattered armor dangling from her, she began, "There are not many of us Aumrarr left, for Falconfar has grown darker. There are ever more Dark Helms, the wizards command fearsome beasts to prowl and strike at will, and..."

Rod found himself staring at Taeauna's front, bared almost down to her crotch. He'd seen her intestines spilling sickeningly out of a great gash, but that wound was now gone. Under a darkening smear of drying blood, her stomach was flat and whole.

"How did you...?" he blurted, gesturing almost helplessly at her.

Her eyes grew larger, and fear came back into her face.

"Have you forgotten everything, lord?" she whispered. "Your blood healed me, just as it healed you. You have that power. The wizards have lusted after it for as long as Falconaar can remember."

Rod frowned. "Falconaar? And my blood heals— why? Because I'm 'Lord Archwizard?' Or the 'Dark Lord?'"

Taeauna closed her eyes, sighed so hard she started to tremble again, and then opened them and said patiently, like a teacher instructing a child, "Your writings change Falconfar, and every sage and wizard knows it. We Aumrarr, whom you created, know it. There have been other writers, many others, before you, but their creations are now but dim shadows before the fire of your pen. Thousands upon thousands of people in this, your world, visit Falconfar in their dreams, and their dreaming gives us strength, too, but it is the scribes of this world that anchor and shape us, and you are the strongest of them all. So strong that we Falconaar, the people of Falconfar, call you the Lord Archwizard, where none have been so named before you."

Rod stared at her, and then looked across the room at the bookshelves he couldn't quite see in the gloom, picturing the row of seven books there, with their familiar, vivid covers, and... and he looked back at Taeauna, at this slender, blood-covered and very real woman kneeling in his bedroom, and forced himself to say, "You called me Dark Lord, too. What's this 'evil' I've done?"

"The rise of the Dark Helms," she whispered, sounding suddenly scared again. As if she expected him to hit her. "Ever more monsters, and the drifting spells that twist hares and stags and cattle into things of claws and fangs that come for us. 'Tis said you've gone mad, mad with power, or that the wizards have struck at your mind with their spells. Even the stones sprout fangs, so men dare not climb seeking mushrooms in the caves anymore."

The Mouths of Stone. More Holdoncorp mischief, like the Dark Helms. Almost all the monsters would be their work, too. In his books, a monster was met, fought, and killed. Only in the computer games did beasts sprout in endless numbers, springing up to menace no matter how fervently players slew them.

Rod looked toward the door and said something rude, spitting out the words slowly and deliberately. The room that held his computer—and the Holdoncorp games—was down a hallway beyond the door.

He'd hated what Holdoncorp had done to Falconfar, hated it enough to reverse and lessen some of their misdeeds in his later books, but their relentless rush to turn his quaint, cozy little world of forests and castles into a few enclaves of desperate knights trying to hold off Hitlerian hosts of marching Dark Helms had soured him on the whole world. Besides his dreams and the odd entry in his notebook, these days he seldom thought or wrote about Falconfar. He'd gone back to the grim-jawed thrillers of spies and missiles and gunfire in the night that sold so head-shakingly well, and...

"Lord?" that soft, purring voice came again, hesitantly. "I came seeking you because we need you. Falconfar needs you. If you turn me away now, the darkness will soon drown us all."

Rod stared almost helplessly at the woman kneeling before him in her slashed and bloody armor. "I... Taeauna, I'm having a hard time believing any of this. I mean..."

He waved empty hands, clawing the air as if he could snatch some sort of answer out of it, but didn't really expect to. Then he started to say more, but knew not what, and settled for shaking his head in helpless dismissal.

Falconfar darkening, just like the real world around him. Society ever grimmer, lawsuits and terrorism and pollution, dire warnings of oil and everything else running out...

Falconfar had been his dream of what he wanted to see. What his dreams showed him, over and over again, bright and beautiful. Glorious skies of magnificent dawns and sunsets above fairytale castles that crowned grassy heights among vast, rolling forests, dragons flying lazily by at a safe distance...

He stared at the woman on her knees before him. Those emerald eyes, grave and anxious, never left him.

Taeauna, she'd called herself. Taeauna of the Aumrarr. She was slender, graceful, and probably taller than he was if she stood up, even without her wings. He'd felt her weight, her touch, even had her blood on him. Right now—he glanced down—it was drying, dark and sticky, on his legs and his underwear. He could smell her. She was real. Falconfar was real.

And suddenly, Rod Everlar very much wanted to see those castles, bright in the morning. And gold at sunset, as soft purple dusk stole in over battlements, and torches and lanterns were lit.

He didn't much want to see Dark Helms, or meet an angry dragon or wizard, but wasn't he a wizard, by Taeauna's reckoning? Couldn't he change things with a wave of his hand?

Christ, he must be going crazy.

He shook his head again, turning away, but those castles wouldn't go out of his mind.

Falconfar.

What if it *was* real?

Rod realized his heart was leaping with eager excitement, like when he was young and looked forward to Christmases and camps… and girls. Before he'd discovered just how cruel real women could be.

"Taeauna," he began slowly, starting to turn around again. And swallowing.

He wanted to see Falconfar for himself more than he'd ever wanted anything before.

And he was suddenly afraid this *was* a dream, and he'd turn and find his bedroom dark and empty, with no blood and no Taeauna. And he'd still be alone.

As alone as he'd been for so many years now, with his family and close friends all dead, losing himself in his writing, laughter and companionship something glimpsed only in books and romantic movies.

Green eyes caught and held his, and snared his breath as well.

Almost angrily he looked away from her, at the bed. Still swimming in blood. Christ, he'd be in trouble if anyone got in here and saw that.

So much blood. He shook his head and peered more closely at Taeauna. Her severed wings, of course, were still missing. "You're sure you're healed? Completely?"

She shrugged, and it was the easy movement of one who feels no great pain. "I feel well enough, lord. Your blood is pure power."

Rod smiled incredulously. "Will it work on me, too?"

"In Falconfar, any wounds that befall you will swiftly heal," the Aumrarr replied, leaning forward with her eyes shining in sudden hope, "but in this world, the swords of the Dark Helms can slay you easily."

As if her words had been a signal, there came a deafening clash of cymbals.

Rod was staggering dazedly back before he realized that the ringing shriek had been made by his bedroom window, bursting into the room in a shattering spray of shards, driven by a thrusting black-bladed sword!

Taeauna ducked under its point as swiftly as a striking snake, to snatch her dagger from the bed.

Rod shouted wordless fear as more windows broke somewhere down the hall. Black-helmed knights were hacking at his window frame, trying to chop the muntins aside so they would have room enough to climb in.

"They mean to slay us both, lord!" Taeauna shouted from beside the bed. "We must hie to Falconfar!"

Rod gaped at her. His taxes were due, and on Monday his editor was sure to call, and...

"I can't!" he started to shout, as there came a splintering crash from the far end of the house, and Taeauna bounded up from the floor, shattered armor clanging. A forest of black blades reached vainly for her amid snarls of anger, and gauntleted fists beat at the windowsill.

"Lord, we must, or we'll die!" She clutched his upper arms fiercely, her fingers like claws, and those emerald eyes blazed into his. "Falconfar *needs* you!"

Booted feet were thundering, far down the hall. Rod looked helplessly at the doorway, and then at a Dark Helm trying to climb through his missing window, armored shoulders splintering and gouging a way through the frame, and shouted, "How?"

Taeauna's smile was like a flame. "Open a dreamgate, as we did to get me here! Think of one place in Falconfar just as hard as you can. See it, dwell on what you see and feel and smell, and keep on doing that, no matter what the Dark Helms do!"

And she whirled away from him to snatch a bookshelf too heavy for him to budge away from the wall, and flung it to the floor. It crashed down, books spilling in a thunderous wave, just as the first Dark Helm raced through the doorway. Tripping on the flood of toppled books, the black knight staggered and stumbled, and Taeauna was on him like a pouncing cat, driving her dagger through the slit in his visor and wrenching his sword out of one massive gauntlet almost in one motion.

Rod's bed cracked under the hard-booted landing of the first Dark Helm through the window. Taeauna whirled around, her gaze like green flames, and shouted, "Close your *eyes*, lord! Watch not me, but *see Falconfar*!"

There was a second black knight in the hall, and a third, but Rod shut his eyes and thought of his favorite castle, thrusting up into the morning sky atop its grassy hill. The one with the great gnarled trees shading the winding lane that led up to it, to where tall, silver-armored knights with long war-horns in their hands stood guard in the sunlight, gazing out over a peaceful valley...

There were crashes, and the loud skirl and *clang* of steel ringing on steel very close by. Rod heard Taeauna grunt with effort, and then there was a ringing crash, the clanging *thud* of someone in armor falling heavily, and the skitter of glass sliding underfoot.

He was just about to open his eyes, expecting a black blade to come racing at him, when the Aumrarr laughed merrily just beside his ear, and cried, "For Falconfar!"

Blue-edged silver fire suddenly flickered around him, and the scene of the castle seemed to rush up larger and brighter before him. "Hollowtree Keep!" Taeauna said delightedly. "Lord, take us there!"

And her arms were around him, a sharp edge of armor clawing at Rod's bare shoulder and the blood-and-sweat scent of Taeauna all around him. The light at the edges of his vision was more blue than silver now, and a hurrying wind was roaring through leaves. Trying to ignore everything else, Rod peered hard at the castle gates—where the knights were now standing up, and looking in his direction.

Suddenly he was stumbling and staggering, bare-foot in the dusty lane, stubbing his foot on a tree root and almost falling, with Taeauna laughingly holding him up. The wind in his face smelled of cow dung and green, growing things, and the bright knell of a war-horn rose into the air.

And behind him, where it was darker, half a dozen black blades crashed together in the empty air of Rod Everlar's bedroom, where he and Taeauna had been standing moments before.

Chapter Two

T HE WIND MADE him shiver, and Rod abruptly realized he was standing almost naked in the land of his dreams. Falconfar!

His dream world.

Alive and vivid and sun-dappled, on all sides, with tree-cloaked hills rolling away to the horizons—and rising into purple mountains, back that way—and woods like he'd always thought Sherwood Forest must look like right beside him, across the lane… the lane that led up to a castle that was towering up into the sky, just over there.

He stared around at rustling leaves and dancing boughs. The dark and mighty trees stood on both sides of the lane, just ahead, and between them the rutted lane ran up from his bare feet, around a snake-like pair of bends, to the castle gates.

Taeauna laughed lightly beside him, and then said earnestly, "Thank you, lord. Oh, thank you!"

Rod gave her an uneasy smile and let out a breath he hadn't noticed he was holding until then. "Uh..."

She *was* taller than him. And slender, long-limbed. Graceful, too, despite her hacked and shattered armor. Bone-white skin visible here and there, where her war-plate had fallen away, sleek curves that... that... God, she was beautiful. Long, tangled night-black hair, those bright emerald eyes, lips like...

"Uh..." Rod began again. Like what? I'm supposed to be a writer, to have the words ready for...

Oh, shit. Staring at Taeauna, he waved one hand helplessly to indicate his near-nakedness, and with the other pointed urgently at the two knights, and at another man in armor who'd appeared out of the castle and was now peering their way.

Taeauna had seen them, too. She turned quickly to Rod. "Please be guided by me, lord." Her voice was low. "Keep silent, give no one your name or the titles I've addressed you by, and pretend you remember nothing of who you are or where you're from."

Rod gave her a rueful smile. "That won't be hard."

Those glorious emerald eyes were serious. "I'm very pleased that you chose Hollowtree—this is a good place—but all of Falconfar is dangerous these days, *goodman*."

"Ah. I've stopped being a lord?"

"Yes. If anyone asks if you're a wizard, do or say nothing that could be taken for agreement, nor familiarity with magic. Just act dazed."

"How will I understand anyth—"

Taeauna made a sharp chopping motion with her hand that clearly meant "be silent!" Rod obliged.

Hastening down the lane were four men: the stout armored warrior who'd stepped out between the two guards, and three bowmen in ragged clothes of what looked like soft, well-worn hides sewn together. The knight in the middle drew his sword as he strode around the first bend, and the archers readied arrows and spread out to either side of him.

Taeauna sheathed her dagger and stood waiting for them, head held high. As the knight approached, slowing warily after his boots slipped twice on moss-covered cobbles, she gently spread her hands wide in front of her, palms out to show they were empty. The archers raised their bows but kept their shafts aimed off into the trees.

All of them were peering keenly at Taeauna and at Rod—especially at Rod, covered in blood and wearing only his boxers.

"You are come to Hollowtree in strange array," the knight said flatly as he came to a halt three paces away. He was a stout, hard-faced man with an air of importance and a belt bristling with silver-hilted daggers.

Rod stared back at him. So they spoke English here. Well of course they would, if his dreams shaped things...

"Indeed, Warsword Lhauntur," Taeauna replied. "Yet we mean no harm to any here, and crave but a night's rest. Unlooked-for magic, not of our weaving, has delivered us out of desperate battle against Dark Helms."

The warsword gave her a sharp look. "You know me?"

Taeauna smiled a little bitterly. "We toasted each other in yon garden last summertide, Lhauntur. I had wings then."

Lhauntur frowned. "Brae... no. Taeauna?"

The Aumrarr nodded. "Taeauna am I. Or what is left of her."

"And this?"

"A man who came out of the fray to fight beside me... with a hayfork. Where he left his clothes, I've no idea, and know not even his naming. Worse than that, though he seems calm enough, pleasant company even, he knows not his own life nor remembrances. Are any healers guesting in Hollowtree, perchance?"

The warsword shook his head, his frowning gaze never leaving Rod. Though he appeared to make no signal, three arrows were suddenly aimed at Rod's head, riding straining bowstrings.

Rod swallowed, tried to smile, and decided it was safer to look at Taeauna than anywhere else. Pleasanter, too.

"Lord wizard!" the knight snapped suddenly, raising his sword, and Rod opened his mouth to answer without thinking. In front of his nose, Taeauna stiffened.

Oh, shit.

Quickly he asked, "Where?"

He turned his head to look behind him first, heart icy as he waited for the hiss of arrows that would slay him.

None came, so he swung around again to look at the warsword. "A wizard?"

Lhauntur sighed, and almost seemed on the verge of smiling. "As artful as a lad caught chewing in the pantry. Down, please, goodman! And keep your hands stretched out flat!"

Rod stared at him.

"You," the warsword snapped, and his mouth definitely crooked into a smile this time. An unpleasant smile.

Rod went down to his knees and then slid onto his belly, keeping his arms spread. The heels of his palms skidded away from him until his chin was resting on the moss. His boxers, now stiff with Taeauna's blood, scratched him as he moved.

The archers hastened forward, and Lhauntur's sword flashed a warning as he advanced on Taeauna.

"You understand our caution?"

"Of course," she replied calmly as she stepped back. Then pointed leather boots were treading firmly on Rod's hands, and men who smelled of rank sweat and forest earth were kneeling over him, fumbling at their pouches. A length of crude cord that looked more like an old root or a knotted length of horse's tail was produced, and Rod's wrists were quickly and snugly knotted together. Then calloused fingers took hold of Rod's armpits and hauled him to his feet.

He found himself looking into Warsword Lhauntur's cool brown eyes—down the shining length of the man's short, broad, and deadly looking sword.

"I'll gag you if I hear even the first sound of what might be a spell, wizard," the knight promised calmly. "And if I find you've been working at that cord, I'll personally break your thumbs and your forefingers." Then Lhauntur smiled and with the same ironic tone that Rod favored when dealing with publicists, added, "So be welcome in Hollowtree Keep."

Rod gave him an empty smile, and then turned to Taeauna and asked innocently, "Lady, are these bad men?"

Emerald eyes widened ere Taeauna said soothingly, "No, goodman. I've been well treated here in the past. Just do as they say." She reached out a finger to his chin, as if to guide him into looking straight into her eyes, and gave him a silent look that said as clearly as if she'd shouted it: "Don't overdo it, Dark Lord."

"Yes," Rod told her, trying to sound vague and yet contented. "Yes, of course."

Only the emerald eye that was farthest from the four Hollowtree men rolled derisively, a feat that left Rod staring at Taeauna in fascination. How did she *do* that?

Probably because I once dreamed Aumrarr could, he reminded himself ruefully, as the warsword made a curt gesture with his sword and they all started to trudge along the lane up to the castle.

THE MAP WASN'T a sheet of weathered parchment at all, but a table covered with faintly evil-smelling mud that had been painstakingly shaped into what was presumably a miniature duplicate of the landscape of Falconfar. Every inch of the terrain close to Rod bore overlapping thumbprints; it had obviously been worked and reworked with care. Large green stains undoubtedly denoted forests, and tiny slivers of wood had been whittled into castles and thrust into place atop hills.

"So, nameless goodman, mark you anything familiar?"

Lord Eldalar's question was sharp, but by now Rod was used to being regarded with suspicion. They'd retied his hands behind him after throwing a loose robe around him; beneath it, he was still barefoot and naked except for his boxers. Taeauna, on the other hand, was being treated with a respect bordering on awe.

She'd stayed close beside him, and made it clear that, wizard or not, the mind-mazed stranger was under her protection. Rod could feel her gaze on him now, watching him almost as closely, no doubt, as were Warsword Lhauntur and the gray-bearded Lord of Hollowtree.

"I'm sorry, but no, lord," Rod replied, looking up to meet gruff old Eldalar's eyes. It wasn't hard to sound honestly bewildered when that's exactly what you were.

The map, however, was fascinating. It reminded him of a wargames table he'd seen in his youth, strewn with tiny model tanks and surrounded by chainsmoking men in suspenders who were waving tape measures in the air and chuckling a lot. If you almost closed your eyes, to make the green stain look more like trees and less like colored mud, this might just be a real landscape that you were hovering over...

As if by magic...

"Where are we?" he asked, pointing with his chin down at the model terrain. "Hollowtree, yes, but where's Hollowtree on this table?"

Eldalar stared at him, frowning, and then stabbed a finger down at one of the smallest castles. "Here, of course." The old lord did everything gruffly and stiffly, it seemed. Even his magnificently embroidered tabard, or tunic or whatever it was, looked stiff.

Right now, he was thrusting his old neck out like a tortoise toward Rod, and harrumphing. "And you, goodman, came from…?"

Rod looked helplessly at Taeauna.

Who leaned forward, still clad only in shards of armor and a few straps, and said firmly, "From somewhere far beyond here, lord. Beyond Dalchace, this road runs to a moot of two rivers, and there are many smallholdings in the wedge of land between their upper courses. We were at one such, a place I saw only briefly, hight Aunduth."

So she could lie like a banker. Hmm.

Rod almost grinned. The candle-lanterns in this dark-paneled inner room stank of tallow, and the flagstones were cold underfoot, but he minded not a whit. Nor did Taeauna's lie or the cord binding his hands bother him overmuch. He was in Falconfar, and this was all real.

And for the first time in years—decades—he was having an adventure. An honest-to-God adventure. If what Taeauna had said about his power was true, he could even heal himself if he got hurt, though he felt no eagerness to let some bowman or knight with a sword test that power. From her brief warning, it seemed as if revealing he was the Dark Lord just might prove very unpleasant.

"You must be tired and hungry," the Lord of Hollowtree said suddenly, his tone a firm dismissal. "Go with Lhauntur. He'll see you both provided for."

He reached for Taeauna's shoulder, as if intending to murmur something more for her ears alone, but she slid gracefully out from under his fingers and said gently, "I thank you deeply, lord. You are as gracious as always."

Rod heard nothing but warmth in her tone, but Eldalar flushed as if she were his mother snapping a firm and well-deserved rebuke at him, and waved them both away abruptly.

As they went out, Warsword Lhauntur's eyes were narrow as he regarded the Aumrarr, but all she said to him was, "I recall days when no hold in Falconfar needed to be wary, and regret that those days are gone."

"As do we all, lady," he replied heavily, as they went back down the dark and curving stair that had brought them to the map chamber. "As do we all."

As THEY PASSED the last lantern hanging above the stair, Taeauna turned as swiftly as a striking hawk, laid a warning finger to her lips, then mimed slumber by bending her cheek onto the back of her angled hand, and then repeated the warning finger.

Rod kept his face carefully blank, because the warsword had reached the bottom step and was already turning to watch them.

"This is a good place," he told Lhauntur slowly, trying to sound vague. "I remember a keep like this, but not this one."

The warsword's reply was a noncommittal grunt. He turned away again, and Taeauna flashed Rod another warning look.

This time, he gave her a grim nod.

He was still nodding in the gloom as they went through a half-open door and along a passage hung with old swords and ancient, rusting shields. He was smiling, too.

Oh, yes. I *am* enjoying myself. The Lord Archwizard of Falconfar has come home. Tremble, dragons! Echo, castles! Die, Dark Helms!

In front of him, Taeauna stiffened as if he'd slapped her across the back. The severed stubs of her wings actually quivered.

And suddenly, Rod Everlar didn't feel like exulting at all. Yes, this was real. Too real.

Taeauna, can you hear my thoughts?

The Aumrarr was walking normally again, and if she could hear what Rod was thinking, she gave no further sign of it.

Oh, damn. What have I gotten myself into?

Into my dreams, of course. But what if they turn into nightmares? What then, over-clever thriller writer?

He traveled the entire length of the next passage, and the next, without coming up with any sort of answer.

Except to discover that he still knew how to shiver.

THEY ATE AT a simple table that was evidently the warsword's customary dining place. The fare was some sort of thick, strongly spiced meat stew ladled over oval wooden bowls full of what looked like Cornish hens on skewers. Gray-green, scorched hens. Taeauna ate eagerly, purring with enjoyment, so after a brief hesitation that he hoped Lhauntur wouldn't notice but knew the warsword would,

Rod fell to. At least Lhauntur had retied his hands in front of him, and even allowed him about a foot of cord between his wrists. Knives and the two-tined forks had been moved out of reach, though, leaving him with a ladle-like spoon and a pair of whittled wooden tongs. The taste was strange—a little like some spiced eel he'd once sampled—but good. Very good.

Lhauntur's meal was one long stream of inter-ruptions, as grim-looking warriors, some in splendid armor but most in motley garb of leather jacks adorned with ill-fitting metal plates strapped on here and there, clanked up to the warlord for instructions. All of them carefully avoided looking at the two guests, and even turned their faces away so Rod and Taeauna wouldn't overhear the terse murmurs Lhauntur traded with them.

When Taeauna was done, she helped herself to more from the decanter whose contents had made Rod's eyes water with a single swallow, leaned back in her chair, and purred, "Lhauntur, I can't help but notice you've a lot of men under arms. Are you expecting an attack?"

The warsword gave her a hard look. "Samdlor and Raeth are good men, and they both swear you appeared in the lane right out of empty air, but magic or no, if Dark Helms you were fighting, Dark Helms may follow you here."

He glanced at Rod for a moment, and then back at Taeauna. "Wizards wield Dark Helms like the rest of us swing swords. And if the Helms come to Hollowtree, this night or the next, we'll have to be very good at swinging swords. Every one of us."

"If they come, Lhauntur," Taeauna said quietly, "I'll swing a sword right beside you."

"And your goodman, here?" the warsword asked, just as quietly. "What will *he* do?"

"Wonder if you have a spare hayfork," Rod offered calmly. "I'm getting pretty good at forking Dark Helms."

A hard and sudden silence fell, and Rod felt the back of his neck prickling. He hadn't noticed more armsmen approaching, nor Lord Eldalar with them.

And then Lhauntur started to wheeze as if he were choking, a rattling convulsion that grew and grew until Rod's mouth fell open in alarm, and the warsword slapped the table and burst into an open roar of laughter.

Laughter that spread, all around Rod, and included Taeauna's high, lacy mirth.

Lhauntur shook his head at last, pointed a finger at Rod, and said, "You're not a wizard. You're worse than that: you're a jester!"

There were groans and some chuckles and mutterings, and then the warsword and the Lord of Hollowtree said, more or less in unison, "Untie him."

Someone hastened to do so, at about the same time as a stout and aging maidservant rushed up to Taeauna with a frilly gown in her hands, spread it out down herself, and asked breathlessly, "Will this do? 'Tis all we could find, lady, seeing as you're as tall as..."

The Aumrarr made a face. "Thank you, but no. I'd rather go naked."

"I'd rather you went naked, too," Rod muttered to the table in front of him in little more than a whisper, but Lhauntur heard him and plunged into fresh bellows of laughter.

Which was when the maid screamed, and men whirled and cursed all over the chamber, and Rod lurched around in his seat in time to see what they were all staring at.

High up amid the guttering candle-wheel lanterns overhead in the lofty-beamed hall, a dark, flickering shape had faded into view. To Rod, it looked like the ghostly images that sometimes faded in and out of view on an old black-and-white television set he'd once owned, way back when; there one moment, and gone the next.

It was a Dark Helm, drawn sword in hand and visor down. It hung there silently, peering around the hall from its height, looking at this man and then at that one. Then it turned abruptly away, as if angry, and... was gone.

"Searching for a wizard and finding none," Lhauntur said grimly, giving Rod another glance. "Wake the stable lads. I want runners going around the doubled guard all night through, making sure no one falls without the rest of us knowing."

"I'll fight at your side," Taeauna promised, shooting to her feet.

"You'll stay here, and your friend with you," the warsword replied curtly.

The Lord of Hollowtree put a hand on the Aumrarr's shoulder—he had to reach up to do it—and this time Taeauna left it there. She even leaned back against him and let the old lord murmur something comforting that Rod didn't hear, that brought a brief smile flashing across her face.

Oh, Christ, Rod thought to himself, there's so little I know about Falconfar. And if anything happens to Taeauna, I'll be alone here, and won't even know what mistakes I'm making.

Hmmm. Not so different from life back in the real world, after all.

No DARK HELMS came that night, and in the morning Taeauna insisted they depart. The warsword and Lord Eldalar disagreed, but not forcefully enough to entirely hide their relief, even from Rod.

Lhauntur sent maids scurrying in all directions as the man who'd thought, just a day ago—had it been only a day ago?—he'd invented Falconfar, went behind the corner curtain to avail himself of the chamber pot.

Rod had spent the night in this cold stone room. Its only other furnishings were a blanket and a heap of straw for a bed that erupted in squeaking mice when the guard who'd brought him there kicked at and then trod on it. It wasn't quite a jail cell, but the door had been firmly locked behind him, and Taeauna had slept somewhere else.

He'd kept his robe on because of the cold, and was glad of it when the door rattled open not long after dawn and the Lord of Hollowtree, his warsword, four bristling-with-blades guards and Taeauna had all trooped in, all fully dressed and with the alert faces of folk who'd been up and doing things for hours. Someone had given Taeauna patched and well-worn leather armor that was tight enough to creak, here and there, but hung loosely in other places. Her welcoming smile, however, lit up Rod's morning like the sun.

The jug of wash-water was icy, and Rod emerged from behind the curtain shivering to find the lord and the guards gone again. Lhauntur, however, stood waving at the bed, and a stream of servants were dumping armfuls of this and that on it.

"Don't stare at yon heap like you've never seen clothes before, goodman," the warsword told him gruffly. "Get dressed in whatever fits. 'Tis yours. There's food coming, too."

Taeauna was already kneeling beside the bed raking through piles of homespun and what looked like buckskin. She cast a critical eye Rod's way, obviously measuring his height, length of limbs, and girth, and by the time Rod had curiously explored the leather shoulder sacks two young and unsmiling maids dumped into his lap, Taeauna had picked out a paltry pile of simple breeches, clumsy boots, tunics, and cloaks.

The sacks were odd pleated things of clanking buckles and uncured, strong-smelling hide that had an arm-loop and a chest-belt; Rod was obviously supposed to sling his over one shoulder and use the belt around his chest to keep it there. Both sacks held a lot of empty space and a sphere of oily cloth bound closed with a rawhide thong. Undone, one of these proved to be two bowls strapped rim to rim: one of wood and the other a battered and repaired war-helm. Inside the bowls were more cloth bundles: a trio of hard, round-domed loaves of dark bread, two disks of sharp-smelling cheese the size and weight of hockey pucks and the color of old yellow soap, and a tiny twist of oiled cloth with a something brown and gritty in it.

"Thoret," Lhauntur explained. When Rod gave him a "what's that?" look, the warsword sighed and added, "Sauce. Very spicy. Dip your finger in it and smear it on bread or cheese or anything you want to cover the taste of. Stains everything." He waved at the other sack. "The other's just the same."

Rod nodded, wondering what the proper way of saying thanks was, when more servants arrived with skins of water and two old, heavy, serviceable swords. They lacked scabbards, and were smeared with what looked like bacon fat. Each had a close-fitting ring collar just below the quillons that was attached to a long loop of chain.

"The chain goes over your shoulder," Taeauna explained before the warsword could. "Now try everything on. If it fits, we wear it or carry it in our laedlen."

"Laed… These sacks?"

"Those sacks."

The warsword turned away, obviously hiding a smile, and Rod sighed and went over to the pile.

"WHAT MADE YOU choose Hollowtree?" Taeauna asked as they paused for a moment on a height crowned with a tangle of ancient, weathered trees. Behind them, a shoulder of a long, high ridge dotted with what looked like sheep had just taken Rod's last glimpse of Hollowtree Keep from view.

Rod had to catch his breath before he could reply. They'd been climbing steadily since they'd left the wagon road just beyond the last guard post manned by Lhauntur's men, to follow a narrow, winding track up through rising hills. The pace the Aumrarr set had Rod puffing long ago.

She strode along gracefully, alert but with none of the manner of someone expecting trouble, and Rod noticed she'd not once called him "Lord" or anything like it this morning. It seemed he'd now fallen to the rank of just a bumbling man.

"I... don't know. You asked me to see Falconfar, so I tried to picture my favorite keep, and... Hollowtree it was."

Taeauna gave him a smile. "I'm pleased nonetheless. I'm known there, hence our relatively cordial treatment."

Rod winced. If that was "relatively cordial," just how bad would everyday treatment be?

And it's very close to Highcrag."

"And what is... Oh. Yes. The high stone hold where the Aumrarr dwell. I remember."

"You should. The sisters will give us shelter, aid, and news. Lhauntur meant to be kind, but," her face twisted in disgust, "these swords!"

Rod grinned. "I've been thinking of mine as a metal club. A greasy metal club. At least it's so dull I can't cut myself when it bounces as we walk."

Taeauna gave him an amused look, and then glanced up into the sky at a small, high speck—a lone bird, flapping along slowly and doggedly— and frowned at it.

"Will you be able to fly again?" Rod asked, watching it. Taeauna stiffened, and he added hastily, stumbling over the words, "I mean: can the sisters give you back your wings somehow?"

"No," the Aumrarr told him softly, coming to a halt and turning to look at him with something— a little flame of anger? Hope? Something else?—in her emerald eyes. "Not unless you can work a new spell that I've never heard of."

"Oh," said Rod apologetically, feeling helpless, and then muttered, "Wingless forever."

For a moment they stood silently together, watching another of the clumsily flying birds following the first toward the row of distant, jagged brown mountaintops ahead, and then he asked, "But why can't you go and charm one of these powerful wizards I heard the men of Hollowtree muttering about, to cast a spell like that on you?"

Taeauna gave Rod a look that blazed with open anger this time. "Rod Everlar, you must stop thinking of Falconfar being just as it was when you wrote about it. To do otherwise is to doom us both."

She waved a long, graceful arm back across the rolling wooded hills they'd crossed, to the fields of Hollowtree and distant rocky crags beyond. It was a magnificent view, but Taeauna seemed unimpressed by its beauty just now.

"The splendid forest kingdoms you dreamed and wrote of have changed. Hollowtree should have shown you that. They're now belike a handful of gems scattered in the dirt: they shine still, but have become small, embattled holds menaced by greater darkness around them."

Rod nodded. "The Dark Helms."

"And more than that. We see and fight prowling monsters grown numerous and bold, more than we do the Helms. Yet we fear Dark Helms more, for they're not just ruthless raid-swords. They serve the Four Dooms." She gave him a twisted smile. "Or rather, three of those four. The three wizards whose tyranny is daily seen by all who venture within their ever-lengthening reach."

Taeauna sketched a brief sign in the air in front of her. It looked to Rod curiously like one of his Catholic friends making the sign of a cross to ward off evil.

In its wake, speaking very quickly, Taeauna hissed, "Remember these names, but speak them seldom if at all: Arlaghaun, Malraun, and Nar-markoun."

She made the sign again, and then continued more calmly. "These three wizards are the greatest in power of the known mages of Falconfar, and they are all evil, grasping men. If they did not endlessly make war on each other, we'd all be in their thrall."

Rod frowned. "That powerful? The first two I created, and Holdoncorp added the third, so they can't have had all that long to—"

"It doesn't *take* long, if no one has magic enough to stop you. Oh, they're not nearly as tyrannical and clever-witted as some of the olden-day mages of legend, yet that may be because they strive constantly, one against the other, each seeking to ensure the other two rise not to supremacy."

Rod frowned, trying to remember. "I made them greedy, and wanting to have absolute control over their own small territories, but what else do they want? Can't they just whisk themselves anywhere, if they just want to snatch gold coins and gems and… and whatever?"

Taeauna smiled thinly. "Smallholdings no more. And each seeks to gather the most powerful spells and enchanted items from the ruined castles of long-fallen kings, and so rise to rule all Falconfar."

"And what's stopped them from doing that, besides each other?"

The Aumrarr shrugged. "Brave men with swords, doing what little they can. Most holds like Hollowtree are ruled by old wolves: hardened warriors who'd be happy to be rid of all magic, and all wizards. Oh, and there's one thing more. Fear of what the fourth and greatest Doom will do, if their deeds awaken him."

"I don't remember including any sleeping King Arthur under the hill in *my* Falconfar," Rod grunted. "So who's this fourth Doom?"

Taeauna gave him another crooked smile.

"You."

"So... ARE THE three wizards watching us now?" Rod asked, much later, when sweat was streaming from him despite the increasingly chilly air, and they were high above the rolling greenery that held Hollowtree, somewhere back below them down there.

Taeauna had finally paused to rest and drink a single swallow of water. She stopped Rod from gulping more of his own with a firm hand, and went back to frowning up at the increasingly frequent flapping black birds. All of the same sort, they seemed to be converging from several directions, and all heading for somewhere not far ahead.

"Mayhap," she replied, "but I doubt it. Working magic's tiring—as tiring as running hard, or fighting, I'm told—so even powerful mages use their spells sparingly. I saw a lesser wizard once, sitting in a chair keeping two magics on his lord from the other end of a market: a disguise and a warding against knives and arrows. He was white and a-sweat and shaking with weariness."

"And I'm supposed to be lord of all wizards?" Rod asked incredulously, wiping a hand across his sweat-slicked brow and displaying it to her.

"Your power is different. You dream and transform things no wizard could. Many things, all at once, large and small. Most mages can burn or blast things, or wreak one transformation at a time on a single person or thing." Taeauna got up, still frowning at the birds. "And your blood heals."

"But doesn't regenerate."

She transferred her frown to him. "What is 'regenerate?'"

"Bring your wings back."

"Oh. No. At least, I think not." She looked away, and her frown deepened.

"Do you want me to bleed on your... on where your wings used to be?" Rod took a swift step sideways as he spoke, to where he could see Taeauna's face.

For just a moment, her calmness broke, and her eyes held as much pleading as they had back in his bedroom. There was more hope in them, too.

And then Taeauna shook her head, and her face was a calm mask again. "Mayhap some day, when Falconfar's need is lesser. I dare not let you throw away your power on me, just one Aumrarr, when so many more may need it, and you may have... limits."

Rod looked into the fire that had returned to her emerald eyes, and then at her back and shoulders as she turned away and started climbing again, threading her way now between rocks as large as men.

Smooth muscles shifted under worn and ill-fitting leather.

He looked back the way they'd come, down across bare, rolling rocks to seemingly endless forests below and behind.

How did I get into this?

Ten years ago, Rod Everlar had been a writer of successful, if unimaginative, Cold War spy thrillers. *Fist of Fire*, *Hitler's Vengeance*, *Thunderbolts of Zeus*, dozens more. Talk to a few old spies or spy wannabes, read a few quirky SF disaster novels, twist ideas from both together, throw in the square-jawed hero, the femme fatale, and the trusted friend or boss who's really a treacherous double agent, and out came the next one. Bang, bang, bang, if that wasn't too trite an expression.

And then had come the dreams. Dreams of swooping dragons and shouting men with swords, and princesses fleeing in diaphanous gowns who turned into pegasi and even more horrific things in mid-stride. And balconies, and flickering torches, and castles—castles looming dark and purple by night or black and sinister by day... And the woman with wings, the one in armor who staggered toward Rod with four evil princes' swords through her, gasping, "I die for Falconfar!"

Her eyes, her amber-flame eyes... *She* had seen him, really seen him, too. And once Rod knew the name Falconfar, the dreams came wild and deep and vivid, one crowding on another, night after night until he was a staggering man by day, so weighed under by sleeplessness and nightmares that he was scarcely alive.

It was an abyss he climbed out of with a single step, one day, when he plucked up a notepad and started writing down what he'd just awakened from, shouting out into his bedroom. The notepad became stacks of notepads, and the stacks turned into binders, and with each page he filled, the dreams were tamed a little more, until they became orderly nightly visits that let him rise again to wakefulness in due time.

Exhausted no longer, but somehow unable to care much about long-hidden Nazis and lost submarine fleets and missile satellites disguised as auto parts, Rod had turned to his notes and crafted a story about Falconfar by stringing together dreams, like a child assembling one of those push-together plastic necklaces. It seemed a trite, even hokey tale, but he shrugged and sent it off to his agent with orders to place it wherever possible, and tried to get back to black helicopters and women in black evening gowns that concealed silencers and little else.

It took him two more books to clear his mind enough to set Falconfar aside, and by then the first one was selling like ice cream on a hot July beach, better than anything he'd ever written before. The clamor for sequels hadn't died down, though the dreams had started to fade; by two summers ago they'd practically disappeared.

Since then, he'd taken care of three of his long-overdue thrillers and plotted the fourth. Holdoncorp's offer for his fantasy world had been staggeringly handsome, and he'd accepted it eagerly, retaining the right to do more Falconfar books just in case. He'd used that right twice, when their blunders had set his teeth on edge enough that he'd strung together a few more bunches of dream-notes around some pointed corrections. Changes that Holdoncorp had of course, calmly ignored, despite the contract.

Making him the Fourth Doom and Dark Lord of Falconfar in the process.

WHEN ROD CAME around the next boulder, Taeauna's sword was in her hand, and her face was grim.

"Tay? What's wrong?"

The Aumrarr pointed with her sword. More of the flapping black birds were flying past. "Vaugren. Carrion birds. Many, where there should be none."

"Gathering to feed after some battle?"

Taeauna sighed. "Undoubtedly. Dark Helm work, this'll be. I was not the only Aumrarr to be harried. Many of our patrols sounded horns the night I sought the place where I go to dream of you, and... reached you at last."

"Dream of me? D'you... uh... often dream of me?"

She regarded him coolly. "All Aumrarr dream of you, Lord Rod Everlar. And pray to you, on our knees. Some devoutly, some, no doubt, mouthing but empty words. Some of us are sworn to bear your child, should you ever appear to us."

Her tone warned him that she was almost certainly not one of the sisters who'd so sworn. It told him a trifle more; that Taeauna would not welcome any smart comment on the matter, or even any words at all.

Not that Rod was far enough away from dumbfounded, just now, to say anything coherent.

In his mind he was seeing dozens of beautiful winged women in armor, kneeling in little glades and on lonely hilltops in front of pristine hardcover copies of *Falconfar Forever*, praying to receive his favor. Or his children. Jesus shitting Christ.

"No GUARDS AT any of the posts," Taeauna whispered, her face so white now that Rod could see a fine web of blue veins all over it. "None." The birds were a flapping cloud now, wheeling and screeching everywhere.

When Taeauna led the way around the last bend to stand on a ledge looking down on the terraced front gardens of Highcrag, they both knew what they'd see.

A field of the dead, lifeless Aumrarr strewn everywhere, lying broken and dead where they'd fallen in battle.

The Dark Helms had slaughtered them all.

Chapter Three

"TAEAUNA," ROD BLURTED, not knowing what to say but knowing he had to say something. "Taeauna, I..."

In grim silence Taeauna stepped off the ledge and stalked down into the battlefield, ignoring the angry flapping and cries of disturbed vaugren. Rod hastened to follow, trying to ignore what he was stepping on. He got one good look at a hooked beak tugging at an eyeball, the flesh that held the orb stretching obscenely yet refusing to part company with its eye socket, and hurriedly looked away, swallowing.

The dell reeked like an open latrine, overlaid with the sweet stink of blood. Armored and half-armored Aumrarr lay sprawled everywhere, some of them so hacked apart they resembled the roasts of a publisher's buffet more than women. Wings that should have soared were crumpled and trodden, bloody boot prints marring the white. And there were feathers, feathers everywhere.

Taeauna was peering intently at one body and then at another, searching for something. From time to time Rod heard her moan softly, murmur a name, or whisper a curse, but she never stopped to weep.

He followed along anxiously behind her, looking around often to be sure no Dark Helm or anyone else was creeping up on them, and because he knew not what else to say, he blurted, "Sorry. Oh, Taeauna, I'm so sorry! This must be horrible for you..."

Taeauna did not reply. When she reached the far side of the dell, she caught up a splendid curve-bladed sword—like a Civil War cavalry saber, only without any sort of basket hilt—and hefted it in her hand. Nodding, she found its scabbard and belt, stripped them from the bloody, headless ruin that had once been a fellow Aumrarr, and donned the sword herself. Then she drew herself up and slammed the old sword Lhauntur had given her into a trampled flowerbed with sudden ferocity, leaving it quivering upright.

Without a word she took a long pace to one side, flung up her chin, and then started back across the dell toward the ledge they'd come from, bending and peering, and from time to time reaching down to draw open a pouch, or roll a body up to see what might lie beneath. Her face might have been carved from stone.

"Taeauna? Taeauna, I..."

Her grim search took her into a heap of bodies, and a cloud of vaugren rose to flutter and flap and screech at her. Rod hastened forward, thankful to have something helpful to do, to shoo them away with wild sweeps of his heavy sword. He stumbled on something smooth and slick—a blood-soaked breast, perhaps, though he was trying not to look down—and almost fell on his face into the fly-buzzing innards of a hacked-open Aumrarr ribcage.

He vomited helplessly then, stumbling and retching until he had to use his sword like a crutch, leaning over weakly to empty his stomach long after there was nothing left there to lose.

Taeauna never paused. Her hands were covered in dark, sticky gore as she gently rolled what was left of old friends over and aside to look at other bodies beneath. Searching, always searching. As soon as Rod's dizzy head and aching guts let him walk steadily again, he hurried to catch up to her.

By then, she was almost back at the ledge, and tugging another curved sword out of its scabbard. She peered critically at the blade, hefted the weapon, and then slammed it back into place, wiped her hands on the tunic of the corpse she was robbing, and set to work on buckles.

When Rod came scrambling up to her, she thrust the sword at him, scabbard and belt and all, without even looking his way. The moment his hands gingerly closed on it, she tugged at his Hollowtree sword, almost dragging him into a face-first fall. Hastily he gave it to her, and she stalked on for a few more paces, past a body sitting against rocks whose familiar face made her sigh, and planted the heavy blade upright, just as she'd done with the first one.

As she stepped silently to one side, to begin another grim journey across the garden of the dead,

Rod moved with her. "Taeauna, I'm—I just want to tell you... I'm so sorry..."

Her newly acquired sword flashed up out of its scabbard and past his nose so fast Rod did nothing but blink at its passing flash and dazzle.

"Dark Lord, be still!"

Taeauna's face was still a web of blue veins, and silent tears were running down her face like water. Those emerald eyes might have been the points of two swords, above a chest that was heaving, but there was no trace of a sob in the harsh voice that snapped, "You didn't do this; spend no breath apologizing for it. Just bide with me in silence, and don't stand in my way when I see my next Dark Helm."

As she stalked past, bending to look at two Aumrarr who lay curled up around each other, broken swords in their hands and agony twisting dead and now eyeless faces, Rod frowned.

Dark Helms. There were no fallen Dark Helms anywhere in the gardens that he could see. He looked down to where the gardens ended and rocks began, and then back the other way, at the open doors in the mountainside that presumably led into the chambers where the Aumrarr really lived, or *had* really lived, but... no black-armored men lying anywhere. Not one.

He started to look more closely among the dead, trying to see if perhaps a man lay among the blood-drenched women. Some of the Aumrarr had been wearing dark leather armor, and the closer he looked, the more beautiful faces and graceful limbs he saw—and gore. Flies, everywhere flies, and those damned birds walking stiff-legged, to peck and stab and tear away...

Rod shuddered and turned away, gorge rising. Even with his eyes closed, he could see a particular Aumrarr face, slack and still with insects crawling on it, but still achingly beautiful. It was staring pleadingly up at him, looking so much alive that he'd almost reached down a hand to... to the severed head whose body, wherever it lay among all the torn and twisted carrion, wasn't within three or four of his strides. No matter how much he shook his head, he couldn't look away from those eyes. Brown, not the fierce emerald of Taeauna's, and never blinking...

"I've seen enough," Taeauna said from beside him, almost tenderly, "and more than enough. But we must go in. There are... things I must see to."

Rod swallowed, trying to banish a beseeching brown stare, and then opened his eyes and said hoarsely, "Taeauna, there're no Dark Helms here. D-did they somehow fight well enough that none of them died?"

Taeauna's face was calm again, and her eyes were dry, but there was a shadow in her gaze that hadn't been there before. "You don't know what Dark Helms truly are, do you?"

Rod blinked. "Uh, evil men in black armor," he said slowly, "whom wizards can control."

"Yes," she agreed bleakly. "Even beyond death." She pointed, and Rod looked and saw the curled fingers of a black gauntlet beneath the distractingly bared hip of a dead Aumrarr. Then she pointed again, and Rod stared at blood-covered black shards for some time before he realized that he was looking at the shattered remains of a black war-helm, its visor twisted up among them like a set of false teeth turned on edge.

Taeauna took a step past Rod, touching his arm with her pointing finger, and then indicated a row of rocks that marked one lip of a tiered garden bed. On the largest stone lay a black hilt, and from it, where the blade of a dagger should have been, stretched a smoke-scar, a scorch mark that ended abruptly, without a point.

"Some of their blades bear spells," Taeauna told him gently. "When broken, they burn away to nothing. A *very* painful passing, if such steel is inside you."

"So… this means…?"

"A wizard was here." The Aumrarr turned, strode a few steps toward the head of the garden and the open doors waiting there, and then stopped to point again.

This time, she was indicating a sister who sat against a low stone wall, arms spread wide in agony, the flesh of her chest melted and drooping like the wax of a burned candle.

"Magic did that," Taeauna added coldly. "And the one who cast it took away his fallen, to bind pieces of ravaged bodies together into men once more and send them shuffling out again to do his bidding another day, dead and beyond dead, rotting inside their armor. 'Tis the armor that truly moves them, not the muscles within. The day a mage improves the spells so a thrust that slays a living man will fail to stop an undead Dark Helm is a day that will doom most folk still alive in Falconfar."

Something in her voice left Rod shivering as she hefted her new sword again and strode on through the nearest doorway. He looked around the dell, and at more vaugren wheeling hungrily down out of the sky to land in it, and then hurried after her.

"Watch behind us," she ordered, the moment he was inside.

They were standing in a high-domed room carved from solid rock, with sunlight shafting down through an oval window high overhead, and dead Aumrarr heaped everywhere. The smell of cooked flesh hung strong and heavy in the air, and several of the twisted corpses were a strange iridescent purple.

"Wizards' work," the living Aumrarr muttered, peering rapidly here and there, as if hidden foes might rise up to blast them both at any moment. The thought awakened an idea in Rod.

"Can wizards go invisible?" he blurted.

"Some know that spell, yes," Taeauna told him, as briskly as one of his long-ago schoolteachers. "It's imperfect, though, unless the mage remains still, and it does nothing about noises like breathing and footfalls. There's no spell-hidden watcher here, if that's what you fear."

She went to one of the niches in the walls where potted plants cascaded lush, waxy green leaves down into the room, and touched a particular spot in the carved stone lip of the opening. To Rod, it looked no different than any of the other shapes amid the running knotwork design, before or after Taeauna's touch. She bent down again to touch another particular spot, in a second lip carving.

There was a soft *click*, and the living Aumrarr went to the frame of an interior doorway and thrust her fingers at it. The doorframe swiveled on hidden pivots, moving top to bottom as a single board, to expose a tall, shallow cavity of many finger-sized niches, most of which seemed to hold keys. She selected two of these, and then bent and took something from the bottom of the cavity.

Rod had just remembered her order to guard their rear, and was turning away. He almost dropped the scabbarded sword she suddenly tossed him, and stood holding it uncertainly until she said, as calmly and as quietly as if she were asking him to pass over a newspaper, "Swing that once or thrice. 'Tis probably a better length for you than the one I gave you earlier."

Before he could reply, she added, "Ah," in far more interested tones, and plucked something small out of hiding. It looked like the sort of tiny box jewelry store purchases came in, only of smooth-polished wood.

And then she'd slipped past him as smoothly as any snake and was heading out the door again, into the death-filled garden. Rod followed, wanting to ask her what she was doing but wise enough to hold his tongue. For now, at least.

Taeauna headed straight for a body Rod hadn't noticed before amid all the others, an Aumrarr on her knees with both hands thrown up in front of her, her face twisted and her mouth frozen open in a shouting position. There was something unnatural about this corpse; Rod stared at it.

Of course. Twisted like that, and rearing back on its knees, it should have fallen over. Something— magic?—must be holding it up, frozen in its contortion.

"Taeauna..." Rod burst out, because he could keep quiet no longer.

"Tried that blade yet?"

"Tay…"

The woman who'd brought him to Falconfar drew in a deep breath, and then said quietly, "This was Marintra. One of my closest…"

Her voice trailed away, and without saying more, she turned abruptly and thrust the wooden box into his hands. Rod dropped the sword as he fumbled with it, hissed a hasty apology, and then got it open.

He was staring at two flat, smooth stones. Nondescript beach pebbles, or more likely streambed stones, if they'd come from anywhere around here. Rod touched one of them with his finger, and a tiny swirl of sparks arose from the stone, to fade away almost immediately.

Which meant that these must be the Holdoncorp creations known as speech-stones. Placed on the tongue of a corpse, each of them would work but once, making the dead say again the last words they uttered when alive.

He nodded gravely and handed the open box back. "She died shouting something that'll be useful to us, you think?"

Taeauna's face was as calm as her voice. Only the fire raging deep in the shadows in her eyes betrayed her fury. "I hope. And no vaugril has yet been at her tongue."

She turned, took one of the stones, and with slow, gentle care laid it in Marintra's mouth.

They saw that pale throat quiver, cords standing out anew, and the flesh around her mouth seemed to creep, as if starting to move with slow reluctance. Then the dead mouth filled with dancing sparks, and moved normally.

The sobbing groan was slow and deep, but its words were quite clear: "Arlaghaun, I die cursing you! By my blood, wizard, may you die a worse death than mine own!"

The sparks promptly died, and the stone was gone. Marintra went on glaring at no one, but her jaw now hung slack.

More so as not to have to look at Marintra for any longer, Rod turned to Taeauna. "I guess... we'll be hunting Arlaghaun now... right?"

Taeauna looked back at him, her face as smooth as stone, and observed quietly, "You're good at guessing things, Lord Archwizard."

Something in her tone made Rod shiver again.

Silently, she turned away and walked back into Highcrag.

THE NEW CHAINS were finer, and tinkled almost more than they rattled when she moved.

The sharp-nosed man in gray smiled approvingly as she came into his many-shadowed study, the angry fire in his brown eyes ebbing, and she took that as a sign to scramble up from her knees to take and kiss his hand, letting her long, honey-blonde hair trail across it first; she knew he liked that. The web of chains joining her wrists to her ankles chimed, and the spells it bore made it wink and flash in the gloom of the old stone room.

"You're troubled, master," she murmured. "Can I help? In any way?"

At another time, her hopeful purr and those ice-blue, almost pleading eyes might have distracted him, but just now the wizard's thoughts were ensnared, returning again and again to that strange stirring last night, that *flow* of force...

Like magic, but not magic. What *was* it?

Something new, something he'd never felt before. Like the fabled storm-dreams of the Shapers, the tumults that led ignorant fools to call the strongest Shaper "Lord Archwizard," when Shapers weren't really wizards at all.

Whatever it was, he must find it and tame it. His rivals couldn't have failed to feel it, and if one of them came to wield it, he could be doomed as surely as if he'd never mastered a single spell, but proclaimed himself king of all Falconfar with nothing to defend himself but a smile.

As empty as the smile he was smiling now.

THERE WERE SOME very artful hiding places in Highcrag, Rod Everlar mused, some hours later. Taeauna knew them all, of course, and was rapidly assembling a pile of small, useful-looking things that seemed too large for their laedlen. When he started to point this out, she reminded him that he still hadn't tried that second sword he was carrying along in her wake. And then she'd gone into a side-chamber and come out with a pair of dark leather thigh-high boots, all laces and feminine points, and tossed them to him with the words, "These should be your size, and far more comfortable than what you're wearing."

Taeauna was foraging for food, too, but no matter what she sought, she mainly found death. Death and more death.

Messily slain Aumrarr were everywhere, long limbs draped over chairs and beds and splintered tables. When one corpse shocked Rod into audible disgust, Taeauna threw him a decanter of wine and told him to drink only a single swallow.

Rod watched her tireless peering and gathering, and wondered when she was going to snap.

If he was in the way, whenever it happened, he was doomed. She could carve him up in an easy instant, probably without even slowing down in her opening of wardrobes and tossing items onto beds.

And then, quite suddenly, she was plucking at his sleeve and dragging him back toward the rooms where she'd assembled the largest piles of items.

"We must be well away from here before night falls. Beasts will come that we'll not want to meet; too many of them."

Rod nodded and hurried after her. A deep anger was rising to choke him, and he felt so sick at what he'd seen that he could barely imagine what Taeauna must be feeling. This was her home; these were her friends...

Dead, every last one of them.

"Tae... Taeauna? Is... Are you the last Aumrarr?"

The wingless woman whirled around so swiftly he shouted in alarm, but all she said was, "I hope not. Not all of my sisters are here. Unless some lie dead in the rocks beyond the gardens that I've not seen yet. I'm not inclined to go looking. Hasten."

Rod knelt and started scooping items into his laedre, his new boots squeaking. Idly, as he stowed and stuffed, he wondered how ridiculous he looked. There'd been a tall oval of brightly polished metal mounted on the sloping front of a mountainous wardrobe in one of the rooms, pretty close to what was sometimes called a "cheval glass" in some of the arty furniture catalogs that came in the mail, but he hadn't much wanted to look at himself.

A mutter of disgust came from close behind him, and one of Taeauna's long arms reached past him into his sack, to pluck something out that he'd just put in there.

"Taeauna," Rod said then, watching her long fingers emerge with something small and metallic that he couldn't begin to identify, "there are…"

He didn't know how to say this, but he had to try. "There are things about Falconfar that I hate. Butchery like this. The wizards. The Dark Helms, and the suspicion. If my books—my dreams—can change Falconfar, *how*? How can I control things, to make just the changes I want?"

In the lengthening silence that followed, her other hand took hold of his shoulder, and turned him gently.

"Lord Archwizard," Taeauna of the Aumrarr whispered, tears glimmering in her emerald eyes as they faced each other nose-to-nose, "I… I don't know."

THEY SPENT THAT night high in the mountains, huddled together in a crevice. Both were wrapped in their own blankets, which did little to make the rocks they were lying on less sharp and unyieldingly hard. Taeauna used a sling made of the sword belts she'd brought from Highcrag to bind the rolled blankets together around her shoulders, and with this crude aid, pulled large stones into the mouth of the crevice, to partly wall it closed.

"Wolves?" Rod had asked, as he chinked the big stones by wedging little ones around them, as he was instructed.

"Worse," she'd told him tersely, and he hadn't felt like asking further. Taeauna had used something from Highcrag that was like a tall metal tankard—only it was as tall as the length of her forearm—to scoop up water from a mountain spring. That and a few berries eaten in grim silence had been their supper, and immediately after that Taeauna had gone to relieve herself and then returned to curtly order him to do the same. He'd been startled, returning to the crevice, to see her standing atop the rocks above it with her sword drawn, obviously having watched over him, but she said not a word as they secured the last rocks in place to wall themselves in, and rolled into their blankets.

Taeauna had fallen asleep almost immediately, but started to whisper names and weep softly. Rod had lain beside her staring up into the darkness, wondering if he should reach out to comfort her, and sleep had been a long time coming for him.

He'd come awake suddenly, later, when the darkness outside the gap-studded wall of rocks was absolute, and something with an unpleasant smell, a low and rumbling growl, and long claws that scratched on stone had nosed around just outside.

It had thrust a snout—at least, Rod assumed it was a snout, though it was too dark to see a thing—between two of the stones they'd wedged, and Taeauna had calmly and silently thrust her sword deep into it, held firm to her steel as it shrieked and clawed wildly at the stones, sending some of them tumbling down her body and bouncing off Rod's blanketed shins, and then gone right back to sleep again.

Her soft weeping awakened him again, later, but when he'd put out a tentative hand to touch her shoulder comfortingly, the cold steel of the flat of her blade had slapped his wrist firmly, and she'd said quietly, "No, Dark Lord."

"Sorry," Rod had whispered into the darkness, drawing his hand hastily back into the meager warmth of his blankets. She'd made no reply.

And now it was morning, and colder than ever, and he was blinking as his breath drifted past his nose like mist, and Taeauna's emerald eyes were regarding him with something like contempt and something like pity.

"Lord Archwizard, reporting for duty," Rod tried to joke.

Her face might have been carved from stone, it remained so expressionless, as she slapped his stiff and aching crotch with the back of her hand and ordered, "Relieve yourself. I'll stand guard. We have much country to walk this day."

He did sorely need to empty his bladder, and rolled out of his blankets into the frigid morning air wincing and shivering. "Much country? Where are we heading?"

"Arbridge," she said flatly.

Rod dimly remembered Arbridge as a pleasant little vale with a castle at one end, a town at the other, and a stream winding through it with farms and little woodlots everywhere. He'd written about a bridge midway along the farm-filled valley where two feuding knights had fought a battle to the death, both drowning in the stream after they'd gone off the bridge tangled together and stabbing each other.

The knight from the castle fights the knight from the town, and no one wins. He'd liked the story, a wrinkle on the old, much-used "making a last stand guarding the bridge" tale. As far as he could recall, he hadn't ever returned in his writings to look at the aftermath for Arbridge.

Which meant, of course, it could be anything now.

A road wandered down the vale, from the town to the bridge and from bridge to castle, and gone up over the hills to other places at both ends, places he couldn't rightly remember just now.

"Why Arbridge?"

"'Tis the fastest way to get down into Galath."

Ah. Now Galath he remembered. One of his creations he was most fond of—if he'd really created anything in this world. A splendid forest kingdom of knights and ladies, old gruff monocled dukes with huge mustaches and pretty ladies riding at their sides, and sinister, oh-so-politely-warring nobles who did each other dirty with poisoned daggers and honeyed words, trying to snatch real power away from a decadent royal family.

"Galath. Yes," he said, smiling.

Taeauna gave him the coldest look she'd yet favored him with, and said, "You'll find it much changed, Lord Archwizard."

Rod looked at her, feeling more than a little helpless. "Taeauna, what have I done to... to..."

"Earn my displeasure? Nothing. I am not angered with you, lord."

"Then why—?"

"I am enraged, lord. Enraged with whichever of the wizards stole your memories from you, furious with the wizard who slew all my sisters at Highcrag, and—"

"Arla—"

"*Speak not his name*! Idiot!"

"Uh. Sorry. Ah, shouldn't that be 'Lord Idiot?'"

Taeauna stared at him for a moment, all the color gone from her face. Then suddenly she rushed forward and flung her arms around him, laughing and weeping at once, so wildly and fiercely that in a hectic instant Rod found himself winded, on his back on the stones, being tugged this way and then that in iron-strong arms as she rocked back and forth.

After what seemed like a long time, her laughter gave way to sobs, and then a sniffle or two. Then she pushed herself up off him, and looked away into the cold morning breeze.

"I wish you hadn't said that. 'Tis in my mind, now; I might slip and call you 'Lord Idiot Archwizard' in the company of others." There was just a hint of what might have been a chuckle in her voice.

"And that plain-tongued honesty would be bad how, exactly?"

Taeauna turned her head slowly to regard him, not smiling. "You *are* different from other wizards. From every other wizard I've ever met. You're... soft where they are hard. Gentle where they are savage. A willful fool where they are haughty and threatening. A—"

"Bumbling idiot where they are capable rulers," Rod interrupted her, adding a wry smile.

Taeauna sighed, and looked away again.

Rod leaned forward to touch her shoulder with one forefinger. "Tay, I—"

"*Taeauna.*"

"Sorry, Taeauna. Uh, Taeauna... I'm sorry I'm not the world-striding godlike cloaked wizard you probably hoped I'd be, able to set things right the moment I set foot in Falconfar."

He felt the stones beside him with his other hand, feeling the coarse, tufted grass between them, and shook his head. "I still can't quite believe I'm here, in this imagin... In this place I never knew was real. But I'm glad I am. And I want to help, however clumsy I am."

He looked around, at other ridges and higher peaks in the distance, and at the great green valleys on either side of the row of hills they were perched atop, groping for the right words. Taeauna was watching him, her eyes on his, waiting in patient silence.

He drew in a deep breath, and said in a rush, "I don't mind being guided by you; in fact, I'd be lost without you and don't want you so much as out of my sight. Yet I... I don't want to just stumble along not knowing *why* we're going to this place or that place. I-I need to know."

The Aumrarr nodded. "Forgive me, lord. It was wrong of me not to have spoken of this with you sooner. I was waiting for a moment of ease, in Highcrag, and then..."

Though her face remained calm, she drew in a ragged breath before adding, "I dared my life to reach you because I was losing it anyway. You were there, dreaming of me, so close. My spilled blood and resolve were enough to open a Way between us. Your power is all mighty, even in your dreams, even when you... know not what you do. You are Falconfar's only hope."

Rod grimaced. "Not to place any pressure on me, or anything like that."

Taeauna shrugged. "I am desperate. I would do anything with you, or," she lowered her voice to a murmur, but kept her eyes on his, "*to* you, to save Falconfar. You are the only sword I know of, to smite the Dooms. *Ach*; the other three Dooms, I mean."

Rod spread his hands. "Very grand. Stirring, even. But what does my having all this power really mean? I've read fantasy novels aplenty where innocent good guys—and gals—blunder along, saved by their own predestiny, to the end of the book, and then suddenly know the Right Thing To Do, and destroy the Dark…" His voice trailed away as he realized what he was starting to say.

"Dark Lord," Taeauna said for him, with a little smile. "Yes. Our Falconaar legends say the same, many times over. Yet I believe you won't be an ignorant innocent when you face the Dooms, if you can reach the right place before you meet with them. Going to that place will break the spell on you, and your memories will return."

"And then?" Rod felt a stirring of excitement within him, a deep, crawling energy that he'd never felt before. This was all so much wishful talk, wasn't it? And yet… and yet…

"When your memories are restored, you should be able to write with power, so your pen can swiftly change Falconfar back to what it should be. Restore we Aumrarr, destroy the wizards and their Dark Helms, make mages who are simply local dabblers in magic and monsters rare beasts rather than nightly prowlers nigh-everywhere. Return wars to disputes that erupt betimes, not the ceaseless warfare that has become the daily lives of all Falconaar."

Well, that was easily *said*. Write what, exactly? Who was to say it would work? Or if his pen could really affect things, what exactly should he write? What if his changes begat consequences that were worse? Or that he didn't even know about, until it was far too late...

Yet in his mind, he was already seeing himself writing the words "No more Dark Helms" on parchment with a quill pen, then watching all of them instantly fade away into empty, collapsing armor and then dust, clear across vast Falconfar.

Enough. Time enough to burn that bridge once he was standing on it. Keep to the specifics, the next step here and now. "What is this 'right place?'"

Taeauna looked very solemn. "I know not," she whispered, "which is why we'll wander after we're away from Hollowtree and Highcrag. But you will know it. In your dreams."

"B-but... I don't remember my dreams! Not since I got here!" Rod protested, staring at her.

Taeauna stared back at him.

"Oh, shit," she said savagely. As all the color drained out of her face, and bleak despair rose into her eyes.

Chapter Four

THEY WERE BOTH on their feet, the Dark Lord and the Aumrarr, striding back and forth in the freshening winds. Huddled against their dismay, they paced among the rocks, back and forth past each other, trying to think.

"So do we just wander the whole world in hopes I'll know this 'right place' when I see it?" Rod Everlar asked incredulously at last, seeing no other possible road. He did, however, picture this "right place" being some jungle-covered ruin slumbering on one continent of Earth while he scoured a busy city on another.

Taeauna whirled to face him. "That's just what we'll have to do!" she said, her voice fierce with sudden resolve. "No matter how long it takes, and no matter how far we must travel! And the reason we'll give to all for our journeying: I'm an Aumrarr guiding you to work off a blood-debt to your family, and you are a man on a death-quest."

These Rod did remember from his writings. The Aumrarr—and only the Aumrarr, as far as he could remember—recognized blood-debts to kin when one of them slew an innocent person through mischance or misunderstanding. A task or service was done, often a rescue or guiding. Death-quests were a widespread Falconfar custom, wherein still-hale elderly folk journeyed to where an ancestor was buried, to arrange to also be buried there. "Aren't I, uh… a little young for a death-quest?"

"You won't look so when I'm done with you," Taeauna replied, giving him a not-so-sweet smile. "Mud rubbed into your face to hide the fire-soot I'll use to draw wrinkles on you, winterleaf in your hair to streak it white, and a kerchief around your head to make you look old and cold, and to keep rain from washing away your wrinkles."

"And where are you going to get a kerchief?"

Taeauna held up one of her blankets, and a dagger.

Rod winced. "Isn't there some other way?"

Taeauna shrugged. "We can burn all we have as a beacon, and lie down here on the rocks to see which of the Three Dooms gets here fastest, to blast us to bare bones."

Rod sighed. "I'll hold the blanket taut, and you cut, okay?"

"Okay," Taeauna replied. Her mimicry of his resigned "why the hell not?" tone was perfect.

Rod hadn't walked this much in a day since he was a teenager, out camping. And he hadn't liked camping that much.

He was tired, he was cold—the breezes were decidedly chilly, up in these hills—and his feet hurt.

Taeauna was still striding along as smoothly and tirelessly as some sort of young acrobat, sleek and supple, ducking and crawling like a wisp of the wind rather than a winded, clumsy, skinning-knees-and-elbows novel writer. Usually she was just ahead of him, but sometimes she turned to look back behind them, then let him pass and followed him with hand on sword, glaring around alertly.

Yet no Dark Helm or monster had come lunging out at them thus far. In fact, aside from tiny, distant vaugren circling lazily high in the sky, they'd seen nothing living that wasn't a plant, all the way.

They soon saw something dead, all right. Their trail led them past the ancient, abandoned ruin of a castle that even the vaugren seemed to shun. Something that stank like old sewage lay rotting inside it, something so large that its ribcage formed arches of bone that towered above their heads as they stalked warily past.

A neck as long as Rod's driveway stretched up a crumbling castle wall, limp and broken, to end in a severed, insect-swarming mess not far from—

"Aughh!" Rod hissed, trying not to vomit. "What's that?"

High above them, crowning the end of a collapsed wall, perched a leathery, many-horned, greenish-brown monstrosity, a little bigger than Rod's body, that looked a little bit like the head of a triceratops Rod had seen illustrated in dinosaur books. If, that is, triceratops had sprouted dozens of dark, corkscrew-spiraling horns, like antelope or mountain goats or whatever, and tusked fangs around a great jaw like an overgrown cane toad or horned devil or—or—

"Its head. This was a greatfangs, when it lived, and that didn't end all that long ago," Taeauna told him, sounding troubled, her sword drawn in her hand. "I know not how it came to be here, in Ornkeep, but..."

Rod was watching her bone-white face. "But you want to," he said, after it became clear she wasn't going to say anymore. "So, do we run like hell, or is it too late for that?"

The Aumrarr shook her head. "Nothing could slay a greatfangs thus except a wizard's spell, or a true dragon; not even another greatfangs has jaws large and strong enough to behead one of its kin." She shook her head again. "I've only seen two dragons in all my days." Looking straight at Rod—a look that laid bare to him just how tremblingly afraid she was—she added, "And I've seen a *lot* of Falconfar. Come."

And she walked into the ruin without waiting for his reply, heading for one of the stone staircases that ascended.

Gagging at the stink of the great carcass they were passing, Rod scrambled to follow, muttering, "Why are we...? What if this damned wizard is lurking somewhere around here, waiting for us? Shouldn't we just...?"

The view of the sprawled, dead greatfangs didn't look any more reassuring from atop the wall, and the stones of that wall, cracked and overgrown with low, creeping plants, literally crumbled underfoot.

Wincing, Rod gingerly followed Taeauna out to the end of the wall. He hoped she hadn't decided she was the last Aumrarr, and she should just hurl herself off it and leave him alone here, up in this whistling wind.

She stopped at the end of the wall, close enough to touch the reeking tangle of sharp, stabbing horns that was the severed head, and stared down at something on the crumbling stone right beside it.

Something that glowed.

Something small, blue-white and bright. Magic, of course.

Rod advanced cautiously to where he could see it properly, and stopped, afraid he might slip and knock Taeauna into all those nasty-looking horns, perhaps to slide messily off into a long, fatal fall down onto the rocks below, and taking him with her.

He was peering at a small, flat stone, and the glow was coming from a complicated little squiggle that had been drawn on it.

"What is it?" Rod murmured, looking all around. He half-expected a dragon, or a wizard— or a wizard riding a dragon—to suddenly race out of hiding, loom up to tower over them, and roar terribly.

Before it ate them, or crisped them with fiery breath, of course.

Gently, coldly, the wind whistled past.

"We were meant to find this," the Aumrarr told him, kneeling beside it. "It's a wizard's rune. The sign of one of the Dooms. Telling us, or anyone passing this way, who slew this greatfangs, to make the way safe for us. It's a trap, of sorts, too; come no closer."

Rod nodded, only too happy to obey. "So you know who put it here?"

Taeauna nodded without replying. She set down her sacks, rummaged in one of them, and plucked forth two stoppered flasks. Pulling the cork from the larger one, she carefully sprinkled an unbroken ring of brown powder that looked like instant coffee around the stone, tapping the flask with a deft finger to make sure she used not a grain more than she had to. She left no gaps, and spilled nothing on the glowing stone.

Restoppering the flask, she returned it to its laedre, and shook the second, smaller flask.

"What's that?" Rod asked.

"Highcrag magic," she replied curtly, pulling its cork.

Rob rolled his eyes. Oh well, perhaps it was incredibly rude to ask such things in Falconfar...

Taeauna put a finger where the cork had been, upended the flask and then righted it again, held her wetted finger over the stone, and cautiously flicked some of the liquid on her fingertip onto the stone.

Nothing happened.

She waited. Still nothing.

"Safe to touch," she deemed, restowing the flask. "Pick it up."

He looked at her doubtfully, and she almost smiled. "It didn't spit sparks, so it won't do you harm," she explained. "Please pick it up. Touch nothing else."

Rod stepped closer, knelt down, and slowly reached out.

"Don't throw it anywhere, or drop it," the Aumrarr warned. "Just hold it, and in a moment or so

I'll ask you to put it back down exactly as you found it, so remember how it was lying."

Rod touched the stone. It felt smooth, cold, and hard; just like a normal stone. He closed his fingers around its edges, still keeping his palm away from it, and lifted it straight up.

The rune flared up into blue-white fire, flooding past his fingers; Rod's hand trembled in a sudden stab of fear.

"Don't drop it!" Taeauna snapped. "Hold tight to it!"

Then suddenly, she was embracing him, her arm around him, bosom against him, and she was shaking, shuddering so hard he had to brace himself to stay upright.

"Put…" she whispered, her eyes flaring as blue as the edges of the glow that was now spilling from Rod's hand, the glow he could feel as a faint, thrilling tingling. "Put it back. Just as it was."

He did so, and the blue-white fire died in an instant, leaving the glowing rune on the stone.

"Rod Everlar," Taeauna whispered into his chest, as fervently as if his name was a prayer. She shuddered against him for several long moments more, and then said briskly, "We should leave this place now. Quickly."

She felt good against him. Emboldened a little, Rod dared to ask, "Are you going to tell me what this, holding the stone, was all about?"

Taeauna looked at him. "It proves you *do* have the power, here in Falconfar. If we can find the right place to free you, and unleash it."

Unleash it?

The Aumrarr slid deftly out from under his arm, rose, and said, "Let's get gone. I enjoy the smell of dead greatfangs no more than you do."

Rod turned and went.

THEY TRUDGED DOWN into Arbridge just as the sun was lowering, leaving the cold breezes of the hills behind them. Rod didn't have to do any acting to stagger like an old man unsteady on his feet, with knees and hips that hurt; they did hurt. He'd lost count of the number of times stones had rolled under his feet and he'd slid bruisingly into various rocks that thrust unfriendly sharp points and edges into the track they were following. A goat track, Taeauna had termed it, but it must have been made by goats about the size of house cats, if its narrowest places and crawl-holes were anything to go by.

Ahead of them, Arvale looked like a great green sward of farms and trees, with the glimmer of winding water at about its midpoint, and beyond it, a line of hills rose again, dark and terrible, as mountains; brown and purple and towering, like the spikes on the back of a sleeping, buried dragon.

Rod found himself nodding and smiling. Why, this would go great in a book.

"There'll be a guardpost," Taeauna murmured, as the rocks gave way to rock-clinging shrubs and creepers, and then to trees, and Arvale opened out green and dark before them. The light was fading fast. "Let me do the talking. You are old and tired, and uncertain of what to say."

"All true," Rod muttered back, and she gave him the briefest glint of a grin as she went on down the widening track, past places where other, larger tracks meandered down out of high pastures to join it, to a fence of heaped stones and stumps where three men wearing swords and a fourth with what looked like a halberd stepped out into the road to await them.

"YOU SUMMONED ME, master?"

"Indeed." The wizard Malraun was as curt as he was darkly handsome. He needed no magic to make his sleek, taut-muscled body striking to ladies, despite his small size. Nor, though he could be glib, did he need to waste time being polite to anyone. If he wanted a particular lady, his spells commanded their obedience. What cared he if they were screaming inside, so long as their responses were eager and ardent?

And if some of them were every whit as eager to kill themselves after he was done with them, what booted it to him?

He rose from his chair to give the lorn a commanding look, and strolled across the rather bare circular tower room toward it.

"You will fly in all haste, permitting yourself no diversions there or upon your return journey, to find and take the Aumrarr who used magic at Highcrag yesterday, and thereafter went up into the hills. They have probably passed the ruins of Ornkeep by now; I slew a greatfangs that had just begun lairing there yestermorn, to keep a certain Doom from getting his hands on it. Take also the one she's traveling with, and bring them both to me. Alive, if you can, but dead if you must."

The lorn's horned, mouthless skull-face nodded. It spread its batlike wings, snapped its barbed tail, and then froze at Malraun's sharp command, "Disguise yourself! Be the largest of vaugren as you seek Highcrag, and use the semblance of a man thereafter. I want to hear of no wild rumors of lorn flying over the Falcon Kingdoms!"

The lorn's tail switched angrily, but it nodded again, seemed to shiver all over, and sank down onto all fours, its wings and head changing shape as its hide darkened. Giving sudden throat to a vaugril's mournful screech, it sprang out of the open window and away, circling Malraun's dark spired tower once before flapping off into the gathering dusk, in the direction of distant Highcrag.

Malraun did not bother to watch it go. He had far more interesting concerns than a mere Aumrarr and her toy. His recent intrigues had brought no less than three thrones to the verge of collapse, and he was determined that two of those realms would be his before another moonrise.

THEY WERE WELL beyond the guardpost, tramping down a rutted dirt road between walled gardens—creeper-cloaked walls of stone with the roofs of thatched homes rising beyond them—before Taeauna took her hand off Rod's arm in a silent signal that they were now far enough from the guards to speak freely.

She promptly did. Beginning with a snort, a shake of her head, and the murmur, "Only in Arbridge would they name an inn so."

"The Two Drowned Knights?" Rod grinned. "I thought it amusing, yes."

"Oh? I thank you for the warning," the Aumrarr said tartly.

She'd done all the talking to win them safely past the wary Arbren warriors, and Rod had been only too glad to stand there looking old and in pain and dull-witted, while the guards discussed him with her as if he were a sack of meat or a placidly deaf ox.

There'd been much discussion, thanks to Taeauna's skillful tongue. They'd learned that a Lord Tharlark ruled in Arbridge now, and that he'd been armsmaster to Sir Sahrlor, the dead knight of Artown, and was a hard-bitten warrior who wanted Falconfar to be rid of all magic and wizards. Tharlark no longer dwelt in town, but had taken Tabbrar Castle at the far end of the vale as his abode, once home to the dead Sir Tabbrar.

It seemed that fear ruled Arbridge now, and kept honest folk abed inside their barred and shuttered homes of nights, but just what caused that fear, the guards had not wanted to speak of, beyond warning the Aumrarr and the old man with her not to camp in a field or hay-heap by night, but to hie themselves inside an inn, pay the coin demanded, and stay there until after sunrise.

"So," Taeauna said, as they reached a moot where cobbled streets of close-crowded stone-and-thatch homes and shops opened out all around them, and men hurrying to get indoors cast them suspicious looks. "Behold The Two Drowned Knights. Old sir, do you again bide silent, and let me talk and pay."

She tapped a purse heavy with takings from Highcrag, and cast a level look at Rod, who nodded silently. Men gazed eagerly upon the Aumrarr, and seemed happy to get her attention and converse with her; whereas he could have been a dusty piece of familiar furniture, too broken-down to use, and too immobile to need noticing.

Taeauna strode across the street as if she lived in Arbridge, and Rod hastened to follow.

The inn was a tall, square, ugly stone fortress of a building, its ground floor lacking any windows that Rod could see. The Aumrarr thrust open its front door and shouldered her way past several muttering local men, into warmth and feeble lantern light. They fell abruptly silent at the sight of the severed stubs of her wings; Rod shouldered through that silence in her wake, meeting the gaze of no one.

The common room was as dimly lit as Rod had expected, and crowded with dark and massive furniture. It wasn't crowded with patrons, though; only a few folk were seated dining and drinking.

Spiced ale, salty broth, or mulled wine: it all came in the same tall, battered metal tankard, and with the same hand-loaves of coarse, dark rallow-bread. Taeauna ordered the wine for herself and the broth for Rod, and they shared them, passing the tankards back and forth like husband and wife.

Not that any of the locals—almost all of them men in leather and homespun, weary after a day's work—cared if the Aumrarr and the old man were a couple or otherwise. They were too busy leaning forward over their own tankards and excitedly impressing a handful of peddlers and traveling wagon merchants with tales of the latest peril to afflict Arbridge.

The Wolfheads, it seemed, had come to Arvale. And the Snakefaces, too.

As the winter past had begun, ran their talk, Dark Helms had suddenly infested Arbridge. Raiding every few days, searching every barn and cottage and swording everyone who didn't flee fast enough, the Helms had scoured the vale from one end to the other, even appearing in Tabbrar Castle. Always they came "from nowhere," apparently melting out of empty air, menacing crofter and lord alike.

In spring the Dark Helms had suddenly stopped coming. The fear they'd brought, however, hadn't faded one whit. For no sooner had the dark-armored warriors ceased to be seen in Arvale, then a new menace appeared: snake- and wolf-headed men who wore masks of living flesh to appear human, and posed as traders by day, but let slip their masks to prowl the vale and murder Ar-folk by night.

For years Arbridge had known few visitors from afar, but the Snakefaces were hidden among a flood of unfamiliar wagon merchants from distant holds and kingdoms, who were suddenly everywhere in Arbridge and Galath, and Tauren and Sardray beyond, too. These merchants sold mirrors, cast metal ewers and decanters, well-made coffers and kegs, saws and hasps and nails, daggers and buckles and cheeses and all manner of things useful and exotic, and bought hides and smoked joints of meat from Arbren.

There had been mages among the traders, too. Not spell-tyrants like the fabled Dooms, but more ordinary folk, both old and young. Bony and fat, they worked little charms and wardings, and sold potions to heal the sick and make the uncaring fall in love.

"None of them lasted long," one drover said darkly from nearby, wrapping both of his large and hairy hands around his tankard as if it were a wizard's neck. "The Vengeful saw to that."

Vengeful? Nothing he'd created, Rod was certain. Taeauna was also listening with that slight frown that meant, he was increasingly sure, that she was encountering something new. And troublesome.

"The who?" a wagon merchant asked, rubbing his chin.

The two men of Ar shook their heads and put up their hands in warding gestures, and just in case the merchant was too dense to take the hint, one of them muttered, "Shouldn't have said anything at all; we don't speak of them."

The merchant nodded, but then leaned forward and plucked at the arm of one of the pair, and muttered, "Well enough, I'll not pry. Yet I'd take it kindly if you'd answer me this: I was seeking a woman who owes one of my business partners quite a debt, and was told in Tauren she was slain by the Vengeful. Now, she could well have been a sorceress, from what some have said. Does this sound right to you? These Vengeful; they'd slay a sorceress?"

The Arbren pair glanced around to see if anyone was listening, making Rod glad he'd just looked away from them and was now peering at their reflection in the shiny, unadorned signet ring he always wore on the middle finger of his left hand. Then one of them nodded curtly and emphatically.

"Good," the merchant said, "I can stop wasting time looking for her then."

"So," the drover said to him, "you've come through Tauren? What news? I've a brother lives there…"

"Finish your broth and come," Taeauna murmured to Rod. "And try to look sad and old and exhausted."

"Behold my stellar acting," Rod said wearily, setting down his empty tankard and rising reluctantly and stiffly to follow her. He hadn't walked this much in a day for years.

"No wings?" asked the innkeeper, as he took her coins and pushed a long-barreled key across his desk to her.

"The first part of my punishment," Taeauna almost spat at him, and then pointed at Rod with the key as if it were a dagger. "The second part."

The innkeeper grimaced sympathetically, shrugged, and said, "Through yon arch, turn left, end of the passage. Match the key to the image burned into the door."

The Aumrarr thanked him with a nod, and motioned curtly with her head for Rod to precede her.

As they reached the end of the passage she stopped outside their door, peered hard at the adjacent walls as if expecting them to bristle with hidden doors, and then muttered to Rod, "Forgive my coldness. I must act the right part to keep you from being suspected of being a wizard. As an Aumrarr working off a blood-debt, I'll be expected to guard you, sleeping across the entrance to wherever you slumber."

She unlocked the door and stalked into the room beyond, hunting around it as if expecting Dark

Helms under the linens and behind every curtain. A dim, dancing light was coming from a candle-end set in a bowl-shaped rock. There was a single bed, with linens and furs and a scattering of cushions, a large window with shutters and no glass, a larger wooden wardrobe affixed solidly to the wall, and two curtained-off corners of the room: behind one curtain was an ewer of wash water standing in a basin on a shelf, and behind the other stood a chipped chamber pot. The window shutters and the door could both be barred from inside the room, and the Aumrarr set bars into place without delay. Then she flung open the wardrobe doors, which were as large as the door they'd come in by, and thumped the back of its dusty emptiness suspiciously. Solid. Then she checked the floors, ceiling, and walls, tapping and sliding her fingers along the mud bricks and broad boards with a thoughtful frown. The bricks were old and crumbling; her fingertips gouged sand from them that trailed to the floor. Their mortar was firm, though, holding them securely in place.

"Find anything?" Rod asked, at last.

Taeauna rose, looking severe, and hastened to him to put a reproving finger across his lips. "Speak as if you're old," she whispered. "And come and whisper to me, like this, whenever you can. Always assume someone is right outside that window trying to hear us."

"Jesus," Rod hissed, "is this what Falconfar's become?"

"Yes. We sleep in our clothes, with our boots on."

Rod shrugged acceptance, and then stood shaking his head. Oh, he'd had knights fighting all over

Falconfar, and fell monsters and nasty wizards, too, but he'd also established beautiful forest glades where faerie magic kept safe everyone inside moonglow rings, and unicorns that galloped through the air to become pegasi, and… and…

He blinked. Taeauna was beckoning him to bed with an imperious finger. Not that she looked as if she had anything romantic in mind, kneeling there atop it fully clothed with her other hand on her sword-hilt, and that stormy frown on her face.

He went to her and whispered, "Yes?"

"Now may well be our only chance to talk freely in Arbridge," she whispered back. "You have been wandering along beside me all day looking lost and upset. I know why, but is there aught you'd like to talk over, lord?"

Rod spread his hands helplessly. "Such as? You can't even name the powerful wizards, if I understand you correctly, and you know as much as I do about this 'right place' of mine, and… and—"

He broke off suddenly, snatching hold of his temper before it flared right out of control, and then hissed, "Yes. Yes, there is something. Tell me more about this part of Falconfar around us. My memory is hazy and it seems everything's been changed around anyway. So we're in Arbridge, a little valley like a trough sliced along the top of a row of hills, right?"

"Right."

"And if we could stroll steadily, about a day's walk that way—er, south, more or less—is a castle that guards the place where Arvale ends and the road goes up over a little lip and then down the slope of the hills into the pastoral but proud kingdom of Galath, with its many knights and castles. That hasn't changed, has it?"

"The lay of the land, no. Galath, yes."

"Later. For now, if there's still a Galath with borders more or less like the old Galath, tell me the layout of things beyond it."

"Yes, lord. The borders are the same. North of Galath is wild forest; south, too, while it's bounded on the east by the same hills as Arvale lies in, only they rise into mountains as they march on south, across almost all of known Falconfar."

"The Falconspires," Rod said, remembering. He quoted the sentences he usually wrote to describe them: "Where dwell the lorn, above, and the deepclaws, in the caverns below. No one gets over that great stone wall easily."

Taeauna nodded. "Only in the west of Galath, where of old was the land of Emmer, fallen so long its songs now fade, does the land lie open to horse and hoof and cart. The River Ladruar winds there, separating Galath from Tauren, on its long way south to the Sea of Storms. Tauren is a small land of merchants and mercenaries, ruled by the Council of Coins. Walled homes, much wealth and bustle, even more intrigue and gossip."

"Yes," Rod smiled. "A nice touch, I thought; guilds richer than any of the lands around, who hire the best mercenaries and so defend their borders against Galath and Sardray."

"Nice, indeed." Taeauna's voice was so dry as to be almost sarcastic. "As you say, Sardray, grassland of the bow-riders, lies beyond Tauren."

"And beyond that?"

"Roads winding through the great wild forest, linking one smallholding to the next; Hawksyl, Darswords, and Harlhoh are the nearest. It's the way you remember it, lord; only the rulers have changed, as the Dooms extend their sway. Most of this great sweep of northlands is covered by Raurklor, the Great Forest, ruled more by the wolves than anyone."

Rod frowned. "So why, if these wizards lust so much for power, do they spend their time contending up here? Surely, in the crowded hot cities around the Sea of Storms, where I wrote that so many folk were wizards…"

"Magic, lord. Ruins. The powerful old magic lies hidden or is guarded by monsters in ruins, or buried in tombs, here, in the North. In the cities of the South every second soul can work magic, and does, but it is the dregs, the everyday spells of illusion and the passing moment and the tiny effect, not the great might they hunger for. The black-bearded Stormar…"

"With their silks and veils, great dark eyes and dusky skin," Rod completed the quotation. What he wrote became true. Whatever he wrote.

So of course to Falconaar, Rod Everlar would be the ultimate weapon.

And the deadliest tyrant.

"Is there any religion in Falconfar now?"

He certainly hadn't written any into his books.

"There were once temples and priests, long ago, but only our most learned elders and wizards remember them. They came from… earlier pens, and have faded before your fire."

"So do Falconaar pray to anyone? And for anything?"

"Many pray in secret, pleading that all wizards may die, and for deliverance from the Dooms. The worship of Aumrarr you know. Lesser wizards pray, too, for more power and that the Dooms who hunt and oppress them be destroyed."

"Oh? And to who, or rather, whom, do all these enthusiastic secret worshippers pray?"

Taeauna lowered herself from her upright kneeling into a belly-on-the-bed dive forward and reached for his hand. She kissed it, and then looked up the length of his arm at Rod.

"You."

DARK-EYED, THE ghostly head rose up out of the coffer that held the gem, and peered into the darkness, head tilted to one side as if it were listening to something. It was bald, yet bearded, a feeble glow in the crypt, and moved in utter silence.

Yet its voice sounded clearly, if a little thin and distant, when it smiled and said, "At last."

"RIGHT," ROD EVERLAR said to the beautiful woman on the bed before him. He let out a deep breath, shook his head, and decided he didn't want to think or say more about being treated as a god just now.

"So tell me more of Hawksyl, Darswords, and Harlhoh," he said instead.

Taeauna shrugged as she slowly sat up on her knees once again. "All much the same. A lordling in a keep, ruling and protecting farms that huddle in a cleared scar in the forest. Each on its own road west out of Sardray. Ironthorn, north of Tauren and northeast of Sardray, is larger and closer to us here, and also consists of farms in the forest, but it has three keeps and three rival lords. Hawksyl for years was home to outlaws from other lands who raided passing wagons, until something—probably something sent by one of the Dooms, for the Council in Tauren denies doing so—raided them. Darswords has been deemed haunted for years; it lies in the shadow of Yintaerghast, the tower of Lorontar. And Harlhoh has fallen under the hand of one of the Dooms who has built his tower there." She drew a name in the loose folds of the bed linens. The moment Rod had read "Malraun," she clawed the cloth back into smooth shapelessness again.

"Who," Rod asked, "is Lorontar? I never wrote…"

"No, lord. Lorontar is long, long dead. He was the only Lord Archwizard before you, a great tyrant and first-feared among the Dooms before your pen was ever known to us. So evil was he that the many wizards who seek to plunder his tower all flee from it in haste, and come not back to try again. So strong was he that his spells keep his tower standing still."

She shook her head, grimacing as if recalling a bitter taste on her tongue, and added, "For centuries he did much as he pleased; no one dared oppose or defy him as he worked ever greater and darker magics. There are some who say he never died, though many tales are told of the brave warriors who dared to hew him down, many dying in that strife. Others say he perished but is not gone from Falconfar, existing still as some sort of walking dead."

She shrugged. "He has not been seen for years. I once saw mercenaries in Bhelraohwsyn showing a skeletal hand and arm in a great glass vessel amongst their battle spoils and claiming it as his. 'Twas hacked from him by their swords, they said, that turned to smoke in their hands in the doing, as they took part in his slaying."

Rod nodded. "And they've not been seen again, yes? Nor the bones?"

"Indeed, they have not. These thirteen summers, now."

"Uh-huh. And where's this Bell-r-oww-sin place?"

"On the east bank of the Ladruar, where it empties into the Sea of Storms."

Rod frowned, genuinely curious. "Whatever were you doing there?"

"A task of the Aumrarr. A secret task."

Rod opened his mouth to tell her that he'd created the Aumrarr, so she should hardly be keeping secrets from him, and then shut it again without saying anything.

Taeauna smiled at him as if he'd done something very noble, and murmured, "Thank you, lord."

Rod shrugged and proceeded to ask the next of the dozens of small questions that were now crowding into his mind. "The Dark Helms, Tay: what are they? Who commands them?"

"Taeauna, lord. They are warriors. Cruel men in dark armor, who obey the orders given them by the one who sent them: a wizard, almost always one of the Three Dooms. Sometimes their swords or their armor or even their touch imparts fell magic on foes, but that is the doing of their sender, not any power of their own. They are slayers, sometimes battle-veterans, but they are men, no more and no less."

"So this 'appearing out of thin air' business?"

"The wizards translocate them, by teleport and tantlar."

Rod frowned. "Teleport is a word I know and have written in Falconfar tales, but what is 'tantlar?'"

"Before you first wrote that word, and the wizards learned to telep—"

"Wait. Forgive me, Tay—Taeauna, sorry—but are you telling me that when I write about a new spell, it falls into the laps, or the minds, I suppose, of the three wizards? Or all wizards?"

Taeauna spread her hands in a "you're asking *me*?" gesture. "Sometimes, it seems so, yes. The Dooms, however, are in a race to master the most magic, so as to destroy each other. They can't wait for your next book to hand them all the same new magic; they need to gain magic their rivals don't have. So they experiment, as all lesser wizards do, seeking to craft new spells."

Rod nodded. "Slow and dangerous."

Taeauna nodded, too. "Wherefore they spend much time and effort—and the lives of their underlings: hirelings and monsters and apprentice wizards they promise magic to, in exchange for service—in exploring and plundering tombs and ruins and anywhere else they think the magic of dead wizards, old magic, may lie waiting. That's what all of this conquering holds and subverting lordlings is about: seizing control of places that might yield up magic. Thankfully, scrying magic is weak, so they must send eyes to watch us if they want to see much. More than one hold and all of the larger lands, has seen knifings and larger battles between the spies of one wizard, and the spies of another."

Rod nodded. "I've used that! The plot of..."

Then he waved that thought away impatiently, aghast at the realization that he'd written about those warring agents without ever thinking the characters might be serving shadowy wizards.

"Sorry," he told Taeauna rather tersely. "You were telling me about teleport magic, and tantlar, whatever that is, and I interrupted. Could we go back to... uh... before I wrote the word 'teleport' and the wizards soon after learned a teleport spell..."

"Yes, lord. Before then, the Dooms, and all wizards, had to send someone to a place to work tantlar magic. After, they often teleport that someone, and it remains some*one*, since they can only teleport one agent at a time."

Rod nodded. "Okay, so what's tantlar, and where did it come from?"

Taeauna shrugged. "I know not; tantlar-work is old. Lorontar is infamous for using it, with his skeletons."

Seeing Rod's baffled expression, she explained. "Lorontar suffered no Dark Helms to fight for him, or stand guard at his tower. He used human skeletons animated and commanded by him to swing swords. There were priests in those days, who went about in cowled robes, and Lorontar's skeletons often used such garb to fool folk until it was too late."

"Charming," Rod grunted. "Okay, so tantlar magic works well with skeletons."

The Aumrarr nodded. "Better than with Dark Helms. The fire, you see..."

"No, I don't see. What fire?"

Taeauna smiled patiently. "Lord, let me explain."

"Er, please do. Sorry."

"Think of a place distant from a wizard; an inn, or a farmhouse, that the wizard wants conquered or searched. Lorontar would send several skeletons, separately, in case they were seen and attacked on the journey by fearful Falconaar. They would move by night, not needing rest nor provender, traveling by day only in wilderlands, otherwise keeping hidden. The Dooms, today, would teleport a Dark Helm instead."

"Right. So one of these skeletons makes it to the inn."

"The skeleton nears the inn, finds a sheltered place not easily seen by folk who might raise alarum, gathers kindling and firewood, and starts a fire."

"With flint and steel," Rod ventured, nodding. He'd written of characters doing just that, many times.

"Indeed. A goodly campfire is lit, and the skeleton then drops a metal token into it that the wizard enspelled earlier, and sent with it. This is the tantlar; the fire awakens it. The wizard has a matching tantlar, magically linked to the one in the fire, but still under his hand, far away, where the skeleton set out from."

Rod nodded again, seeing where this was going.

"Any creature induced to touch the wizard's tantlar can then be transported across Falconfar in an instant, to the tantlar in the fire, by a far lesser spell than a teleport. So the wizard can cast many tantlar spells, and send dozens, even scores, of creatures swiftly to a distant tantlar."

"I should use this in a book," Rod muttered. "I could…" He stopped as fear flared on Taeauna's face, and said quickly, "Right. I see why arriving in a fire could harm skeletons less than living men, who have feet that burn, in boots that burn."

"Yes. The tantlar can be retrieved from the fire without ending the magic, though the chance of sending more warriors is instantly ended, but when that fire goes out, all of the transported creatures, alive or dead, no matter where they are, get magically 'snatched back' to the first tantlar, or the wizard's tantlar. Along with everything they're wearing, carrying, or holding that isn't alive, and is smaller than they are."

"Hmm. What if someone doesn't want to go back?"

"They have to cast a spell to sever the link. I don't know what such magics are called, or how they are worked, but I know they have been worked. So enraging the Dooms, in both cases, that they teleported new agents to the spot, to bring other searchers by means of another pair of tantlar, and hunted down the wayward apprentice… it was one of their apprentices, seeking to escape, in both cases."

Rod shook his head, feeling as wary as Taeauna looked. "I see. I also see that what I don't know about Falconfar is going to get me killed, if I'm not careful."

"I will defend you with my life, lord," the Aumrarr hissed at him fervently. "You are Falconfar's last hope!"

"Your last hope, you mean," Rod murmured, smiling to try not to alarm her further. "Falconfar doesn't know I'm even here. Thank God."

"What is this 'God?'"

"Never mind. Just something I curse by. So are all wizards evil?"

Taeauna hesitated. "All wizards are... dangerous. Their power makes them impatient for more, and they can easily become evil."

"But magic isn't evil; you Aumrarr use magic, and are good. I know you are, I..."

Rod fell silent. It felt wrong, somehow, to say, "because I created you that way." He wasn't going to get to the verge of saying so again, if he could manage it.

Something like gratitude flashed through Taeauna's eyes before she nodded solemnly and replied, "Magic is but a sword. The wielder does good or ill, not the blade, unless the blade is a shapechanged wizard or beast, free to think, and can work on the minds of those who bear it."

Rod rolled his eyes. "I never thought I'd end up thinking that I wrote too much about Falconfar. Right, tell me more about Galath. That's where we're going, isn't it?"

"Yes," Taeauna said slowly, eyes almost imploring, "because that's the land you've written most about, and so thought most about, wherefore, I'm hoping..."

"That this 'right place' that will bring back my memories is somewhere there." Rod seemed to be doing a lot of nodding. "Well, I hope so. I always liked Galath, and dreamed most about it, and wrote more about it than anywhere else in Falconfar. It was a little like England, to me."

"England?"

"Well, not the real England, but how I imagined England in the time of knights and castles, when I was young and saw Robin Hood movies and—"

"Robbing…?"

"Never mind. Tell me about Galath. It's still all those happy folk on their sundappled farms, each village with its castle up on the hill, wherein dwell all those crusty old nobles with their soup-strainer mustaches and monocles and galloping hunts, right?"

Taeauna sighed. "No longer, lord. Galath is too large and powerful for any of the Dooms to conquer; whenever one tries, the other two join forces to defeat him. All three have been harshly taught this lesson by the others, so they no longer try. Instead, stepping around each other save when their spies happen to come within dagger-reach, they have been busily plundering the many castles of the realm for magic, slaughtering nobles to do so."

"Christ," Rod snarled. "Now I *want* to have a pen in my hand that can transform Falconfar!"

"More than that; the royal family is all but slain entire."

"The Rothryns? 'All but?' So who's left?"

"Well, some are fled, or gone into hiding, but it's hard to hide from a Doom unless you truly go far and never return, abandoning all trace of heritage and privilege; most of those have been found and killed. Then, quite openly, Lordrake Rarcel and Lordrake Bellomir, the brothers of the king you knew, and all the princesses, then Queen—"

"The king I *knew*," Rod said bitterly. "So they got Arbrand, too."

"Yes, lord. Last summer, in Terth Forest. Prince Keldur, soon after. So now all the Rothryns have been murdered except King Devaer."

"Oh," Rod said. "The youngest son, the one I cast as the weakling and wastrel." He sighed, and then shrugged and said, "Well, at least there still *is* a king."

Taeauna nodded. "The Mad King."

Chapter Five

"**M**AD KING?" ROD Everlar ran a hand over his eyes. He was tired, damn it, and this just about...

"So Galathans call him. Whether he's truly mad or not, no one knows but himself and the wizard who's enthralled his mind with spells, if he's not too far gone."

Rod groaned. "One of the Three?"

"Of course."

"So, is he a stone-faced killer now, or a brawler who snarls royal commands? Or does he stagger about mumbling, trying to fight the spells?"

Taeauna sighed. "You'd best hear it all, and properly. Hearken. Last of the Rothryns or not, Devaer has seen but ten-and-six summers. No one has ever observed him to gibber or drool and stagger, and he has no odd habits or pursuits. He seems older than his years, as if the crown about his brows has made him wise. He simply gives orders—coherently and with dignity—that are wild in the extreme. Commanding this noble house to make war on that one is a favorite, and has cost the realm the Sunders and the Hammerfells."

Rod felt suddenly sick and empty. He'd loved both families. He'd dreamed of the Sunders as sneering, sophisticated beauties. The men he made purring, grudge-pursuing villains, and poured his own lust-fantasies into lush descriptions of the tall and dark-haired, cat-graceful, never-sated Sunder women. The Hammerfells had been his bulging-thewed, amiably roaring "good old boys," salt of the earth like that squire in *Tom Jones*; what was his name again? Worthy? Big, brawling, lusty hard-drinking types, with necks and shoulders like prize bulls, and a laughing, bellowing love of battle.

"All dead?" he heard himself asking, without much hope.

"Perhaps not. Both families were wealthy and had holdings all across the North, and they fled in tattercloak haste after the dragon fell into the lake."

"The dragon? I never put... Holdoncorp! Yes, they did, *damn* them. So, let's hear it: are dragons infesting the skies all across Falconfar?"

"No. At least, not yet. Just the one appeared, by night, and was slain by a spell-lance that lit up the sky clear across Galath, but I'm sure you remember the legend—"

"That I wrote? Of course. 'Dragonfall dooms the realm.'"

"Indeed. A lot of nobles saw it as a sign to be heeded, and fled the realm without delay. Thereby they managed to cling to their lives, at least for a time. They were still galloping for the borders when King Devaer took to commanding one noble family to butcher another 'traitor' family, and then announcing that his appointed slayers were themselves traitors, and sending another family out to kill them in turn. Rumors of this or that wizard compelling him to do this are a dozen a day, but there's never been any agreement as to just which wizard."

Rod groaned again, but Taeauna went right on.

"After his seventh naming of a new 'traitor house,' the nobles stopped heeding him and departed the court. Most of the courtiers and royal servants fled Galathgard on their heels, abandoning Devaer; the rest were devoured by all manner of monsters that started appearing in the castle thereafter."

Rod winced. "Is there anything left of Galath at all?"

"Of the countryside you remember? Much. Of the court and any true rule over the kingdom? Nothing. Several of my sisters dared to fly into the upper towers of the royal castle of Galathgard, earlier this season. They saw Devaer wandering alone there, shunned even by the prowling beasts, no doubt thanks to magic. Dark Helms and ever-more monsters are gathering there now; it's become a place no one who serves not that Doom…" Taeauna slapped the bedding in front of her, traced "Arlaghaun" on their folds, and as swiftly raked that name away "…dares go."

Feeling as angry as he could ever remember being, Rod snarled, "Except us."

And he reached out and put his arms around Taeauna.

She stiffened, and started to pull away, but he tightened his embrace, just holding her tightly in his arms, not moving his hands at all.

After a time, he started to hum, deep and low, as he remembered his father doing when comforting his mother; a gentle, endless, soothing tune, sad, slow and majestic rather than happy or bouncy.

And slowly, ever so slowly, he felt Taeauna relax against him. He dared to move one of his hands, then, lifting it—*slowly*—to stroke her hair, taking great care to keep away from the stumps of her severed wings. God, the muscles she had back there...

Slowly, and without a sound, she was yielding, sinking into his chest. They both reeked of sweat, they both had matted, tangled hair, and Rod was acutely aware that he was comforting a woman who was stone to his damp mud; she could literally tear him limb from limb, whenever she wanted to.

Taeauna sank her cheek into his shoulder, bending over to do so, and suddenly gave a great shudder, followed by a sigh that seemed longer than Rod could ever hold his breath, even long ago, as a strong young man, when he was training to be not a half-bad swimmer.

This time, when she pulled gently away, he let her go. She sat back, looking away from him, her eyes bright with unshed tears, only to toss her head, look directly into his eyes, and whisper, "Thank you, lord. I... thank you."

"So, IS HE? Or not?"

The voice outside the window was gravel-rough and impatient, but the innkeeper's shrug held no trace of fear.

"I cannot tell. He is suspicious, and so you should know of him. What you do cannot be my affair."

"Urrhh." The grunt held neither agreement nor dispute. "The Vengeful shall be told."

A boot shifted on loose stones, and then the night outside the window was empty. In the pitch darkness, the innkeeper shrugged and slid the window panel closed.

ROD EVERLAR CAME awake suddenly and painfully, out of a dream that seemed to involve his blood-drenched bed at home, when a hard and heavy boot took him in the ribs.

"Rod Everlar!" Taeauna shouted. "Up, and defend yourself!"

Blinking in the darkness, Rod was dimly aware of Taeauna leaping over him to his left, so he flung himself to his right, trying to grab at the hilt of his sword as his body rolled over it.

Swords clanged together on one side of the bed as Rod fell off it on the other. Someone or something hissed like a snake, steel rang on steel again, and a horrible wet-throated squalling burst on Rod's ears out of the darkness. He fumbled for his sword and tried to get to his feet, as swords skirled musically and blades glanced off each other from where Taeauna must be fighting. The squalling died down into wet coughing near the floor, and two or three short, angry hisses sounded at once, one of them from right in front of Rod.

He stopped trying to get up, and used both hands to sweep his blade across in front of him, angled upwards, as if he were trying to bury an axe into a tree looming above him, or better yet, slice that axe right *through* a tree.

Halfway through its swing, Rod's blade hit something solid and meaty, jarring his hands to numbness, and... cut through, spattering him with unseen but swamp-reeking wetness and causing a bubbling-wet shrieking overhead that was startlingly loud and near.

As swords clanged again across the room, and he heard a sob that might have been Taeauna—*Taeauna!*—something bumped against Rod's left boot, so he rolled hastily to his right again, coming up against the wall.

"Taeauna?" he shouted desperately.

Behind him the unseen creature he'd wounded fell heavily onto the edge of the bed and thumped to the floor, its shrieks dying into squalling. Rod turned and lashed out with his sword again, hacking wildly at what must be lying beside him.

He couldn't see a thing, couldn't—

"Taeauna!"

She hadn't answered! Hadn't...

Wetness fountained audibly under the edge of his sword, and the squalling stopped, trailing away into a lowering *hiss*. Across the room, blades clashed again, and there was a sudden wet growl of anger. Taeauna cried out a short "*huunh!*" of effort, as if she'd done something strenuous that caused her pain, and then a loud hissing arose, and a body thumped rapidly backwards, off balance, and fell to the floor with a *crash*.

"Rod?" Taeauna panted. "Lord Rod?"

"Here," Rod replied uncertainly, raising his sword straight up. "I can't see a thing."

"Get to the window," she gasped. "Crawl across the bed."

Rod pointed his blade down to the floor and prodded gingerly ahead with it, finding feet almost immediately. He went around them and found the bed. "The laedlen?" he asked, remembering that Taeauna had tossed the inn's cushions to the floor and used their sacks as pillows.

"Bring…" Taeauna panted, "them."

She was hurt, all right.

"Tay, do you need my—"

"Not here," she snapped. "Help me… The window bar…"

Rod clambered across the bed, encountering something smooth and scaly that shouldn't have been there—it was wet and sticky, but thankfully didn't move—and found the floor on the far side.

"Tay," he muttered, to let her know it was him as he reached out. His fingers met with something solid. Leather. "Your leg?"

"My leg," she sighed, and he felt a trembling under his fingertips.

Rod rose, hastily. "I'm here."

"Hurry," she whispered. "Please."

Rod felt for the wall, found the wooden bar, and lifted it. It was heavy; the far end wavered as he wrestled with its weight.

"Just drop it," the Aumrarr murmured. "I'm clear."

Thankfully, Rod let go, remembering to jerk his own boots back just in time.

The bar landed with a crash, and bounced onto his toes anyway.

Its landing brought a few weak hisses out of the darkness behind them, but Taeauna was already pushing at the shutters. "Get the laedlen. We must leave."

"Out the window?"

"Yes, wise old man, out the window." Her snap was as half-hearted as it was quiet.

Rod thrust the window shutters open, smacking someone in the face who was standing outside in the night, who responded by swinging a sword right past Rod's nose.

Rod snatched up his own sword from where he'd left it leaned against his crotch, and thrust it out into the dark bulk. Hard.

It went into something, a little.

That brought a loud and furious *hiss*, and the blade swung back to clang against Taeauna's. She sobbed in pain, and Rod angrily thrust with his sword again, aiming for where the hissing was coming from.

Again, his steel met something solid, slicing past it into air. The hiss burst into wet squalling.

Rod pulled his sword back hastily, feeling Taeauna straining beside him to hold the foe's sword with hers, and started to hack and chop wildly, putting his strength into it.

The dark bulk abruptly fell away, thumping solidly onto the ground, its squalling ending in a wet spewing sound that quickly faded.

"Dare we...?" Rod whispered.

"Get... the... laedlen," Taeauna snarled, and half fell out the window.

Rod hurried to obey, joining her with an awkward somersault that brought him down hard on the body of whatever he'd just felled, and sent his sword bouncing one way and the two laedlen the other.

Taeauna staggered up to him. "Bring them," she gasped. "I can't carry..."

Rod brought them.

THROUGH THE HALF-OPEN door, the knight's face was grim. "Dursra the peddler, lord. We got her drunk, as you ordered, and she's talking. I came straight. As you ordered."

Lord Eldalar of Hollowtree gently set aside the reluctant-to-let-go arms of his wife, and rolled out of the welcome warmth of their bed with a grunt of irritation. "Aye, she would be. Nothing good, I take it?"

"Something you should hear, before I lock her away in the old turret so her words reach no one else."

The Lord of Hollowtree threw on his breeches, stamped his boots onto his feet, shrugged on his grand tunic, scratched at his gray beard, and reached for his sword. Never let your folk see you half-dressed. Or less.

Fastening the tunic as he went, he followed Lhauntur along the dimness of the secret passage into the room of the ledgers, and thence to the long passage that led to the back chamber. Grim-faced guards nodded at their approach and stood aside.

Fat old Dursra lay on her back on the cot where prisoners were usually shackled, unbound but in no state to stand, let alone go anywhere and work any menace on anyone. The sour reek of Durraran's wine was strong in the room, and Durraran himself sat on a stool nigh Dursra's head with a bucket, awaiting the inevitable time when she'd spew.

She was babbling. "'Ware all, from one end of falcons' flight to the other, for the Fourth and greatest Doom is come... walking with a wingless Aumrarr, as humble as a frightened shepherd... as powerful as all the other Dooms together... slipping into Falconfar... stumbling until he awakens, when it will be time for wizards and kingdoms to stumble..."

Lord Eldalar listened grimly as these words were repeated. Thrice. More slurred, sometimes, but with not a word changed.

"That's all she says," Lhauntur told him gruffly. "We were right."

The Lord of Hollowtree shrugged. "We treated him well." After a moment he added, "Taeauna called him our last hope."

"Fortunate us," the knight grunted, sounding unimpressed.

Eldalar shrugged again. "My thanks, Lhauntur. I'm for bed. Rouse me if the Four Dooms start tearing Hollowtree apart around our ears. Anything less can wait for morning."

THE SWORDBLADE THRUST through the chink in the ramshackle wooden wall without warning. The fat man blinked at it for a moment in the feeble light of the candle-lantern, and then brought one of his great hairy fists down on it, as hard as he could.

The sword broke off with a ringing *clang*.

"Cheap stuff," the man rumbled. "This'll be the gels' father, come calling."

He shuttered the lantern, snatched up the doorbar, flung the door open, and rammed one end of the door-bar out into the night, hard.

It struck something solid. There was a wet, strangled cry, something small and light bounced off his boots, and then the scream started; a long, raw, descending cry that was punctuated by several crashes of the railings of various flights of stairs being struck on the way down.

The fat man slammed the door, dropped the bar back into place, and snatched the lamp off the table to peer at what had hit his boots. A human tooth, trailing several threads of bright red blood.

The fat man grinned, ere turning to bellow, "Isk, he's caught up to us again! Start packing!"

The stream of profanity that came from the other room made him grin all the wider. Ah, dainty ladies these days...

SUDDENLY THE MOON showed itself through fast-scudding, smokelike clouds, night going from gropingly dark to merely dim in an instant. Rod and Taeauna could suddenly see that they were staggering along an Arbridge alley together, rather than merely feeling their way along it. There came an angry *hiss* from far behind them.

Rod turned his head and saw snake-headed men, scales gleaming in the moonlight: three of them, with drawn swords in their hands.

"Shit," he spat, "I don't remember..."

"This would be something else you can blame on Holdoncorp," Taeauna said grimly, leaning on him even more heavily. "Just keep going. Head for those trees ahead."

Rod obeyed. "Looks... Looks like a cemetery." He glanced back over his shoulder again. "They'll catch us long before we get there."

"I know not 'cemetery,'" the Aumrarr said calmly. "Yon's a burial yard, if that's what you mean. Where folk lay their kin to rest under enspelled stones."

Rod frowned. "Enspelled stones?"

"To keep the dead down," Taeauna explained. Rod could see dark wetness all down her belly and legs, and she was using her sword like a walking stick as well as clinging to him. He looked back again.

"They're—"

"Keep going," the Aumrarr snapped. "Drag me."

"I… yes, Taeauna."

Her grin was more a grimace of pain than anything else. "That's better," she said. And then staggered, her face twisting, and she gasped, "Rauthgul!"

Rauthgul. Rod's invented Falconfar equivalent for the f-word.

Rauthgul indeed, damn it!

There was no way they were going to reach the yard before the snake-men caught them, no way! And the burial yard was just that: a yard, an open plot of grass and trees walled on three sides but open to a street that Rod and the Aumrarr would soon be crossing. Or would try to; there remained the little matter of winning the sword-fight that would erupt right in the middle of it, when the snake-men caught up with them.

There were grassy humps in that yard that must be tombs, and little stone houses, too, dark with moss and age; crypts? The trees were old and gnarled giants, and it all might as well have been on the far side of the Falconspires, for all the likelihood Rod Everlar had of ever reaching them alive.

They were going to die here, a handful of minutes from now. He and Taeauna were going to be sliced and hacked apart, butchered very messily by swords Rod hadn't a hope in Hades of stopping.

Dark-armored figures suddenly streamed out of a side alley, hacking and thrusting, and a snakeman went down, making those horrible squalling sounds. Dark Helms!

"Hurry!" Taeauna gasped, clutching at the throat of Rod's tunic, all of her weight hanging from her claw-like fingers. "Lord, hurry! Please!"

Her last word was a sob of pain, as tears came and she shuddered all over, sagging against him.

Rod swore and gasped and got an arm around her, struggling to shift her weight to his hip so he could limp along in clumsy haste.

Swords rang off each other behind them, someone groaned, there was some hissing, and then they were out onto the dust of the street, Taeauna hanging like a dead weight. Surely there'd be Dark Helms pelting this way in a moment or two.

When they reached the grassy unevenness of the burial yard, Taeauna clawed her way up Rod until she was upright and peered into the night gloom.

Trees and crypts and their shadows were all around; Rod glanced back at the battle now going on. There seemed to be more snake-men, yet the Dark Helms weren't retreating. Fighters were sagging down with wounded groans or slumping dead, but the fray wasn't getting any closer. There just might be a chance for...

"That one," the Aumrarr said wearily. "Slide the stone aside."

Rod looked at the dark slab of stone, then at her pain-wracked face, and shook his head in disbelief. It was about the size of a door and as thick as his hand, lying on the ground on a lip of stone blocks set into the grass.

"Let me down," Taeauna whispered, "and *move that stone.*"

Rod did as he was told, leaving the Aumrarr sitting facing the fight back in the alley with her sword across her knees. He tapped the stone with the toe of his boot; it was heavy, all right.

Thrusting his sword into the turf near at hand, he knelt down, put his fingers along the edge of the slab, and heaved.

He managed only to overbalance face-first onto the stone, skidding along on his nose to the accompaniment of Taeauna's ragged, pain-ridden laughter. When he rolled onto his side to glare at her, she was clutching her belly and wincing at the pain of her own mirth.

"Don't…" she gasped. She then put her head on her knees and managed to say, "Don't make me laugh again, please. It hurts so."

"It may astonish you to learn this," Rod growled, as he got up, "but Lord Archwizard Rod ruddy Everlar wasn't trying to make you laugh. I can't move this rauthgulling thing. It must weigh as much as a car!"

"Car?"

"Oh, never mind," Rod snapped wearily, going back to the slab to try again.

"Lord," Taeauna hissed urgently through clenched teeth, "look for a stone among the rest, around the edge, with a slot in it. Put your sword in the slot, and thrust sidewise to the slab. Across, if you take my meaning. Don't twist, or you'll break the sword."

Rod stared at her wordlessly, then shrugged and looked for such a stone. It looked to be right by his foot. "This slot; can it be full of moss?"

"Yes. Very likely."

Rod snatched his sword out of the ground, looked back at the fight, and saw that the snake-men seemed to be down to an agonized handful that the Dark Helms were toying with, stabbing the scaled hides at will. Several Dark Helms had turned from this to start stalking toward the burial yard. They were still some strides away, across the street. Rod thrust his sword into the slot and heaved sideways, toward the slab.

For once in his life, he'd guessed right. There was a moment of stony grating, when not much happened. Then the slab swung aside, moving on some sort of hidden pivot, and leaving him staring down into a hole.

The feeble moonlight showed him stone steps leading down into darkness, then promptly went away as fingers of cloud slid over the moon.

"Taeauna?" Rod turned to the Aumrarr. He could just see the glint of her sword in the returned darkness; it wasn't moving. He stumbled over to her. "Taeauna?"

She was slumped over her blade, silent and unmoving. *Great*.

Hearing the boots of the Dark Helms crunching on the gravel of the street, Rod sheathed his sword, tucked Taeauna's under his arm, and started tugging the limp, heavy Aumrarr toward the hole. He could move her, but could he get her down those stairs before a Dark Helm diced them both? Darkness didn't seem to much bother them, as far as he could tell thus far.

Huh. Thus far. As if there were going to be any "later" for him to leisurely observe the Dark Helms.

He got Taeauna down the hole by the simple stratagem of tripping on the edge of one of the lip-stones and falling into the unknown, her body tumbling atop his.

The landing hurt, his shoulders and elbow slamming numbingly down on very hard stone, before Rod bumped and slithered sideways down unseen steps to the sound of loud stony grating overhead.

Silence fell. He was lying on his back, on hard and smooth stone, somewhere cold and damp, with Taeauna lying half atop him. His own breathing was loud in his ears, but he could hear none of the faint night sounds of Arbridge, and the faint touch of night breezes was gone. That grating noise must have been the tomb closing.

Had the Dark Helms shut him in here to die slowly in the dark? Or had he hit something in his fall that moved the slab, and the Helms were waiting above it right now, swords poised to stab?

"Happy choices," he said aloud, hearing his words fall into dead and empty darkness.

Well, at least nothing felt broken, and he hadn't clonked his head. Until greeting the slab with his nose, he hadn't even...

Taeauna! God, he must have hit his head to forget her!

She was dying, or dead already, leaving him alone in the dark in a tomb in Falconfar. Some Lord

Archwizard and Doom he was! Hah. Doomed, yes, but...

Her sword was lost somewhere in the darkness—he remembered it clattering during his fall—but she was right here. Lying on top of his scabbarded sword, limp and heavy.

He couldn't bear to deliberately slice himself with a sword anyhow. He would have to use his dagger, or one of hers; whatever he could reach. He found her mouth with his fingers, traced the line of her jaw, and trembled at the sudden thought of losing her. His other hand, scrabbling awkwardly up and back along his ribs, found the pommel of his dagger.

He slapped it, to fix in his mind where it was, and began the heaving and wriggling process of getting Taeauna off his other arm without cracking her head on anything, or losing track of her in this pitch darkness.

When he could move both arms, he drew the dagger, reached with his other hand to her mouth again, and found that she still wasn't breathing, but at least her lips were parted. He then put the dagger against the back of his hand, his gorge suddenly rising, and... sliced.

It made him feel sick; he thrust the thumb of his dagger-hand into the warm wetness to make sure he was bleeding, and then put his cut hand to Taeauna's mouth, rolling over to make sure his blood could drip between her lips.

Blue fire kindled on her tongue, and grew like a blue-white candle, showing him her face, blue fire trickling down her throat.

She coughed, convulsed, swallowed, and whooped for air. Then her hands came up and gripped his cut hand like two iron-hard gauntlets, forcing him over onto his face as she turned his hand so she could suck… suck greedily, blue fire leaking out around her mouth as she shuddered, twisted, and sucked more.

Only to fall back, panting, letting go of Rod's healed hand. Her eyes were closed, and she moaned.

A moan of pain and… hunger?

The blue glow was fading fast; Rod fumbled with the dagger and stabbed himself through his palm.

"Arrghh!" Jesus, it hurt! God damn!

He found himself sobbing, drenched with sweat and over on his face again on the stone, bright blue ribbons of blood running down Taeauna's cheeks as she sucked at him so fiercely he thought skin and flesh, tendons and all were going to be drawn out of him and down her throat.

Rod's glowing blood slowly pooled on the stone beside his face, flowing outwards to seep down old cracks in the stone.

And the stone suddenly heaved under them!

Taeauna tumbled out of sight, over the edge, and Rod found himself pitching off the tilting slab, too, as a cold and eerie light flooded up into the tomb from below.

Rod rolled over, fear sudden and icy rising in him. Fingers of bone, trailing tatters of grave shrouding, were curled around the edges of the slab, thrusting it up from beneath. The slab was cracked across in two places, and was beginning to come apart…

"Shit! Oh, God bloody shit!" Rod scrambled to his feet and away, almost weeping those words. He'd never realized they'd fallen onto the top of a huge stone coffin, not the tomb floor, and now… and now…

He pounced on Taeauna, who was lying in a limp heap just two strides away, and shook her, yelling, "Tay! Taeauna! Wake up! What do I do? What do I do?"

She groaned, her eyes still closed, and in a frenzy Rod turned his back on whatever was rising out of the tomb, refusing to look at it, and stabbed at his hand again.

Blood spattered Taeauna's face, then glowed blue once more as he slapped his hand across her mouth and held it there. She made a muffled moaning sound, and moved feebly in his grasp. "Wake up, damn you!" he cried.

Which was when something bony and very, very cold touched Rod Everlar's shoulder.

Chapter Six

ROD'S SCREAM WAS lost in a loud and sudden grating of stone overhead that brought back the moonlight and Arbridge—and a Dark Helm, hastening down the tomb steps, gleaming sword first.

The black-armored warrior's face was hidden behind his helm, but the trembling-in-terror writer saw that helm lift to regard whatever cold and bony thing was behind Rod, pass over Rod with eyes glinting in excitement, and fall on the blue fire of his blood, running down Taeauna's chin as she sucked.

The Dark Helm descended another two steps. Face to face with Rod, he hissed, "So! The Master must know! You are the Dark Lord!"

HER CHAINS CHIMED and winked again, which meant that she had moved.

"Stop that," the wizard Arlaghaun commanded coldly, not looking up from the thick tome of spells. The symbols moved—by the Shapers, they did!—so pages he'd studied many a time before suddenly revealed new magics...

More chiming, a gasp of pain, and the candles flickered.

He looked up to give his apprentice one of his sharper glares. In the mirror behind her, his reflection glared too: the man in gray with a nose as sharp as a sword, brown eyes blazing and lips thin with anger.

She trembled under his glare, her tear-filled eyes very, very blue beneath sharp black brows. He could smell her cooked flesh. The candles she was holding were filling her palms with hot wax as they melted, but what of that? The strength to ignore pain is vital to casting spells in battle. Perhaps he should affix barbs to her chains, or weave fresh nettles through them, to truly teach her suffering.

She tried to smile at him through her tears. "S-sorry, master."

"You will be," he told her calmly, letting his gaze slowly wander the length of her bared body, to see if shame still made Amalrys blush.

It did, but far more slowly, this time. Perhaps she was getting used to wearing only chains, under the eyes of every Dark Helm who met with him.

Hmm. Time to let the dogs take their pleasure with her? A matter for consideration, certainly, but—

"You are the Dark Lord!"

The cry was faint but clear, rising like a war-shout from the third crystal along of the row of seven under the window.

Arlaghaun stiffened, of course. What wizard wouldn't?

When he whirled to stare at the glow in that sphere's depths, he knew his eyes were flashing, betraying his own eagerness to his apprentice; giving her a tiny weapon at last.

Uncaring, he hurled down the book and strode across the room toward the crystal. He'd waited years for this moment.

IN AN ALLEY in Arbridge, a dozen Dark Helms turned their heads as one, helms snapping around in unison as they all stared across a street and beyond into a burial yard.

An underground crypt stood open. One of their fellow Dark Helms was crouching over it, but the cry that had sung so loudly in their heads had come from another who must be down inside the tomb.

A few swift, brutal thrusts slew the snake-men they'd been tormenting. Hurrying, the Dark Helms turned and stalked down the alley, heading for the crypt.

"Dark Lord," rose their murmur. "Dark Lord, Dark Lord, *Dark Lord*."

THE CANDLE-LANTERN ON the table was almost entirely hooded. Only a thin line of feeble light shone up off the tabletop onto the masked Arbren merchants and shopkeepers huddled around. This cloak of concealment was more by choice than necessity; Lord Tharlark encouraged the Vengeful, as hounds he need not pay, who did his work for him: finding and slaying all wizards.

Yet the Vengeful dared not relax. Lordlings had turned on even their most faithful hounds a time or fifty before, and in the end Tharlark would, too, if they were any judge of men. He was too full of rage and suspicion, and too swift to draw sword, that one.

Wherefore the Vengeful kept their own suspicions honed sharp; hence this meeting, late at night in an upper room above a shop owned by one of their number.

A man had come to Arbridge, and taken a room for the night at the Drowned Knights. A man no one had heard of, said by his companion to be old, who said little. And that companion was an Aumrarr.

"...and Aumrarr seem always to be near anyone who wields magic," the shortest, fattest masked Vengeful hissed fiercely, tapping the table with his forefinger as if it were a drawn dagger.

"An Aumrarr without wings," one of the men standing in the shadows put in, his voice almost resentful in its puzzlement.

"Aye, what does that mean?"

"Well, someone cut 'em off her, look you!"

"A lover who didn't want her to fly away!"

"The man we're speaking of, to force her to stay near!"

"Bah! Did ye not see the two of them? She could break him into bloody bones with her bare hands, even if she bore no sword! He's a blundering innocent, like a seer or a herb-cook!"

"Or like a wizard," the short man snarled, waving his finger.

A tall, grim Vengeful standing in a corner waved a hand in disgust. "So because he walks with an

Aumrarr, that's enough to make him a wizard to you? She told Orstras she was working off a blood-debt, and I'm inclined to believe the winged sisters when they say such things. So, tell me now: if an Aumrarr owed a blood-debt to a babe in arms, you'd suspect the babe of being a wizard?"

"But this one's not a babe. And, aye, if what they say is true, they do owe him a blood-debt. Why? Isn't it likely that the kin of his they killed was deep in magic, somehow? The Aumrarr are fascinated with magic; they seem to smell it, as my hounds nose out scamper-rats, and wherever there's magic, there are Aumrarr, flapping and wheeling and hovering."

"Just like vaugren."

"Just like vaugren, indeed."

"Well," another of the masked men at the back of the room spoke up, "you are all of Arvale; if these two travel on, come morning, they pass off your platter and become a problem for other Falconaar. I'm traveling on to Galath with my wagons, and I suspect they will be, too. I'll watch them, and if your suspicions are correct, do what has to be done."

"I'm bound for Galath, too," the only woman in the room put in, scratching thoughtfully at her mask. "I'll do the same, and as a woman may well learn more from the Aumrarr through friendly chatter than you can with your blade. You know how Aumrarr are with ladies."

There were chuckles. "Aye, we know," the short, fat Vengeful said meaningfully.

* * *

THE CHILLING HAND on Rod's trembling shoulder thrust him firmly aside and let go; Rod Everlar cowered away, whimpering, but could not keep from looking at what strode past him.

A skeleton, tall and terrible, its bones black and shimmering with blue fire at every joint, the rotting tatters of a shroud clinging to its limbs as it climbed up two stairs and jabbed one bony hand into the Dark Helm's face—actually *into* it, blue fire swirling, piercing helm, flesh, and bone alike.

Those skeletal fingers closed together and pulled back, tearing away the front of the man's head, leaving his skull like... like Rod's mailbox, gaping open after he'd pulled all the letters out.

The Dark Helm's body pitched forward, collapsing down the steps, and his fellow Helm rose from crouching over the top steps with a frightened curse, whirling around to flee.

"Stop him!" Taeauna cried feebly. "He must not live!"

The skeleton clambered down a couple steps and bent in one fluid motion, for all Falconfar as if it were a sleek and strong giant serpent rather than a thing of bones, and plucked up the huge stone lid of its coffin. Rod glimpsed an elaborately carved likeness of a warrior in battle, sword raised in victory, above a long and flowery inscription, before the skeleton leaned forward and threw the great slab of stone up the stone stairwell as a warrior hurls a shield, edge-on and spinning, at foes in battle.

It struck the Dark Helm in the back of the neck, smashing him off his feet and up into the air, head almost severed. When man and stone slab crashed on the stairs together, and bounced wetly once, there was little left of the fleeing warrior's head.

As an onrushing crowd of Dark Helms came to a wary halt, Taeauna crawled hurriedly up the steps and plucked up the grisly crushed helm from the broken body under the slab.

She bore it, dripping with its contents, back down the crypt stairs to Rod. "Drip some of your blood on it," she panted, "and the magic that compels it should burn away."

Wonderingly, he did just that. The metal hissed and smoked, Taeauna hurriedly let it fall to the stone steps, and together they watched the helm melt away to nothing.

STANDING OVER HIS crystal, the wizard Arlaghaun arched over backwards with a startled cry of pain, and clawed at the air as the sudden agony of being burned raged up within him.

With a shriek and a rattle of chains, honey-blonde hair flying, his apprentice flung down the guttering candles and fled.

Unnoticed, the book of spells on the floor glowed and started to turn its own pages, tiny voices hissing out incantations that went unheeded.

THE DOZEN DARK Helms roared in common pain, clutched their heads, and staggered away into the night, some of them dropping their swords and all of them hurrying.

"Come," Taeauna whispered. "Swiftly! Take up my sword; let's be up and out of this place of death!"

Rod did as he was told, grinning wryly at how used to swiftly obeying her he was getting, and pleased as Punch that she was awake and alert and with him again.

As they went up the steps, Taeauna sucked greedily at Rod's fast-vanishing wound, seeming to gain strength with every step. Behind them, the dark and gaunt skeleton reached out beseeching hands and begged hollowly, "Shaper, give me life again! Raise me to the living, and I'll serve you! I—"

"You can't," Taeauna whispered in Rod's ear. "You musn't!"

Rod was hastening up the last few steps, swallowing down a fresh surge of horror that threatened to choke him. "I... I don't know how," he admitted helplessly, "even if I wanted to."

"Noooo!" the skeleton howled, hurling itself desperately at his ankles. "Don't leave! Master of All, don't leave me!"

Rod flung himself up onto the grass and rolled away from the crypt and up to his feet. He sprinted out into the street, with Taeauna running hard at his heels, and dared not turn to look until he was in the alley.

At the top of the steps leading out of its crypt the undead was straining to follow and starting to crumble. As Rod and Taeauna watched, huddling together, it collapsed into dust with a last, helpless wail.

Shaken, Rod drew in a tremulous breath, shook his head, and asked, "Dare we go back to our rooms at the inn?"

"When I'm stronger," she murmured. "Lord, I need more."

Setting his teeth, Rod put his arm around her, handed her back her sword, and drew her back against him. Then he took his dagger and drew it steadily along his forearm that was around her stomach, cutting deep.

The fingers of his cut arm suddenly felt like ice, and then as if they were on fire. He loosened his grip around Taeauna, and felt her pluck his arm up to her mouth and start to suck hungrily. Glowing blue fire pulsed around her mouth as she leaned back against him.

God, her mouth is beautiful.

Watching her, Rod felt sudden desire rising in him. His body stirred, and he knew she must be feeling it, against her leg.

She ignored it so he said nothing, as the pain in his arm slowly sank into an ache, and then into nothing at all.

Abruptly the Aumrarr spun out of his loose embrace, took his hand with a mysterious little smile, and tugged it gently, bidding him follow.

Along the alley and back to the inn, trotting swiftly, swords out and peering this way and that for any sign of Dark Helms, snake-headed warriors, or anyone else who was up and about in the waning moonlight.

Nothing. Arbridge might have been deserted, empty buildings under the moon. Even the inn-yard doors were firmly latched and barred, and inns were customarily open but well lit and guarded in the dark hours. Rod and Taeauna went around the back, finding the window shutters of their room gaping open, just as they'd left them.

Inside, the room was crowded with the sprawled dead: a Dark Helm, hacked to death, atop too many snake-headed men to count. Many of them had been felled in the wardrobe they'd entered the room through; its back stood open, slid aside to reveal the dark mouth of a secret passage beyond. Taeauna went right past it to the entrance door of the room, waved a stern finger against her lips to warn Rod to be as quiet as possible, and took down the door-bar, taking infinite care to be silent.

When she gently tried to open the door, the Aumrarr found it had been boarded firmly shut from the inn-passage side. She turned to Rod, took hold of his nearest ear, and whispered into it, "As I expected. We must be gone from Arbridge by morning."

"Or?"

"Or tarry and be slain. With every slain wizard, favorable regard in Arbridge for Lord Tharlark grows. He never misses any chance at a mage-slaying."

"But I'm not—"

"That matters not to him. Come. We have a long walk ahead of us, in the dark. A cold swim, too."

"There's something wrong with the bridge?"

"'Tis guarded by the lord's armsmen. And watched by Dark Helms and the Vengeful, too."

"The Vengeful again," Rod said thoughtfully. "Local crazies?"

At Taeauna's puzzled frown, he hastily amended his question. "Local mad-folk?"

She shook her head. "Spreading now, and ordinary folk who are frightened more than touched in the wits. Some of my sisters believe—believed—the

Dooms were encouraging the Vengeful, to scour the lands of hidden and lesser wizards, to drive the survivors to seek apprenticeship with the Three to save their own skins, and exterminate all unpleasant surprises. None of the Dooms wants someone unknown bursting into their lives as an ally of another Doom, who could overwhelm defenses they've prepared to stand against the rivals they know."

"As I could be," Rod whispered.

She nodded on her way past him to the window. "Let's be going; despite how it may feel, thus far, this night won't last forever."

"BY THE FOUR sinister Dooms!" the tall masked man snarled. "You found it just like this? Nothing's been moved?"

Both of the other Vengeful nodded. "Just like this," one of them offered.

"Nothing," the other confirmed.

The tall man stared down at the headless body under the huge tomb lid.

"A Dark Helm." Unhooding his lantern, he stepped carefully around it, peering closely at the corpse-dust on the top step and stone lip of the tomb, and went down the crypt steps to peer into the open coffin. Empty.

He looked back at the body under the lid, then up at the other Vengeful. "Get to Olnar's and fetch four pry-bars... and Olnar, too. We've a body to dispose of, an empty coffin to fill, and a crypt to close before the womenfolk are up and seeing things and screeching about them."

The other Vengeful hesitated.

"Go! Unless you've the stomach for explaining all this to half the women in Arbridge, and listening to the other half gossip about you as liars who must have been 'up to something.'" He spread his hands, smiling. "The choice is yours."

Both men turned and started down the street that led to Olnar's.

HERE IN THE shadow of the trees, the black, rushing waters of the stream looked very cold.

Taeauna moved a little way along the bank, peering.

Rod waited, figuring she was seeking the best footing to cross, but eventually she nodded, plucked a few flowering rushes, took off her sword-belt and then various daggers in their sheaths from all over her body, laid them on the bank, and started to strip.

Rod blinked and retreated a few steps, half-turning away, but she paid him no heed at all. When she was done, she bundled her clothing and boots together on the bank, took up the rushes, and climbed down into the stream.

Rod stared at her as she scrubbed at her armpits and crotch with the broken-off ends of the rushes, and then quickly looked away when she looked up at him and said quietly, "Is anyone coming? Either side of the stream? Look well, mind."

"I..." Rod gazed hard past the trees and across moonlit fields, this way and that. "No. Ah, no. Uh, isn't the water cold?"

"Icy," she confirmed tersely, scrubbing hard. The rushes seemed to be oozing a sort of foam; Rod watched with quickening interest as she lifted one breast and then the other, thrusting a rush under them both.

When she shot another quick look up at him, he didn't look away. "How can you do that?" he protested. Darkness descended on them, as a racing cloud hid the moon.

"Shh!" Taeauna hissed at him, and in the same whisper added, "I stink. And so do you. Now get those clothes off and use some of these rushes. Soon we'll have half the prowling beasts in the North following us if you don't. They track by scent, look you!"

"I…"

The moon chose that moment to come out again, full and bright and clear. Bare and beautiful in the moonlight, the Aumrarr put her hands on her hips and stared up at him.

"Lord Rod Everlar," said Taeauna, somehow contriving to make her whisper sound like a sergeant's bark, "get bare and get down into this water right now. Or I'll come up there and bring you down and wash you myself."

Rod tried to grin and say something snide about welcoming that, but somehow, now that this was happening to him, it didn't seem even the slightest bit erotic. Not like in good fantasy novels.

Or even his. Wincing, Rod Everlar looked around for approaching foes in the bright moonlight, as a cold breeze rose gently out of the east and slid numbingly past him. Finding none, he sighed and started undressing.

THE FRESHENING BREEZE stabbed into them like daggers of ice; the guards on the bare stone battlements of Tabbrar Castle drew their weathercloaks more tightly around their shoulders, cursed softly, and started tramping toward each other, the better to keep warm.

"Any marauding dragons your end?"

"Not just now. Yours?"

"Not a one. It's the invading hosts of lorn that's scared them off, that's what it is. Lorn painted pink, dancing with each other."

"Lorn? I dream of seeing a few lorn. Just to pass the time. Watching the castle wall crumble away with age gets old after a time. If you take my meaning."

"I do, Jorduth. Indeed I do." The older guard leaned on a lichen-spattered merlon and peered over the lip of the rampart, looking out at the moon-drenched and utterly empty road below, winding up out of Arvale past the castle walls and then over the lip of the stone ridge, to begin the long descent into the kingdom of Galath.

Jorduth rested his elbows in the next embrasure, stared down at the same serene expanse of road, and said slowly, "The Dooms alone know who Lord Tharlark thinks will come galloping up here at this time of night—in either direction. Fair freeze your bones off, to be out riding just now." He lifted his head to stare at old Blaurin, more to goad an answer out of the veteran than for any other reason.

Blaurin shrugged and spat thoughtfully over the edge with the easy aim of long, long practice. They both paused to watch his offering land.

THE COLD ALMOST seared his hand. Rod snatched it away from the wall, turned to Taeauna, and shook his head. "Wherever my 'right place' is, this isn't it. I knew there was a castle here, but come to think of it, I don't remember having ever heard of Tabbrar Castle before. It must be Holdoncorp work."

The Aumrarr shook her head. "Older. Far older." She drew the dungeon key back out of her scabbard again. "Come. Some journeying yet awaits us, this night."

Rod wearily followed her back into the secret passage. As they left the dungeons, Taeauna carefully locked up behind them again.

BLAURIN'S SPITTLE LANDED with a *splat*, dead center, atop the great iron swivelpost of the barrier that guards below could swing out to block the road, and scratched his chin-tuft of a beard.

"Seems to me," he ventured, "that as long as we watch, no one will come. The moment we nod off, or go down off the walls, that's as when smugglers will come through the vale and down into Galath, or an army will come up out of Galath."

"The latest noble fleeing the Mad King. They'll want to get far and fast, not tarry here."

"Oh? If all that dooms them are his orders, so all as hunts them—half-hearted, like—will be other nobles. Why not stop here, one boot over the border out of Galath? Only a noble house that has a feud going with whoever took this castle would bother to break blades outside the king's writ."

"Well, isn't that most of them? I mean, aren't they all feuding with each other, every last one of them?"

Blaurin shook his head. "Not anymore. The old families, with all their chests full of good gold broons and blood-kin beyond counting, are all dead or fled; they were the ones as saw feuds as daily entertainment. All that's left now are the younger houses, and a few survivors."

Grimacing against the cold, Blaurin lurched upright and started walking again. "Not that I 'spect we'll be seeing any armies this night, nor slave-takers or the like, going either way."

"Oh? Why not?"

Blaurin pointed down into Galath. By night, to guards on the wall, it was just the vast darkness beyond the reach of the huge, chain-hung castle lanterns in one direction, as opposed to the lesser darkness of Arvale in the other direction.

"You can't see them now, but earlier on I marked six banners at the Galath guardpost. Double strength tonight, for some reason. Usually it's the king thinking some poor hunted fool is going to try to crawl past the guards and escape his clutches. There's not a silent cat as will manage to slip in or out of the Realm of the Rothryns this night."

Rod yawned and stumbled again.

"God, Taeauna, if it wasn't so damned cold, I'd have fallen asleep walking an hour ago!"

"Quite likely."

Jesus, she sounded more like a primly disapproving schoolteacher than ever.

A tireless, deadly, magnificently beautiful schoolteacher who had scrubbed Rod's backside, as firmly and briskly as if he'd been a pig or a pony she didn't think much of. And she'd been completely unconcerned about her nakedness while his face was flaming.

She went on into the darkness, drawn sword in hand, ducking and weaving among the low branches and brambles that kept whipping across Rod's face as if she really could see them. The only time she'd slowed was when he'd really torn his face open, and she had turned to lick and suck it distractingly. She wasn't slowing now.

"Taeauna, where are we going?"

"Into Galath. Whose folk aren't deaf, so be still!"

"Are we going to walk all night?"

"If we must. Now shut up, lord."

That at least made Rod snort in wry amusement. Ah, yes, always address the Lord Archwizard of the world politely, after you've snapped an order at him.

He managed to keep silent for most of the way down a difficult hillside of rocks and thorny vines and trees whose gnarled, many-jointed branches grew damnably low to the ground, before he fell down an unseen drop about the length of his own legs to land bruisingly on a jutting rock.

"Where are we heading, anyway? Galath, yes, but where in Galath?"

Taeauna whirled around so swiftly that he almost shrieked, her sword-tip glinting back moonlight right beside his ear.

"Rod Everlar," she said softly, leaning forward to fix him with solemn eyes from less than a hand-length away, "if I answer you now, will you promise—and keep your promise, by the Dooms!—to not speak again until I bid you to? We are very close to being discovered, now, and slain out of hand."

Rod swallowed. "I promise," he whispered, so softly that he could barely hear himself.

Taeauna nodded approvingly, leaned even closer, and breathed into his ear, "A particular haystack."

"A—?" Rod swallowed the "what" even before her finger came up to tap him sternly on his lips.

The Aumrarr dropped her hand down his chest to his arm, and trailed down that arm to his wrist, which she pulled on, gently, and led Rod into deep, branch-tangled darkness.

He concentrated on ducking and weaving as best he could, to avoid shattering every branch, and kept his mouth shut, even when Taeauna lost her balance and sat back hard on his shin and the boot below. She patted his knee by way of apology, and towed Rod on into the night, leaving him smiling at nothing and thinking about how he'd been alone and quite happy about it three nights ago, and now couldn't properly recall how he'd never had Taeauna the Aumrarr in his life.

He blinked. He didn't even know her last name. If she even had one. No, he hadn't ever given the Aumrarr surnames, had he?

Or to put it more honestly, he'd never even thought about it.

Quite suddenly, they came out of the woods, and over a low stone wall made up of boulders and smaller stones, all heaped together in an overgrown ridge, and into a field that was like a bright blanket of silver under the moon.

And there, halfway across it, was a haystack.

It was a heap of hay bigger than some of the cottages they'd walked past, leaving Hollowtree. Taeauna took firm hold of Rod's hand, pointed down and gestured until he understood what she was indicating. He was to walk between the rows of whatever crop had been sown here, following her lead.

There was even a ladder waiting for them, leaning against the huge, shaggy mound. Taeauna stopped him, shaped the haystack with her hands, then moved one hand to indicate that the stack was hollowed out like a bowl on its top. Then she mimed sleeping, her head on her hands. Right, they'd sleep up there. Then she pointed at Rod, at the ladder, and then up.

He shook his head, pointed at her, and then up the ladder. Ladies first.

She repeated her gestures more firmly, frowning at him.

He shook his head, and repeated his gestures.

She shrugged, waved one hand in a contemptuous "whatever" gesture, and went up the ladder. Rod noticed she carried her sword ready in her hand, something he certainly couldn't have done without falling off the ladder.

As Taeauna reached the top of the ladder and clambered forward into the bowl of the stack's summit, there was a sudden commotion.

This particular haystack, it seemed, was occupied.

Chapter Seven

As Rod stared up into the moonlight, fear growing in his throat again, Taeauna's elbows thrust up into view, one after the other, one of her feet kicked, and…

A Dark Helm, helmless and trailing blood from his stabbed face, came hurtling forward off the top of the stack and crashed headfirst into the field right beside Rod. His neck broke with a loud and horrible splintering *crack*, he convulsed for a flailing moment, and then lay still.

There was a grunt of effort from atop the stack, a *gasp*, and another Dark Helm fell into view, sagging over the edge of the stack with his arms dangling. And more blood spattered down from his fingertips and then from the rest of him. His throat had been opened like a slaughtered hog's.

Taeauna grunted, high and sharp, and then her bloody face appeared over the edge of the stack so she could order Rod curtly, "Get out of the way."

He stepped back, taking care to keep in the rows, and she shoved the dangling Dark Helm, and then a third one, off the stack to crash down in front of Rod. Then she came back down the ladder, dug into the side of the haystack, and started thrusting the bodies in, crawling atop them and tugging at them unconcernedly.

She didn't move as if she'd been hurt, but Rod asked her anyway, when she'd finished shoving the last boot out of sight beneath the gently tumbling hay. The stack hadn't taken kindly to all her tunneling, and now sagged a bit on the ladder side.

Taeauna pointed at her sliced and streaming forehead. "Just that. One of them had his dagger out to cut his nails."

Rod solemnly drew his dagger, sliced the palm of his hand, and held it out to her.

She swallowed. "Lord, waste not your power. We may both soon need so much more."

"Stop being so cheerful," Rod growled, "and drink up. You think it's easy for me to just cut myself open?"

She thanked him with her eyes, bent, and sucked.

Rod watched the blue fire lighting her hollowed cheeks from within, felt desire stirring in him again, and... the moment passed. She was healed, his wound was gone, and she gave him a grateful smile and started up the ladder again.

Rod rose from his knees before he realized he had even sunk down on them. "Where are you...?"

"We're sleeping up here, as I told you."

"B-but with them down here, lying dead right underneath us?"

She stared at him blankly for a moment, and then shrugged. "Yes. Why not?"

Rod grimly started to climb the ladder. "In Falconfar," he growled aloud, "I guess you—uh, that'd be *I*—can get used to anything. I hope."

"LORD, DAERN AND his men are missing from their posts! I—"

"I know," came the cold reply. "They are elsewhere at my command."

The burly seneschal in the doorway swallowed a startled curse. "Lord?"

Baron Murlstag sighed, his yellow eyes gleaming a warning of rising irritation, and turned from his lamplit desk and the ledgers spread open on it. "If you must know, Authren, I sent them to the Arvale border. To a haystack."

"A haystack?"

"Seneschal, I do not take it unto myself to question His orders, and I suggest you also refrain from doing so. They are to intercept two travelers, a wingless Aumrarr and a man walking with her, and bring them here. If you are wiser than I was, you will not ask why. If you are a fool and ask anyway, rest assured I cannot give you an answer; I was furnished with none except a promise to take my life from me slowly and painfully, if I dared ask again."

"Oh," the seneschal of Morngard told the floor in front of his boots gruffly. "One of those matters."

Baron Murlstag nodded. "One of those."

ROD'S EYES FELT as if someone had poured sand into them, his mouth was as dry as a clay kiln, and his throat itched. Inside.

Something very bright was trying to leak in, all around his eyelids, and something else was pinching his left earlobe repeatedly. He brushed whatever was pinching away, or tried to; it seemed to be made of unyielding, unmoving stone.

"Come down," shouted an unfamiliar voice—a rough, mature man's voice—from somewhere nearby, "or we'll loose our bows!"

Whatever it was pinched Rod's ear again.

He yielded, rising into wakefulness with an irritated swat at that something. Which caught his hand in an iron-strong grip and announced firmly, in Taeauna's voice, "Stop flailing around, lord, or I'll throw you off this haystack."

Haystack? Oh. Oh, yeah. Oh, shit.

Rod sat up suddenly, blinking in the bright morning sun. He could barely see over the edges of the untidy bowl of hay he and Taeauna had slept in. At least, he presumed they'd slept; he remembered nothing at all after lying down on his back and turning his head slowly to stare up at the full canopy of unfamiliar stars overhead.

The haystack was surrounded by unfriendly faces, of armsmen in chainmail and helms, with loaded and aimed crossbows in their hands. Aimed at Rod, now.

Only one man in the ring didn't have a bow; he was the one on a horse, with a drawn sword in his magnificent gauntlets. He glared at Rod as if sleeping on a haystack was a torturing-to-death offense. He was a broad-shouldered, burly sort, with a jaw-fringe-with-little-point beard, and he wore a golden gorget and the largest gauntlets Rod had ever seen, even including all the more fanciful sword-and-sorcery illustrations that adorned the covers of his books and everyone else's shelved in the same section of the bookstores.

This was the boss, obviously, of somewhere. Probably here.

Then the man's face changed, for the better, and Rod became aware that Taeauna had sat up in one smooth, sinuous motion.

Then he became aware of something else. She'd removed her clothing down to the waist. And was preening.

"Taya!" the bearded man on the horse grinned. Then his face darkened again. "What happened to your wings?"

"Dark Helms cut them off," Taeauna called calmly, starting to dress again.

"These three?"

"No, but those three came within reach so I slew them instead."

The man grinned again. "Ah, lass, lass! Who's your... friend?"

"He is no danger."

"Good to hear," the man called, "but you should know that you are both in danger, every moment you tarry up there. Things are much changed in Galath, and lorn fly over my lands at will. Come down, and let me take you to Wrathgard!"

"Wrathgard?" Rod said slowly. "Is this... Lord Darl Tindror?"

Taeauna nodded, crawling across crackling hay to the top of the ladder. "Not a lovely name, is it?"

Rod winced. "Best I could come up with at the time. I was in a hurry."

They climbed down, armsmen moving forward to offer the Aumrarr a hand down from the ladder. She thanked them, smiling.

"Good greetings, lads. I've not forgotten your kindnesses."

When Rod reached the ground beside her—no hands reached out to assist him—she indicated the man on the horse and then waved at the armsmen, and announced, "Lord Tindror and his personal bodyguard."

"Who are almost all the armsmen I have left," Tindror leaned down from his saddle to mutter urgently. "Mount up behind me, Taya, we must ride!"

"Has Galath become that bad?"

"Worse. The sooner you're safely out of sight inside Wrathgard, the better."

Taeauna sprang into the air as if she still possessed wings, caught hold of the noble's shoulder in midair and turned herself, and landed lightly behind him on the high, arching back of his saddle.

This made the horse snort, buck once, and then toss its head and complain. As the lord held its reins firmly, the Aumrarr settled herself against him, slipping her arms forward and around his chest.

"Your wings!" Tindror said, shaking his head in wincing disbelief. Then he looked down at Rod again, suspiciously.

"This man is under my protection," Taeauna said quickly into his ear. "He's a traveling companion I'm charged to deliver somewhere safely. Nothing more."

Rod gave Lord Tindror a friendly smile and a nod; calculating gray eyes measured him, and then the smile was returned, to the accompaniment of a finger pointing down the row of armsmen. "Mount up with Jarth; he's the smallest of us."

Rod turned his head to look at where Tindror was pointing, and beheld Jarth standing behind the other armsmen, in the shadow of a tree. Grim-faced, a white sword-scar across his cheek, he was holding the reins of all fourteen horses, which between his glove and the horses were wrapped, pulley-style, around the trunk of that tree.

Clever. Rod grinned and started the short walk toward Jarth. By the time he reached his new sad-dle-mate, all of the other armsmen had mounted and started to ride, and he and Jarth were standing amid hoof-dust with the last horse. Its nose was gray with age, and it was giving Rod a half-bored, half-suspicious look.

"You and I look at Falconfar the same way, I see," Rod murmured to it. That earned him a real smile from Jarth who had said not a word, and looked likely to keep silent for days to come. He gave Rod a hand up into the saddle.

A snatched breath later, Rod was wincingly remembering why suits of armor all seemed to have such heavy codpieces.

And then they really started to gallop.

"AND DO YOU mean to tell me," Lord Tharlark inquired icily, "that a wingless Aumrarr walked into Arbridge with a wizard at her side, calmly spent the night at our lone inn, the two of them butchered about a dozen men and robbed a tomb in the burial yard in the crown-cobbled center of town, and no one saw where they went?"

"Uh, well, ah, *magic*, my lord! They took themselves off elsewhere like that! Faster than… uh…"

"Than you can snap your fingers, Gelzund? And how many more times will you have to snap them before the two of them are standing before me in chains? Hey?"

Gelzund's red face went white, but he knew better than to attempt a reply. Not that he could think of one.

Tharlark leaned forward in his high seat and stared around the dark-tapestried great hall of Tabbrar Castle, sterner displeasure than usual riding his hard face, and said coldly, "My dislike of those who work magic should be very well known by now. It is my fond hope that more of the loyal folk of Arvale shall come to share my views, and soon. Wizards are a curse and a bane, who wither and despoil the lands they rule, even as they rule them more harshly than the worst king or lord could ever hope to, no matter how many gibbets and dungeons, swords and flogging-frames he has at his command. This Aumrarr and the wizard with her will be hunted from end to end of this vale, though I suspect they are long gone. Thereafter those who call themselves the Vengeful, and meet masked in shadows, will come before me publicly, and I'll send them outside the vale, to hunt down and slay the two foulnesses who have so casually offended our justice and our peace."

He stared around at the many Arbren in the hall, who all stared back at him mutely.

"I suspect," he added, standing up, "that the two we seek have gone on into Galath, with no magic at all to take them there, just walking by night. The

Vengeful will follow them, and find them, and slay them, bringing back the heads here as proof. Whereupon we'll have a feast, and bid minstrels to sing throughout the lands that in Arvale we suffer no wizards to live, and hurl challenge to the Dooms that so many cower in fear of, that they will find no welcome in Arvale, and show their faces here upon pain of fitting death. All Falconfar will then know of Arvale, and admire Arvale, and those who hate wizards as I do will flock here and make us great!"

He paused for applause, staring down at the assembled Arbren, who stared back at him in silence.

"Then we'll have many more feasts!" he thundered, waving a fist in the air.

Silence.

Rage rising in him, Tharlark turned, his magnificent new half-cloak swirling, and strode down from the dais his high seat surmounted. At the bottom he turned again to face the silent Arbren, and snapped, "Well? You'll like that, won't you?"

They gave him only more silence.

It deepened, somehow, seeming very heavy on his shoulders, as he marched across the back of the hall to the door that led to his private chambers. Stupid dolts. Couldn't they see?

Or did a wizard already have them in thrall?

THREE BONE-JARRING HILLS later, the hard-riding band's gallop slowed and faltered as the horses struggled up a very steep switchback of a trail to the gates of a tall castle that Rod had no trouble in identifying as Wrathgard, just as he'd described it.

Atop a very steep-sided green hill that was bare of all trees and shrubs stood a frowning, unadorned stone fortress. A simple, massive squared stone tower, tapering slightly as it rose to a crenelated height, soared up out of a semicircle of five slender cylindrical towers. The towers shared a crenelated wall, but only a dry ditch as a moat, and that wall came together to join the window-studded front of the great central tower, so the front gate gave straight into the tower. Crowning the lofty battlements of that huge and baleful tower was a tall, elegantly spired room with windows all around it. Not the best castle to withstand a siege, and more strange than beautiful, all told, but it was quite distinctive. And just the way Rod had written about it.

Yes, this was definitely his Wrathgard. Seat of power for Baron Tindror, at the heart of his meager lands along the eastern border of Galath, which stretched south to Sword Pass, a bandit-haunted, perilous mule-route through the rising Falconspires. A few hills west could be found Tarmorwater, a winding stream that kept widening into little lakes and then narrowing again to crossings that needed only the most modest of bridges or fords.

Before they hastened through the front arch of the castle, Rod looked out from the height they'd gained, but got only a brief glimpse of pleasant green rolling hills, of fields studded with many woodlots. And in the distant sky, rising up above those trees…

"Lorn!" Jarth shouted, as they entered an inner courtyard and grooms bustled to take the reins of all the horses. "Lorn, aloft!"

"Nigh Old Forge?" Lord Tindror called back.

"Aye, lord!"

The bearded baron merely nodded, looking utterly unsurprised. Pointing at Rod, he said to Jarth, "Show him a garderobe, then see he gets to the map chamber."

Then he was gone with an arm around Taeauna's shoulders and both of them hurrying through a door in less time than it took Rod to blink.

He blinked several more times, just for practice. Since when did everyone in Galath—sorry, in Tindror's demesne, which would be Tarmoral if no one had changed the name he'd given it, back in *Broken Blades of Falconfar*—do everything in such an all-thundering hurry?

Or was this yet another change that Holdoncorp's games had done to the land? *Click, click, whisk, whisk*, kingdom felled, time for lunch?

Two narrow, steep stone flights of steps up, and out into a hall. He was grateful for the garderobe which he more than needed, and when Jarth waved at it, Rod thrust aside its curtain thankfully, strode through the archway and around the corner, and froze. Taeauna was standing waiting for him, her face serious.

"Does this feel like your right place?" she whispered.

Rod blinked. "No. Uh... no."

She nodded, slipping out past him. "If you get that feeling, anywhere in Wrathgard, tell me immediately."

Then she was gone. Rod stepped to the seat shaking his head and wondering what Jarth would say when he emerged.

As it happened, the answer to that was: nothing at all. Jarth uncoiled himself from where he was leaning against the wall, scarred face expressionless, and led the way along several passages to a grand and guarded door. The guard there was obviously expecting Rod; he nodded, opened it, and waved Rod inside.

The far side of the room was a row of arched windows looking out over southern Tarmoral, their bottom sills at about waist-level, with bookshelves beneath them. The room was filled with a magnificent, smooth-polished wooden table that could seat forty but was currently in use by only two: Taeauna and Lord Tindror. There was a tall, fat cut-glass decanter of fire-hued liquid between them, its upended stopper beside it, flanked by two half-full glasses. The seat right in front of Rod was pulled out from the table, and an empty glass stood waiting for him on the otherwise bare table in front of it.

Tindror pushed the decanter toward Rod. "Sit down, drink, and speak to me. Who are you? Why are you with Taeauna? And why come to Galath just now, when all is in uproar?"

Rod decided to take those commands literally. With a polite smile he sat, took up the decanter, and filled his glass, hoping some convincing lies would come into his head before he was done. Or Taeauna would…

Taeauna did. "We Aumrarr owe a blood-debt to this man," she said smoothly, "whose mind has been harmed by a hostile wizard's spell. He cannot remember some things, such as his name, which is Rodrell, and can't say others. He is on a death-quest, to a place the magic afflicting him would prevent his ever reaching, for he can neither say nor remember it."

"Wherefore you're guiding him." Tindror nodded and put out a hand for the decanter; Rod pushed it back to him and raised his glass in salute. The baron gave him a smile that precisely matched Rod's.

"Wherefore I'm guiding him," Taeauna confirmed. "You may speak freely in front of him, and please do, because if Galath's that much changed, I must hear of it, and he should know what he's walking into, too."

The bearded baron regarded Rod thoughtfully, nodded slowly, and refilled his glass. "Well enough, where to begin? The king. Devaer is king now, as you know, and is either mad or, as many Galathans believe, is enspelled by some wizard who compels him to issue decrees that seem mad to us all. House after house is outlawed or set against rivals until the butchery bleeds the land white. Crops stand untended in the fields, monsters—not least the lorn, who serve and spy for wizards—and brigands roam freely, and the road ahead seems bleak."

Taeauna nodded slowly. "Dark Helms?"

"Everywhere, and serving many masters; they often clash with each other in the farm fields, despoiling crops with their deaths."

Taeauna looked less than surprised. "And which noble houses survive? Who's in favor, and who's otherwise?"

"Of the great families, only Hornsar, Mistryn, and Deldragon still hold their castles and rightful place in the realm without being the crawling servants of the king."

"And those servants would be?"

"The houses of Bloodhunt, Brorsavar, Lionhelm, Dunshar, Blackraven, Windtalon, Stormserpent…" Baron Tindror paused for breath and lifted a finger to wag in the air, marking off those still remaining. "…Pethmur, Snowlance, Nyghtshield, Mount-blade, Duthcrown, and Teltusk all now serve the king. Which is handy for him, as all the courtiers and royal servants have long since fled, or were devoured by the beasts roaming Galathgard. In some rooms, their gnawed bones litter the floor."

"Charming. And whom do you think compels the king to their own bidding?"

Tindror shrugged. "That's no secret, but we say his name not aloud, of course." He put a finger into his glass, drew it forth dripping, wrote "Arlaghaun" on the tabletop, and wiped it swiftly away into a fire-hued smear.

"Quite a list. You made no mention of where you stand, or any of the other—"

"Rabble? We barons are beneath notice, until one or other of the greater nobles wants our land or just decides to gallop an army through it. There were something more than sixty of us, and more than forty are now dead, their lands seized or laid waste. Many of those left survive only because they are the tools of other wizards, who move them about to stand three or more together against any threat sent by the king. In this manner, once-great Galath lurches from month to month, leaving a bloody trail of the dead. The land is so empty of common folk that it may soon fall to the wolves, leaving the king ruling naught."

There came a soft, respectful rapping at the door. The baron held up a cautioning "say nothing" hand to Taeauna and Rod, and called, "Enter in, and set it before us!"

Servants came in with covered platters of food and decanters of wine, whisking away the old decanter and setting out warmed plates. Rod watched; though he'd never even thought of such a detail in his writings, it seemed honored guests were personally served helpings of this and that onto their own oval plates. His was now covered with a heap of thin slabs of meat in their own drippings, a bundle of green vegetable spears that looked something like asparagus, and a cluster of small green vegetables that looked like raw figs but prickled his nose with their high spicing. This was accompanied with a little flared bowl of some brown soup that smelled wonderful.

The servant bowed; Rod had just noticed Lord Tindror and Taeauna both inclining their heads in response to similar bows, so he did the same, straightening up again in time to see the baron plough into his food like a starving dog.

He was happy to do the same.

The meat tasted a little like venison, the green spears were like munching solid split pea soup, the fig-like things tasted like someone had married fried green tomatoes (seeds and all) with the hottest tabasco sauce he'd ever put tongue to—big gulp of the new wine there!—and the soup was like drinking gravy. Very rich, lovely gravy.

Damn, but he'd been hungry. He hadn't quite realized just how hungry until he'd had a good smell of what was on his platter, but it was all gone now, scant moments after being laid before him, and if it hadn't been for the fact that both the baron and Tay were holding their plates up in front of their faces and busily licking them, he'd have been worried that his ravenous haste would have been seen as bad manners.

Shoot, bad manners? Here he was worrying about bad manners, like... like... God, he was tired. A yawn... mustn't yawn again, no...

Rod sat back from his plate to avoid plunging face-first into what he hadn't yet licked off of it, and found himself staring at the magnificent vaulted ceiling of... What was this room, again? The... the chamber, the... the...

That was when the map chamber either swam away from Rod into white mists of oblivion, or he stopped worrying about what it was called.

THE SUDDEN FLAPPING at his window startled Baron Murlstag into a cursing, scrambling rise from his chair, yellow eyes blazing, as he tried to claw out the ornamented sword at his hip. By then, the leaded casements were swinging open, letting light and a cold breeze flood into the gloom, and setting the lone lamp to flickering wildly. Murlstag's sword rang free of its scabbard.

"Oh, don't bother," the lorn plunging over the wide stone sill told him contemptuously, its tone making clear what its mouthless skull-face could not. "I'm not here to offer you violence."

"This time," the baron grunted angrily. "Yet your kind are not known for being... trustworthy."

"On the contrary," the lorn replied, its barbed tail lashing air in irritation, "we carry out orders precisely. If you seek untrustworthiness, look to your own kind."

It turned back to the window, wriggling its slate-gray shoulders; bat-like wings smoothly half-unfurled and as smoothly drew together again. "Murlstag, hearken: I bring orders to you. A wingless Aumrarr and a man with her have been seen being rushed into Wrathgard. They are to be seized at once, alive. The castle and all else in it can be destroyed."

Yellow eyes blinked. "Tindror took them in?"

"So it would seem," the lorn replied coldly, its tone making it clear that only someone as stupid as Baron Murlstag might have trouble grasping that obvious circumstance. It ducked its horns and sprang to the windowsill, then launched itself into the high cold air beyond, wings snapping out, without waiting for a reply.

Baron Murlstag stood in that window, the highest in his castle, and watched the flying thing dwindle into the distance.

Damned insolent beasts. He hated them almost as much as he hated Baron Darl Tindror.

THE VAULTED CEILING of light stone, as magnificent as ever, faded slowly into view out of the mists, and swam around above him.

Rod Everlar had always liked vaulted ceilings, and had ended up with a stiff neck staring up at far too many of them as a teen, trudging around various historic European cathedrals in the wake of his parents, and he remembered putting them in various feasting halls and great chambers in his Falconfar books. Hammerbeam ceilings, too, but the fan vaulting had always seemed to him the most beautiful. Holdoncorp's artists had been delighted to discover he'd included them...

"Rod! Rodrell!" Taeauna snapped, sounding angry, her voice echoing strangely and coming from a long, long way away...

"It worked, lady, let me assure you! It worked!" an unfamiliar, frightened male voice was gabbling from very close by.

The ceiling went on swimming, circling around above his eyes more slowly now...

He was lying on something hard. Hard, smooth, and flat.

He was... Rod was lying on his back on the table in the map chamber at Wrathgard, staring up at its ceiling, with someone whimpering beside him.

He turned his head and found himself looking at a young man in robes—a priest or monk or wizard, but Falconfar had no monks or priests, so this must be a wizard—who was bone-white and chattering in fear.

"What're you afraid of?" Rod asked curiously.

The man stared at him, and then said in a rush, "That the Dooms felt my spell-work on you! And will hasten here to take or slay me!"

"What spell-work?"

"P-purging that which afflicted you."

"The wine was drugged," Taeauna told Rod furiously from the far side of the room; he turned his head in her direction, and saw that she was standing over the baron, holding her sword to his throat. Tindror, grimly pale, was still in his seat. "How do you feel?"

"I... fine. I think."

"T-there are no spells on this man," the wizard stammered.

Taeauna nodded grimly, never taking her eyes from the baron. "It is as well for you," she told Tindror softly.

"L-lady, I am sorry. Who is he?"

"Better that you not know. He is… important." Her voice was now very soft. "As you now know."

Rod saw tears well up in Tindror's eyes.

"I meant no harm, Taya. Please believe me!" the bearded noble hissed, starting to weep. "I never wanted to do anything to… darken what we share."

"You truly mean that?"

"Yes," he said fervently. Taeauna looked across the table at the wizard, caught his gaze, and pointed meaningfully at Tindror.

Nodding nervously, the wizard cast a spell, a short and careful incantation that ended with his eyes closed and his arms spread wide.

The man stood in silence for what seemed like a long time to Rod, who was holding his breath, and then confirmed, "He means it. His intention was to send this man into slumber so he could… he could…" He blushed, and pointed at Taeauna, then hesitantly waggled his pointing finger back and forth between the baron and the Aumrarr.

She nodded her thanks, and told Tindror crisply, "Then, Lord of Wrathgard, you may just have retained your life." She gestured with her head, a sharp lift, bidding him rise. "The secret passage," she commanded, her sword never wavering from the baronial throat.

"Yes," the baron said huskily; he'd started to nod and promptly felt the cold point of her steel. He backed carefully away, Taeauna moving with him so her sword never left its menacing position, until he'd passed the windows and reached the tapestried wall beyond. He did something to the paneling behind the first tapestry that made it shrink back into darkness, leaving a narrow opening that someone thrusting the tapestry aside could enter, to step around the section of paneling.

"Rodrell, bring the wizard and follow us closely," Taeauna commanded. When they'd crossed the room, Tindror silently led the way up a long, very steep secret stair.

The door at its top stood open, so they could step right into a palatial bedchamber, windowless but hung with many lamps, and aglow with sunlight streaming down a spiral metalwork staircase in one back corner. The room was soft underfoot with overlapping furs, and was dominated by a huge round bed where four beautiful women lounged sleepily, clad in alluring scraps of silk or even less, until they sat up to stare at their lord and the three intruders in shock.

"Turn out your... maids," Taeauna ordered the baron. "They can sleep elsewhere this night, and perhaps really sleep for a change."

Tindror flushed angry red, but obeyed silently, pointing at his maids and then down the stairs, and standing over them as they plucked up various robes, found footwear, and hastily departed.

The Aumrarr turned to Rod, pointing at the door the four maids had just vanished through at the head of the secret staircase. "Lock and bar yon door," she commanded, "and share the bed with the mage. I promise you he'll be no trouble after you put him to bed, bind, and gag him."

Rod tried not to stare at her with quite the shock Tindror's playlasses had done, but wasn't sure he was succeeding. "But... where will you—?"

Taeauna gave Rod a look that silenced him in an instant, and then whirled back to the baron, sword up to point at the spiral staircase.

"Get up there," she ordered, "and then toss every last hidden weapon in your bedchamber down here. Then I'll come to your bed. And do all you ask. Try not to scar me too badly."

Chapter Eight

ROD EVERLAR WAS awakened by the screaming. Shrill, agonized shrieking from overhead that sent him bolt upright in the near-darkness, and wakened the bound wizard beside him into a squirming frenzy of frantic muffled calls through his gag.

Rod was still blinking and trying to gather his wits when Taeauna and the baron, both unclad, burst into view at the top of the spiral staircase, bloody swords in hand. Tindror half-ran and half-fell around the first curve of the stair, fetching up against the rail and turning to face whatever might be following them, and the Aumrarr vaulted over the rail to crash down feet-first on the edge of the bed, tipping it up wildly in a great groaning of wood. Rod and the struggling wizard were hurled into the air, and the bundle of boots and clothing Taeauna was carrying burst apart in all directions.

Taeauna's landing was hard enough to hurl her across the room into a wardrobe; it rocked, boomed against the wall behind it, and flung its doors open in protest, but didn't topple as she caromed off it into a run.

The wizard squalled through his gag as she sprinted right at him, but she merely freed him with two swift slices of her gore-dripping sword and whirled away in search of her boots, hissing at Rod, "Get dressed! Find your sword! We're under attack!"

Tindror joined the hunt for clothes, panting hard and snarling, "They must have emptied the Falconspires of lorn! There must be hundreds out there!"

"There'll be hundreds in here, once they hew through all the furniture," Taeauna panted back at him. "Sorry about your bed!"

The bearded baron shrugged. "Just so long as we both live to see you help me warm the next one." He found his belt and fumbled at the buckle, which started to glow, lifting the darkness they were all groping in to mere dimness. "Can't find my damn boots in all this gloom! Why can't they attack after morning soup, like decent bandits?"

Rod stared at him.

"'Twas a joke, silent man!" Tindror snarled, while hopping on one foot as he struggled, one-handed, to tug on what must be Galathan underwear. Then the baron saw that Rod's stare was fixed on his sword, which was dripping bright blue ichor. Tindror waved it. "Hoy, silent man, haven't you ever seen lorn blood before?"

"N-no," Rod admitted. "We don't put it in *our* morning soup."

Baron Tindror blinked at his guest, and then roared with sudden laughter.

"Ho, but that's the spirit! That's the flaming backbone, by Galath!"

He whirled suddenly to wag a finger in the half-dressed wizard's face, and said, "Don't let me catch you trying to hurl spells at our backsides, or use them to slink away, either! That motherless rump-licker Murlstag is out there with all his knights, nigh a score of Helms against every one of ours, ringing Wrathgard all around, and lorn by the score are roosting on all our roofs and turrets and battlements! You know as well as I do which Doom is behind this, and if you don't know by now what Dooms do to lesser wizards when they catch them, trust me thus far: you don't want to find out!"

The wizard whimpered, gabbling his words twice before he could say them clearly. "Isn't this the safest place to stay, right here? With the long staircase Baron Murlstag's swords will have to fight their way up."

"It would be," Tindror snarled, "if the lorn hadn't burst in on us up there! When my father's grandsire built Wrathgard, there were no lorn in Galath, none of us had ever seen such a beast. So my bedchamber has eight windows, each as tall as two men—or *had*; they just smashed them all, coming in at us all at once!"

He lowered his voice into a fierce muttering, and added, "The only reason they're not down here clawing and biting at us right now is that Tay and I pulled my best suit of armor down into the top of the stair after us, and chanted nonsense over it; the lorn think it's enspelled and waiting to do them harm if they so much as touch it. No, we have to get down and go deep, to the cellars where our well is, and the granary and armory around it, where old spells are laced through the stones and no wizard of today, Doom or otherwise, can make those stones walk to thunder into battle against us, or melt to fall on our heads! Come, while we still can!"

By then, Tindror was speaking to three hastily dressed people. He and Taeauna traded looks, she lifted aside the bar across the door, Rod handed her the key to its lock, and they started down the steep, narrow staircase and into the growing din of battle.

Murlstag's men had won past the gates and were already inside the castle.

"Oh, shit," Taeauna whispered, and turned to Rod. "Lord, this is not the ending I hoped for. I am sorry."

Tindror and the wizard both looked at Rod, startled at that "lord."

He kept his eyes on Taeauna, and told her fiercely, "We're not dead yet. You… you have nothing to apologize to me for. I… I'm starting to like this. Even with all the blood and doom."

Her sudden smile made her eyes flame. "Oh, I can give you more of that."

"I don't doubt it," the wizard said suddenly from ahead of them, slowing as they reached the bottom of the staircase and the *clash* and *clang* of swords grew suddenly louder. "But what of right now? What should—?"

"Stand aside," Lord Tindror told him brusquely, "and save your spells until I ask for their hurling. 'Tis time to fight! Good old butchery, carving up foes like carcasses for the kitchens!"

He thrust himself past the shuddering wizard and sprang down the last few steps, bellowing, "For Wrathgard! For Tarmoral!"

The stair opened into blood-drenched tumult. Bodies lay sprawled in spreading pools of blood everywhere, and rats were boldly scurrying from one corpse to another, unheeded in the desperate fray. There was no sign of the baron's maids or any other women of the castle, except among the dead, and the few men of Tarmoral were busily swarming and hacking down two foes in full plate armor, holding their arms and feebly kicking legs as daggers worked at armor joints and snarling men wrestled against locked-down visors to open breach enough to slip a knife blade in.

The baron rushed over to the nearest enemy knight, dug his fingers under the edge of the man's helm, and tore at it, twisting viciously. The neck inside it cracked just before he got it far enough up that his men, stabbing past him, could bury half a dozen daggers into the exposed Murlan throat.

Blood fountained, and streamed down Lord Tindror as he turned and stalked over to the second Murlan knight, snapping, "Belgard! Guard yon door! Gethkur, I want every stick of furniture you can swiftly lay hand to packed—and packed tight, in a real tangle—into the forehall, and its doors barred and braced, both ends!"

His men leaped to obey. Their fellows kept stabbing at the second knight who was dying by the time the baron reached him.

"The least of Murlstag's hounds," Tindror said sourly, "have better armor than any man of Tarmoral has ever owned. And for years the bulk of our crops have been demanded by the Throne of Galath, while all they ask of Morngard is a dozen new-forged swords and shields every harvest-tide. 'Twill be a pleasure swording warriors who invade us at the behest of the king."

"I've been busy at that pleasure since before dawn," a graybearded Tarmoran panted, rising from the task of tugging armor off a dead Murlan knight. "Murlstag is out there; I saw him myself, sitting his saddle under his banner. No one else this side of a field hawk has those yellow eyes. We think he brought a few hundred more than a thousand with him, under arms; we've taken him down under the thousand, all right, but… then there're the lorn."

Tindror nodded. "There are," he replied curtly. "How much of Wrathgard do we still hold? Are all the lower floors—?"

"No. These and the rest up here came up a ladder to that big window in the Shields Hall; the lorn broke it and held the upper end of the ladder firm, against our shovings and hewings from within. They still have Shields Hall, but we've forced them back to its doors. Down below, the main doors are still shut against them for now, but a few of the Murlans who came up the ladder are skulking about, swording anyone they can reach. We're hunting them."

"Well done, Lemral. The lorn: have any of them dared to enter Wrathgard?"

"Not that I know of, lord, though they could be swarming through the upper rooms of all six towers and I'd not know it. I have seen them out windows, just as I ran past; they're perched on our roofs and ramparts like trees in the forest!"

"The North Stairs?"

"Still ours. The Purple Stairs, too. We're going below, lord?"

Tindror nodded.

"Good. Torl and Baereth have been guarding the well since first warning was cried by the wall-watchers."

The baron smiled. "Good and better. Have—"

Faintly, from outside the walls, came a sudden swell of sound. Angry shouting, cries of alarm, a thundering of many hooves, and then a long, rolling succession of dull, meaty, heavy crashes, laced with the screams of horses and men.

Then a war-horn sang out, high and clear, in a distinctive three-note call. It was echoed by two more, and they were all answered by a rising din of shouts and steely clanging, the ringing of hundreds of swordblades striking each other.

"Deldragon?" Tindror snapped, wild hope in his face. He and Lemral sprinted off down a passage.

Taeauna followed every bit as quickly, taking firm hold of Rod's elbow as she passed, to tow him along, and snapping at the wizard, "Come, wizard! Come, or I'll hunt you!"

They all pelted along the passage, through one door and then another, into a room where lorn were perched on the sills of shattered windows, and dead Tarmoran guards lay sprawled and silent on the floor.

The lorn took flight, hissing, as Lord Tindror charged right at them. He fetched up at the broken window, panting, to stare past his raised sword, out and down.

In the morass of churned earth that the Murlan horses had made of the ditch and great slopes around

Wrathgard, the men of Murlstag were dying in their dozens under the lances and blades of even more magnificently armored knights, a great sea of moving steel that had charged into them without warning from behind and smashed through their ring, trampling and slaughtering, before the war-horns had sounded.

Through that breach the newcomers were now flooding in all directions, charging besieging Murlans. Tindror laughed aloud as he beheld Baron Murlstag's own banner flapping raggedly, far off to the left in frantic flight toward the mountains. A small and dwindling knot of Murlans around it were being ruthlessly harried and hacked down by hard-riding knights, and three dragon banners streamed above those pursuers.

Everywhere the baron looked, he could see busy butchery of Murlans, their maroon banners with white stag heads falling here, there, and over yonder. And everywhere the eye turned, steel-hued banners emblazoned with a crawling red wyrm were advancing.

He held up his sword to them in salute before turning from the window.

"Deldragon," Lord Tindror announced slowly, deep satisfaction in his voice. "Deldragon has come to save us all."

CRIMSON DRAGONS FLAPPING on steel-gray banners fell into liquid shapelessness as the scrying-spell faded, and left the wizard Arlaghaun watching nothing at all.

"Amalrys," he ordered his chain-girt apprentice flatly, "cast it again. I must see if that fool Murlstag survives and manages to return to Morngard."

She nodded in the gloom of the old stone room, eyes downcast for fear of drawing his ire. They both knew how displeased he was at Deldragon's sudden appearance, and how had that meddlesome, oh-so-valiant velduke known of Murlstag's ride on Wrathgard, anyway? What wizard was whispering in *his* ear?

Her cruel master sat silently watching her casting, as he often did, looking like a sharp-nosed warhound in his gray garb, his brown eyes ablaze. At first she'd thought he watched her so intently because his chains were all Arlaghaun suffered her to wear and he enjoyed indulging his lusts, but she might have been bared down to her bones for all the man-reaction his face betrayed right now.

That sharp, thin-lipped face was a mask of calm as her chains chimed around her. Amalrys made her casting as graceful a dance as she could, swaying her hips and tossing her head to make her long, unbound honey-blonde hair swirl about her shoulders, thrusting her breasts and hips at him in as sinuous a manner as she could manage, offering herself to him with longing in her eyes, just as he preferred... but when at last she was done and turned to face Arlaghaun, fingers spread in the last gestures, he wasn't looking at her at all.

He'd been busy casting his own spell, all this time. A compulsion magic.

Her master gave her an expressionless nod. And then he did something surprising. Though he'd never bothered to tender her any explanations before, he did so now.

"I have worked a compulsion," he announced calmly, "to draw all the nobles under my control to

Galathgard, to receive the king's next decrees. It will take some days for all of them to reach the castle; you and I shall use that time to work tantlar magic. A *lot* of tantlar magic. When Deldragon arrives home, he will find his wells and flour poisoned, and every last item of magic in his castle gone."

Amalrys couldn't help herself. She went white and started to shake.

Arlaghaun smiled slowly, obviously enjoying her terror for what seemed to her a very long time before he added gently, "Calm yourself. I will not be requiring you to test the magics we seize. Klammert and Yardryk are both more expendable than you; they can see to braving any traps and unforeseen discharges."

"HAS HE?" TAEAUNA murmured. "You're sure he's not ridden by a Doom, who sent him here to slay or capture us?"

Tindror sighed and waved his arms wide, his drawn sword still in his hand. "I can be certain of nothing, Tay; you know that. Yet he's the last noble in all Galath I'd suspect of doing any wizard's bidding. Yes, yes, I know that makes him a more suitable wizard's pawn than the rest of us, but somehow I just can't believe... no. No."

The bearded baron shook his head, and then shrugged. "And if he is? How can we stand against him? Murlstag's men were more than my loyal blades can handle; Deldragon can bury us in knights, all of them better armed and armored than we are. So when this fray is done, and he comes to our doors, I'll let him in, and welcome him as the friend he has always been to me. And if he then seizes you and your silent lord, or butchers me where I stand, and all of my household with me, then… he does so. Whether I like the fate he hands me or not, what can I do?"

FOUR DIRTY-BOOTED MERCHANTS crouched behind spreading sallva branches and peered out over a battlefield at the distant towers of Wrathgard. They wore no badge or colors to tell Falconfar they were of the Vengeful, but they didn't need to. Real merchants would have been fleeing as fast and as far as they could from this pitched battle, not sitting on a ridge, albeit in bushes, staring down at it. The screams of horses and men and the clang of steel on steel drifted up to them all too clearly.

"So what do we do?" the oldest, deepest-voiced one asked. Thrayl was seldom at a loss for what to do next, but this was one of those rare occasions. "Go back to Lord Tharlark and tell him all Galath is risen in war? Or that the two we were sent to find must have been captured or slain? Or go not back at all? Or go on into this?"

"I'm not lying to Tharlark," small and sly Carandrur put in, his whining voice sounding affronted, almost bitter.

The third Vengeful, a coffee-colored man with a row of small, simple earrings riding each of his ears, shrugged. "Well, I'm not getting myself killed because Tharlark wants to collect heads of folk he's never even met, who passed through Arvale and were gone out of our lives where we should safely leave them." The fourth Vengeful, a darker, taller man, nodded silently.

"Dombur, I don't recall the lord asking your opinion of his commands," Carandrur snapped. "Nor you, Pheldur, if you stand with Dom."

"Carandrur, I don't recall the lord making you any sort of commander over us," Dombur replied flatly. "Nor did I tell Lord Tharlark I'd do as he directed. Both you and he seem to forget I'm not of Arvale; nor is Pheldur, here. He seems forgetful indeed to me, Tharlark does, as he's obviously forgotten something else, too: that the Vengeful are not his to order about as his personal servants."

"Aye," Pheldur rumbled. "I haven't the hips, nor the breastworks, come to that, to be one of his 'personal servants.' I'm more the simple 'wizard-hating, get on with my life, slay all magic-dabblers when I find them' sort. Let strutting lords hire, train, and pay their own skulk-swords, if it's slayings they want done of travelers who eluded them and might, or might not, have magic."

"Are you two mad?" Carandrur hissed. "Have you forgotten how many Arbren the two we're hunting slew, back in Arbridge?"

"Friend Carandrur," Thrayl snapped, "I don't count Snakefaces or Dark Helms as proper folk of Arvale. Now, how would things be if you were abed in an inn with your woman, and in the dark of the night men with blades burst in to slice you up, and you happened to be awake and have your own sword to hand? Are you telling me you'd not defend yourself, nor hotly proclaim your perfect right to do so, if you survived? Hey?"

Carandrur grimaced, then shook his head and spat, "I obey my Lord of Arvale, as any loyal Arbren should. If he is mistaken, then he is mistaken; it's not my place to pause and ponder if he is or not."

"Oh?" Thrayl folded his arms across his chest. "Lord Tharlark demanded that a wingless Aumrarr and a wizard who'd passed through his lands, and were clean gone, be hunted and slain outside our borders, and their heads brought back to him. Well enough: he is my lord, and I'll obey. Yet what if I find this Aumrarr and the man with her isn't a wizard at all, what then? And since when do thinking folk want to slay Aumrarr, who do good for all, albeit in a way that often rubs lords a-wrong? Are we to murder passing innocents, because my Lord Tharlark's bloodlust is up and he feels the need to count another wizard in his tally? Or because he's angry that two folk slipped through his fingers, and feels the need to show Arbren he's in firm charge of all that befalls in the vale, and will hunt beyond our borders what he missed seeing when they were standing under his hand? And what if word gets around to more way-merchants, of how Arvale will hunt down any of them that Arvale's lord gets to thinking might be a wizard? How many merchants will come into our vale at all, then?"

Carandrur's face darkened, and he folded his arms across his chest in exaggerated mockery of what Thrayl had done. "I didn't come here to the blundering edge of a battle, Thrayl, to bandy words with you."

"Well, now, think on those words you've just said a moment, Carandrur. That's just it; we're sitting on the edge of a great fray, and find this end of Galath, at least, roused to arms and rushing about killing each other with right bright enthusiasm! What boots it if our hunt for two folk we only think came this way, remember, rouses one of these warbands below to hack us to the ground and ride in anger right up into our little vale—defended only by Tharlark's sharp tongue and a handful of guards, mind—and lay waste to all Arvale, end to end, because we dared stride into Galath to hunt and slay?"

Thrayl sat back and added quietly, "Just think about it a little more, Carandrur. That's all I'm asking. While we still have our heads on our shoulders to do some thinking with."

BY THE TIME Deldragon's war-horns blew a triumphal flourish, Lord Darl Tindror had led his wizard and his two guests down to the towering front doors of Wrathgard, and ordered them flung wide.

Some of his men gave him grim looks, but hastened to obey, dragging out the huge beams that barred and braced the doors against rams, and thrusting the huge doors open, the ponderous arches groaning deeply as they were moved.

Tindror sheathed his sword and strode to stand where the two doors had met. His timing was perfect; Deldragon's knights had cleared the dead from before the doors and formed two rows, astride head-tossing horses, to give the velduke's bodyguard an avenue to ride along, forward to Wrathgard with Velduke Deldragon himself shielded from attack behind them.

The bodyguard, four stout-armored knights twice the height of some of their fellows, rode right up to Tindror and then parted, turning aside with cold, alert gazes, to leave the bearded baron standing staring up at a fair-haired, familiar figure in dazzling enspelled armor, mounted on a magnificent horse covered in mail and barding-plate.

From his flaxen mustache to his piercing ice-blue eyes, Velduke Darendarr Deldragon might have been a shining hero straight off the cover of one of Holdoncorp's game boxes. Bareheaded, he waved a gleaming gauntleted hand at the baron and called, "Darl! I hope you don't mind this intrusion. I felt a hunger to hunt Murlstag, and the spoor led me here!"

"Murlstags are bad at this time of year," Tindror observed, smiling. "I thank you for this and stand in your debt."

"Not at all, not at all. Murlstag fled, I'm afraid. My men are chasing him, but running is something he's very good at, and lorn came down like a cloud as he got near the Spires. He may make it home to Morngard yet."

"Wrathgard yet stands, and I have you to thank for that," Tindror said quietly. "Will you come in?"

"Alas, but I cannot stay. A certain wizard watches Bowrock, and means to do mischief whenever I am away from home."

"You have much to do with wizards?"

"As little as I can, friend Tindror. As little as I can. I have no love for the thought of ending up dancing to any spell-tune, if you take my meaning."

"So you smelled Murlstag in the air?"

Deldragon grinned. "No, nor used magic either. I have spies in that boar's wallow, and they have ways of signaling me swiftly. When I saw he'd gone to war, it fell to a simple matter of taking to horse and following him."

He looked up at the walls and towers of Wrathgard, drew his snorting horse nearer, and said more quietly, "Darl, to these eyes it looks as if Wrathgard is breached, and your healthy armsmen are now… but a handful. Need you sanctuary, at Bowrock?"

Lord Tindror's chin lifted. "Thank you, Darendarr, but no. I'll bide on my own lands, defend my own, and take my chances."

His voice was curt, but he held out his hand as if pleading, and added, "Yet I have two guests I can no longer give fitting shelter to; guests a wizard watching from afar might well send a stag to fetch. They could use your sanctuary."

He turned and pointed to Taeauna and Rod. The Aumrarr gave Deldragon a solemn nod, so Rod did the same, and endured a moment of feeling as if he was being skewered to the heart on a lance of ice-blue eyes before the velduke smiled and nodded.

"I extend my offer to you both, if you are minded to ride with me to Bowrock. Begging the pardon of my Lord Tindror for saying so, there's no finer castle in the land."

"I should be honored," Taeauna said loudly, "just as I was deeply honored by Lord Tindror's hospitality, aid, and friendship." She looked at Rod, and said, "I speak also for my traveling companion, Rodrell, whose wits have been spell-twisted. There are things he can't remember, and others he can't utter. He is on a death-quest, and can neither say nor remember the place he seeks. We Aumrarr owe a blood-debt to him, wherefore I am guiding him."

Deldragon's brows lifted. "Ah. Entertaining guests, I see. Be welcome in my home, provided, of course, we get there. Once the very rock of peace, justice, and order, Galath has become a rather more interesting place."

Without turning his head, he raised a voice a trifle and called, "Parl?"

"Lord Velduke?"

"How many Murlan horses can be ridden?"

"We have ten-and-nine, lord."

"Provide our two guests with one apiece, keep two as remounts, and give the rest unto Lord Tindror, in payment for disturbing his tillage."

He looked down at the baron, who nodded and said, "Deldragon, you are a decent man."

"Galath demands, Darl. Galath demands."

The velduke watched horses being brought to Rod and Taeauna, and Deldragon knights assisting them to mount by cupping gauntlets around their boots and through sheer strength lifting them up onto their horses. Deldragon nodded, let his own restive mount trot in a tight circle, and came back to Tindror to murmur, "You're sure you'd not want to feast tonight in Bowrock? Natha would be glad to see you, and Laranna, too!"

Baron Tindror stared up at him. "Tempting. Thanks. I find myself strong enough to stay. Where I belong."

Deldragon inclined his head. "Darl, you're a decent man, too. Fare you well, in the days ahead; they bid fair to test us all." He looked across the churned slopes of dead and dying men and horses, and added, "You've weathered the first test handily. I wonder if there's such a thing as a lorn-slaying spell?"

Tindror shrugged. "There's such a thing as too much magic in a kingdom, that much I know."

Deldragon shook his head, watching servants hasten out of Wrathgard to hand his two new guests each a small, half-full laedre. "Too much magic? That's like saying 'too much boar' or 'too many knives.' 'Tis not the magic... 'Tis those who wield it; their weakness, that they get so seduced by power as to use it for their every whim. But this is converse for a fairer day, another time." He turned his head and cried, "We ride!"

"We ride!" the Deldragon knights roared in chorus, and set about turning their mounts in thunderous unison.

Deldragon nodded to Tindror, raised his open hand in salute, and said to Rod and Taeauna, "Guests, will you ride with me?"

"Bright Lord of Galath, we will," the wingless Aumrarr replied, framing her words in the tones and serene dignity of a noble lady of long years and high standing.

The velduke flashed his teeth at her in a delighted smile. "I believe I'm going to enjoy this ride home even more than usual."

Taeauna inclined her head to him, and turned to raise her hand in salute to Baron Tindror, who was still standing with his arms folded, in the open doorway of Wrathgard. He lifted his hand in response, face carefully expressionless.

Aside from Taeauna, who was watching for it, Rod was the only person who saw Tindror's lips move, soundlessly framing the words, "I love you."

Then Wrathgard and its bearded baron were behind them, Deldragon knights closing in around them in a jingling, clottering forest of trotting riders.

The velduke leaned close to Taeauna and said, "A good man; one of the few. You have just seen the pride and folly of Galath. If we were all a bit less noble and high-minded, and a bit more surly and... and..."

"Pragmatic," Rod murmured, earning himself a startled look from Deldragon, and then a fierce nod.

"Come," the velduke cried then to the knights all around, spurring his horse into a canter. "Ride in earnest! Lances up! 'Tis a long ride to Bowrock!"

Chapter Nine

THE RIVEN KEEP stood on a ridge deep in the wild heart of the Great Forests; already young trees were sprouting up amid its blackened and tumbled stones, and older ones thrusting out branches to cloak it in their greedy reachings for sunlight. The winged Aumrarr stalking grimly through the seared ruin moved slowly, for they were weary from a long flight, and battered from battle.

"Well, 'tisn't called Shatterjewels for nothing," Juskra said fiercely, impatiently brushing matted blonde hair back from her scarred face. "Of course the Dooms blasted every likely-looking stone and wall to powder! They'd cook and eat their own grandmares in hot-gobbling haste, if they thought doing so would win them one more spell!"

"Sister," the youngest and most beautiful Aumrarr replied quellingly, "tell us something we don't know. Years upon years of sisters before us swarmed all over this keep looking for magic, any magic!" Dauntra waved her arms at the devastation around them. "I don't know what you were thinking to find that they couldn't."

"A stone or two of the keep still standing," Juskra snarled back. "Do the Dooms have to wantonly despoil everything they touch?"

"It seems so," dark-robed Lorlarra sighed, coming into the shattered room from the dark opening that had brought her from the well-chamber. It had been a tight fit, even with her wings folded tightly around her. "Just be glad they've raged over this place so often, and thoroughly satisfied themselves that no magic remains but the echoes of what is lost. Otherwise, the power Ambrelle and I just used would have them all here in a trice, hungry for battle and new magic to call their own."

"It worked?" Dauntra's usually impish voice was sharp.

Ambrelle was the tallest and oldest of the four, and had fought hard and long. Her severe face was pinched with pain as she came out of the well-chamber in Lorlarra's wake, her purple-black hair hanging across her face as she nodded wearily. "Thus far," she said. "Malraeana and Phandele float in spell-sleep, and the healing has begun. It will take days, sisters mine."

"There are our own hurts to see to, after that," Juskra muttered. "I'm in no hurry to leave these glows that blind the Dooms to what we do here. Where in all the Falcon Kingdoms are folk free of their sway now?"

"And Highcrag and all our sisters are gone," Lorlarra whispered, hugging herself as if a chill wind had just thrust past her, "or twisted by those spell-tyrants."

"Twisted? Who? I thought they slaughtered everyone at Highcrag."

"They did." Lorlarra's voice was sadder than ever.

"Then who?"

"Taeauna. Wingless, now, and seen walking the world with a wizard."

"Taeauna? A *wizard*? Who?"

Lorlarra shrugged. "An unknown mage. From afar, perhaps."

"So how is it we know he's a wizard?"

Lorlarra shrugged again. "Who else but a wizard could tame her, sear off her wings, and have her so enthralled that she'd travel with him?"

Dauntra shook her head. "I'll not believe that until I see it myself," the youngest of the four Aumrarr said wearily. "There are wild tales enough whispering their ways ar—"

"This is no wild tale," Juskra said bitterly. "I heard it, too. From a trader who's one of the Vengeful."

Dauntra clapped her wings angrily, her large brown eyes darkening in anger. "Ah! The Vengeful, who see fell wizards under every stone and behind every face that so much as looks at them!"

"The Vengeful," Juskra snapped back, "who have found so many wizards these last few years and sent them to swiftly dug graves."

"Yes, and what has that given Falconfar? Three Dooms who tower over all the lands like god-colossi; three Lord Archwizards in the making!"

"Sisters!" Ambrelle said severely. "Cease this wrangling! I myself cleave to the thinking that we cannot be certain, from here in this ruin in the green wild heart of nowhere, whether or not Taeauna is a traitor and the man she's traveling with is a foe or a wizard, nor rightly deem them peril or no."

Tall and tired, she stormed into the midst of her fellow Aumrarr, hands on hips, and added crisply, "I believe our time will be much better spent making a meal, devouring it, and talking over Falconfar as it is, not Falconfar as one maimed sister and a mystery man walking with her may or may not make it, in time to come. There is much to discuss, sisters mine."

Juskra nodded a little sullenly, and scratched at the stiff, stained bandage that covered most of her breast. "Well said. So talk. I'll suffer you to do so just as long as we ride over new ground, or speak of what is happening now; I've little stomach for trading words we already know, about places all of us have seen time and again, year in and year out. For instance, it should come as no surprise to any of us that Hammerhand of Ironthorn has come out as clear and strong in his hatred of wizards as Tharlark of Arvale has ever been, nor that Eldalar of Hollowtree cleaves to the same view. I do not care to sit through all of us listing such well-known lore one more yawn-inducing time."

"Fair enough," Dauntra said flatly. "Know, then, that the newest of the Dooms—'N'—has successfully bred and spell-changed the beasts he calls 'greatfangs.'"

"The three-headed dragons?"

"They're not—oh, never mind. Yes, the three-headed dragons."

"And we know this because...?"

"Because he risked one on a daylight raid on the docks of Irkyn, in Rornadar, riding a second overhead to watch what befell. He'd not have risked them both had he not possessed others. Moreover, the two seen by the Irkynaar were younger and smaller than the lone greatfangs seen over Sardray a month back."

"He's breeding them," Lorlarra agreed.

"Yes," Juskra echoed. "I judge his thinking much as you do; he'd never risk both if they were all he had. My new lore is nothing like as dramatic as that, yet will be the more lasting."

Ambrelle's eyes twinkled. "Well, with a teasing like that, we're certainly listening. Say on."

"When we were all but younglings," the badly scarred Aumrarr began, rising from where she'd been sitting with hands clasped around knees to pace restlessly, wings stirring, "there were no priests in Falconfar, no churches. Holy places, yes; altars, aye. We murmured a few words to fading gods more or less for luck, and most Falconaar counted themselves lucky there were no sacrificial pyres anymore, no priests scourging and damning and striking unbelievers down dead. For kindness and sick-tending and rescues unlooked-for, Falconaar had us."

"I know where your words are leading," Dauntra murmured. "Say on."

"First came the Forestmother, worshipped in the Raurklor holds, who warded off wolves and worse, and guided home those lost in deep woods. And who could speak out against aid like that? Or fear a few young lasses who went barefoot, and nurtured mosses growing on their own skin?"

Juskra turned slowly to meet the gazes of each of her three sisters, and added softly, "So they are here to stay, and growing stronger. They talk now of Holy Moots, and 'Calling Up the Mother,' and having a say in who rules a Great Forest hold and who does not. Which is more than enough to rightfully alarm Falconaar. The way-traders who travel far with their wagons are already wary and muttering, warning each other of holds to be avoided if one travels alone. This much, sisters, you know already, or should."

She turned her head slowly to survey the faces of her fellow Aumrarr again, and added fiercely, "Hearken now to my news, out of southern Scarlorn. A new god is rising, darker by far than the Forestmother. 'Gluth,' they call it, the Black Beast, a gigantic padding thing of claws and fangs that stalks the wild places, and hunts humans left alone. Hunts those its worshippers bid it to, they believe, staking sacrifices out to die and going on hunts of their own to bare and wound and leave helpless victims of their choosing, for the 'Holy Jaws and Claws' to find... This is evil, sisters, and rising, and many *want* to believe in it."

Juskra stalked across the riven room, folding and unfolding her wings in her rising agitation. "I tremble for the day—and it will come soon—when one of the Dooms sees that the way to exalt himself over his rivals, and us all, is by using his spells to shape such a beast and use it to command all who worship Gluth. And where men hate and fear wizards, those same men will cower before a god."

"Shit," Lorlarra whispered, white to the lips. "Juskra, you certainly know how to make this particular Aumrarr wish she'd died at Highcrag. If you're right—and I'm sure you are—this is a shadow over all Falconfar, and we will live out the rest of our lives in its gloom. Not that it sounds like our lives will be all that long."

"They won't be, the moment some priest of the Black Beast or the Forestmother decides Aumrarr are an evil to be hunted down to earn divine approval," Ambrelle said softly, running her hands absently through her purple-black tresses. "Oh, sister, can this be true?"

"Can and is," Juskra said darkly. "Deny it or refuse to see it, and you endanger us all. I begin to think the best service we can do Falconfar is to fly swift and hidden to every last Falconaar ruler and elder we can find, and warn them against the worship of these two deities, speaking as if the Dooms are already controlling them, but doing so in places where they are too busy to rule or conquer directly. We need the rulers to be scared enough to act, but not too scared to act."

Dauntra nodded. "That will work. I like it not, and it will be both difficult and dangerous the moment the Dooms learn what we're doing, but it is our best road ahead. Sister, I thank you for this warning." She rose, strode slowly across the room to what was left of a wall, thrust her hand gently against it in slow anger, and then turned, eyes flashing.

"So we must together do the tongue-march across Falconfar, here and now, and decide where to go and what to do. Ambrelle, conjure the map."

Ambrelle looked to Juskra. "Promise you'll not storm out if we chew over holds and rulers?"

Juskra drew back her lips to show her teeth in a mirthless smile. "You have my word. Make the map."

Ambrelle drew forth a pendant from its hiding place in her bodice, clasped her hands together around it, closed her eyes, and whispered, "Show me."

The shattered and tumbled stones before her began to glow an eerie emerald hue, a glow that rose in threads from them, drifting like smoke. In a few silent moments it had formed a horizontal disc in the air, a circle as thin as parchment and as far across as a wagon... a circle of blue and dun brown and dark green, that spun and flowed and then quite suddenly became sharp-featured. There were seas in three places, one of them vast enough to fill a third of the disc. A great spine of mountains arose that almost split the disc into two halves, trailing off into that large sea in a string of isles like the barbs of a dragon's tail. The rest was brown land or great ragged stretches of green forest.

The other Aumrarr all leaned forward as Ambrelle opened her eyes, sighed, and put the pendant back in its warm haven.

"Begin where we go most seldom," Dauntra suggested, "east of the Spires."

Juskra nodded, extending a long, sleek pointing arm to indicate a huge stretch of land that filled the southeastern arc of the disc. "Sarmandar of the Manykings. Large, rich, deep-historied, and not worth a moment of our time. We could spend our lives—long lives, mind—just going from one self-proclaimed king to the next. So long as they make war on each other—and that is all they do, sisters!—words of ours are wasted on their unhearing ears. Let fabled Sarmandar go its own way and find its own doom; let us keep to the north of the Wyrmsea."

Her pointing finger moved north, across a narrow sea that bounded Sarmandar to the coast of the huge landmass that covered most of the disc.

"On that north coast are the Spellshunned Lands," Lorlarra murmured, bending forward in her tattered black war-harness. "Perfumes and silks, and old, old magics gone wild and wrong. They'll not welcome the Dooms in black-towered Inrysk and proud Marraudro."

"Wherefore they have no defenses against the Dooms or any wizard of might," Juskra warned. "Moreover, with magic denied yet at work, all awry, those who hunger for order will find the promise of order—and so, a new taste for their own hunger—in the Beast and the Forestmother."

Ambrelle frowned. "So who rules there?"

Juskra sighed. "Beyond what all know, that the Lion-Knights rule in Marraudro, I know not. Inrysk has local lords and some sort of council of lords over all, as I recall, but of today's names and faces, I know none."

Ambrelle nodded. "Shall we leave them to last, sisters mine? Whispering to rulers takes longest when one must learn who and where each ruler is, and with our wings, we stand out, and may easily be used as unwitting pawns by the malicious, to work mischief by our very approaches to the ears of kings."

"Well said," Dauntra agreed. "So, trending back toward us, west of Inrysk along the shores of the

Wyrmsea, we come to Harfleet, Sholdoon, and Zancrast; all but names on the map to me."

"I've been to two of the three," Lorlarra said quietly. "All are bustling ports on Ommaun the Wyrmsea, their wealth ruling small territories around them. Uneasy neighbors, but too greedy for daily gold to leave off trading long enough to take up arms against each other. I'm sure the Dooms would love to rule them, and they would welcome wizards and the cultists as they welcome everything: as tools to earn them even more coin."

"The Dooms and priesthoods are hardly tools to be governed for long by mere greedy traders," Juskra disagreed.

"True, sister, but the folk of those ports won't know that until too late. Taraun Zaer is High Lord of Zancrast, a vain, purring, oh-so-jaded man whose wits are keen, but far feebler than he thinks they are." Lorlarra rolled her eyes. "Tall, slender, trim-black-bearded, and thinks himself irresistible to all women and any man he puts his mind to conquering."

"Charming," Juskra said venemously. "Well, Belrikoun is a lesser evil, then. He's the Ruling Scepter of Sholdoon. A fat man who looks like the former pirate and everyday greasy glutton that he is, but just and kind when he wants to be, and nobody's fool. He will listen, I think."

It was Dauntra's turn to frown. "Wasn't Sholdoon the place with the oh-so-sneering merchant nobles, who feud with everyone who comes within reach, and allow their own pride to rule them?"

Juskra nodded. "It was, but Belrikoun tamed them, by wooing the younger ones and slaughtering their elders but making the deaths seem richly self-earned. They love him not, but they do obey him, and now see and judge the world as it is, and not as they prefer it to be."

"Which proves that one man can change attitudes within his lifetime." Dauntra held up a hand to stop her fellow Aumrarr interrupting as she pondered. "Hmm. For my part, I have been to Harfleet. Arl Hraskur is the Waveking of Harfleet, and has received Aumrarr before in friendship. The more beautiful we, the more friendly he, if you take my meaning."

Lorlarra sighed. "Sister, we do. A night in his bed will mean he listens, then, but will he heed?"

Dauntra nodded slowly, her expression thoughtful. "Like Belrikoun, he's too wise not to pounce on any hint of a threat to his rule. He is wary, and has his spies, and plans ahead. He will know what to do. And do it."

"Which brings us to Scarlorn, just the other side of the Falconspires from us," Juskra said briskly. "Huge, pastoral Scarlorn."

"Land of farms, swamps, and more decadent satraps than I can count," Ambrelle sighed. "Must we visit them all?"

"But of cour—"

"No, Juskra. Here I disagree with you," Dauntra said firmly. "I have done sister-work in Scarlorn a time or two. Visit the right handful of satraps, and the spies of the rest will carry word to their masters better, and with it more apt to be believed, than if we came to whisper it ourselves."

"Fair enough," Juskra granted, scratching at her bandages and wincing. "So who are these 'right handful?' Vorl Dhaerar? Mrauker Zael? Harem-mon?"

"Mrauker, Haremmon, and Imb Trar. Vorl's palace is haunted by his aunts." Dauntra rolled her eyes again. "Their ghosts strangle spies, and most of Scarlorn knows that by now."

"Right, that's Scarlorn. Important enough, after we've dealt with the mess in our laps. Galath. If we fail there, it won't matter which god or goddess this kingdom or that chants to, or what way-hold bows to which Doom; we'll be dead and Falconfar will be lost," Lorlarra said quietly.

"And Taeauna and her pet wizard are in Galath right now," Juskra snarled.

Lorlarra shook her head. "He'll have to be far more than a pet, this mage of hers, if he's to have any hope of surviving for long in Galath. Arlaghaun rules in Galath, his spells right up the Mad King's backside, controlling every word that comes out of Devaer's mouth."

"Every noble of the realm has been summoned to Galathgard, to hear the king's will," Dauntra said grimly. "All who attend not will be branded traitors, their lives and lands forfeit."

Juskra shrugged. "Who of the Galathan nobles isn't his already? Deldragon, old Hornsar, Mistryn, and a handful of barons; Tindror, Ammurt…"

Ambrelle smiled mirthlessly. "Ammurt was killed a few days back, with all of his kin and most of his household. His tower collapsed on his head. 'Mysteriously,' they say."

"Aye, 'mysteriously' as in spell-blasted," Lorlarra sighed.

"So that's—what?" Juskra snarled. "Three vel-dukes and a baron, out of them all? While Arlaghaun sits on the throne of Galath, with Devaer a puppet in his lap!"

"Indeed," Dauntra agreed. "The king is his, two of the veldukes, all of the ardukes, every last marquel and klarl, all but one baron, and any number of the border knights. Against four men who may not ride together or agree on anything, save bending the knee to a king they deem mad. So, sisters, do we throw our lives away swording all who gather in Galathgard?"

Juskra shook her head fiercely. "Trying that would be just what you called it: throwing our lives away. If we don't slay Arlaghaun, then Galath is doomed. And we may have to do it several times since he may have spells set to bring him back from death. Then swiftly must we serve Malraun the same way, for he's sniffing around Galath, watching what Arlaghaun does and awaiting his chance. The nobles are but shouting brutes on horses, the king reduced to a drool-wits; 'tis the wizards who matter."

Ambrelle sighed, her face grim. "Sisters mine, it's always been the wizards who mattered."

"WHY THE HURRY?" Rod muttered through clenched teeth, as his saddle rose painfully to meet his descending crotch one more time. "Who would dispute with a velduke of the realm, and all these knights?"

Deldragon glanced at Rod with those ice-blue eyes for a moment, and then pointed up into the sky.

"They will," he said shortly, and then bellowed, "Lances up, lads! Gallop! Lorn!"

Rod's horse knew that barked command, if Rod didn't, and leaped forward. Rod hastily caught hold of the high horn of his saddle to keep from falling off, as the world suddenly became a blurred din of pounding hooves. Looking up, he saw a descending cloud of lorn, like a twister he'd once seen in the sky but lacking a dark cloud above it… a lowering, questing snout…

There was a terrible majesty in that slow, ponderous turn in the air, and then the swift and quickening dive, gray wings snapping back like the feathers of an arrow, claws extended, impassive skull-faces staring…

Hundreds of skulls, staring…

We have no lances, we three, Rod thought, or said in apprehension, in the instant before the lorn struck.

"I can't go on alone," Carandrur snapped. His eyes glittered; the sly little cobbler was seething. "So, are you all traitors to Arvale, then?"

Thrayl turned to Dombur and Pheldur; the three men exchanged dark glances, but kept silent, their faces expressionless. Thrayl looked back at Carandrur, his face a mask that betrayed nothing.

"Well?" the cobbler spat.

The three taller men went on giving him silence.

"Thrayl, when I get back to the vale and tell Lord Tharlark of this, what do you think he'll do to you? Hey? Kill you and your wife and daughter, and seize your shop and home, of course, but how will he hand you death? Do you really think he'll be merciful about it? That it'll be quick? Hey?"

"Lorn, yonder, diving out of the sky," Dombur said quietly, lifting his head in a gleam of earrings. "Lots of them."

Carandrur went on glaring at Thrayl, watching the shopkeeper's eyes leave his and lift to stare where Dombur and Pheldur were looking, up into the sky.

After watching their intent faces for some time, he turned to look, too.

Thrayl's sword was already in his hand; he stepped forward and swung, in one swift movement.

His steel bit deep into Carandrur's neck before the cobbler had even started to turn back.

Carandrur's head flopped loosely and his body spasmed, writhing wildly off Thrayl's blade into the dirt.

Thrayl stood like a statue, and watched the cobbler die.

He didn't look at Dombur or Pheldur until he was straightening from wiping his blade clean on the dead man's vest.

They looked back at him expressionlessly.

"Shrewdly struck," was all Dombur said, before they turned together, to begin the long trudge back to Arvale.

VELDUKE DELDRAGON LOOKED every inch the warrior hero, twisting and hewing in the heart of a cloud of flapping lorn, standing up in his saddle to deal flickering, darting death in all directions, as Rod stared at him open-mouthed.

His sword was like a great flashing fang as it swept up into a lorn breast, slicing open the squalling, clawing thing even as it tried to gore him. Entrails and blood gouted down the withers of his mount, and on the ground and horse behind. All around them, horses were starting to scream.

Brushing Rod's hip as their horses bucked and started to rear, Taeauna leaned perilously over in her saddle, exposing her side to the lorn that would have torn her open if it hadn't struck Deldragon's lorn and been hurled past, to slash with her blade at the lorn that was menacing Rod. Hissing, it batted at her blade and then was past her, great wings flapping, barbed tail lashing at Rod's face, before being severed by Taeauna's snarling slash. Blue blood spattered their faces as the lorn arched and squalled, fading away in the distance as fresh lorn swooped in.

It was all a blur to Rod, as he crouched low and fought to hold on to his saddle horn with all his strength, staring in astonishment at the forest of knights' lances ahead of them that were thrusting at the sky, impaling and slicing lorn here, there, and blood spraying everywhere.

"'Ware! They're coming around again!" Deldragon roared, reaching out a gleaming gauntlet to take Taeauna by the severed stump of one wing, where it protruded through her armor, and haul her back upright.

"No!" Taeauna shouted back almost merrily, eyes bright. "They are? You surprise me!"

Deldragon stared at her for a moment, then bellowed out surprised laughter, as lorn wheeled overhead and swooped down.

One was coming in low at Rod, this time from the side, almost kissing the ground before soaring up at his leg, head bent to lay open his thigh, tip him out of his saddle, or both. He snatched out his dagger, not knowing what else to do, and then Taeauna was there again, her shoulder ramming him as she flung herself across the curving back of his saddle to hold out her sword two-handed like a lance, giving the lorn the choice of impalement or shearing off.

It chose the latter at the last tail-lashing instant, hissing in fury. Again her blade met the barbed tail, but this time the lorn won free.

"They'll be after our horses next," Deldragon growled. "Time for some family magic."

"Magic?" Taeauna's head snapped around in a flurry of hair. "You're a wizard?"

"Hah!" the velduke snorted. "Hardly. I'm a man with something the wizards that bedevil us want. I have an enchanted ring!"

"I see," Taeauna panted, as her racing horse hit a hollow and bounced her in her saddle, hard. "What does it do?"

"This!" Deldragon called, thrusting out his hand at the next wave of lorn.

The sky in front of his spread fingers seemed to catch fire.

An instant later, the lorn did, too, howling in agony as they swept down, trailing crimson flames. In the air, those raging fires seemed to tug at their bodies, curling them in upon themselves like hide-head beetles, dragging them aside in ragged arcs from the bucking Deldragon horses.

Whereupon the burning lorn exploded—and horses, knights, wingless Aumrarr and all were hurled forward into the air, amid a great wave of searing flame.

"Isk, YOU AWAKE? Galath at last," the fat man growled from the front of the wagon. "Look dead, now."

The skeletally thin woman inside the creaking wagon made a rude sound by way of reply, shrugged off the cloak that had been keeping her warm, and laid herself down in the coffin.

Arranging the thin shroud over her naked body, she composed herself with her hands folded over her mouth. Between her fingers was the pinch of powdered arsauva that would leave her senseless the moment it touched her tongue; she held her fingers firmly together and waited. No sense wasting good arsauva if lazy border guards made its use unnecessary.

"I'm ready, Gar," she announced, closing her eyes. "Try to sound convincing, for once."

"I thought he'd never stop chasing us," the fat man muttered, as an armored Galathan warrior stepped out into the road and held up his hand in the signal to halt. "Still, we're here now. Driven to take refuge at last in the most law-abiding kingdom in all Falconfar. Strong king, proud nobles, lots of guards and coins. Bugger it all, anyway. Well, at least we'll be safe here."

"TAUREN'S MERCHANTS WILL do whatever they see best for preserving their own backsides," Juskra said flatly, running thoughtful fingers along the three old, white sword-scars that crisscrossed on her left cheek. "If that means deserting Tauren and taking themselves down the Ladruar to the Ports of Storm, that's just what they'll do. As allies, they are useless, and they'll never order their mercenaries into Galath to so much as lift a finger to aid someone else, not even if all of the Dooms lay wounded and helpless, for the ready slaying, because it will cost them coin."

"Yes, and they have no warriors but hireswords," Dauntra agreed, anger sparkling in her great brown eyes. "And their loyalty is to the purse, not a realm or kin or family hold. I know a dozen of the lords of Taur by name and face, and would be known to them if I flew to their gates, but they'd sell their own mothers and daughters for coin, let alone friends and allies."

"And Sardray keeps to Sardray," dark-armored Lorlarra put in. "As their elders never tire of saying, 'What comes to the windy grass matters; what befalls elsewhere matters not.'"

"And none of the forest holds," Ambrelle said quietly, "have either the battle-might to make any difference, nor the will or strength to push through two lands to reach Galath." The senior Aumrarr stretched her wings, tossing her long, glossy mane of purple-black hair. "So Galath, as we all knew, all along, is the cauldron. If Arlaghaun rises to rule it unopposed, the rise of the cults will hardly matter; Falconfar will be lost."

"We must work against him, and hope Taeauna's man *is* a wizard, and we can turn him into a blade against Arlaghaun."

"It all comes back to the wizards," Juskra said bitterly, scratching at her bandages again.

"Always," Dauntra agreed. "Well, there're Four Dooms, and four of us. A fair fight, I'd say."

They laughed then, the bitter laughter of despair.

Chapter Ten

ROD'S HORSE LANDED an instant before he did, wherefore he smashed his face hard into its neck. Which pleased it not at all.

As he fought to stay on its back, and it reared and bucked and lashed out in all directions with its hooves, there was similar rearing and screaming all around him, amid much knights' shouting.

The air around him was a-shimmer with heat and thick with the sharp smell of smoke, but the flames had faded, and war-horns were sounding. The wavering forest of upraised lances ahead told Rod that Deldragon's knights were still on the road, three abreast. Lorn wheeled and shrieked overhead, but none were swooping.

"That's done it, for a time at least," Velduke Deldragon said with satisfaction from somewhere, near to Rod's left. To Rod, the man looked completely untouched; flaxen mustache as neat as ever, eyes still that serene and icy blue. "They hate fire."

"I'm not surprised," Taeauna said tartly, from nearer. "So do the horses, to say nothing of me. Have you anymore little tricks of magic we should know about, Lord Deldragon?"

"No," came the flat reply. "None you should know about."

"I see."

"Lady of the Aumrarr," the velduke replied calmly, "these are troubled times, and I have a duty to Galath and to the folk who dwell under my hand. To keep to the right road and do his duty, a man must do what he must do."

"Agreed," Taeauna said pleasantly. "Words to remember."

Rod had just managed to catch hold of both his reins and his saddle horn, and felt secure enough to risk turning to look at Tay and the Galathan noble.

And then wished he hadn't. The glances they were giving each other included polite smiles, but their eyes looked as if they were crossing swords to begin a duel.

A duel to the death.

"My best firedance for the Lord Blackraven," Marquel Ondurs Mountblade said grandly, adjusting his new monocle, "and I'll have the same. Bring a large decanter, the old vintage, mind!"

The servant bowed low, spun around still in his crouch, straightened with an audible snap of dagger-coat tails, and hurried off past Mountblade's steward, who stood as still and expressionless as a statue, hands clasped behind his back, carefully out of earshot of seated lords.

Marquel Larren Blackraven had only just arrived at Mountgard; he'd still been clapping the road-dust from his hands when he'd been led up the path from the stables. Sighing in his ease, the tall, hook-nosed young nobleman leaned back in his chair to look out over the trim green gardens falling away from the terrace. He hummed under his breath for long moments, as he turned his head to peer; Mountblade smiled silently and watched his guest.

To their right rose the weathered stone bulk of Mountgard, but directly before them the greenest lawns Blackraven had ever seen sloped gently down to pleasant clusters of spire-shaped evergreens, little bowers of winding flagstone paths, and beds of flowering shrubs cloaking sculpted stone maidens. Beyond their shapely, endlessly beseeching limbs gleamed the tamed waters of a smoothly curving stream; from where he sat, he could just see the curve of an arched bridge in the distance, spanning somewhere beyond the sculpted forests. Beautiful.

"Nice," Blackraven said at last, and meant it, as he turned gleaming emerald eyes back upon his host. "This must be a delight to ride home to."

Monocle gleaming, Mountblade smiled widely. "It is. Not the grandest gardens in Galath, and far from the largest, but mine, and well suited to me. The stream, in particular; I've had the banks sculpt-ed this side, to make it perfect for strolling or bedding down with a lass, and I use the horse trail on the far bank every morn. Everything just as I want it. That's why the new wall; guarding all of this seems my best bet for keeping it. If battle comes, I don't want some ill-bred, motherless dog of a warrior galloping his nag through my beds, hacking at the trees as he fights off those who chase him, and winding up lying dead with his horse and a lot of others, tangled in the stream—just as rains come, so I get flooding!"

"Good thinking," Blackraven replied, rubbing the bridge of his hooked nose and nodding a little grimly. "Aye, I fear war is coming; strife that will purge Galath, cleansing our realm as never before."

Mountblade nodded glumly. "And tearing what it is to be of Galath asunder in the doing. Galath will never be the same again."

Blackraven stared at his fellow marquel, who was as young as he was, though the monocles he affected made him look older. He hummed absently under his breath for a moment as he considered what to say, and then shrugged. "My father said as much, and so did old Velduke Barrowbar, when I was a lad. The kingdom is always changing; none of us can ever have back the Galath of our youth."

"The king grows wroth more and more often," Mountblade muttered. "And titled folk who've not blood-sworn anew to him are down to... what? Three veldukes? A border baron or two?"

"Just one baron, now. Tindror, hard by the Arvale way through the Spires. He'll not last long. Nor, I'm thinking, will the others. We'll be summoned into the Presence soon, and mustered to arms by royal order."

"Hunting unbowed veldukes."

"Indeed. Yet so much is obvious, Mountblade; what has you worrying?"

"When all who might defy His Majesty are swept from the realm, what then? Will we be turned on each other again? Or sent against Tauren?"

"King Devaer does seem stirred by battle," Black-raven said carefully, "and why not? He seems good at it, no?"

"Ah, here's the wine," Mountblade said, by way of reply, seeing the returning servant slowly and carefully bearing a platter dominated by a gigantic decanter.

Blackraven turned to watch the approach of the firedance, and so missed seeing Mountblade collapse forward on his face onto the table between them, monocle clattering. Yet he would probably have failed to witness the fate of his fellow noble no matter which way he'd been facing, because he also slumped into slumber at the same moment, head lolling.

The astonished servant blinked and faltered in his measured stride, the platter swaying dangerously, until the steward stepped forward to deftly and firmly steady it and its oversized decanter.

"Wh-what has happened to them?" the astonished wine-bearer whispered.

"Worry not," the steward replied a little sourly. "I've seen this before. 'Tis magic. They'll wake in a moment, all afire with the same notion; whatever thinking a wizard's just thrust into their heads."

"What wizard? Do wizards rule in Galath now?"

"Of course, lad, but it means your death to speak of it. So, mind: I did not say 'of course,' but rather, 'Of course not.' Got it?"

The wine-bearer opened his mouth to reply, but ended up leaving it agape without uttering a word.

The two marquels awakened as suddenly as they'd fallen asleep, straightening without seeming to notice they'd nodded off. They stared at each other with identical smiles, brought their fists down on the table in perfect unison, and declared as one, "Galathgard it is, without delay!"

His monocle dangling, Mountblade looked at the steward and roared, "Horses! Full guard, to ride with me!"

"Y-your wine, lord," the wine-bearer offered.

"No time!" his master bellowed, springing up from his seat to stride for the nearest door into Mountgard, and thrusting the servant aside. "We must ride! We are required, before the throne, without delay!"

The steward, still nodding acknowledgment of his master's command, caught the decanter out of midair, even as the wine-bearer, the platter, and the two ornate metal flagons crashed to the terrace.

Marquel Blackraven was already up and out of his chair; he snatched the decanter from the steward's hands as he hastened to follow his host. The steward ran with him as the noble drained the decanter in one long, loud quaff, and calmly accepted it when Blackraven wiped his elegantly trimmed mustache with the back of his hand, still running hard, and handed it back to the steward with a great satisfied sigh.

Reaching the doorway just behind the visiting marquel, the steward of Mountgard snapped a stream of orders to the door-servants, handed one of them the decanter, and strolled back to help the wine-bearer up.

The younger man was still on his knees, retrieving fallen flagons and wincing over his bruises. He looked up a little fearfully to find the steward smiling crookedly down at him.

"And *that*," the older man said ruefully, "is how Galath is ordered these days. I used to think we lived in the grandest realm in the world…"

A FEW LORN were wheeling high overhead, like vaugren circling over something that had died in the open, but most of them had fled after Deldragon's fire burst. The knights had ridden hard and steadily since the attack, seeming to ignore streaming wounds, loose-flapping armor, and a handful of empty saddles, but a certain tension hung over the three riders at the heart of the long column of Deldragon knights.

Rod knew not what to say, and Taeauna had given Velduke Deldragon only tight smiles, and not a word of reply, since their words about other magic the velduke might be—no, almost certainly was—carrying.

This seemed to alarm Deldragon, who'd tried several times to begin pleasant converse, and was now stroking his flaxen mustache repeatedly.

"We're well onto my lands now, and very near to my home," he announced, as they started around a high green hill crowned by a banner-fluttering watchpost; a horn rang out from it, and was answered by the war-horns of the knights at the head of the column. "If I've offended you, I desire you to remember this: duty drives us all hard."

"Certainly, Lord Deldragon," Taeauna said warmly, rescuing Rod from silent helplessness.

Well, what does one say to such a large, handsome hero of a man? "Hi, I created you, glad you've turned out the way you did?" "You're certainly more impressive in person than how I just described you, in a few overblown sentences?"

"I am sorry if my reaction has discomfited you in any way," the Aumrarr said smoothly to the velduke riding at her hip. "Your dedication to duty is admirable; one of the rocks that folk must be able to stand upon and trust in, if there is to be any peace in Falconfar. You are quite correct in keeping your secrets and weapons ready but known only to you. I would do the same, were I riding in your saddle."

Darendarr Deldragon peered closely at her face, those ice-blue eyes intent, seeking any hint of mockery, but Taeauna gave him a real smile and the words, "Lord, I mean what I say. Truly. I am an Aumrarr, remember?"

"I believe you," the velduke said, matching her smile, "yet feel moved to comment that I have met sisters of yours before, and known both sarcasm and playful deceit to fall from their lips—very prettily, and not without cause, but with the shrewd power to wound nonetheless."

"Ah. Yes. I can speak in that wise, too, when moved to. I meant rather that Aumrarr deeply understand duty and dedication to it, given how our own lives are spent."

"Indeed," Deldragon replied, inclining his head politely and leaving Rod settling deeper into safe silence than ever. Then, as they rounded the bend, the velduke swept out his arm grandly and said, "Welcome to Bowrock!"

Rod Everlar had seen Bowrock before in his dreams—or had he created it, his dreams causing the castle to be? He was going to have to understand that part of things better, and soon—but that first sight of it, soaring white and splendid across a broad green valley, still took his breath away.

It was huge. A mottled stone city crowning a hill, girt about with tall white stone fortress walls that thrust out into two massive gate-towers to greet the road they were riding down; identical, side-by-side towers that soared straight and bright up into the sky like something out of a fairy-tale, only bigger. Much, much bigger.

"It doesn't look as if it could ever be taken," Rod mumbled, and saw Taeauna hide a smile as, beyond her shoulder, Deldragon's brows rose.

"No, it doesn't!" the velduke agreed heartily. "I sit taller in my saddle whenever I ride around this bend and gaze upon it. I was born and reared in Bowrock, and have always known it would be mine. Yet somehow, when looking upon something so grand, one is always aware of those who dwelt before you. In Bowrock, it seems to me that I walk cloaked in the ghosts of my ancestors. Not unfriendly haunts, nor anything I or you or anyone can see and hear; but I can feel them. Always."

Taeauna nodded as if that was a familiar feeling to her. Rod nodded out of respect and because his mind was busily picturing Deldragon sweeping down staircases with a ghostly escort, streaming out pale and wraith-like behind him like an impossibly long bridal veil...

More horns sounded, from the tall towers of Bowrock this time, and were answered by the knights riding up ahead. The road went on past the gates, Rod could now see, forking to descend into the valley and to wind through hills and on south and west, to other velduchal lands in Galath.

The road also broadened, and acquired traffic. Carts were drawn up along its verge, selling everything from remounts and draft-oxen to trinkets, and a lot of heaped greens and root crops. Folk strode back and forth shopping, many of them towing rumbling-wheeled handcarts, but this sea of people parted miraculously to let the knights trot straight through without hindrance or a word spoken.

And many of the people, as Deldragon rode past, thrust their hands to their chests in some sort of salute, standing tall and gazing at him with respect. The handsome velduke nodded to as many of them as he saw, unsmiling, his head turning this way and that constantly so as to miss no one.

Rod's heart lifted, and he found himself, suddenly and silently, close to tears.

So this was what it was to be revered and genuinely looked up to. He'd written plenty of fictitious, heart-wrenching scenes down the years, in book after book, but this... this was real. There wasn't a shred of fear in those faces; this was no tyrant coming home and marking who genuflected and who did not. This was real.

"Jesus," he whispered under his breath, shaking his head in awe. To be so, well, "loved" probably wasn't the right word for it at all, but...

Then they turned into a huge archway into a narrowing stone chute, a rising cobbled ramp between walls bristling with stark, menacing arrow-slit windows, that led to a second arch.

Rod glanced up and found himself looking at a forest of massive spikes; rows of portculli just waiting to thunder down, and beyond them, just before the inner arch, a massive wooden scoop or hinged basket full of what Rod thought were ball bearings could be seen. To pour down the ramp and make every foe and their horse fall, yes, but where did Falconaar get ball bloody bearings?

Not from *his* writings, that was for sure... oh. Holdoncorp. Of course. If a trap would be visually fun in a computer game, he'd better assume Falconfar had that trap. And all of its clanking, spiked, blood-dripping, cigar-smoking variants, too.

So did that mean that ball bearings appeared magically, in smiths' back rooms and castle armories and market stalls? Or that overnight some Falconaar conceived of them, and how to fashion them round and nigh perfect, and awakened driven to make some, and not cease until they were being snapped up all over the Falcon Kingdoms? How did this... what had Tay called it? Oh, yes, "shaping." How did this shaping really work, anyway?

Beyond the inner archway, the way widened into a huge open space where many cobbled streets met. A busy moot was fronted by three guardposts where hard-eyed guards manned crossbows as large as wagons that hurled quarrels larger than the knights' lances. The crossbows were aimed right at the archway, to fire down the throats of anyone trying to storm the castle gates. Beyond, the crowded, many-balconied buildings of the city rose like a dirty gray-brown wall, but one broad street ran on through them, straight and true, rising at its far end into...

"My home," the velduke said, pointing. At a large, spartan-looking stone keep up on a hill, crowning the highest point of the hill covered by the city, right at the back, beyond all the crowded roofs.

"Jesus," Rod hissed again, as the knights started the long trot down the avenue. It was one thing to blithely write about tall buildings and crowded cities and reeking dung-wagons, but quite another to ride through the heart of it all gawking around, seeing and smelling and...

He saw washing hanging from balcony rails, and stout women with weathered faces securing it with wooden pegs bristling from their mouths. He saw scores of men and children trudging or even struggling under the weight of laden caskets and coffers and sacks; the trade in every shop seemed to involve carrying lots of things. And everywhere Rod saw folk pause in what they were doing to glance down at the procession of riding knights, recognize the bareheaded velduke, and straighten to smartly bring their hands to their chests in salute. Jeez, that was impressive.

He glanced over at Deldragon; as before, the velduke was nodding back to everyone he saw saluting him.

Flies were everywhere, and horse dung underfoot, though children with scoops or using just their hands and stained old sacks were darting out between horses and hurrying folk to scoop up the steaming droppings. Rod turned in his saddle to see where one of them—a dirty-faced girl in a rag of a dress—went, and saw her hasten down an alley and in at a door.

Then they were past, and he could see that alley no more, and the streets were rising and growing broader and less crowded. The houses were grander, now, some of them having little stone walls and arched metal gates enclosing tiny garden-yards, rather than opening directly onto the street. He'd seen nothing that could be called a sidewalk, nor…

A sudden, strident war-horn fanfare jolted him upright, blinking.

He was in time to see the knights in front of them parting, turning aside and bringing their horses to head-tossing halts, to let the velduke and his honored guests enter Deldragon's castle first.

They rode through an arch wide enough for six riders abreast, in a crenelated wall perhaps thirty feet high, into a wide cobbled area in front of a grand door at the top of wide stone steps, with another archway into the gloom of some sort of interior coachyard, beyond.

Uniformed servants were waiting for them on those steps, and grooms to take the reins of their horses, crimson dragons bright on many steel-gray breasts. It was impressive; Rod sat uncertainly in his saddle until Taeauna and the velduke both started to dismount. Then he promptly discovered how stiff and sore his legs were as he tried to do the same and ended up half dismounting and half falling out of his saddle, wincing.

The horse was led away while he was still limping over to Taeauna, and in a sort of daze Rod found more smartly uniformed servants than he could count bowing low to him in unison and then whisking him up the steps with the Aumrarr at his side. To his confused, wonderstruck look she replied with a wink and a grin, and Rod found himself being smoothly conducted along dark, grandly paneled passages where countless servants averted their stares to bow low, up a grand-bannistered flight of stone stairs to ornate double doors that waiting servants in daggercoats flung wide, and into a suite of brightly lit rooms where the grand procession suddenly ended, leaving him blinking in the sudden stillness.

"Your rooms, gentles," a grandly liveried servant murmured from behind Rod and Taeauna, as he withdrew, softly drawing the double doors closed again as he bowed and departed behind them.

More servants stood waiting in the doorways of five—no, six—inner rooms, and now smoothly bowed in unison, and... and...

Taeauna stepped forward, and then saw something (what, Rod could not tell) and stopped dead.

She whirled to face Rod, eyes flashing a "be still" warning, and as swiftly spun right back the way she'd been facing, turning her head to look intently around at all the servants. She clapped her hands briskly, and announced, "We thank you very much for your kind attendance, but now most urgently require you all to depart and leave us."

No one moved.

The Aumrarr drew herself up and said curtly, "Go. Now. All of you."

Rod saw heads turning, junior servants looking to those ranked above them. Taeauna saw who they were looking to, and leveled her own cold gaze on those four senior servants.

They coughed, nodded, and kept their reddening faces carefully expressionless. One by one, they bowed again to Taeauna and then to Rod, and slipped away, the other servants melting away with them.

Rod tried as hard to keep from looking puzzled, as all of them obviously were; try as he might, he couldn't see anything in all the luxury surrounding him that should spur Taeauna to suddenly act as she was.

He could see nothing at all alarming or unusual.

"I dismissed all of you," the Aumrarr said firmly, her voice colder than ever. She raised it a trifle to add, "Including you who watch and listen in the walls. Just go, and tell your master that I ordered your withdrawal. For your own protection."

Rod shook his head, bewildered. "What—?"

Taeauna's hand closed on his, quellingly, as she said to the walls around them, "I jest not. Now go."

Rod heard the slightest of sounds off to his left, and a faint stirring, clear across the room. Then silence.

"Staying, still?" Taeauna asked, her gaze fixed on just one wall now. "Well, I warned you. Your doom is of your own choosing."

She turned then and embraced Rod Everlar like a lover, her body melting against his, her lips nuzzling his ear.

"Is this your 'right place?'" she breathed.

Rod kissed her jaw just above the chin, and let his lips trail along it to her ear, heart pounding. (Hey! I'm like a suave secret agent, kissing the girl! Not that he could recall many stories where the beautiful Russian lady spy was sporting the stumps of recently clipped wings.) "No," he whispered, as quietly as he knew how. "What's up?"

Taeauna's arms went up and around his neck, as if in quickening lust, so she could bury her lips in his ear and whisper, "Stay away from yon table for now, and don't look at it with any interest at all. Those are enchanted things, laid out to show Deldragon's spies by your reactions if you're a wizard or not. Whatever you do, don't pick any up, handle them, or take them. Just leave them be; overlook them. They bore you and mean nothing to you. Except that veldukes put some odd decorations in their guest chambers."

Rod had vaguely noticed a glossy-polished table ahead with a row of small objects on it. He firmly quelled his impulse to turn his head and look at it properly, and settled for moving his mouth to a shapely Aumrarr ear and breathing into it, as softly as possible, "Deldragon's spies? Is he a foe, then?"

"He's… careful. As all Galathan nobles must be. The careless lords are already dead."

ANY VELDUKE'S CASTLE has many rooms, not all of them grand or well used, and the personal keep of Darendarr Deldragon was no exception. There were dozens of dark stone rooms on the damp southern side of its cellars that had been left to the rats and dust for years, and in one of them now, the air suddenly started to glow.

The glow grew, becoming many small points of light that silently spiraled around each other. They whirled ever-faster, rising up from the floor into a tall, thin column, spinning and… suddenly coalescing into a young, alert-looking man in robes who clutched a large and bulging sack.

Taerith Saeredarr peered all around, turning quickly to look in all directions for signs that anyone else was about. Seeing nothing but darkness, now that the glow that had delivered him had faded, and hearing nothing but his own breathing, he put the sack on the floor, held it there with one hand, and pivoted again, more slowly, listening very carefully this time.

Nothing.

Leaving the sack, he went to where he knew the door was. It stood open with only more darkness beyond; he looked and listened again.

Silence stretched, and Taerith slowly relaxed. It seemed there was no life nearby; possibly there was no one on this level of the cellars at all, just now.

Which was ideal. He returned to his sack and raked a heap of kindling out onto the floor, surrounding it with sticks and framing it with two small logs. Leaving the rest of the firewood in the sack and pushing it aside to stand as a barrier of sorts between the flames he was going to make and the door, Taerith drew forth a flint and a steel striker from behind his belt buckle, and set to work fire-starting.

He got sparks almost immediately, into his waiting, bone-dry tinder. He let it smolder until it caught, fed it more kindling, and then blew on it at just the right moment. His fire flared.

His hand went again to his belt, and drew forth a small metal token shaped like a coin. Twigs were snapping, now, and smoke began to rise as his blaze quickened. Taerith dropped the tantlar carefully into the heart of it and stepped back, drawing a dagger so he could cast a manydaggers spell if a Deldragon knight or servant burst into the room.

Then he waited, heart racing. Fear was raging in his dry mouth and pounding innards, but he had been an apprentice to Arlaghaun long enough to fear his master far more than intruding into a castle whose folk would probably seek to slay him on sight.

The fire freshened, building into a small, steady snapping of sparks and streaming of flame, smoke drifting out and away, stealing from the room out into the passage beyond.

And something ghostly started to appear in the air above the little fire. Shoulders, a helm-covered head... that head turning to glare, a raised sword slowly melting into view...

Faint and distant sounds arose, from far beyond the passage outside the door, and Taerith's head jerked up. Fast, *thump-thump-thump* sounds; someone in boots, running. No, several someones!

Getting closer fast. Deldragon's guards, for all the coins in Galath. Smoke does have a smell that carries...

Taerith raised the dagger in one hand, kissed it and then kissed his other hand, lifted that hand with the fingers curled just so, and waited.

They'd not use bows, not indoors, in such small, dark rooms. Wherefore he could afford to wait until just the right moment.

Which was... *now*!

A knight burst into the room, lantern waving wildly in hand, sword out and seeking the fire.

Taerith cast the spell, his first murmured words bringing the man's head snapping around to stare at him. The knight charged and Taerith stepped carefully away from the wall and fed him a stream of phantom daggers, blades of magical force flashing out like half a dozen arrows fired nose-to-tail to thud home in the man's throat and face, shredding it into a red cloud and tatters of flesh.

The headless body ran on, stumbling, and Taerith kept walking, striding aside to let the dead knight collapse into the spot where he'd been standing.

The Dark Helm above his fire grew solid, muttered a curse, and hopped hastily out of the flames as Taerith made his daggers loop around the walls of the room, to await another foe.

Another foe came, and then another; two Deldragon knights burst through the doorway, waving their swords. They shouted a challenge to the Dark Helm and charged, even as a second Helm started to appear in the fire.

"Tantlar magic!" one of them shouted, and clawed a horn from his belt. Its call came out as a weak, wavering blurting as Taerith sent all of his flying daggers arrowing into the knight's neck from behind, almost severing his head. The other knight felled the Dark Helm and rushed at Taerith who fled along the wall, willing his conjured daggers to strike.

The second Dark Helm stepped out of the flames and lunged at the running knight, who struck aside the blade reaching for him, reeling and hopping to try to keep his balance. Taerith's daggers caught up with him as he regained it, parried the Helm's sword, and slashed his foe's head so hard that the helm went flying.

Those daggers sank home, and the Deldragon knight groaned, staggered, and went down, but when Taerith willed his flying weapons up and out of the dying man, their blades were dwindling and wreathed in swirling smoke; the magic of the spell was fading.

Another Helm was materializing above his fire already. Taerith hurried forward to nudge the logs closer into the flames and heard more shouts in the distance. They sounded like names; someone was calling for the missing knights, wanting to know what they'd found.

Well, strolling through the cellars to give them the answer "death" hardly seemed practical now, when they could be shown it firsthand.

Taerith grinned at his own gallows humour, daring to start enjoying this foray at last. The third Dark Helm stepped out of his fire, gave him a nod, and headed for the door, even as the shadow-shape of the fourth began to form above the flames.

A horn sounded, echoing from far off in the cellars, and Taerith lost his smile.

The tantlar wasn't bringing through his master's warriors fast enough to defeat a lot of knights. Oh, shit.

He had another teleport spell to take him home, but certain death at his master's hands awaited him if he used it now, with the task not done. The well to poison, all the other lesser apprentices to bring through, the entire keep to be scoured of magic items...

He had another manydaggers spell, too, and conjure armor that would slow swords striking at him, but not much else. If it came to fighting knights, he was doomed.

"No," Taerith hissed, fear starting to rise in his throat.

"Oh, yes," the fourth Dark Helm disagreed gleefully, shouldering past him into the passage beyond.

Taerith watched the fifth one slowly form with a growing sense of dismay. Too slow, much too slow...

The room was thick with smoke, now. Should he dump out the rest of the wood around the fire in a ring and move to another room?

Perhaps he could hide, and let the Dark Helms battle all the knights he could hear hurrying this way. Perhaps...

The passage lit up with the light of many lanterns, laced with racing shadows. Taerith cursed in earnest and hurried to the back of the room. He dare not teleport without putting up a proper fight. He discovered his hands were shaking just about the time the fifth Dark Helm charged at the door, the sixth appearing wraith-like above the freshening flames, and the doorway erupted in Deldragon knights, a dozen or more—yes, definitely more!

Taerith frantically cast his manydaggers spell and tried to destroy the faces of the foremost knights with his racing blades, as they swiftly and ruthlessly hacked down the fifth Dark Helm and swarmed forward, kicking the sack aside.

They were going to destroy the fire, they were going to—

There was a shrill, high, but oddly faint scream from those flames, as four or five Deldragon blades met in the still-forming sixth Dark Helm, who toppled sideways and faded from view. Taerith saw some of his racing daggers struck to the floor with swords, and stamped on to keep them there, as unsmiling men in armor closed in on him.

With trembling hands he ended the manydaggers magic and tried to cast his teleport spell, twisting desperately aside from the first sword thrusts.

"Farewell, Taerith," Arlaghaun's voice said quietly from his belt buckle.

Those dreaded words were the last thing the apprentice ever heard, as Falconfar exploded into bright crimson around him.

THE EXPLOSION IN the cellars rocked the keep with a deep shuddering, blasting three Dark Helms at the other end of the tantlar to dust. In the cellars of Bowrock, what little was left of the ceiling cracked and fell into the whirling dust, spilling the contents of the storeroom above down into the deep pit that the cellar room had become. A few hands, fingers, and twisted fragments of sword blades bounced and rolled far down the passage from the riven room; in the room itself, nothing was left but roiling dust, busily adhering to cracked walls that were now covered with a red mist of blood.

Taerith Saeredarr had always wanted to make a splash in Falconfar, and he'd certainly achieved his fondest wish.

Chapter Eleven

SWORDGUARD MARKOUN DARFEST'S head was ringing as if all the war-horns in Bowrock were
blowing at once, close around him, and some
how he kept staggering bruisingly into the wall. His
sword-arm felt like it was on fire, just above his
elbow, but when he stared at it he could see only
blood and torn armor, no flames at all.

So he must be dazed, then, as well as wounded, and
no wonder. He'd been far down the passage from the
room where the firelight and all the fighting was taking place, at the back of a long line of Deldragon
guards, but what a blast!

He'd been hurled back and around a corner, smashing into the roof of the passage, with his fellow guards
all around him in a meaty tangle that had shielded
him even as their bones and helmed heads shattered
and crunched around him. They had died, all of them,
leaving only him to stagger out of the slaughter.

Nothing could have survived that blast, nothing. Yet his orders were clear: "Find out what lurking foe is down there, slay or capture, and report back." There was no one left to find out anything but him, now.

Markoun rebounded off the wall one more time, shook his head ruefully, and devoted all of his effort to walking down the rubble-strewn passage without kissing its walls every fifth or sixth step.

He managed it, and was quite proud of himself as he left the shattered rooms behind, certain that no foe was still alive to do anything to anyone. A few more limping strides brought him to the passage-moot where a left turn would take him to stairs up, when something sharp and sudden and cold as ice slid across his throat, leaving him breathing only blood.

As his choking started and his slayer dragged his head ruthlessly around, Markoun Darfest found himself staring helplessly at the helmed and visored head of a Dark Helm, thrust forward almost nose-to-nose with him.

There was a malicious grin behind that gleaming black metal; Markoun could feel it. As the darkness rushed in, the last thing he saw was a fire in a cellar room behind the Dark Helm's shoulder, and Dark Helm after Dark Helm striding out of it.

ROD EVERLAR WAS lying on a vast and very comfortable bed, dozing in the largest, fluffiest bathrobe or "warming-robe," if he'd caught Tay's murmurings properly, he'd ever encountered. Dozing, but hoping he'd not fall really asleep.

He was waiting for Taeauna to finish in the big round pool of smooth stone that served guests housed in these chambers as a bathtub. He sorely needed a bath of his own.

Earlier, she'd been splashing and murmuring in contentment, and Rod had half-hoped she'd call him in to help her scrub or wash her hair, but she'd settled down to mere occasional sighs of contentment. He suspected she was dozing, too.

Ah, well, at least they weren't—

From behind the wall just to Rod's left, there came a short, choked-off cry, followed by some heavy thuds and bumps.

A man being murdered, inside the wall? That's certainly what it sounded like.

The bathroom erupted in a sudden crash of sheeting water, and Taeauna burst out into the bedchamber, bare and dripping.

"Get dressed and armed, now!" she snapped, snatching up her sword from where she'd laid it ready on the bed. "Throw me your robe; I'll dry myself with that!"

Heart pounding, Rod scrambled to obey.

No BANNERS FLUTTERED from the turret-tops of Galathguard, and no horns rang out in greeting. The gates stood open with no sign of guards or any living person within, at all.

Birds darted, perched, and flew as if there were no humans near, and a lone, statue-like perched vaugril was the only living thing visible on the battlements.

As Baron Margral Nyghtshield and his bodyguard of knights rode in through the grand gate and looked around at dark doorways, the hooves of their horses echoed back emptiness. Weeds and saplings sprouted amid the stones, and no servants came running, no one stood watching; there was not one stick of furniture or a lantern in sight.

"Looks like a ruin," Nyghtshield muttered to his shield-knight, peering about with the one eye he had left; the battle that had robbed him of the other was so long ago that he'd almost forgotten it. He hadn't, however, forgotten the shambles that the once-grand Galathgard had become. "Even worse than before."

The knight pointed to a distant gaping archway. "We're not the first here, lord."

"Oh? How so?"

"Horse dung. Fresh. There, just inside the arch."

"Hmmph. I've seen better stables." The baron urged his horse forward at a careful walk; the shield-knight turned, waved a swift signal, and watched knights dismount and trot ahead, one of them stepping away from the horses to ready and light a lantern.

Galathgard certainly wasn't the most welcoming of royal palaces.

TAEAUNA DIDN'T TAKE much time drying herself. She was dressed before Rod was, had retrieved their laedlen from a side-chamber, and was tugging at the bed-furs while he was still sitting on one corner of them, dragging on his boots.

By then, sounds of battle—clanging swords, shouts and screams—were rising all around them.

"Well, that didn't last long," Rod muttered. "Who do you think's attacking us this time?"

"Whomever Arlaghaun could send or compel to swing swords here," the Aumrarr told him bleakly, tossing him a fur. "They're searching for you."

Rod shook his head. "Have they nothing else to do with their lives?"

"To master more than a few of the lesser spells, one must hunger for ever more magic; ever more power," Taeauna replied. "They see you as the most power to ever come within reach, so they grab for you."

Rod rolled his eyes. The din of battle was growing almost steady, now, coming faintly but steadily through the walls. No one came to their doors, and no servants or anyone else came rushing out of hidden back ways. Yet.

"What's this for?" he asked, holding out the fur. It was so heavy that he needed both hands.

"Put it over your shoulders like a cloak," Taeauna replied, settling a fur around herself and whirling a second atop it.

Rod shrugged his fur on. It was very heavy.

"Tay, how am I supposed to fight, with this—"

"Just shrug it off, lord, right away, if you have to use your sword," Taeauna replied, her tone also telling him to stop playing the idiot.

"Yes, but what am I wearing it for?"

"To keep warm. The cellars will be cold, too cold to sleep comfortably without it."

"The cellars?"

The Aumrarr whirled impatiently to glare at Rod, their noses almost touching, and thrust both laedlen into his hands. Collectively, they were heavy, too.

"Lord Archwizard," she said flatly, "as much as I'd love to debate each and every breath we both take with you, as the days pass around us, we'd best get out of these rooms where many folk may know we were housed, and get into hiding. If the keep is full of warring men, the cellars will be the best place to hide. So come with me, try to stop asking questions, and start looking for lanterns or torches as we go."

Rod nodded. "Yes, Tay."

"And stop calling me... Oh, never mind."

"Yes, Tay."

Sword drawn, she ducked gracefully past him, their hips brushing for the briefest of instants, heading for gloomy side-chambers many of the servants had come out of, upon their arrival.

"What're you looking for?"

"Back ways in and out of here," Taeauna said curtly. "Stay close behind me, keep your sword sheathed until I tell you otherwise, and try to shut up. Lord."

Rod obeyed, quelling a sudden urge to chuckle at her last word. Ah, such respect he was now getting. Just keep quiet and carry the sacks, dolt.

Taeauna found three back ways, all of them concealed by sliding panels behind tapestries. She opened each one a trifle and listened intently to the darkness beyond, closed two of them, and then beckoned Rod through the remaining opening behind her.

The man who'd thought he'd created Falconfar followed her, and found himself in pitch darkness, with cold stone walls close by on either side of him. Taeauna was just ahead and was moving away from him; he hurried to follow.

The second time he ran into her, the Aumrarr captured his hand with her own in the darkness, guided it to her belt, and murmured, "Feel your way along to where the belt crosses my spine... there! Now hold on, right there. If I stop, kindly have the basic wits to stop, too."

The sounds of hard-raging battle were growing louder, everywhere around them, but they seemed to be alone in the narrow passage, and the only sounds they could hear ahead seemed to be the pounding of many boots, of men rushing past them from left to right. The Aumrarr seemed in no hurry to get to that cross-passage, wherever it was; she kept stopping and feeling around, with Rod feeling increasingly like a small boy playing at being a train, as she towed him this way and that in the darkness.

"How can you—?"

"I can't," she hissed. "So I must feel. Whenever we come to where another passage joins ours. Now hush."

They went on, Taeauna trailing her fingertips along one wall, until the sounds of running men seemed very close. Then the Aumrarr stopped, and Rod could feel her reaching, this way and that, tracing the panel at the end of their passage with her fingertips. She seemed to find something, and went still until the running men seemed fewer. When the sound of boots died away altogether, Taeauna thrust gently at the panel, sliding it an inch or so open. Then she stopped, leaning on her sword as if it were a walking stick, head drawn back from the door at an angle, and went still, obviously watching and listening.

Rod carefully moved over to the darkness in the lee of the rest of the panel so he wouldn't be seen;

the cross-passage was only dimly lit, but seemed very bright compared to what they'd been groping in. He also let the laedlen gently down to rest on the floor but kept hold of them; carried together in one hand, they were heavy and feeling steadily heavier.

Soon the sounds of more hurrying, approaching boots could be heard, and two armored warriors rushed past. Then another, and a trio.

Taeauna turned, reached for Rod's chin, took hold of it and turned his head so she could whisper in his ear, "Dark Helms, all of them. Coming up from the cellars. Our duty is clear." He felt like a small boy being firmly handled by a disapproving teacher.

"It is?" Rod's mutter was lost in the sounds of more boots; the Aumrarr sighed.

"Yes. We must get down to the keep's well and guard it. They'll try to poison it, to doom all Bowrock, but not yet. Not when there's a chance they can vanquish all, and seize Deldragon's seat. When all of Bowrock rises to arms against them, and they are forced back, and know they must lose, then we must be ready, and cleave to our duty."

"And defend the well, the two of us, against most of an army?" Rod's incredulity made his whisper much louder than he'd intended it to be. "Christ! Is my time here going to be one long series of fights, chases, and running and hiding?"

"Welcome to Falconfar," was her dry rejoinder.

LANTERN LIGHT GLIMMERED in the distance. "Who's that?" a deep voice challenged out of the darkness.

"Nyghtshield," the one-eyed baron called back. "Who are you?"

"Lionhelm. Duthcrown, Snowlance, and Pethmur are with me. Welcome to Galathgard."

That last sentence had been decidedly sarcastic, which was a long stride in daring beyond what any noble of Galath had made so loudly at court before. Whether His Majesty was englamored or just sinking into madness, levity had long since ceased to be safe in Galathgard.

So had tarrying there a breath too long, after royal dismissal. Wherefore Galathgard's great halls were now deserted. Not to mention cold, dark, and echoing. They stank of mold and animal leavings. Two gigantic open archways beyond where Baron Nyghtshield stood now was the throne hall, the largest and grandest chamber in all Galath, and if there had been a single lamp lit in it, or fires in its hearths, he would have been able to see and feel it long since.

He strode toward the lantern, and the circle of faces around it. Great lords of the realm, all.

"Huh," he said aloud, as he approached them. "It feels more like we're visiting a tomb than the Court of Galath. Where are all the courtiers? The servants? The bustle, the waiting feast, the errand-riders hastening in and out?"

He knew the answers, of course. They all knew the answers.

The courtiers were all dead, or long since fled. Hungry beasts prowled the halls, Dark Helms dwelt in armed camps in the outlying wings and towers, and the king walked alone.

Mad as a drool-wits.

"Speak not so freely," Arduke Halath Lionhelm replied warningly, his handsome, hawk-eyed face stern. "Galathgard is not so deserted as it seems in these few halls. You'll find fresh blood in many corners; the Helms were probably set to slaying or driving out the monsters, to empty the main rooms for our arrival."

"Grand and grander," Nyghtshield muttered, finding himself suddenly more than impatient with the ordering of Galath by the Mad King. He looked around the ring of noble faces with his surviving eye, and nodded politely to everyone, seeing mistrust and weariness to match his own in every gaze, and outright dislike in some.

There were nine faces in all; while he'd been walking to Lionhelm's lantern from one direction, it seemed other lords had been arriving from other rooms. Lionhelm was the only arduke, but there were three marquels: Blackraven, who was humming to himself as usual, Duthcrown, and gleaming-monocled Mountblade; two klarls, Dunshar and Snowlance; and three barons, loud and fat Chainamund, yellow-eyed Murlstag, and stone-faced Pethmur.

Dunshar, a cruel, burly man Nyghtshield had never liked, was glaring at him, as were the barons. Young but white-haired Duthcrown was looking sourly at everyone.

The glimmer of a bobbing lantern shone into the gloom from a side-arch, out of the Hall of Lions. It was borne by a servant using a loft-pole, who strode toward them with measured pace, intoning like a doorwarden, "Behold! Velduke Aumon Bloodhunt, Velduke Melander Brorsavar, and Arduke Tethgar Teltusk are come among you."

"Behold, indeed," Duthcrown grunted. "We all stagger under the weight of titles, I daresay."

"Yet let us cling to this small measure of courtliness," Velduke Bloodhunt snapped, eyes blue and sharp, but his old face gone as gray from the pain the long ride had brought him as the hue of his thinning hair. "It is so very nearly the last vestige left to us." He nodded across the ring of lords in the brighter lighting, and murmured politely, "Lionhelm. Snowlance."

"My lord," the hawk-eyed arduke replied with a nod, and lifted a hand to indicate another archway. "More of us arrive, I think."

Nyghtshield turned to look where Lionhelm was pointing, and saw two tall, muscular men striding out of the darkness. They looked like warriors, and increasingly familiar as they approached, but the baron turned to the servant. "Well?"

The man with the pole-lantern acquired an expression of uncomfortable uncertainty, and looked to Velduke Bloodhunt, who was evidently his master.

"Introduce them," Bloodhunt said shortly.

The servant cleared his throat and announced, "Arduke Laskrar Stormserpent and Arduke Yars Windtalon."

"It seems likely this is all of us, leaving aside the border knights," the other velduke growled. "We should go in."

The servant looked at his master again, who gestured silently in the direction of the throne hall. The servant straightened his shoulders, lifted his lantern, and started to pace in that direction, and the great lords of Galath drifted after him, their chatter dying away.

Arduke Lionhelm, with his lantern, brought up the rear, and Nyghtshield peered through the darkened archways they passed and saw more than one pair of gleaming eyes staring back at him. Oh, yes, Galathgard still had its beasts. He was suddenly glad that his handful of knights was standing in the same stables as the far larger bodyguards of the vuldukes and ardukes.

Until he remembered that the new royal decree that armed underlings remain out in the stables meant their swords were no deterrent to monsters prowling here, in the main chambers of state.

In grim silence the lords of Galath paced through the vaulted halls, boots nigh-silent on the dusty marble, ignoring stains and bones and the rubble of crumbling adornments fallen from on high since their last visit.

When they stepped into the vast throne hall, the pole-lantern's light showed them a little of its high, arched ceiling, and below that the two tiers of dark and deserted high galleries, their archways like so many empty eyesockets in rows of watching skulls. Below the galleries were the rows of little round, shell-like stone balconies stretching down both sides of the hall, supported on their impressive clusters of pillars.

The servant strode to the stone stand that had held pole-lanterns and braziers since his grandsire's great-grandsire's day, and raised his pole to slide it down into one of the waiting sockets there.

Whereupon the stone spoke, in a cold and crisp voice that so startled the servant that he nearly dropped the pole. "Depart this place right speedily, and take your light with you."

Lantern swaying wildly, the servant cast one fearful glance at his master, and fled.

The lords looked at Lionhelm, who took his usual place on the tiles. He stood facing the throne, swung open his lantern, and looked back at all of them, a silent look of command riding his handsome, hawk-eyed face. The other lords hurried to their preferred places; the moment they reached them, the arduke extinguished his lantern, plunging them all into near-darkness.

"And who was that, who spoke to your man?" a lord's voice muttered. "Sounded like a woman, not the king. No voice I know, anyway."

The darkness hid old Velduke Bloodhunt's shrug, but he'd barely finished making the gesture when a distant, startled shriek arose from the direction the lantern-bearer had taken—and ended, as abruptly as it had begun.

"Doomblast!" Bloodhunt snapped, blue eyes blazing with anger. "I liked that lantern."

Someone chuckled in the darkness, and Bloodhunt growled wordless anger in that direction.

"Nice to know we're as well behaved as young lads at play," someone with a reedy voice observed.

"Speak for yourself, Klarl Broryn Snowlance."

Snowlance snorted. "Such candor, Mountblade. Pity you showed none of it last summer, when the king wanted to know who'd raided the Hammerfell granaries."

"Baseless—"

"Not at all," came the sour tones of Marquel Oedlam Duthcrown, who had plucked forth a comb from some hidden place about his grand garments. "You were seen by many, Ondurs. His

Majesty knew the truth when he asked." He began tidying his prematurely white hair. "Enjoy your leash; it grows shorter."

Marquel Mountblade busied himself with polishing his monocle, and did not reply.

"SHALL I END it, master? The darkclaws hasn't eaten much more than the head of Bloodhunt's servant, yet; it's still hungry."

"Not yet, Amalrys. Let them savage each other awhile longer. I'm enjoying this."

PETHMUR MIGHT BE one of the poorest barons, a sheepfarming warrior whose face was customarily as hard, gray, and expressionless as stone, but when his temper rose, his normally closed mouth erupted.

It was erupting now. "And who stole the Sunder jewels, before the king's agents could get to them? Baron Glusk Chainamund, that's who."

Chainamund was a fat, florid man who seemed to swell up when he was angry, his large straw-yellow mustache quivering like the barbels of a monstrous catfish. He was swelling up now. "That's a lie! I was never near that tower!"

Pethmur's stony face seemed almost to crack as it creased into an unaccustomed sneer. "Ah, but 'tis amusing, isn't it, to stand in the presence of a belted baron of the realm so stupid that he condemns himself out of his own mouth? And just how did you know, Chainamund, the Sunder women kept their jewels in the tower? When their rooms were all in the new wing, which was terraces and low halls, with nary a tower in sight?"

"You shut your mouth, Lothondos!" the fat baron bellowed, his face a deep crimson. "You lie like a dragon-shitting rug!"

"Now, now, Chainamund!" a burly klarl interrupted sharply. "Baron Pethmur may indulge in falsehoods, or may not lie like a dragon-shitting rug—such a colorful phrase; I thank you for the entertainment!—but he does raise a telling point. The whereabouts of those jewels was a deep Sunder secret, not something all Galath knew; yet you were seen to ride right to the tower doors, and have your men force them, paying not the slightest attention to the inviting windows and easily opened doors of that new wing we'd all exclaimed over and strolled through, before the Sunders... fell out of favor."

That overlarge, straw-yellow mustache curled. "Oh? How would you know, Dunshar?"

"I know many things, Baron Chainamund; I make it my business to know things. For the good of Galath, of course. In this particular case, His Majesty had ordered two lords of the realm to watch over the seat of the Sunders, to guard against unauthorized visits. And, of course, to watch each other. One of those lords was myself, and the other was Baron Mrantos Murlstag. Murlstag?"

"I confirm," Murlstag said heavily, his yellow eyes flat as he looked up at the fat baron. "I and Klarl Annusk Dunshar did watch over Sundertowers, and you, Chainamund, rode right up to the old tower and forced entrance, just as Dunshar says. We reported as much to His Majesty. Ask him if you believe us not."

"Oh?" The red-faced baron threw wide his arms. "All that will prove is the lies you told him! And did he not remind us all, at our last conclave, that lying to the crown is treason? Was not Marquel Larren Blackraven, who stands not three paces from you now, charged by the king to enact justice on the knight Harlbrace, of Harl Keep, for that very crime? And did so, bearing the traitor's head back here? By the way, where is it, Blackraven?"

The hook-nosed marquel broke off his quiet humming to smile easily. "It was yonder, on the spire atop yonder balcony, but something has eaten it," he said, pointing with one hand as he stroked his neat mustache with the other. "I see the jawbone on the floor there. A little gnawed, but still recognizable."

"So something is dining well at court," a lord commented sarcastically. "Behold, all is not lost in Galath yet."

"Well," broad-shouldered Velduke Brorsavar said gruffly, "that's a comfort. Of which I have all too few to cling to, in these my declining years. I—"

"Hold!" one-eyed Baron Nyghtshield interrupted sharply, throwing up a warning hand. "Someone comes!"

"More than one," Klarl Dunshar put in, striding to one of the lesser arches of the hall. The burly noble peered, and then turned back. "Yes, far more than one; more than a dozen."

"The border knights," old Velduke Bloodhunt said dismissively. "I believe, my lords, that we can now cease to wag our tongues quite so freely. Hmm?"

By way of reply, his fellow nobles all fell silent, so the border knights of Galath entered the throne hall in an uneasy stillness that was broken only by the faint scrapes of their own boots and the creaking of their best war-leathers.

It didn't take them long to assume their places down the sides of the hall, cough, peer warily into the beast- and decay-smelling surrounding darkness behind them a time or two, shuffle their boots, and then settle into the deepening tension.

Whereupon, with a sudden flash and roar, two bright columns of flame erupted up out of the smooth, bare marble tiles on either side of the archway through which the lords had entered the throne hall.

Between them, framed by their sun-bright roarings, came striding a young and handsome man, grinning haughtily under the glint of a gold crown worn askew on his lank black hair. He was clad like a noble youth at ease, in a flowing open-fronted silk shirt with fluid sleeves, black breeches with scabbarded sword and matching dagger, and warriors' boots.

"All bend the knee to His Majesty Devaer, King of Galath and Lord of Falcons!" commanded the same crisp, cold, and loud female voice that had earlier instructed the lantern-bearer.

The lords and border knights of Galath stared and listened in startled silence for a moment, and then went to their knees in leather-whispering unison.

AMALRYS TURNED, HER chains chiming. "Very impressive."

Despite the biting dryness in her voice, Arlaghaun smiled at her carefully expressionless face—by the Falcon, those eyes of hers! As deep and bright ice-blue as ever—letting his real mirth show.

"As I intended," he told her gently. "Silence, now. I must speak for this puppet of mine, for the next while."

Brown eyes blazing, the gray-garbed wizard made a steeple of his hands, rested his chin on them, and sat motionless as the rising sparks of his magic rose around him.

Amalrys hastened to assume one of the poses that would let her chains hang silent, and waited to be noticed again.

"YOUR SWIFT AND attentive attendance upon us here at court warms our heart, loyal lords of Galath," King Devaer purred.

Behind mask-like faces, more than one of those lords wondered how their hitherto blustering and profane monarch had managed to acquire such glibness in the short time since their last conclave. Oh, they'd all heard the talk about his mouth being directly controlled by the wizard Arlaghaun, greatest of the Dooms, but then, wild talk races across lands like the light of the rising sun, and about as often.

Or was there a cabal of wizards, who for their own amusement took turns making His Majesty dance? That would explain the changing royal eloquence.

"My lords, you will have heard of the unfortunate fate of Baron Ammurt, late of our loyal company," the king continued. "It is our belief that peace and order in fair Galath are best maintained by loyal lords in every castle, with no break in rule that may lead to lawlessness through brigandry, marauding wild beasts, the evil done by invaders who desire Galath to fall, and the treason of the disloyal. And make no mistake, my lords, we are watched by many who would prefer Galath to be swept away for their own rapacious gain. Wherefore I want Castle Ammurt rebuilt and a strong and loyal Baron Ammurt dwelling in it and dispensing our justice—and mercy—in the Ammurt lands, before the snows fly again."

Devaer paused to stare briefly down the hall, at carefully impassive face after carefully impassive face.

"As Gustras Ammurt's heirs perished with him, we find it necessary to create a new Baron Ammurt. The chance to reward faithful servants of Galath warms us even as the unfortunate passing of a family bright in history and brighter in service to the realm saddens us."

The king paused, stepped forward, and threw up his right arm with a dramatic flourish. He held it aloft for a long moment, looking around the hall again, and then brought it down to point at one man.

"Tauntyn Lhorrance, stand forth!"

Childish though the pointing and bellowing was, most of the lords blinked at Devaer with new respect. They hadn't known he could thunder.

The border knights ranged down the sides of the dark and lofty hall stirred, and from among them hesitantly stepped forward an obviously startled man, tall and pockmarked. "M-majesty?"

"Here and stand before us, Lhorrance. You have sworn fealty to us as Sir Tauntyn Lhorrance, but we now require your personal loyalty to us as Baron Tauntyn Ammurt. Do you, before the titled lords of Galath, in the throne seat of Galath, swear to serve us with personal, absolute, and utter loyalty, foresaking all other ties and obligations?"

"I... I do."

"Accepted. Do you swear to serve us lifelong, and hazard your life without hesitation, at our command?"

"I do." The pockmarked border knight had gone pale, as if realizing where this oath might well lead. Soon.

"Do you swear to uphold our laws and decrees absolutely, showing neither variance nor exception?"

"I do."

"Do you swear to obey us in all things, without question or offering debate or disagreement?"

"I do."

"Then put out your hand."

Slowly, struggling not to frown, Tauntyn Lhorrance extended his right hand. Devaer shook his head and pointed to the knight's left hand; Lhorrance hastily proffered it instead.

The King of Galath produced a small vial out of one silken sleeve, drew his dagger, sliced a line along the fleshy part of the knight's palm, and filled the vial from the blood that welled forth.

"Go forth from this place as Baron Tauntyn Ammurt!"

"I... thank you, your majesty."

"Go under our command, Ammurt. You are to take your handful of armsmen, scout the lands of Baron Tindror and Velduke Deldragon, and report back in all haste to us here, ere returning to the Lhorrance lands. There, you shall speedily train a knight to administer those lands for you, as you secure the Ammurt lands and make habitable Castle Ammurt. Go, and tarry not in the performance of any of these crucial duties!"

Pockmarked face pale, the new Baron Ammurt turned and marched out of the throne hall, his hand dripping blood.

Smiling crookedly, the King of Galath watched him go, and then raised his voice again.

"Veldukes Aumon Bloodhunt and Melander Brorsavar; ardukes Halath Lionhelm, Laskrar Stormserpent, Tethgar Teltusk, and Yars Windtalon; marquels Larren Blackraven, Oedlam Duthcrown, and Ondurs Mountblade; klarls Annusk Dunshar and Broryn Snowlance; and barons Glusk Chainamund, Mrantos Murlstag, Margral Nyghtshield, and Lothondos Pethmur, attend us!"

Without waiting for any reply, he ordered, "You are all to return to your castles and there, within three days and nights, muster all your knights and armsmen, and more, every last man and woman on your lands who can swing a sword or fire a bow. Marshal them all, and on the fourth day march them. As directly as you can, through each other's lands without brook, delay, or resistance, you are to march them to the lands of the traitor Deldragon, defeating all resistance and foraging on what you can seize there, and make war on Deldragon, besieging Bowrock and slaying every last dog, cat and servant within its walls, excepting two persons: an Aumrarr whose wings have been severed,

Taeauna, and a man who walks always at her side. They are to be brought before us alive and unharmed; the man who harms either of them is himself a traitor to Galath, and his life is forfeit."

The king stopped speaking, and silence fell. And deepened.

Until one raven-haired lord, Arduke Tethgar Teltusk, found enough boldness to ask, "Your majesty, if we all go to war, who will maintain order in our own lands, against brigands, prowling monsters, drunkards and other malcontents, and even wild dogs?"

The king smiled softly. "The lorn. They obey me, now."

Several of the border knights ranged down the hall laughed, in disbelief or wonderment.

Lorn plunged down out of the darkened upper galleries of the throne hall, dived on those knights, and tore them apart bloodily, limb from limb.

Most of the nobles whirled and grabbed for their swords as the knights shouted and screamed, but froze and did no more than watch as the doomed men died.

The lords of Galath paled still more when more lorn descended out of the upper darkness to perch on the balconies above them, one for every noble.

Chapter Twelve

IN THE DARKNESS of the highest galleries, a lorn perched on carved stone adornments like a statue, watching fellow lorn rend border knights of Galath far below.

Without warning, another lorn struck like an arrow out of the darkness, claws first, wrenching the perched lorn's head around with such swift violence that its neck broke in an echoing instant.

Another two lorn soared up from the gallery below as the dying lorn's body was snatched off its perch by the fatal strike, to take hold of the body and bear it across the throne hall, wings beating within inches of the ceiling, into the other gallery.

The lorn that had done murder did not relinquish its hold, and its razor-sharp claws had nigh-severed the head of its victim by the time it was dragged into the gallery across the hall, still clutching the head.

The head came off by the time the body landed, flopping bloodily down onto bird-dropping-littered stone. The murderer calmly wiped its claws clean on the body, and flew back to the perch where its victim had been. The other two lorn stood wary watch over the body, staring intently for any signs of movement or revival.

Thanks to the violent deaths of the knights and the attention given those passings, none of the men below noticed a thing of what befell above their heads.

"So passes Malraun's spy," Amalrys spat, turning again to her master with those startlingly blue eyes ablaze.

Time for some taming. Again.

Arlaghaun took hold of a fistful of chain and dragged her back against his gray-clad breast, snaring her long blonde hair in his other hand and tugging down, to force her head up and back.

She gasped at the ceiling, arched back and trembling. The chains cut into her softest place, and her neck-manacle half strangled her, but she knew better than to hiss out her pain.

Especially when his thin lips were smiling, and coming down on hers so tenderly.

"Well done, my dearest apprentice," the sharp-nosed wizard murmured. Then, his expression changing not a whit, he cruelly jerked the chain straight up, hard, sawing deep between her legs, heaving her right up off her feet.

When her bare feet returned to the floor, spots of blood dappled it between them, and they came not from where she'd been biting her lips to stifle a shriek. Those blue eyes pleaded with her master.

"Just remember you're my apprentice," Arlaghaun whispered, his eyes like two blazing brown fires. "Mine to show kindness to... and mine to destroy."

"YOU'RE FALLING FOR her, Arlaghaun," the darkly handsome wizard sneered, sinking back into his grand claw-footed chair with a weary sigh, and wiping the sweat from his face. Listening through ward-spells by means of a deep magic was draining; doing so while linked to two other minds—lorn minds, at that—was utterly exhausting. "And thereby," he added in satisfaction, "building a bridge that will lead to your own doom."

Malraun wiped his face again and lounged back in the chair, swinging his booted feet up, and smiled at the precious vial of the maiden's blood, harvested so daringly and so long ago, anticipating the chance she might become Arlaghaun's apprentice. The fire of his warding-spell raced swiftly around the vial, once, awakening answering glows in the great green tapestries that hung on the walls all around. Nodding in satisfaction, he reached deftly down behind his chair and slipped the vial back into its hiding place under the loose stone.

Only when Amalrys bled monthly, or from a wound, could he awaken his deep spell and "hear," albeit poorly, through her skin. Thanks to Arlaghaun's cruelty, his love of biting and hauling hard on chains in particular, Malraun the Matchless could listen to choice moments of converse fairly often. If fuzzily.

The lorn had been able to hear Arlaghaun speak through his human puppet rather better. Not the lorn he'd left perched so obviously for Arlaghaun to find and destroy, but the two better-hidden ones whose minds he'd been listening through.

The lorn he'd sent to hunt the Aumrarr and her mysterious companion, whom she might well have fetched from some magical otherwhere, and who just might be a minor Shaper, had not returned, and was either dead or in hiding, not daring to return to him. Either way, it had clearly failed.

It was now time for a more direct try, to snatch the man the Aumrarr was guiding, or see him and decide if he was worth no further attention, by using strong magic to burst into Bowrock himself.

Before Arlaghaun did, or all of Galath's sword-swinging armies.

THE COLD STONE room had been dark and deserted for a very long time.

Yet not completely dark, and not completely deserted.

There was the oval of glowing magic on one wall, and there was the dust that lived.

The dust that was swirling together now, on the floor in front of that glimmering oval, to form the eyeless planes and curves of a human face, a face that rose up, as if on a building ocean wave, into the shape of a human head.

Fleetingly, before it collapsed back into drifting dust again, that head seemed to be watching the oval.

As the dust settled, it again moved into the outlines of a face, a visage of dust that rose at the forehead end just a little, this time, to regard the magic of the oval.

The oval in which colored shapes moved and talked, showing the young, sneeringly smiling King Devaer of Galath addressing the nobles of the realm in the gloomy throne hall of Galathgard.

Then the oval flashed, and the scene within it was of a tall, gray-clad, sharp-nosed man roughly dragging a nude, manacled woman to him by means of her chains, her very, very blue eyes staring up at him pleadingly.

It flashed again, to show a darkly handsome man in robes slipping a vial into a recess and replacing a stone atop it, then rising to fetch a wand and start to cast a teleport spell.

Quite suddenly, the face collapsed back into a smooth, moving heap of dust. Dust that flowed purposefully across the floor of the deserted room to swirl around a bright metal warrior's gauntlet lying on the floor. As the dust circled it, moving faster and faster until the faintest of hissings could be heard, motes of light blossomed here and there about the gauntlet, winking and glowing. They multiplied into a flickering, pulsing glow, and then, all at once, vanished.

The dust glided to a stop, lying motionless in a ring, as if exhausted.

Then, very slowly, it started to move again, drifting back across the room. Quickening as it returned to the floor in front of the oval, surging up into a heap as it reached where it had been before, a heap that reshaped itself once more into the watching face.

The oval stopped showing an empty chamber that the robed man with the wand had vanished from, flashed, and then displayed a dark stone passage that Dark Helms were running along, black blades drawn.

The dust settled down to watch.

"WHAT SAY, ISK? Safe to go back to the Stormar ports yet?" the fat man rumbled. "I miss the sea."

"You miss painted lasses and easy thievery, you mean," the bone-thin woman seated beside him on the wagon said tartly. "And having a dozen-some waterlogged scows to escape on, when things go bad."

"Can't hide on a wagon," the fat man growled, looking around at endless rolling hills and the few poor farms adorning them. "Can't we sell this one?"

"We'd better, before the man we stole it from catches up to us. Then go north again."

"North? But the sea's south of here!"

"And the lands of the Velduke Deldragon, who hates the lord of where we are right now, are north of here. So angry wagon merchants wanting to catch us will receive no help at all."

The fat man cast a thoughtful look back along the weathered board roof of the wagon, his gaze lingering on the six arrows embedded there.

"North it is, then," he said, and spat on the aromatic behind of the ox just in front of him.

The ox kept right on plodding, and did not respond.

THEY'D FLOWN THIS high before, but this time the air was colder, somehow. The fiercest and most scarred of the four Aumrarr faltered in her flying, turning in her customary position at the fore to hug herself; the others saw that Juskra was shivering.

"Once we've done this," she said, absently stroking her bandages, "and shown ourselves to all Galath, what then? With these wings, sisters, we can't exactly hide!"

Dark-armored Lorlarra nodded. "And I'm in no hurry to lose them as Taeauna did. Think you: a life without wings? Now that would be true doom."

"We'd best be ready to flee fast and far, then, sisters mine," Ambrelle warned, her unbound purple-black hair streaming out behind her. "The wizards vying for rule in Galath haven't shown much mercy to anyone."

Below them, Galath was a carpet of lush greens, adorned with ribbons of silver-blue water and a brown, wandering spiderweb of cart-roads and lanes. The four Aumrarr had decided to fly high over the realm, seeking armies on the move, and had just soared over its border.

"What's that?" Dauntra snapped, pointing, her usually impish brown eyes sharp with concern. "Yonder!"

Something was rising from the high, tree-cloaked ridge of Darragh Forest, well ahead of them, in the heart of the kingdom; something like a storm cloud.

Dark, and menacing, and...

"It's coming in our direction," Ambrelle warned, slowing.

"Lorn!" Lorlarra said suddenly. "Those are lorn—thousands of them! And they're coming for us!"

Juskra slowed, the better to turn an incredulous face on her sister. "They can't be! Lorn can't see that well, to hunt us at this distance!"

"They don't have to see," Dauntra said bitterly, "when a wizard sees for them, and commands them aloft. Sisters, we must flee!"

"Flee?" Juskra spat incredulously. "I will not! I've had enough, and more than enough, of fleeing and hiding whilst sisters are slain here, there, and everywhere, and the slayers face no harm nor even blame! I—"

"Will die alone here, in the air, then," Ambrelle said sadly. "Torn apart by lorn. To stand with you is to throw our lives away needlessly, achieving nothing, and that avenges or brightens the memory of our dead sisters how?"

"You will all turn back?" Juskra cried, rage making her weep. "And fly away, craven? All of you?"

"All of us," Lorlarra replied sadly.

Juskra turned in the air in a whirl of wings. "I can't believe what I'm hearing. I—"

"No, sister," Dauntra said sharply, "you don't want to believe what you're hearing, which is far different. You want to die here, don't you? To go down fighting!"

"I—no! No! *No!*"

"Yes," Ambrelle said gently, reaching out for Juskra's arm as her sister burst into a flood of tears that robbed her of coherence. "Come, sister."

The cloud of lorn was much nearer, now, stretching broad and dark across the sky.

Dauntra swooped in under Juskra's wings, on the other side from Ambrelle, and took Juskra's other arm. "Come," she added, rolling over on her side to find air enough to beat her wings without getting tangled in Juskra's broad, resisting ones.

"Sisters," Lorlarra said urgently, "we must away. They're coming so fast."

"Juskra," Ambrelle said firmly, "don't throw your life away just yet. Sacrifice yourself only if it's going to at least bring down a Doom, and make things better for Falconfar."

"And if we find such a chance?" Juskra howled, through her tears.

"Then, sister, we'll rush to die with you," the oldest of the four Aumrarr promised grimly, purple-black hair billowing in a sudden side-gust. "None of us live forever, but like everyone who thinks about such things, I want to die knowing my death achieved something."

"And in the meantime," Dauntra said grimly, her words sounding almost foul when set against her young and striking beauty, "I'm going to slay every Dark Helm and every lorn I can catch alone. Every last one."

OFF TO THEIR right, in the direction the Dark Helms were running to, there were sudden shouts, and the ring and clang of swords meeting shields and armor and other swords rose to a deafening din.

More Dark Helms rushed past. Taeauna turned and whispered fiercely to Rod, "Lord, stay here."

Then she was out into the passage, sliding the panel almost closed behind her, and gone, darting to the left. Rod stepped forward to stand right where she'd been, nose near the narrow gap so he could look out. Taeauna was down at the corner the Dark Helms had been rounding, presumably on their way up from deeper levels of the cellars. Her shoulder was to the wall, she was crouching, and her sword was out and ready.

More Dark Helms burst around the corner; Taeauna gutted the last one with a perfect thrust through the side-seam of his armor plate, where a row of descending buckles under his arm attached the back to the front.

The other Dark Helms whirled in surprise, stumbling over their own haste. Taeauna slashed open the throat of the nearest one while he was still turning; he fell into the one beside him, slamming the man helplessly into the wall. Taeauna carved a new smile across his eyes before he could move, took out his throat on her return slash, and whirled back to face the corner, just in time to meet the next trio of racing Dark Helms.

They saw the sprawled bodies, and stumbled and swayed trying not to trip over them; Taeauna's blade was in the neck of the nearest one before he even saw her. The other two hacked at her, off-balance and wading in ankle-deep dead warriors, and she managed to batter one's blade aside and bury her sword in his face because his visor was still half-up.

The other one sprang over bodies to reach the wall right beside Taeauna, and swung his sword viciously.

She thrust herself against him like a lover, belly to belly, to get inside the reach of his sword, hooking her leg behind his. When he tried to pull back so as to sword her properly, he crashed over backwards and she pounced, stabbing ruthlessly.

Which meant she was down on hands and knees, with her back to the next Dark Helms, as they came rushing around the corner and started falling over bodies and cursing and reeling aside.

Taeauna was turning, but there were four swords reaching for her this time, too many for her to ever hope to turn aside. No! Rod Everlar thrust the panel open and burst out into the passage, the heavy laedlen dragging him wildly off-balance at his first step into a helpless sideways stagger that ended in him tripping on a downed Dark Helm and toppling onto that body, hard and ingloriously.

Yet Dark Helms had turned at his arrival, blades swinging around to him, and that had given the Aumrarr all the chance she needed. Black blades were already clattering to the floor as Taeauna darted here and there like some sort of Olympic fencer trying to out-dance an acrobat, and by the time Rod had heaved himself upright again, two throat-slit Dark Helms were falling dead at his feet.

His stomach heaved, and he promptly emptied it, all over them.

Taeauna reached out a long arm as the last Dark Helm she'd been fighting fell over backwards, throat fountaining, and dragged Rod over now-heaped bodies to stand with her against the wall.

She gave him a disgusted look, wrinkling her nose at the smell of his sickness. "The hidden passage where I told you to stay," she said pointedly, gesturing with a sword dark and dripping with fresh blood, "would have been safer. And less upsetting."

"And if something happened to you?" Rod panted, as the Deldragon battle far down the hall rose to fresh heights of frantic hacking and screaming. "I'd be alone, and doomed, and utterly lost. 'Welcome to Falconfar,' indeed."

Taeauna shrugged. "Yes, lord; welcome to Falconfar. Just the way you wrote about it."

"It is not! I never wrote about Dark Helms! They're Holdoncorp's invention!"

"Well, *un*invent them, lord. Write with power!"

Rod flung up his hands in helpless exasperation. Unexpectedly, the Aumrarr gave him a wry smile, grabbed one of those waving hands, and used it to tow him around the corner. "Come. We must find that well."

Before he could reply she suddenly staggered, the air around her glowed and sang, and a metal gauntlet appeared, silently and out of nowhere, on her sword hand. Its appearance gently thrust her bloody blade out of her fingers, to clatter to the stone floor.

Taeauna stared at the massive, gleaming wargauntlet with just as much gaping astonishment as Rod was. Then she let go of him to use her free hand to try to snatch the heavy thing off without success, despite a few moments of hard-panting struggling. The gauntlet just wouldn't budge.

Rod watched all the color drain out of her face. "Where did it come from?" he couldn't help but ask. "Does it feel magical? What's it for?"

"Yes, it feels magical!" the Aumrarr told him, eyes large and dark in a snow-white face. "As for your other questions: I don't know! I don't know!"

Then boots were pounding toward them, out of the darkness of the far end of the passage.

Rod set down the sacks and drew his sword; Taeauna had just enough time to scoop up her blade before five Dark Helms burst into view, and they were fighting for their lives.

Rod flinched back as a sword struck his own blade so hard that his hand went numb. The Dark Helm pressing him stumbled on the edge of one laedre, and Rod hacked desperately at his head, clumsily and sideways, catching the man's helm and wrenching it around.

The warrior screamed through the metal as his ears and nose were torn, and then a second Dark Helm lunged at Rod over the shoulder of the first one. Rod backed away so swiftly he almost fell, and the second Dark Helm fell over the first as the blinded first warrior blundered sideways into his charge.

Rod sworded the backs of both of their necks as hard as he could, feeling his sword bite in. It came back red and dripping, and his stomach lurched again.

He threw up right in the visor-covered face of another Dark Helm, who staggered back in disgust. Taeauna used the space that gave her to dance away from the wall where she'd been frantically parrying three shoulder-jostling foes, and tossed her sword to her free hand to stab around behind a sword-arm, into its leather-covered armpit. Even as that foe sobbed and dropped his sword, another Dark Helm's blade was darting at her. She slapped it aside with the gauntlet, and at the touch of her gage, the metal of that blade melted away into curling smoke.

The Dark Helm stared at the stub of his weapon in astonishment, but Taeauna never slowed; she drove her gauntleted fist in the other direction, into the ribs of the man she'd just wounded.

His breastplate was suddenly gone—just *gone*— and Taeauna whistled in amazement and slapped the man across his visored face.

An instant later, he was staring at her in pain and fear, bare-headed. She broke his jaw and struck him senseless with her next blow, and then turned back to the warrior whose blade she'd first melted away. The third of the Dark Helms she'd been fighting had already fled back down the passage.

The swordless Dark Helm was backing away, hauling out his dagger. Taeauna glared at him, but took the time to gingerly put her blade back into her gauntleted hand.

It did not melt away; she sighed in relief and headed after the Dark Helm, who kept on backing away, waving his dagger warningly.

Taeauna broke into a sudden run, to catch her foe, and Rod hastily scooped up the laedren and ran after her.

When she caught the man, it was his turn to desperately parry, the dagger bending under the force of her cut. Rod skidded to a stop beside them and used the momentum of his run to bring the laedren looping around like a huge sap, crashing into the Dark Helm's arm and shoulder and sending him staggering. Taeauna sprang at him, clutching, and his greaves, breastplate, and gorget all melted away before he got his dagger up into her face where her waiting gauntlet caught it. The man's moan of fear ended abruptly when Taeauna's punch crushed his throat and bounced his head off the stone floor with brutal force.

"Come on," she gasped at Rod, "or we'll be standing right here all day and night while they come at us. We've got to get to that well!"

"Do you know where it is?" he asked, as they started running again.

"Certainly," Taeauna replied, and pointed at the floor. "That way."

"Thanks!" he responded sarcastically, as they trotted down the passage into steadily deeper gloom, and found the first descending stone staircase. The first flight was bare and empty, but as they turned at the landing, about a dozen Dark Helms came trotting up the steps toward them.

"Don't let any of them get around behind me," Taeauna panted. "Just swing those laedlen!"

So Rod did, timing his first buffeting blow to catch a lunge headed for the Aumrarr. The warrior was strong; Rod's attack just moved his arm and blade aside a foot or so, but it was enough. Taeauna's sword was like a flickering flame among the black blades, and Dark Helms were reeling, clutching at slit throats, and tumbling back down the stairs, driving down the warriors behind them into a stumbling, fighting-for-balance chaos. Rod waded into that with his swinging sacks, making sure off-balance men fell back onto those below. The Aumrarr punched aside swords, destroying them halfway down to the hilts at a touch.

"There are only two!" someone snarled from several steps down. "Stand and fight! Just charge, and hurl them back, and swarm them! Come on!"

Taeauna waded down the steps in the direction of that voice, punching and slapping, then driving her blade home wherever armor vanished. A voice cursed aloud as its owner turned and fled back down the stairs.

That started a rout; suddenly everyone was running, leaving only the wounded and dying behind on the steps. Ruthlessly Taeauna descended from body to body, turning the former into the latter.

Rod did not want to see that bloody work too closely. He hung back, settling the laedlen properly over his shoulder and gingerly wiping the blade of his sword clean on a body clad in leathers that had been under now-vanished armor, that thankfully had its head turned away.

"Come!" Taeauna called at last. "The well, remember?"

Rod sighed and hastened down the steps to join her, carefully skirting the slumped bodies.

The Aumrarr stared up at him consideringly. "You're fine in a fray, but hate the blood the moment you've time to think about it, don't you?"

Rod nodded. "I'm a writer, not a—"

A Dark Helm came running up the stairs, and Taeauna coolly turned, parried the man's blade with her gauntlet, and drove her sword under the edge of his visor and into his throat.

"And I'm an Aumrarr," she said a little sadly. "Perhaps the last one. Killing Dark Helms is what I do, now." Then she shrugged, and added, "Well, 'tis more purpose than some folk have in their lives. Let's find that well."

"And fill it up with blood," Rod murmured to himself. He took care to speak so quietly that she couldn't possibly hear him.

WARSWORD LHAUNTUR LOOKED up at the fat trader's cheerful hail. He recognized the man: Reskrul, who came over the mountains from Scarlorn once a year, his mules heavy-laden with tools and buttons and fastenings that the folk of Hollowtree bought eagerly.

"Be welcome in Hollowtree," he said cheerfully, "and have a tankard. We're just about to ride out on the night patrols. What news?"

"Hah! Big news. Recall a wingless Aumrarr who came through here some days back?"

"I do, indeed."

"Well, seems she laid waste to Arbridge, and went on down into Galath swording barons and besieging castles right and left."

Lhauntur raised a disbelieving eyebrow. "All by herself? That'd be a feat worthy of a god."

"Ah, but she wasn't alone. There's a man traveling with her."

That brought forth snorts of amusement around the warriors' table, and one jesting comment. "He's deadly with a pitchfork, that one!"

"Oh?" Reskrul said happily, pulling himself a tankard. "Well, the traders I met outside Arvale said she slaughtered hundreds forcing her way into Wrathgard, and enslaved poor Tindror!"

He peered around. "Looks like she didn't do all that much damage here."

"We're better fighters than the Galathans," Lhauntur said dryly. "*We* enslaved *her*."

TAEAUNA STRODE RIGHT up to the Dark Helm at the doorway. When his sword came up, she backhanded it aside and thrust her own blade unceremoniously into his throat.

He sagged to the floor, spewing blood, and she stepped inside the room with Rod on her heels.

"The well," she said with some satisfaction, indicating a circle of stone blocks overhung by a stout timber frame sporting two cranks and sets of descending ropes. Six Dark Helms looked up from what looked like a game of dice, rose hastily, drew their swords, and came over to her.

Taeauna stepped around the first one, touched the blade the second one was raising uncertainly to menace her, spun swiftly to slap aside the first warrior's sword that was on its way to plunge into her back, and then fed that warrior her own sword, right through his throat.

She ran around him in a swift circle as she did so, swinging his choking, staggering body between herself and the rest of the Dark Helms. Their charge parted to come around the flailing man and at her from both sides. Taeauna calmly tripped one warrior as she shouted, "Lord!" and then lunged in the other direction, parrying a blade and then melting it to nothingness with a slap of the gauntlet.

Rod swallowed as he ran forward. He was supposed to slit the sprawling warrior's throat, he knew, but winced at the very thought. The Dark Helm still had hold of his sword, and swung it viciously at Rod's ankles, so he hopped over it and brought the laedlen together down on the man's head, hard.

The man shuddered and fell still. By then Taeauna had slain two more, the one she'd disarmed was sprinting around them all in a wide half-circle, seeking to escape the room, and the last Dark Helm was shouting in fear as Taeauna advanced on him. "Lord!" she called. "Don't let that one get away!"

Rod obediently trotted over to where he'd be in the running warrior's way; the Dark Helm greeted him with a sneer and a wild roundhouse slash that would have severed Rod's head from his body if it had connected. Rod ducked, stumbled, let go of the sacks right against the running man's ankles, and tried to step aside to ready his own sword.

The Dark Helm tripped over the sacks, staggered, and ran into the wall. Bouncing off it, he reeled right into Rod's desperate, teeth-clenched slash that sliced deeply into his neck and left him wobbling unsteadily to the floor, groaning.

Rod tried to be sick again, but there was nothing left in his stomach. He was still heaving when Taeauna strode past to slit the throats of the Dark Helms Rod had fought, giving him a disgusted look as she did so.

"You're going to have to learn to kill without becoming ill," she told him. "Now help me drag this dead meat over to the door. We'll heap them up there to win us time to be ready for the next Dark Helms to show up, and believe me, there will be more."

Rod believed her, even before sudden sounds nigh the doors heralded the arrival of forty—no, something nearer sixty Dark Helms that were crowding into the room before he and Taeauna could shift a single body.

"Get around behind the well," Taeauna ordered, shifting her sword to her free hand so she could flex the fingers of the gauntlet.

"We're going to die here, aren't we?" Rod asked, as he hastened to obey.

"'Tis quite likely," the Aumrarr replied. "Unless you can picture your bedchamber again, very vividly."

"I..." Rod couldn't see anything but the cruel grins of Dark Helms who were moving into the room, walking slowly and carefully, forming a wide arc of armored men as they drew their swords and lowered their visors.

So this was it. He was going to die in Falconfar.

Chapter Thirteen

"I WILL TRY to use the gauntlet," Taeauna murmured, "and shield you. But you must have the will to use your dagger on your own hand—deeply, slicing the palm, not your fingers—and thrust it around to my mouth, so I can drink lots of your blood. If I am sore-wounded, and collapse, hold tightly to me and try to vividly remember your bedroom."

Rod shook his head. "We're going to die here," he muttered, watching more than seventy Dark Helms closing in. The menacing black-armored warriors were crowded together, filling that entire end of the well-chamber. Step by careful step, they were moving forward, forming a curving wall like giant living pincers closing in around the Aumrarr and her mysterious companion.

Taeauna looked straight into Rod's eyes and said softly, "Very likely, lord. Know that it has been an honor."

She stepped forward and tenderly, then passion-ately kissed him, her tongue darting in to thrillingly caress his.

Sudden passion flared in Rod, a tingling excite-ment he hadn't felt since his first kiss. Taeauna's mouth was sweet, and hot, and *hungry*...

She pulled back just enough to whisper, "Your feelings are strong enough, I think, that if you could think of your bedroom, hold its image in your mind, and wound me without letting that image waver..."

Then the air tingled, suddenly as cold as ice. Taeauna stiffened and Rod winced, feeling a searing chill despite her body standing as a shield to his; what must *she* be feeling?

They staggered apart as Taeauna whirled to see the cause of the cold and stiffened again.

A short, slender, darkly handsome young man in flowing robes was standing not an arm's length away. He was facing away from them, aiming a wand at the Dark Helms who were suddenly sprint-ing forward, swords raised and faces tight with fear, starting to shout.

The wizard snapped a word that struck all ears like a blow, and echoed weirdly around the room, and from the wand erupted a wide fan of racing flames.

Dark Helms screamed, writhed, and died, flames blazing briefly and hungrily along their limbs as the wizard calmly turned to make sure he fried all of them. Leather under-armor blazed up as the metal armor atop it twisted, buckled, and melted, the men beneath both shrieking and sizzling loudly as they died. A horrific stink of burnt leather and cooked men—akin to roast boar, but rank with sweat and urine—arose before all the Dark Helms, their reaching swords falling just short of their slayer, were slumped dead on the floor.

The man in robes turned to Taeauna and Rod as smoothly as a tavern dancer, smiled a coldly commanding smile, and said, "I am Malraun, and with my wizardry, we can—"

That was as far as he got before the gauntlet on Taeauna's sword hand came alive, rising and reaching out, and dragging her unwilling arm with it, as she trembled in a vain struggle against it.

As its metal fingers spread, an unseen force snatched the wand from Malraun's hand and plucked it whirling through the air into the grasp of the gauntlet, which closed around it.

Fighting to wrench her hand free of the gage or maintain some control over her fingers, Taeauna sobbed aloud in her exertions, arching her back and heavily muscled shoulders to twist and pull.

The wand blossomed into a flaring glow, and from that glow streaked a bright and sudden bolt of racing flame, no longer a wide cone now, but a lance aimed to pierce Malraun the Matchless.

The flames flashed, struck, and were gone, leaving Malraun wet with sweat and staggering in their wake, smokes swirling from him in a dozen places and his hair an ashen ruin. He gasped for air through a slack mouth, bent over in pain... and then was gone, in an eye-blink, as if he'd never been there at all.

"Teleported," Rod said tersely in the instant before the gauntlet turned, still towing the unwilling Taeauna, and touched him with the end of the wand.

Rod set his teeth against pain that didn't come, wincing away from... no attack at all. No flames, nothing.

Nothing but a strong and vivid image flooding into his mind, as bright and detailed as his clearest memories.

Yet he knew it was a place he'd never seen before.

A castle that looked old and sinister, a tall black needle soaring up into a milky, cloud-filled sky in front of hundreds of trees. It was a castle of unique and striking appearance; a slender, soaring hall of obsidian hue that sprouted a spire offset to one corner.

Then the vision was gone, as abruptly as it had come, and Rod was blinking at the same thing Taeauna was.

The wand and gauntlet had both vanished, in a winking instant, leaving Taeauna's sword hand bare, empty, and unmarred.

Rod stared at her, and she stared back at him. "Are you... all right?" they asked each other, in perfect unison.

Then they both shrugged. "I saw things inside my head," Taeauna blurted, while Rod was still struggling to find the right words.

"Yes!" was what he settled for. "I saw a dark castle; some fortress I've never seen before. What did you see?"

Taeauna shrugged again. "I..."

More warriors came running out of the darkness, lots of them, the thunder of boots almost deafening. The Aumrarr gave Rod a weary look and turned to face the doorway again, hefting her sword.

The warriors flooded into the room. They wore motley armor, not black with identical visored helms, and Velduke Deldragon strode at their head, flaxen mustache bright and ice-blue eyes peering everywhere.

He stopped, very suddenly, when he beheld Rod and Taeauna standing guard before the well, and dead Dark Helms piled up in a great arc around them.

"How by the Falcon Aflame did you get down here?" Deldragon asked, his voice slow and deep with amazement.

"Darendarr," Taeauna snapped, "first tell me: is there a place down here in your cellars where three passages meet like this," she gestured swiftly, "and then a fourth comes in a little way along, about up here?"

Deldragon frowned, and then nodded. "Yes."

"Send a score or more of your knights there, to the room in this angle of the three-way moot. It holds a tantlar-fire; that's where these Dark Helms are coming from!"

Deldragon spun around and started snapping orders.

"That," Taeauna murmured to Rod, pointing to her own head, "is what I just saw."

The velduke's orders were sending most of the knights who'd come with him racing off again. When he was done barking instructions, Deldragon turned back to them with a smile. "My thanks. So, tell me now: how come you to be here, instead of in the rather better appointed guest chambers I provided for you?"

"I thought it most unlikely that Dark Helms would be welcome in Bowrock," the Aumrarr told him. "So when I saw them rushing past in such numbers, it was clear this keep was beset. Either they would prevail, and we'd all be too dead to care, or you would beat them back, whereupon defending your well during their withdrawal would be crucial. So we sought it."

She went closer to the velduke, and added in a voice that was little more than a whisper, "I learned of that tantlar in a vision, just now. Darendarr, have you ever seen a gauntlet appear magically on someone's hand, here in your keep?"

Deldragon shook his head, and answered in a similarly guarded voice, "It seems we three have some matters to discuss. Later. Right now, we of Bowrock are preparing for a siege. Several nearby Lords of Galath have been seen mustering all the armsmen they can. I strongly suspect they intend to come here, and that the rest of the surviving lords of the land will be joining them, and bringing their own armies along, too. I gave you my protection, but I must now lay a choice before you. Some of my best knights will be escorting certain persons here in Bowrock south out of Galath just as fast as they can ride; would you two like to be among them?"

"No," Taeauna replied firmly. "Deldragon, we will stand here with you."

"We are well provisioned, have other wells, and are well-trained for war, but if all the armies of Galath come to our gates, the siege may not end well," the velduke said quietly.

"If that befalls, so be it," the Aumrarr murmured, looking at Rod.

He shrugged and told her, "I stand with you, Tay. If you are staying here, so am I."

Deldragon bowed. "I am honored. Come with me, please." He gave some swift orders that made most of his remaining knights take up positions around the well to guard it, and told two of them to "Fetch the waterboys, and tell them the way is clear to come down again and start dipping."

That pair of knights hastened away, and the velduke led Rod and Taeauna out the door and in another direction, through doors and up short flights of stairs and along passages to more stairs.

They climbed many flights of stairs and traversed many passages before the velduke shouldered through a door that opened into a small, bare chamber, nodded at Taeauna to close it, leaned back against the wall, and asked, "Lady of the Aumrarr, tell me more of this gauntlet you spoke of. Please."

Taeauna shrugged, and held up her sword hand.

"It just appeared, out of nowhere, here on this hand, and I could not get it off. A large, heavy wargage. Well made, in good repair, and magical. The air glowed around my hand, and... well, *sang*. Like high harp strings that call on and on, without sounding like they're being plucked or strummed."

As the words left her lips, the air promptly started to glow and sing, just as it had before. This time, however, the glow enshrouded an alarmed Rod Everlar.

Taeauna and Deldragon turned to stare at him in time to see something small, dark, and horsehead-shaped appear in the air above the quiet man's hand and fall into it.

Rod juggled the thing for a moment, as if he might drop it. Then he held it up in his right hand to peer at it.

He seemed to be holding a model or statuette of a horse's head, cast and then worked in some dark olive-hued metal to bring forth fine details. It was surprisingly heavy.

Then he wasn't seeing the thing in his palm at all, but the black, odd-spired castle once more, suddenly and so vividly that he might have been standing in front of it, with a cool breeze rising around his shoulders.

"It's the same place," he whispered again, in bewilderment. "The dark castle."

AMALRYS TURNED TO her master in a chiming of chains. Under dark brows, her ice-blue eyes were frowning. "Master, something in Bowrock is thrusting my scryings aside. I was seeing into the velduke's keep without hindrance, but now, just like that, I cannot. Something within leaves me gazing at empty sky, or south out of Galath, whenever I try."

Arlaghaun looked up from the old and heavy metal-bound tome he was studying, preoccupation giving way to uninterest on his sharp-nosed face.

"Deldragon has hired a few lesser mages," the gray-clad wizard mused. "Wherefore it will do you good, Amalrys mine, to wrestle against them a time or two. So try your scryings again, and yet again, for the practice will do you good. And bother me not."

His thin lips shaped a mirthless smile. "After all, there's nothing of consequence the good velduke can hide from us before he dies."

* * *

"Put it down!" Taeauna snapped at Rod, eyes blazing. "Throw it down!"

He regarded her calmly, cradling the heavy thing in his palm as he thought. "No."

He put it in his laedre instead. "Its magic won't help us in fighting, or a siege, but is too useful to just throw away."

Taeauna gave Rod a sharp glare. "You know what it does?"

"I do now."

"So you are a wizard," Deldragon said softly.

"No," Rod replied, meeting the velduke's ice-blue eyes steadily. "No, I'm not. If you held that horse-head, it would tell you what it does, too."

"Well?" Deldragon asked, holding out his hand.

"No," Rod told him. "Not now. If we survive the siege, yes, but it would be bad for you to touch the thing at this time."

Taeauna was still watching Rod intently. "It showed you something else, didn't it?"

"Yes."

"What?"

Rod looked at her, then nodded his head in Deldragon's direction, and looked a silent question at the Aumrarr.

"Tell us both," she replied quietly.

"I saw the castle again."

"The castle? Which castle?" She frowned. "What other times have you seen this castle?"

"The castle I saw when the wand touched me. I'd never seen it before then. It's tall and black, and has a thin spire rising out of one corner."

Taeauna went a little pale, drew in her breath sharply, and then asked carefully, "A squared-off tower, with four turrets at its corners, three of them just bulges that rise no higher than the battlements joining them, but the fourth a cylindrical tower that rises above the turrets for half again their height, then narrows to a smooth needle-pointed spire?"

Rod nodded.

The Aumrarr added grimly, "And this castle has no moat nor outbuildings, and stands in the heart of a green, growing forest. The trees close around it are dead and bare. Yes?"

Rod nodded again.

Stroking his flaxen mustache, Deldragon looked a silent question of his own at Taeauna.

"Yintaerghast," she whispered, in reply. "Lorontar."

Then it seemed to be the velduke's turn to shiver, go pale, and take a step back from Rod.

AMALRYS STIFFENED SUDDENLY, and then erupted into wild spasms, her chains clashing as well as chiming, her honey-blonde hair lashing the air as she jerked her head about, her hands like wriggling claws. Then she slumped over in her chair, head lolling and drooling.

Arlaghaun looked up in annoyance, brown eyes flashing, and closed his book with a sigh. Thoughtfully, he tapped his sharp nose for a moment, then cast a careful spell over his apprentice.

She neither moved nor spoke.

The gray-clad wizard shrugged. Good. No rival mind was infesting hers. Her will must have failed under the strain of fighting to command her scrying-probe through Deldragon's hired defenses.

Such things happened. Such would happen to her again, until enough practice strengthened her mind sufficiently.

Shaking his head, the greatest Doom of Falconfar went back to his book. He'd been working out a cleverly hidden message in a particularly fascinating passage...

NARMARKOUN SMILED SLOWLY. "Always they forget about me. Arlaghaun the Arrogant-Beyond-Belief and Malraun the Matchless Dolt. Far too powerful to concern themselves even with the notion that someone else just might, *might* have mastered magic enough to be a match for either of them. And, in time, the greatest wizard of all. Ever."

The tall, blue-skinned wizard shifted on his smooth and shifting bed of ice-cold wenches, their dead bodies responding to his will. They began to caress his scaly body and accept him in, their eternally grinning skulls regarding him with eyes that were no longer there.

"I'm not the greatest yet; not even close," he told one skull, as the body attached to it started to stroke him and grind ardently against him, "but already I have achieved far more than either of my oh-so-exalted rival Dooms. Where they fiddle with spells that were old before their grandsires were born, adjusting tiny details of casting and result, I breed greatfangs."

He raised his voice, clenching his scaly fists, and told them proudly, "I augment greatfangs. I tame greatfangs and ride greatfangs and take the shape of greatfangs... and know the love of greatfangs. I can hide in the form of a greatfangs if ever I am beset, and I can steal the loyalties of apprentices without their masters even noticing. Arlaghaun, your precious Amalrys is mine now!"

He frowned and peered around his womblike bedchamber of dark red velvet, but found no answer to what was now troubling him. When he spoke again, his voice had fallen to a thoughtful murmur. "But I wish I knew what mage is protecting Deldragon. Malraun fled from him, Arlaghaun didn't even notice him, Amalrys was casually foiled by him; who is he? Deldragon has coins aplenty to spend among the Stormar, and has spilled more than a few of them on spells and black-bearded, bright-robed spell-hurlers, but I've heard of no wizard among them that has such power, and casual mastery of it."

He reared back from the skull-headed wench embracing him far enough to catch hold of its shapely shoulders, and shake it fiercely. Its jawbone rattled.

"Can another Doom have arisen?" he demanded of it. "Has the fourth Doom come at last, and none of us noticed him?"

Grinning silence was its customary reply, and grinning silence was what it gave him now.

"WELL, SOMETHING'S UPSET them," Iskarra said peevishly. "Just look out there: bees from a kicked-over hive! Now, it can't be Deldragon being foolish enough to make war on someone; he just came back from doing that, and the going then didn't take half this fuss. And he won, didn't he? So there'd be not the urgency, this time."

She pointed a little unsteadily out the cleanest window of the dingy taproom, and waited for the grunt that would tell her Garfist had looked and seen what she'd been watching over his shoulder.

Thirsty from all that talking, and not sure if she'd said everything clearly thanks to all the drink already aboard her, Iskarra shook her head, looked into her almost-empty tankard as if it might hold some inspiration, found nothing promising, and clunked it down on the tavern's dirtiest table again. When would these lasses who danced on tables while hauling off their clothes learn to wipe their boots first?

Garfist grew tired of staring at running knights and frantically trotting drovers and turned back to face her, his own tankard almost invisible in his huge and hairy fist. "I'll tell ye what it is, Isk, dearie. It's a siege they're preparing for, that's what it is."

Iskarra stared at fat old Garfist Gulkoon as if he'd suddenly grown another three heads, all of them beautiful and feminine and eagerly trying to kiss each other, and protested, "But it can't be! We'd've heard! Besides, so would they, out there! You can't march an army around Galath without giving everyone else in the realm more than plenty of warning." She waved one long-fingered, spiderlike hand in the direction of all the bustle out in the street and snapped, "And that is *not* 'plenty of warning.'"

"Aye, I'll grant ye that. I'll grant ye that." The onetime pirate belched loudly, farted just as thunderously, turned his head in the direction of the bar, and bellowed, "More ale! And none of yer stingy tankards this time. Bring a keg, man!"

The master of the Gauntlet and Feather was privately of the opinion that the two uncouth, dirty visitors from the South had already taken aboard more than enough ale to rot their insides, and it in turn had already done its work on their brains. Yet they were his only customers, looked to already be past the point of destructive belligerence, and if all they did was spew all over the table, floor, and each other, and then flop face-down in their own mess and start snoring, well, he had maids enough to clean up after that.

Wherefore he called, "Of course, Master Gulkoon! I'll go fetch it," and hurried into the back to get Narjak to help him carry up the oldest, flattest, wormiest keg of soured ale from the cellar. These two must have been too far gone to taste what they were downing six tankards ago.

If Iskarra and Garfist had known the tavern master's opinion of them, or what he was now planning to pour into them, they'd have been neither annoyed nor surprised. Tavern masters were all heartless bastards, and besides, this latest one hadn't judged them far wrong.

They made their livings largely from thievery, these days. Wherefore their presence here in Bowrock, where they'd fetched up after a hasty flight from justice in three Sea of Swords ports. This was certainly the unlikeliest place for anyone to seek them.

The persistence of that Arlsakran merchant had really surprised them both. After all, the man had fourteen daughters; couldn't he spare the best-looking three to a life of tavern dancing and pleasuring men, rather than staying home digging daily in the mud of the family farm and pleasuring their father nightly, all in the same gigantic, groaning bed? And he'd looked too fat to chase anyone through three cities, too!

Almost as fat as Garfist himself: a onetime pirate who'd promoted himself to forger when his girth made him too slow for deckfights, then a hiresword all over the lands east of the Spires, thereafter a panderer for a long time, and now a thief. He was still covered with a pelt of the same thick red hair, all over, that had adorned him since his youth, but in the years since he'd lost almost all of his teeth, and broken his shovel-sized hands so often that they looked like gauntlets of spiky bone, calluses, and corded veins.

Iskarra "Vipersides" might look as fat as Garfist, but her bulk was all magical crawlskin, not her own itching hide. Under it, she was the skinniest, boniest living person Garfist had ever seen; all warts, wrinkles, and gray skin, she looked like a withered corpse, not a woman. Not that he hadn't tasted her favors a time or two; a man has needs, after all. And she did know spices—and poisons, and antidotes—better than anyone he'd ever met, besides being uniquely gifted for thievery.

Years back, somewhere way out east, she'd stolen her crawlskin: the magically preserved, semi-alive skin of a long-dead sorceress. It melded to her own hide when she wanted it to, and held the shape she gave it, so she could be all hips and breasts a man would hunger for, or as stout as Garfist, or barely larger than her own naked hide-and-bones. It could also part when she wanted it to, allowing her to reach in and hide gems and coins and other stolen things in leather bladders she strapped to herself. Right now it was carrying a surprising number of coins, all folded in flesh so they wouldn't clink together. It could even turn into a long fleshy rope or worm, and reach farther than her arm could, turning like a snake and clutching at her bidding. Without it, she was as skinny as a lance and as desirable as a corpse.

Best of all, she liked Garfist, and he liked her, and they trusted each other; something neither of them had dared to do with anyone else for years and years.

Iskarra's looks were slipping, but her face still had some of the dark-eyed beauty that had caught men's eyes when she was younger, and her body was wrapped in enough clothing to fool them. And that profane mouth still had the skills of a Stormar pleasure-lass.

To say nothing of her wits and fearlessness, that both outstripped Garfist's own. And were both good things, when one was stealing magic.

Here in Bowrock, houses seemed full of enchanted gewgaws and even the occasional battle-wand. Moreover, many of them seemed to have been turned inactive, and left in the keeping of folk who didn't even know they were magical. Garfist and Iskarra could scarce believe their good fortune, and hadn't yet dared to snatch much.

Yet the only wizards they'd thus far seen in Bowrock were strutting Stormar alley-mages, who knew a few tricks, four or five real spells, and how to make and peddle "charms" and enchanted oils that might or might not do what they claimed to do.

"Grow us a really striking bosom, old Viper mine," Garfist rumbled now, reaching across the table. "I need to remember how to fondle."

Iskarra gave him a disgusted look, and dealt his hand a half-hearted slap. "No biting," she snarled. "Like last time."

Garfist tried to chuckle, but it erupted into a choking snort that quite spoiled his leer, so he settled for thrusting one great paw of a hand into the open front of her leather bodice, and squeezed.

She gasped and shuddered, half-closing her eyes and moving under his hand with her lips caught in her teeth, moaning as if in need, and then stuck out her tongue at him, made a rude sound, and snapped, "Where's that ale? Are they all out back pissing into a keg to fill it for us, then?"

"D'wanna stay here for the night? I think they rent rooms, Isk."

"Not if you're going to try to crawl on top of me. My love for being crushed is fading." Iskarra belched loudly, and then winced. "Gorge rising, throat afire," she croaked. "Get them to bring that glorking ale!"

Garfist growled in agreement, swung himself around, and heaved himself upright. The movement was heralded by great creakings from the stout chair beneath him.

The deserted taproom of the Gauntlet and Feather heaved and rolled for a moment under his boots, like the deck of a ship in heavy seas, but he was used to that, and just kept striding, reaching the door beside the bar at about the same time as the master of the house and a sweating Narjak started through it with a full keg between them.

Garfist scooped it out of their shared grasp with one hand, and bore it away back to his table with a satisfied purring sound, leaving Narjack open-mouthed in awe, and gaping, a moment later, when the decaying woman at the table stood up eagerly and held out an empty tankard, her bodice fell open, and he could *swear* he saw the nipple of one bared breast grow a tiny hand and tug the bodice back up. The tavern master hastened along in the keg's wake, anxious to prevent spillage when it was tapped, or utter disaster if it got dropped.

Garfist sat down with the keg in his lap, as if it was a giggling tavern maid, and roared, "Where're all yer other patrons, friend? All upstairs bouncing the beds? Or are they out there running around in the streets like all the rest? Ye'd think there was a siege coming, the way they're preparing!"

The tavern master managed a weak smile.

"W-well, as a matter of… aha… fact, there, ah, is."

Garfist looked up and dropped his own jaw onto the keg beneath it. "Well, shit me! Who're the belligerent would-be conquerors?"

"Ah, well… almost all of the Lords of Galath, they say. They're not here yet, mind."

The tavern master half expected the two drunkards to explode into profanity and swaying, doomed attempts to hasten out of his establishment and flee the city.

He did not at all expect Garfist to slap the table, grin broadly, and growl, "Well, that's grand! Always wanted to be lord of somewhere, and sounds like some vacancies're going to open up soon. Lord Garfield Gulkoon of Galath; has a ring to it, don't ye think?"

The tavern master of the Gauntlet and Feather prided himself on being a seasoned, unflappable professional, and proved it to himself then and there. He managed to entirely quell his strong and instant impulse to shudder.

Chapter Fourteen

T HE SOUP WAS wonderful, a rich broth thick with onions and the leavings of many spit-roasted fowl. Taeauna and Rod both ate heartily until they were more than full; Rod was amused to find that Aumrarr belched and groaned and sat back in chairs holding their bellies just like everyone else did.

They'd expected their summons to the velduke's table would mean sitting at a long table in a lofty and echoing hall feasting with a lot of haughty people, but instead they'd been shown into a cozy, book-lined study with a magnificent map of Falconfar on the wall that Rod spent a long time studying.

The room had no guards or servants or anyone but the two of them in it, and held books on shelves all around the walls, and a littered desk that had a lone dagger floating point-down in the air over it.

("Guard-blade," Taeauna had murmured. "Don't go anywhere near yon desk, even if papers blow off it by themselves.") It also held a table with four stout chairs drawn up around it. The soup had been served to them at the table, along with lemon-scented drinking water, a fragrant-smelling fresh loaf of bread, a sharp saw-knife to cut it with, and a bowl of garlic butter to spread on it. Rod could remember few meals as good, in all his life.

They'd sat over the remains of the repast until the last heel of the bread was quite cold, and Rod was fighting back yawns and wondering when a servant would appear to guide them back to their bed in those distant guest chambers.

"Shouldn't we…?" he got as far as asking Taeauna.

Her response was a sharp look and a firm, "Patience."

As if that had been a cue, a bookshelf swung open and Velduke Deldragon strode in, stroking his flaxen mustache. He nodded a silent greeting to them, his ice-blue eyes seeming somehow dull and washed out, and scaled the helm under his arm into a corner where it thudded down on a cushion Rod hadn't noticed before.

Suddenly the room was full of silent, deftly hastening servants, bringing a housecloak, wine and a platter of goblets and sugared nuts, and steaming platters of roasted meat. Just as suddenly, they were all gone again, and Velduke Deldragon was wearily forking meat running with red juices onto his plate and saying, "Lady of the Aumrarr? This is choice young stag; I smoke and hang my own."

"I'd love some, Darendarr," Taeauna said gently, "but let me carve and serve. You look tired."

"I am tired. I've been rushing around all day talking. I'd prefer to swing a sword daylong, any day. By the Falcon, it's tiring giving orders and explaining, explaining, explaining! You'd think my people of Bowrock would know about catching rainwater and bringing in hay for the beasts and all of that by now, but every time—"

"I know," Taeauna said sympathetically, and it sounded to Rod as if she really did.

Deldragon ran a hand through his flowing hair, and then gave Rod an apologetic grin. "It's a lot of work, preparing for a siege," he said, "but you don't want to hear all about that. Nor do I find I want to talk all about that, one more thuttering time."

He attacked his stag like a starving man, and then looked straight at Rod and asked, "What do you know about the Dooms?"

Rod was aware of Taeauna's sudden glare at the velduke—she was bristling as if she wanted to draw sword on him—but kept his eyes steady on Deldragon's before replying. "Not much," he said. "That there are three of them, maybe four someday, and that they're powerful wizards, really powerful wizards, who want to rule all Falconfar. Each of them, so they fight each other. And I believe I heard in Arvale that one of them is trying to rule Galath. The Dark Helms serve them, and maybe the lorn."

Deldragon nodded. "Three evil wizards at war with each other. Each of them seeks the magic of the past, for sorcery has fallen far in reach and mastery since the days when Lorontar butchered every wizard who wouldn't bow to him. So today the Dooms scramble to gather the most powerful spells and enchanted items from tombs, and the ruined castles of long-fallen kings, and the vaults of Galathan nobles. One of them does rule our king, and through him orders nobles slaughtered or banished, so their magic can be seized. Hence this siege; it comes now because I dared to aid Tindror, but it was coming anyway. Bowrock is awash in magics."

At that moment, a glow kindled in the air above the table, air that started to sing, high and faint. It grew very quiet around the table as the glow grew, and something small and wraithlike materialized into view on the polished table, right in front of Rod.

Something that became more solid, until all hints of wraith-smoke were gone, and they were all staring at something that looked like a little jewel box, that might comfortably fit in a lady's palm. It had a tail of fine chain, that ended in a finger-ring. The glow and singing sound faded, leaving it gleaming brightly against the dark, smooth wood.

"Don't touch it," Taeauna snapped at Rod. "Please."

She shot a glance at Deldragon, who was staring at the box in mute astonishment. "I was going to accuse you of producing these enchanted trinkets, as a test to see if my companion here is a wizard."

He tore his gaze from the jewel box at the word "accuse" and looked up at her.

The Aumrarr's gaze, on his, was both hard and cool. "Those curios on the table in our guest chambers were just that, weren't they?"

The velduke blinked, sighed, and nodded. "Yes. They were put there at my command by hired Stormar wizards; magelings of no great accomplishment, which is the only sort of wizard I can afford. Yet you just said you were going to accuse me this time… but?"

The Aumrarr's gaze softened. "But 'tis clear you're as surprised as we are. Wherefore this isn't your doing. Someone else has reached into Bowrock with their spells. Someone who knows this man is here."

"Someone who can reach freely into Bowrock, past the wardings cast by my hired mages," Deldragon added grimly.

"Or someone who is inside Bowrock, already here in this keep, hidden among your folk," Taeauna said quietly.

They watched the velduke slowly go white.

"BLOW ME HARD, Isk, if I can think of a good reason for us being allowed inside yon keep," Garfist growled. "They're preparing for a glorking siege, aren't they now? What idiocy could induce them to let two outlanders who look like us anywhere near their precious velduke?"

Iskarra pointed one long and bony finger at two wagons being drawn slowly up a distant cobbled slope that led to a gate somewhere on the far side of the keep. "Food. They'll want wagonloads of food in there. Turnips. Lar-fruit. Bloodbuds. Wheels of cheese from far Zharlay."

Garfist's gut rumbled like storm-thunder. "Huh. I wouldn't mind a wagon of cheese from far Zharlay."

He waved one shovel-sized hand in an expressive gesture of futility, keeping the other wrapped tightly around what was left of the keg of ale. He'd brought it with him out of the tavern despite its sour taste, because, well, it was beer. "And just where are ye going to get a loaded wagon of plenty from, hmm?"

"Behind the market, of course. They're still arriving now."

"And the drovers as owns it? They're just going to hand it over to ye, I suppose?"

Iskarra triumphantly bared her breasts and belly, plunged a hand into her navel which split apart vertically, into a wide, bloodless opening, reached up inside herself, behind her bulging breasts, fumbled with something there, and triumphantly drew forth two tankards. Theirs, from the tavern.

Garfist looked incredulous. "Ye're going to seek someone stupid enough to trade us a loaded wagon—and dray-beasts, mind—for two empty tankards?"

Iskarra rolled her eyes. "Stick to brawling and spewing and rutting, old Gulkoon, and leave the thinking to me, hmm?"

She nudged one of her breasts with a tankard. "With these, we distract the men we choose. You smite them to sleep, we leave the tankards in their hands and them propped sitting against a wall, and you half-fill the tankards and drench the rest of them with yon ale, and off we go. Everyone who sees them will think them drunkards. That much is so easy it's barely worth saying aloud. What's got me foxed and witless is what happens after we're inside the gates; what then?"

"Then we help unload, discover our beast-harness is broke, and say we're too tired to deal with it now, we've come all this way, it can wait until morning. Should we sleep in our wagons, is there anywhere around here to shit, and by Galath we're hungry; are there kitchens still open?"

Iskarra smiled crookedly. "You can still think!"

"O'course, lass! That's how I get all the gels, and their coins, and then peels the one away from the other, remember?"

Iskarra rolled her eyes. "Peeling gels," she murmured. "All you ever think about..." She stowed the tankards away where she'd produced them from, and did up her clothing again, peering pointedly all around. She even looked under her own feet and around behind Garfist.

"What're ye playing at this time?" he growled. "Ye're being clever again, I know ye are! When ye get that look on yer face..."

"I'm looking for the gels," she snapped. "And the coins, too."

Garfist made a very rude gesture that ended with him noisily licking three adjacent hooked fingers clean.

Iskarra struck a pose, and made her crawlskin fashion lush curves with naughty areas of spectacular size. "You can do that if you can catch me," she said, sticking out her tongue at him, "but it's been years since you've been able to do that."

"If I was a rutting Doom of Galath," Garfist said heavily, "yer ass'd not be laughing so loudly!"

"If you were a rutting Doom of Galath," Iskarra replied tartly, "most Falconaar would be dead, and the rest of us'd all be in hiding."

Garfist grinned. "That's true. Heh. Let's go get us a wagon."

He peered again up at the soaring walls of the keep. "If there's one place in Bowrock that'll have magic, and coins, and gels, lying around for the taking, it's in there. Where the bloody velduke is probably snoring away, reclining on heaps of them right now."

"Heaps of coins or gels?"

"Both, Isk." Garfist belched so violently he filled his mouth with searing gulped-once ale, and had to swallow it down again. "Both!"

TAEAUNA SET HER boots ready beside the bed, drew her sword, and got into bed with it. Thankfully, she put it by her sword hand, to the outside, rather than between them.

Which left her free to roll over on her side, head propped on one elbow, and ask Rod, as he struggled to keep his eyes on her face, "So. Are you going to show me these magics that have been appearing out of nowhere and dropping into your hands?"

"No," Rod said shortly. "Not yet. I don't want to touch them again. Yet."

"You're scared of them," the Aumrarr murmured, her gaze sympathetic.

"No, I'm not scared. Okay, yes, I am," Rod admitted. "I... that castle. I'm afraid if I do anything with them, even handle them too long, I'll somehow get taken inside that castle."

"And what do you fear will happen to you there?"

Rod looked at her. "That someone will hand me all this power you keep saying I have."

"And?"

"And I'll do the wrong thing, and wreck Falconfar."

"'Wreck?'"

"Kill everyone, hurl down kingdoms, make the mountains erupt, the seas drown the land, that sort of thing."

"But what you write, everything you do, you can reverse by writing more. You can put it all back."

"No, Tay," Rod whispered. "You can't. I can't. One can't. No one can ever put it all back. Once something's done, it's done. You can try to put it back, but the damage is done; you can never repair it all."

Something sad and terrible rose in Taeauna's eyes, and she whispered, "You're learning. Lord Rod Everlar, you are learning, and finally handing me hope thereby."

And she turned and blew out the last lamp.

Her voice had sounded as if she was on the trembling edge of tears; hesitantly Rod reached out a hand for her, in the darkness, meaning only to comfort.

It was captured in her fingers, and firmly turned over. Her lips brushed his palm in the softest of kisses before his hand was firmly returned to him.

"Please, lord, let me sleep," she whispered, sounding even closer to tears.

"Of course," Rod mumbled, rolling over.

He lay there as still as he could, listening for her to settle into sleep, but Falconfar's god of slumber—if Falconfar had a god of slumber—got to him first.

* * *

"WHICH ONE, OLD viper?"

"Well, we don't look like the most respectable traders, now do we?" Iskarra whispered hoarsely. "So then, we need one of the better-looking wagons. Not too grand, or we'll seem out of place riding it. But solid, respectable; all the things we aren't."

"Huh. I'm solid enough," Garfist growled, thumping the large, descending slope of his belly. "The other, I'll grant ye. Not that I see—"

"That one," Iskarra said, pointing across the walled wagon-yard. "Off by itself, there, hard by the wall."

Garfist promptly hefted his keg to a more comfortable carrying position under his arm, and set off across the yard.

Iskarra's choice was a larger wagon than most, nondescript and solid. It bore no badge nor painted name on the gray side or end she could see, and the two men busy around it were hitching its team of four draft horses back up, rather than unhitching and hobbling them for the night.

Iskarra turned her back, pulled out her tankards—it wouldn't do to bare all her secrets before she had to—and trotted hastily after Garfist, calling softly, "Ale? A quaff for the night? Only one copper tarth."

"No sale," one of the drovers said curtly.

"Begone," the other suggested, in no more friendly a manner.

Garfist sighed heavily and set down his keg.

"Blast and bugger-all," he growled. "Ye, too? What's a man got to do, to sell any ale in this— whoa!"

The drover beside him had drawn his sword. "See this? Get gone!"

"Well, now," Garfist growled, "that's not friendly!"

"It's not meant to be." The man showed his teeth, and jabbed the point of his sword in the general direction of the fat man's belly.

Garfist swiftly plucked the keg up and thrust it forward, catching the point of the drover's blade in its staves. When he flung the keg down, the sword was wrenched out of the man's grasp, and Garfist reached out with one ham-sized hand, caught the man by the throat, and snatched him off his feet to dangle in midair, kicking and strangling.

"Must be valuable, whatever's in there," he growled at Iskarra, as she darted past him to confront the second drover, who was advancing menacingly from his end of the wagon with drawn sword in hand.

"Likely," she agreed over her shoulder, running straight at the man and hurling her tankards, hard and accurately. His blade deftly struck them aside, and then thrust ruthlessly at her; she slowed not a whit, but twisted herself sharply sideways as she snatched a hairpin out of the tangled mess of her hair.

The sword went right through Iskarra, piercing the crawlskin back and front, plunging through her false breast and back, but thanks to her twisting, missing her emaciated real body within. By then her arms were around the drover, and she was stabbing his back hard and repeatedly with the hairpin. His leathers prevented it from going in that deep, but it didn't have to; Iskarra had dipped it plentifully in the strongest sleep-inducing drug known in Falconfar.

Nose-to-nose, the drover grinned mirthlessly at her, and then kissed her. "Skaekur, huh? Never forget the feel of it, bubbling through the body. Pity I'm spellguarded against it."

Iskarra tried to pull free, but there was suddenly something in her head, like a dark purple cloud stealing across her thoughts, dark and heavy… She couldn't seem to think straight, to care about anything anymore, but she could see, as if from a great and numb distance, that she was now energetically embracing the drover, and returning his kisses.

With a furious effort she managed to swing their locked-together bodies around until she could see along the wagon to where Garfist had been happily throttling the other drover.

Her mountainously stout partner had set the man down and was now gently massaging the drover's bruised throat and dusting him down as carefully as a mothering-maid. Garfist turned and gave Iskarra a smile, and she saw that his eyes had gone purple.

Nodding a respectful farewell to the drover, the fat ex-pirate came lurching along the wagon. The darkness in Iskarra's own head was forcing her to gently disengage herself from her drover, now, and spread her legs to accept his hands on haunch and crotch, boosting her up the back of the wagon to open its rear doors wide.

She did that, swinging them clear just as Garfist rounded the wagon and boosted himself inside, with a great rolling grunt and a heave that shook the wagon and made the hitched horses snort and paw.

Then the force in Iskarra's head was compelling her forward into the darkness of the wagon, between the stacked wooden crates of swords and arrows, to pluck aside a central stack she shouldn't have been able to budge an inch.

The end of the stack proved to be false, a single panel adorned with sawed-off ends of stacked crates. Behind it, smiling rather unpleasantly at her, sat an unkempt man with curly hair of dirty gold, and unruly eyebrows and a jaw-fringe beard to match.

His large, dark purple eyes were in her head already, floating dark and heavy and all-seeing. He was the source of the magic now ruling her and Garfist. Yardryk, his mind identified himself, apprentice of Arlaghaun. He was young and supremely arrogant and overconfident to a fault, she could tell; neither his name nor that of the great wizard he served was information she was supposed to know. He seemed unaware of how much his thoughts were leaking into her head.

Yardryk was hiding among all these swords and arrows so he could get into the velduke's personal keep; the wares had been chosen to make them irresistible to warriors facing a siege. The idea was Arlaghaun's, but the schemings and details had been Yardryk's own, and he was very proud of them.

He was also greatly pleased, now, by the unexpected arrival of Garfist and Iskarra, now that he had made sure no rival mage had sent them to him as lures, or was lurking in their mind. They were just what he needed: outlanders not of Bowrock or of Galath, who had been drovers before and could serve so again now, freeing his warriors to pose as guards of so precious a load.

This would enable Yardryk and one of the warriors to slip off into hiding, once the wagon was inside the velduke's keep; thereafter, they could work much mischief. Leaving one guard for the load, and two owner-drovers up front to flog the goods and suffer the daggers of the Bowrock warriors, if the velduke wanted to escape paying or grew overly suspicious of so convenient an arrival of weapons.

Yardryk saw no reason not to take the wagon to the keep right now, seeing as other carters, despite the coming of night, were still running their wagons of food and casks of wine to the velduke's buyers. Food and wine that, properly handled by the velduke's cooks and cellarers, could not help but be preferable to what wagon-merchants could buy from the market fry-stalls, come morning. Oh, yes, the luck of the Falcon was with Yardryk Brightrising just now, making his family name proud truth at last...

He gave Garfist and Iskarra one last sneering smile as they fitted his false crates back in place in front of him, and the stout former panderer heaved and grunted a real stack of crated swords into place in front of that.

The two grinning guards then pulled up crates in front of the stacks to sit on, Garfist and Iskarra closed and fastened the doors on them, and before long the solid gray wagon was rumbling through the cobbled streets of Bowrock with two silent, mind-ridden drovers at the reins, heading for the velduke's keep.

* * *

THERE WAS A small, round skylight in the domed ceiling, high over the huge guest bed; Rod had never noticed it before.

He found himself blinking blearily at it now, however. The first sun of morning was blazing above it, making it a bright blue eye staring down into a room that was still dim, and cold, and very, very still.

He was naked, of course, and lying flat on his back in the bed, but there was something small, heavy, and hard on his chest, and he was otherwise bare. Where were the linens? The sleeping furs?

And where was Taeauna?

Rod lifted his head enough to see that he was alone on a bed that didn't seem to have any furs or linens on it anymore. There was a small metal *something* on his chest that looked somewhat like an ornate brass-finish sink faucet handle that a television design show host might have chosen or sneered at, not something of Falconfar at all. It looked like it had been welded onto three mock miniature dagger letter-openers, splayed out at angles. It must be another "gift from nowhere" thing of magic, fallen on him while he slept.

So he'd missed the whole glowing air thing, or had he? This looked almost as if he'd been arranged, for some sort of ritual.

"Taeauna?" he asked softly.

Silence. He couldn't even hear her breathing.

He put a hand up and took hold of the metal thing on his chest, and was abruptly aware of a reek of smoke and a flash of heat.

Not from it, but inside his head… and linked to it, or caused by his touching it. Yes, definitely. His fingers told him it was cool, his nose told him it smelled of nothing more than metal and possibly a little whiff of long-ago oil of some sort, but his mind was telling him that it had erupted in some sort of intense heat, and something had burned, swiftly and sharply, leaving behind smoke.

Rod sat up, holding the enchanted gewgaw carefully, and peering all around the room. No servants, and no guards. Bars across the insides of the doors, where Taeauna had put them last night, and—

"Jesus!" he spat, flinging the metal thing down and hurling himself forward off the bed, landing hard on his knees and clawing his way across the rugs. "God, *no!*"

Taeauna of the Aumrarr was as naked as he was, and was lying sprawled and senseless on the floor halfway across the room, face up, and not breathing. Her face looked empty, her eyes blank. And the fingers of her left hand, stretched out toward him, were charred to ash.

"Taeauna!" he cried, touching her cheek. "Taeauna!" Her skin was cold, and when he shook her gently, she moved loosely under his touch, as if he were rocking something empty. She wasn't breathing!

Frantically he tried to remember that CPR course, the mouth-to-mouth business of wiping the plastic dummy with a foul-tasting alcohol wipe... hyperextend neck, mouth sweep with his finger—*shit*!

There was soot on her tongue; it turned to black slime on his finger when he wiped at it. He'd let her head fall back as he stared at it, and there was more soot now, like black powder, leaking out of her nostrils. She was dead, she must be.

Rod Everlar burst into tears.

He had to do something, had to... Through a watery, blinding rain of weeping he clawed his way across the room, around the room. Where was her goddamned sword?

His dagger! Yes! There, with his clothes, yes, yes!

He snatched it up, raced across the room to her. Slice the palm, the fingers not the palm, so cold and easy, blood welling out red and fast, fingertips dripping...

Get them in her mouth, you idiot, her mouth!

Cursing, he crouched over her while beating his fist with the dagger still clenched in it on the rug. Rod thrust his fingers into that open, slack mouth, rubbing his blood into her tongue, holding the tongue down with his fingers so it wouldn't fall back and block her throat... feeling it well out of him, trickling, trickling; surely, if he could get the blood to flow down her throat...

If she wasn't stone cold dead already, and his precious special healing powers were too late and no good, that is.

His heart leaped; the blue-white glow! The glow! He pulled his fingers out, but found the glow was coming from his palm as it healed itself smoothly; from that open, motionless mouth, nothing.

Feverishly he slashed himself again, twice this time, deep crisscrossing cuts that almost christened the rug before he could get his cupped palm back to her mouth and pour the blood in.

"Tay," he pleaded, trying to curl himself around her cold curves, "live! Live, damn you! Please, please!"

He felt weak and sick; all that blood, flowing out of him. It would pass, this feeling, as soon as he healed. He knew that, but still… still… he was alone in Falconfar, all alone, his life empty, its heart and center gone, just like that. He didn't even know what had happened to her!

"Tay," he sobbed. "Tay…"

She quivered, suddenly, under him. Again, a sudden spasm that shook her. Rod clawed at her. "Tay? Taeauna?"

He could see the blue-white glow in her mouth, rising like fire; she was lapping weakly at his hand now, like a kitten.

Rod's tears blinded him, he gulped and sobbed helplessly, saying her name again and again until she said weakly, "Yes, 'tis me, lord. I'm not likely to forget my name now, with you bawling it over and over. I'll live. I think."

Rod snatched her up into an embrace, frantic to kiss her, to hold her, which was when he became aware that someone was pounding on a door, close by, and sharp womens' voices were calling, "Taeauna of the Aumrarr? Taeauna? Lady of the Aumrarr?"

"Help me into the bed," Taeauna gasped, into Rod's ear, "and throw some furs over me. Don't let anyone in until your hand is whole again. They must not see what your blood does, or half Galath will know you are a Shaper before nightfall, and every Doom, lackspells-wizard, and petty tyrant in all Falconfar will be in here trying to seize you!"

Chapter Fifteen

THE HEAD-SWORD of the velduke's guard was a tall, stern knight in magnificent armor, whose face had just gone from cold and professional to open-jawed disbelief. "New swords and arrows? You tongue-teasing me?"

"Not yet," Iskarra purred at him, like a Stormar alley-lass.

The knight looked at her weathered face, misjudged her age a trifle, and took her flirtation as a jest.

He grinned, still shaking his head at what fair falcon's fortune had brought him, and said, "Well, good traders, I'll have to ask you to step down and have a sit, yonder; there's ale. We'll unload your wares, go through them, and pay good gold roezels, counted out to you on yon barrelhead—fair market price, as good as you'll get anywhere—when we're done. My men will take your wagon from here."

Iskarra and Garfist climbed down, rather stiffly. They had spent much of the night sitting in a jammed, unmoving line of wagons seeking to enter the keep; dawn had come while they were still outside the gates. The dark cloud left their minds as suddenly as if it had been chopped off by a cook's cleaver, as their boots touched the cobbles of the gloomy keep courtyard. Too weary to be thankful, they started the trudge over to where promised ale waited.

Their wagon was backed to a dock, posts were fitted into sockets in the cobbles and the horses tethered to them, and the wagon doors were swung open. One wagon-guard trotted down from the dock to join Garfist and Iskarra, giving them a "just watch yourselves" look as he arrived and held out his hand for a tankard.

A gang of burly, sweat-soaked men who'd obviously been heaving cargo for most of the day strode wearily forward with some of the velduke's knights, and the gray wagon's load was inspected and brought out onto the dock in an astonishingly short time. Garfist, Iskarra, and the guard carefully refrained from looking at each other as it became apparent that the men of Bowrock had found no wizard, second guard, or false front of stacked crates.

Yardryk, it seemed, was as clever as he thought he was. Thus far, at least.

The head of the guard was as cheerful as if dozens of lasses far younger and more beautiful than Iskarra had just agreed to tongue-tease him for days on end, when he strode up to them and pronounced that their arrows were, "The best I've ever seen, and the blades aren't far behind that, either!"

Bright gold coins were counted out and bagged under the watchful noses of the two scruffy drovers and the wagon-guard, the tall stern knight clapped Garfist on the back like an old friend and pronounced trading with them "a proper pleasure," and they were requested to depart.

The wagon-guard took firm hold of the sacks of coins; Garfist and Iskarra, uncomfortably aware of the watchful eyes of many Bowrock guards, were forced to shrug, exchange glances, and head for the horses without dispute.

Garfist went around back to swing the wagon doors closed, and was unsurprised to find the guard's sword out and raised to menace him.

The guard remembered Iskarra in time to spin around as she slipped through the wagon from the front, but his spellguard against skaekur did him no good at all against the hairpin she kept coated with lursk. He slumped to the ground without hesitation, and Iskarra shrugged and let his head bounce. What need have cruel bastards for brains?

It took her a short, fumbling time to tie the coin-sacks together and drape them over her neck before concealing all under the crawlskin, and a little while longer to drop her breeches and empty her bladder into the guard's half-full wineskin, drop a pinch of one of her powders into it, restopper it, and shake vigorously.

By then, Garfist had searched the man for weapons and found what he'd hoped to find: a dagger engraved with a smith's mark from somewhere else in Galath. He flung the wagon doors wide again and bellowed, "Aid! A spy from Murlstag, sent to harm Bowrock!"

Knights were swarming the wagon almost before Iskarra could get down from it and point back up at it with a trembling hand.

When they shouted questions at Garfist, he pointed with one massive hand at Iskarra. When all eyes were on her, she cried, "Yon guard, inside; we hired him in the market outside the gates of Wrathgard. Paid him good coin, too. And just now, our lawful and honest trade here done, we're securing the ropes inside the wagon to leave, and we catch him hauling out his wineskin and saying he needs to get to a well, somewhere in this keep, before we go! When we tell him that sounds witless, he draws steel on us. So Gar here lays him out a-dreaming, but you'd best take and bind him, and that wineskin, too!"

Frowning, knights rushed up into the wagon in a thunder of boots and a flashing of swords. Iskarra and Garfist watched them, backing away slowly and casually, until heavy hands fell on both of their shoulders, and they turned their heads to find unsmiling Bowrock guards saying rather coldly, "Our wizard would like you to give him some answers."

"Answers?" Garfist rumbled, eyeing the ring of swordpoints that had suddenly appeared, to encircle his throat.

"To questions he's bound to want to ask," a knight told him, indicating where they'd sat to take ale before. "Why don't we all just sit down and—"

The ear-shattering explosion that erupted behind them just then sent the gray wagon and its unfortunate horses whirling in all directions in many pieces. One of them was large enough to behead

Garfist's knight, and the blast itself heaved the cobbles underfoot and hurled Iskarra and some of the smaller guards right in under the wheels of other wagons. Garfist received a blow on the shoulder that sent him spinning like a top, so he had many brief whirlings of time in which to see a variety of spectacular fires erupt amid the other wagons in the courtyard, and watch broken men and the gore spatter across the keep walls and then start to drip back down again.

Where the wagon and all those knights had been, there was nothing, nothing but scorch marks radiating outwards from a shallow pit in the cobbles. An unseen giant had taken a great greedy bite out of the front of the loading dock, and there were cracks in the floor that hadn't been there before.

As Garfist came whirling toward her, spitting a stream of curses as he plunged, bounced, groaned, and came skidding to a stop just the other side of the wagon wheel hard by her head, Iskarra rolled over, her head ringing, and wondered if she'd ever be able to hear anything again.

It seemed the wizard Yardryk was clever enough, after all.

ROD EVERLAR SAT down heavily on the edge of the bed, wrapped in a housecloak embroidered with dancing unicorns—dancing unicorns? In Falconfar? Oh, right, there had been a row of them on the box of the very first Holdoncorp game—and said, "Tay? That's the last servant gone again, I think. You can come out now."

Taeauna smiled and reached up a hand to him; Rod drew in his breath sharply in wonder. It was the hand that had been fingers of ash and bone the last time he'd looked, but now it was whole again, as perfect as if it had never swung a sword or done any rough work, let alone been crisped in magical flames.

He took hold of her offered hand and peered at it closely, running his own fingers over its unblemished softness. "It was the gewgaw, wasn't it? You reached for it, and it burned you?"

"Hush," the Aumrarr murmured. "Be careful. We must speak as if a servant stands over us always, listening to what we say and writing it down. Come to bed."

Rod raised his eyebrows in such stunned astonishment that Taeauna giggled, and put the bed-furs to her mouth hastily to muffle her mirth. Then she lowered them enough to say in mock indignation, "By the Flying Falcon, do men think of nothing else? Really!"

At least, Rod hoped it was mock indignation.

Pointedly keeping the cloak on and wrapped around him, Rod slid in under the furs beside her, muttering, "Your lord obeys your command. So what am I supposed to be thinking about?"

In response, Taeauna ducked down under the furs, crooking her head in a clear signal for him to join her. When they were both entirely under the covers, she threw an arm over him, pulled herself close against him, and whispered, "Move about a little, and moan, as if we're… you know."

"What is this, method acting?"

Taeauna gave him a puzzled frown, and Rod shrugged and tried an amorous moan. The result left her fighting not to giggle again, a struggle she promptly abandoned.

"Tay," Rod murmured patiently, "I love being in bed with you, even if, you know, nothing happens, but like any other guy, I find the teasing gets a little wearing. What is this?"

Her face went serious in an instant, and she nodded. "Lord," Taeauna whispered, "this is the best way for us to talk together frankly, just now. The way you found me, the 'gewgaw,' as you call it; you should know what it does before anything else happens."

Rod moved his arm over her, growled as if in passion, and whispered into her armpit, "So tell me."

Taeauna firmly pushed his head away. "That tickles. Know then, lord, that I awakened before you, and sought the chamberpot. You were then—forgive me—flat on your back and snoring."

"Nothing to forgive," Rod said, carefully rolling over atop her but keeping his weight on his arms and off of her. Under him, Taeauna deftly rolled onto her front. "Say on."

"The usual glow in the air, and that... that thing appeared, above your chest, about the length of my leg—and *don't* go feeling along the length of my leg, lord, thank you very much. I climbed back onto the bed and stretched out my hand to catch it as it fell; not to take it from you or pluck it out of the air, but to shield your chest from it. With those little points it has, and its weight, I saw it as no better than a dagger aimed at your chest. So I tried to catch it."

"And things didn't go well."

"Indeed. It fell, flamed the instant it touched my fingers, and as I let go, it spat lightning at me. You saw what it did, yet we were no more than the thickness of my hand above your chest, and it touched you not; not even one hair is scorched, and yes, I've looked. The bolt went down my arm and into me, and hurled me right off the bed, furs and all, and left me as you found me; wounded unto death."

Rod reached down under the linens and furs on his side of the bed, to where he'd slipped the gew-gaw under discussion to keep the servants from seeing it.

Taeauna winced as he brought it up between them in the darkness, to peer at it curiously and turn it over and over in his hands.

"Are you seeing something, now?" she asked softly. "That castle?"

"Yes," Rod muttered. "Yes, and now, for the first time, I feel as if I very much want to go in there."

"Oh, shit," Taeauna whispered. "Oh, Rod."

SOUNDS WERE RETURNING in waves, like surf pounding on Stormar shores. Iskarra winced and tried to move her fingers and toes. Thank the Fal-con, everything responded, and there were no knife-like stabs of agony.

The dark, pitted curve of a well-traveled wagon wheel was hard by her head, and a stunned or unconscious Garfist was drooling on the other side of it. As she gazed at him, his eyelids fluttered and his lips shaped a disgusted, "Too bloody typ-ical. Always I get the whack. Always."

Iskarra read his lips more than she properly heard those words, but hearing was coming back to her. Yes, it was coming back.

She risked turning her head, looking back to where the gray wagon had been. A few knights were standing looking grimly down at the shallow pit, but most activity and attention was on the fires flickering on other wagons, and the buckets of sand and water being dashed over them.

The courtyard gates had been closed, and there were more hard-eyed knights standing with their shoulders against them. A lot more hard-eyed knights.

She reached out a hand past the curve of the wheel to dig her fingers into Garfist. Who stiffened and rolled over to glare at her.

"Oh. Isk. I can't hear anything, Isk!"

She tapped an imperious and bony warning finger across her lips, then pointed at him and at herself and then upwards, miming a set of steps with her hand, and then pointing up again.

It was time for them both to slip away and up into the keep, before all the tumult died down and they were noticed again.

Thank the Falcon, Garfist was nodding agreement.

As THE TWO roads converged, and the many-bannered armies riding along them drew very close to meeting, one commander gave a signal, and war-horns rang out again. They were promptly answered from the other glittering host.

One last reassuring exchange of "peaceful parley" notes. Good. Arduke Tethgar Teltusk did not allow himself to relax, however. He didn't think even a weasel like Glusk Chainamund would risk treachery after Devaer's stone-cold-simple orders and threats, but one never knew.

The wits one wizard could twist one way, another mage could as easily turn another way, after all.

"Ho, Teltusk!" the fat baron called, from beneath his fluttering, yellow-and-scarlet horned ox-head banners, all joviality in what looked like new silver-bright armor studded all over with great round rivet-heads. "Any sign of Deldragon knights?"

"None," the raven-haired arduke called back, in as affable a tone as he could muster. "I think he's hunkering down inside his best armor and just waiting for us to come a-battering!"

"Good!" Chainamund bellowed, straw-yellow mustache quivering. "Let this be a grand day for battering, then!"

WALKING AWAY FROM the courtyard of wagons down one of the dark stone passages slowly and casually, as if they belonged in the keep, had taken all the nerves Garfist and Iskarra had left to muster. By the time they reached a long, dark, rotting-food-stinking passage somewhere behind the kitchens, they'd been trembling and only too glad to break into a run.

That brisk sprint took them down the rest of that passage, around a corner, and into an even darker passage, where Garfist's winded state brought them to a panting halt.

Iskarra sniffed. "Mildew. Well, better than rotten meat and eggs."

Garfist waved such trifles away with one hairy fist. "What made the dratted cart explode, any-way?" he growled.

"Your wits did get scrambled, didn't they?" Iskar-ra asked sharply, tapping his forehead with one bony finger. "The wizard. Taking care of his man, who might be made to talk."

"Shit. He'll come after us, won't he?"

"Not if he doesn't think we're still alive," Iskarra snapped, tugging open the front of her clothing one more time. "So you are going to wear the crawlskin as a pair of fittingly huge breasts, and become the heftiest washerwoman in all Falconfar, and I'm going back to my skeletal self. And we're just going to have to hope he hasn't left some sort of magic in our minds that will let him find us and rule us at will."

Garfist stared at her. "Oh, shit," he rumbled. "We're right back in it, aren't we? Even worse than fleeing an angry Arlsakran, this is. Running around a keep hoping a skulking wizard doesn't see us while a siege sets in."

Iskarra smiled and shrugged, as the crawlskin rose and wrapped itself high around her bare chest, shaping huge breasts that rose invitingly toward him. "You want to live out your life sitting in boredom, Gulkoon, growling about the adventures of your youth as they fade in your memories? Let's live a little!"

Garfist's hands clamped down on her proffered false flesh, and by those shapely handholds tugged her against him. "Oh, 'tisn't adventurous living I'm so wary of, Viper. 'Tis more the dying that's got me worried!"

"I WISH YOU hadn't put your blade through him," Yardryk snapped, his dark purple eyes sharp with anger. Running his hands nervously through his curly gold hair, he looked down again at the

Bowrock servant sprawled on the floor. A bright ribbon of blood was wandering lazily over the stones from the just-slain man's throat to wherever a low spot would make it pool.

"Next time, when I say 'strike him senseless,' I expect a loyal swordsman of the master we both serve to do just that."

"You know magic, wizard," the warrior said curtly, "and I tell you not how to do that. Kindly leave the brawling to me. He was about to scream, and my blade prevented that."

Yardryk sighed and turned away. "Very well," he said curtly.

The warrior watched him, glowering. Arrogant young hightrews!

The least of Arlaghaun's apprentices, but still, one of the Master's apprentices.

Thinking dark thoughts about idiot warriors, Yardryk bent to the satchel he'd carried since he'd teleported them both out of the wagon that he'd just been forced to destroy, throot it, though at least he'd had the pleasure of obliterating a dozen-some of the most eager Bowrock knights, along with it. He undid the clasps, and plucked out two metal spheres. They were smooth, they were heavy, and they more than filled his palms. He turned to the warrior.

"Korryk? I need you to hold these."

The warrior stared at him coldly for a moment, and then strolled slowly forward and took the spheres into his own hands, his every movement a slow, eloquent shout of "you're no better than me" insolence.

Ah, but to be a wizard was to be unloved.

"Thank you," Yardryk told him expressionlessly, turning back to his satchel. "Please, for your own safety, take great care to keep the spheres apart."

He wasn't certain how much Korryk knew of the task they were here to do, or how much the veteran could correctly guess. Arlaghaun wasn't in the habit of telling warriors all that much, but then veteran warriors in his service didn't live long enough to be veterans if they were stupid.

Yardryk drew in a deep breath, took the little braziers out of the satchel, and then the little sack of powdered steel—shavings and filings that had once been tempered swordblades; naught else would do—and silently thanked the Falcon that he had no need of flint strikers and kindling and the messy business of blowing on sparks just so. Filings in brazier, will the flame to flare at his fingertip, murmur the words that would make the iron burn readily, touch and step back. One brazier, and then two.

Yardryk made a little show of placing one burning brazier in just the right spot on the floor, stepping back to frowningly survey it, stepping forward to move it a few inches, stepping back again, and finally nodding. Yes.

The other brazier he left where it was, hoping Korryk would heed it not. He busied himself over the first one, getting out a dummy wand (a simple stick of wood, not magical in the slightest) to wave as he used his other hand to trace the runes in the air that mattered, murmuring after each the word that would make it take fire and glow, building on the previous runes in a long, faintly humming chain that rose up from the brazier like a column of purple flame.

He walked around it, peering at it as if seeking flaws. Stopping finally on the far side of the shaft of purple magic from the warrior, Yardryk nodded as if satisfied with his work, and commanded, "Korryk, I need those spheres now."

The warrior ambled over in a slow slouch this time, giving a gusty sigh to make it very clear that magic bored him. He thought it was scarcely as useful as a shrewdly swung sword, and for something treated with such wary awe, it seemed to need a lot of help.

Yardryk gave the sullen warrior a tight little smile, and pointed at one rune in the humming column. "This one; I need you to touch that ball to this rune. Gently. Don't worry, nothing bad will happen."

Reluctantly, giving Yardryk a glare that was heavy with suspicion, Korryk rather gingerly extended the sphere.

The column bulged to take it in, for the first time giving the impression that the purple air, or whatever it was, was rushing up and down past the runes, and now rushing around and over the metal ball, too.

By now, a tingling should be rushing through Korryk's arm. Nothing painful or even uncomfortable, but... unusual.

"Do... do I let go of it?" the warrior asked, sounding more wary than sneering. At last.

"No," Yardryk said warningly. "That would be bad."

He stepped forward, drew another rune, and chanted a swift incantation.

For a moment, as Korryk stared up at the rushing purple column, nothing happened.

Then, as swiftly as a striking snake, the column
bent over, swooped down from on high toward the
second brazier, and swung sideways in its plunge at
the last moment to race at the second sphere Korryk was holding. It swirled around the sphere for a
rushing moment that left the warrior's arms shuddering and his mouth open in rising fear, and then
swooped away, to bury its end in the second brazier.

Yardryk smiled tightly and lifted his hand with
the careless indolence of an indulged and haughty
emperor.

And the purple snake rose and straightened into a
smooth, high archway, rooted in the two braziers,
and hauled Korryk off his feet, still clinging to the
two spheres that were now embedded in the curving purple arc of magic, well off the ground.

"I—*help*, Yardryk! I can't let go!"

"No," the wizard replied, almost purring in satisfaction. "You can't."

There was a crackling in the air, a sudden tension
and heaviness that shouted silently that something
powerful was about to happen.

As the warrior started to kick wildly, thrashing
his arms in increasingly frantic attempts to get free,
the air along the inside of the purple column started to shimmer, like the air above a raging fire.
Within its shimmering, the shadowy dimness of the
cellar room split apart like tearing canvas, to reveal
a larger, slightly better lit chamber beyond, a cavernous space that was certainly not visible outside
the purple arch.

Something was moving in that larger hall, something—no, several somethings—that flapped and
glided, flying swiftly nearer...

A trio of lorn, and then another, swooped through the arch and soared up to circle the cellar room of Deldragon's keep. Then they shot out of its doorway, wings raked back, heading elsewhere fast.

More lorn followed, and Dark Helms, too, a score or more of men in black armor, drawn swords in their hands and visors being swung down into place as they stepped into the gloom of the cellars.

"You see, Korryk," Yardryk said gloatingly, "just as you were ordered by our master to serve me, I was ordered to complete a specific task here: to construct a magical gate between our master's keep and this one. Unlike a tantlar, many living things like lorn and Dark Helms, for instance, can traverse a gate swiftly, at the same time. A tantlar-link can be destroyed very easily, by extinguishing the fire its destination tantlar is being warmed in, or removing that tantlar from the flames. This gate, however, feeds on magic hurled at it, and can even survive these braziers being extinguished or removed; it will only collapse when what powers it is gone. And it's powered by the life force of a living human, or humans."

"No!" the warrior shouted. "Noooo!"

"One such could have been the servant you killed," Yardryk added, with a ruthless smile. "Now, it's going to be you."

He turned his back and walked away, heading for the doorway of the cellar, where the trapped warrior's screams would be less deafening.

If Arlaghaun had been telling the truth about how many creatures he was going to send through the gate to overrun Deldragon's keep, those screams might not last all that long.

Gates were hungry things.

"WELL," GARFIST RUMBLED, "I don't exactly look like someone even a starving sailor would lust after. I mean, look at this face! Tits can only do so much."

"Yes, but what tits," Iskarra grinned.

He cuffed her playfully across the forehead. "Now we have to steal something that'll do up over them. All this for a bit of food and wine."

"Lantern, don't forget the lantern," Iskarra reminded him, earning herself a sour look from the feminine travesty Garfist Gulkoon had become.

"Look at me!" he snarled, waving two shovel-sized, hairy hands. "Who'm I supposed to fool, eh? I mean, how many blind folk am I likely to meet on my way to the kitchens? Blind folk without hands to feel these—and then the rest of me—with?"

"Gar, don't be surly. We have to eat. The occasional man still looks at me, remember."

"Aye, but... but..." Garfist became aware of Iskarra's dangerous glare and the dagger that had very suddenly appeared in her bony hand, very close to him, and settled for saying, "but there's no safe thing I can say just now, is there?"

"Well, you could say 'Dearest Iskarra, whose body I will worship fervently and often in these days ahead, you are right in all things, always, and of course in this, so how can I best pass myself off as a woman, I who am not worthy to be counted among womanhood no matter how hard I try?' But somehow I doubt you're going to say that."

"I can't say that," Garfist rumbled. "Ye lost me after 'fervently and often.' I sorta got... got..."

"To thinking about that. Of course." Iskarra's voice dripped with acid. "Things will go much better, Gar dear, if you just stop trying to think and start trying to do what I tell you to do. Whenever you don't, you wind up finding one thing with frightening speed: trouble."

"Found a lantern," Garfist replied sullenly, pointing.

"Good. Go fetch it. Yes, with your front all hanging out like that; if someone sees you, just leer at them, and don't run or look furtive or guilty. And bring the lantern back here. Then we'll talk about finding clothes."

Garfist nodded and trudged off down the passage. Iskarra watched his broad-shouldered figure dwindle toward the distant lantern, hanging from a beam where two passages met, and winced. He looked less like a woman—even a large and lumbering woman—than anything she'd ever seen.

Garfist reached up for the lantern, and then lowered his arm again and peered intently down one of the side-passages. He thrust his head forward, sinking it between his shoulders like a vaugril, and then stalked down the side-passage, slowly and intently, hunting prey.

Iskarra flattened herself against the cold stone wall, wincing. "No, you great stupid ox!" she hissed. "Don't try to get clever. Just get the lantern and get back here. Don't..."

Garfist burst into view around the corner again, running hard, his false crawlskin breasts bouncing up and slapping him in the face with every pumping stride. There was a gutted boar carcass in one of his hairy hands, still trailing the hook it had undoubtedly been hanging from.

Right behind Garfist, and running hard, was a red-faced, snarling cook with a great cleaver flashing in his hand. Followed by another four—no, seven—other cooks and scullions, waving various knives and skewers and pans.

Iskarra whispered every profanity she could think of as she waved to Garfist and then turned and ran.

Deeper into the cellars, where there just might be a place to hide.

Chapter Sixteen

"Fair morn, Lord Deldragon," Taeauna greeted the velduke gravely, striding up to him. Rod kept a careful pace behind her, as if he were her faithful shadow. "How best can we…?"

Deldragon was wearing a smile as he lifted his hand in greeting and opened his mouth to speak, but his face fell into astonishment and anger as he looked past his two guests, his ice-blue eyes seeming to catch fire. Rod and Taeauna were turning to see what disaster was behind them as he bellowed, "Lorn! Raise the alarum! Lorn in the keep!"

Bowrock knights and armsmen erupted out of passages and doorways by the dozens, and the velduke roared, "Bows! Guard every archer we have, from this moment on! I don't want a single one harmed by lorn, and I want every glorking archer out here and filling these lorn with arrows!"

Even before the nearest knight could shout a warning, the velduke whipped around, sword leaping into his hand to precede his turn, and so, without even meaning to, spitted a lorn that was diving at him, claws spread wide and poised to rend.

Taeauna hacked at one of those claws to make sure it didn't fold up around the velduke's blade and rake him as it died; Deldragon struck its other aside himself.

It shuddered and started to curl up in death; as Deldragon shook it off his steel, kicking it toward the floor, the thunder of many hastening boots was heard in the passage the lorn had erupted from. Bowrock knights formed a line of bared steel across the passage even before the first Dark Helms burst into view.

The velduke groaned aloud at their numbers, for the passage looked to be filled for a long way back with a seemingly endless flood of gleaming black armor. "Fall back!" he shouted. "Fight and fall back, fight and fall back to the Warhorn Chamber! We'll make a stand there!"

More lorn swooped at him, over the heads of the surging army of black-armored warriors, and Deldragon pointed his blade at them as if it were a bow, whispered something, and then vanished behind a sudden bright blossoming of flame from its tip. In an instant that fire filled the air before him with a roiling sphere of fire, and started to spit forth long tongues of flame.

Those tongues lashed out thrice the length of a lance to sear and sizzle lorn after shrieking lorn, until they circled away from that offered death, squalling. The velduke bellowed, "Men of Bowrock! Get out of the way!" and leveled his sword, even as knights and armsmen scampered aside, aiming it right down the throats of the onrushing Dark Helms.

Who staggered, screaming and writhing, as they cooked in their armor and flames raged among them. The velduke calmly moved his blade back and forth, seeking to immolate as many as he could. Some Dark Helms tried to struggle on into the inferno, but most turned and tried to flee, pushing and even hacking at their fellows behind them.

Yet all too soon, the flames flickered, faltered, spat, coughed, and went out, the velduke's sword going dark.

"Men of Bowrock!" he shouted. "Form a line! Spears to the fore!"

A few of the Dark Helms raced forward to try to surround the velduke, before Bowrock's knights and armsmen could block the way, but Deldragon retreated even as Bowrock spears and hurled shields struck and assailed those few bold foes, and Taeauna stepped forward in front of him like a champion, sword raised.

"Lady of the Aumrarr," Deldragon said approvingly, "again you risk yourself in my battle!"

Taeauna shrugged. "I am an Aumrarr; I fight Dark Helms. That blade of yours can't burn every last one of them."

"True," the velduke agreed grimly, as the men of Bowrock clashed with the Dark Helms in front of them. "I can't call up that power many more times ere it's exhausted; I doubt it will last through this siege. Even if I do."

"None of us will survive to see the siege begin if we don't deal with what's in your cellars now," Taeauna warned.

"The well, again?"

"No. The lorn, all these Dark Helms; look at them! This can be no new tantlar, lord. There's a wizard somewhere in your keep who's just opened a gate. And all the armies outside your walls will pour right through it, if we don't destroy it."

Darendarr Deldragon went white and said a very dirty word. His hand shot up to stroke his flaxen mustache, as unnecessarily as always.

"Come!" said Taeauna, clapping him on the shoulder. "Leave the battle here to your knights; someone else can rally them in the Warhorn Chamber. Bring two of your best blades, and show me a way down into the cellars that isn't already full of Dark Helms!" She waved at the passage full of fighting, hacking, and dying men in bright armor and in dark. It was a hopeless tangle of shouting combatants, heaped corpses, and the sagging or writhing dying.

The velduke stared at her for a moment, shaking his head. Then he bit his lip, whirled around, and bellowed, "Tarsil! Amandur! Belros! To me!"

"Lord, I come!" someone shouted, through the din, and "Lord!" someone else echoed; Rod saw a tall knight pushing through the milling Bowrock knights from one direction, and two armsmen doing the same from another.

The knight got there first. "Lord?"

"Tarsil," Deldragon snapped, "take command here. Try to hold the Helms, and have the archers save their shafts for any lorn they see. If many lorn break past you, or the Dark Helms press, fall back to the Warhorn Chamber and make a stand there. Do it!"

"Lord!" Tarsil acknowledged with a bow, and the velduke clapped him on the arm and turned to the two armsmen.

"Amandur, Belros! Come, out of this! With me! We're going hunting!"

Deldragon waved to Taeauna, and she nodded, ducked around some trotting Bowrock armsmen, and sprinted across the passage, Rod right behind her, and the velduke and his two armsmen right behind Rod.

The Aumrarr plunged into a side-passage that seemed, by the smell, to lead past kitchens, and slowed for the others to catch her up. "Darendarr, if you wanted to get back down to the well-chamber but not take yon passage, all choked with Dark Helms, which way would you take? And is there a goodly choice, or only a few routes?"

Deldragon shook his head ruefully. "There are dozens. My great grandsire did not build this keep with thoughts of defending it floor-by-floor, up or down, in mind. Do you think haste on our part is most important, or descending by a way least likely to meet with our foes repeatedly, along the way?"

"The back way," Taeauna snapped. "As 'back' as you can fashion for us, lord. We must not get buried in lorn or Dark Helms before we find that gate!"

The velduke nodded. "Then this way!" he said, darting into another passage and starting to run. They all plunged after him. Rod kept his sword in its sheath and devoted himself to just running; he suspected he was going to be rushing around in dark stone hallways for quite some time.

Almost immediately Deldragon saw something ahead that made him snarl a startled curse and duck through a door into a very dark room. Wrenching open a door on its far wall, he led them out into a narrower, dimly lit passage, growling, "Getting more and more 'back' as we go. 'Ware! Stairs down!"

Then he seemed to plunge into the floor and disappear.

Enthusiastically, everyone followed, Rod running hard to keep up and frowning as he caught hold of an aging iron railing and swung himself around and down, plunging deeper into the stone roots of the velduke's keep.

From what he'd seen thus far, all Galathans seemed to be in a very great hurry to get themselves killed.

THE GREAT CLEAVER had hewn through boar and oxen many a time, but boar and oxen seldom wore armor.

So when the furious cook swinging that cleaver puffed his way around a corner, snarling out obscenities as fast as he could breathe, and came face to face with a trio of chuckling Dark Helms, the hard-swung cleaver rebounded from the black breastplate of the foremost warrior, ringing in protest and trailing sparks.

Boar and oxen seldom thrust swords at a cook, either.

The head cook of Deldragon's keep would then have perished swiftly indeed if a second wave of Dark Helms hadn't charged out of a side-passage beyond the grinning trio, roaring triumphal roars, and thrust forth a forest of gleaming blades that forced the incongruously bosomed Garfist Gulkoon to desperately windmill his arms into a wild, skidding stop.

Spitting out fervent curses of his own, Garfist tried to turn and flee back the way he'd come and blundered right into the backs of the trio of Dark Helms menacing the cook, sending them toppling and sprawling helplessly.

They shouted in fear. So did the cook whose cries doubled in volume and fervency a moment later, when his seven undercooks and scullions ran right into his backside, hurling him helplessly forward atop the three Dark Helms.

Whom Garfist shed like a cloak of tumbling men as he burst out and upwards from beneath all the wallowing, flailing bodies, to lumber away down a thankfully empty passage, gaining speed as he went. The boar carcass, looking a little more ragged and worn, still trailed behind his large and hairy left hand.

No sooner had he vanished into the distant darkness than Iskarra "Vipersides" burst into view out of the passage he'd turned back from, running hard and panting harder.

"Old blundering ox," she gasped, "you'll be the glorking death of me yet!"

The wave of Dark Helms who'd set Garfist to flight were butchering their way enthusiastically through the kitchen staff and the trio of their fellow Dark Helms alike, gleefully hewing a clear path forward. They promptly tried to make Iskarra's breathless observation true, reaching for her with their blades.

She leaped forward into a somersault under those swords, yanking a hairpin out of her hair in mid-tumble, and sprinted off down the passage after Garfist.

The few surviving cooks and scullions, shrieking for all they were worth, pelted after her. A flood of Dark Helms ran after them, slashing and stabbing at the air, and as they caught up to each kitchen worker in turn, they butchered screaming, sweating flesh, too.

As cook after cook was loudly murdered behind her, Iskarra ran on, hoping the Dark Helms now pursuing her weren't spellguarded against skaekur. If fair fortune was with her for once, she'd not have to find out, but fair fortune so seldom rode escort with her these days that...

Her pessimism was promptly proved well founded. She came to a passage-moot at last, and had to stop to peer wildly, trying to see which of the three diverging ways Garfist had taken.

He'd turned down the last passage she shot a glare along, of course. Looking took just enough time that the foremost Dark Helms pounced before she could get started down that passage, roaring bloodthirstily and hacking at her like woodcutters impatient to split kindling.

Iskarra flung herself at their ankles, tripping one into his fellows. That took two black-armored warriors to the floor and left a third clawing his way free of them, off balance and with sword swinging wildly to try to regain his footing.

Iskarra sprang up from the floor like a leaping frog to crash into his chest with both bony knees and stab his face repeatedly with her hairpin. The

Dark Helm went down hard on his back, shouting, and she bounced up from his chest to her feet and sprinted hard down the passage after Garfist with the Helm's shouting dying into slurred gurgles in her wake.

Three or more Dark Helms, by the sounds of running boots, were right on her heels, after her like hounds.

"Gar!" she shouted. "Gar?"

There was a lantern somewhere around a corner to the left, ahead in the passage; its light was spilling out along the walls and ceiling in the distance. Iskarra ran toward it as hard as she could, almost winded now, panting raggedly, wondering if she'd tire enough that they'd catch up to her in the open passage and hack her down from behind, too.

She could hear a lot more boots, running behind her closest pursuers, now. Great. How many Dark Helms does it take to kill one ragged, slightly tipsy, seen-brighter-days woman?

"Gar... fist," she gasped angrily, reeling around a corner. "I sure hope you... went this... way."

Garfist reached one shovel-like hand out of the darkness of a side-passage and swept her past him. Then he put his shoulder against a tall stack of wooden crates where it had been before and waited.

"Stay. Catch yer breath," he muttered. Iskarra reeled against the wall and bent over to gasp in earnest, nodding thankfully. She just needed a moment or two.

Dark Helms came thundering up, not slowing. They were headed for the next side-passage, where the lantern light was coming from.

With a grim smile on his face, Garfist Gulkoon leaned forward, grotesque false breasts bouncing and bobbing, and toppled the crates.

They crashed down on the shoulder of the nearest Dark Helm, smashing him to the floor instantly. The Dark Helm right behind him ran into them with his upper body, lost his racing feet forward out from under himself, fell hard, and got the rest of the crates crashing down on him just as the next Dark Helm ran into him, and the one behind in turn crashed into them all.

Broken-bodied and senseless, the four Dark Helms said nothing at all, and by then, no one was paying them the slightest attention, because the crates had been full of ball bearings that were now flooding out into the passage with a thunder of their own, as a small, sprinting army of Dark Helms ploughed into them, shouted wildly, raising up arms and swords in a vain attempt to keep from falling, and skidded helplessly… everywhere.

"Come on!" Garfist snarled to Iskarra, turning and peeling her off the wall with one great sweep of his arm. "I can scarcely see down here, but there're crates all along both walls, full of all sorts of—"

With a wild shout, a skidding Dark Helm made it around the corner into the passage, fetching up against one wall with a crash. A second Dark Helm struck the wall right beside the first, narrowly missing impaling himself on the first Helm's sword.

Garfist spun around, caught hold of a tall stack of crates, and heaved.

The stack crashed down across the passage with a roar mingled with shrieks of splitting wood as the crates burst open, spilling forth a clanging metallic chaos of hasps and handles and hooks, dark and smelling strongly of oil. The Dark Helms fought for balance among this slithering metal, and the foremost caught hold of the next stack of crates and tried to swing his legs over and past the iron-mongery.

He got halfway through his swing before the crate he was clinging to came free of its stack and pulled the stack over in his wake; helplessly he slithered feet-first into the darker passage beyond, that crate slamming into his head.

Garfist was already stepping forward, to almost delicately drive his dagger up under the warrior's helmet, into his foe's throat and up behind the jaw. Ignoring the fountaining blood, the fat ex-procurer grimly twisted his knife in deep before wrenching it forth again.

Iskarra shoved another stack of crates over the already-fallen ones, in a flood of debris that filled the passage chest-high. "We should go," she hissed. "'Twould be a pity if that next passage ran down and cross-connected with this one up yonder, and the Dark Helms just ran around and came at us that way."

"Indeed, Viper," Garfist growled with mock flourishes of dignity. "The same thought had occurred to me."

He hefted the boar carcass in his hand to make sure none of it had torn free in all the tumult, then nodded, bent to wipe his dagger clean on the leather war-harness of the Helm he'd just slain, and started off down the passage. "Isk, are ye... unharmed?"

"Only my pride, Gar. To think these young louts almost ran me down, in all that armor, too. Let's go. And before you ask: somewhere deep, cold, dark and deserted in these cellars, where we can hide for a bit and let these crazed Galathans fight their battles over our heads."

Her brisk stride turned into a trot to keep up with Garfist, before she asked, "Carve me a slice of cold, raw boar to chew as we walk, hey?"

"That's my Viper," Garfist grunted. "Any chance to sink yer teeth into raw meat."

He set to work with his dagger, and then grunted, "Come to think: ye can claim this crawlskin back any time right soon, mind. There's raw meat, if yer jaws need some work."

"Gar," Iskarra said coldly, "that's not amusing. Not at all."

Garfist shrugged. "Killing folk, I'm good at. Making them laugh, less than good."

He strode on for a bit, and then asked, around a mouthful of boar, "These Dark Helms; think ye they were sent here by 'our' wizard, since he vanished from inside the wagon?"

The woman trotting beside him stopped abruptly and put a hand on his arm, her face going pale.

"Oh, steaming dragon shit," Iskarra cursed slowly, staring up into his eyes. "Yes. He came here to open a gate, to bring them through. And he's managed it. This keep could be doomed from within, even before the siege begins!"

KORRYK'S FEEBLE SCREAMS stopped not long after his struggles. He hung limply from the spheres he was now bonded to, too weak and helpless to do anything else.

The youngest of Arlaghaun's apprentices stood calmly watching the captive warrior shrivel and wither away. From time to time, Yardryk stroked his curly, dirty gold beard, his dark purple eyes thoughtful.

It would not be long now before the insatiable gate took the last of his life-force, and when it was drained, the gate would flicker violently with bloody consequences for creatures caught in it, and then fade out.

And the flow of running Dark Helms and swooping lorn would end, long before the Master desired it to. Which would have grave consequences for Yardryk, even "fresh waiting grave" consequences, one might say.

It was time to find Korryk's replacement.

Turning his back on the gate, the unkempt apprentice stalked away, murmuring a spell over the glass eye cupped in his palm. The glass started to sear his flesh as it liquified, and then, just before the pain would have made him sob and fling it away, shaking his hand to be rid of the agony but not the blisters and later scars, it vanished, and he could scry.

It was as if a curtain was drawn back in his mind, enabling him to see rooms and passages around him at will, spread out in his mind while his eyes saw only darkness and solid stone walls all around.

Yardryk first saw the Master's forces; not so many lorn, now, but Dark Helms beyond counting, streaming forth from the gate, rushing along the largest passages and ascending every stair or ramp they saw. They were like a river, all rushing together, so he looked elsewhere. Were there other folk down in these cellars? Guards on patrol, coming closer, perhaps?

No, nothing like that. A few stray bands of Dark Helms, chasing and slaughtering Bowrock folk, a few cellarers, far away from the sound and the rushing Dark Helms, shifting some kegs and oblivious to the fighting... hold! What were these, much nearer?

A pair, standing alone, conferring in the darkness. A tryst? One of them small, a boy or a slender woman, the other, huge! Yes, huge and hairy, but breasted like a woman, both of them standing eating something in the darkness.

Never mind what or who they were; that large one should have life-force enough in her or him to feed the gate for a good long time. More than enough time as would be needed to bring through all of the Master's forces, anyway.

Yardryk smiled and stepped forward to hail and command the next few lorn to appear out of the gate. Five or six Dark Helms, too: force enough to fetch back this new gate-fuel alive.

And more or less unharmed.

ROD EVERLAR FETCHED up against yet another wall, this time bouncing off it more than bruisingly slamming into it. Swallowing a sigh, he ran on.

If this was one of his own fantasy novels, he should—would—now do something bold and heroic, something Falconfar-shattering. Turning his modern real-world knowledge of eclipses or electricity or the tactics of Talleyrand into some dramatic, decisive, witnessed-by-all act that would make Falconaar stop and gasp in awe and then kneel before him.

To live happily ever after, ha ha bloody ha.

In a book, it was all so easy. With a few sentences he could be a god, or a superhero, or the Lord Ha Ha of Falconfar.

Here, all he could think of doing was staying close to Taeauna, keeping his mouth shut, and doing whatever seemed best as this world threw one danger or crisis after another at him.

He hadn't run so much in years as he had these last few days. Or been as frightened. Just staying alive was probably going to be his lone awesome act, if he could manage even that. Not that anybody beyond Rod Everlar would even notice, let alone be awed.

Crazy world.

He found himself fighting for breath again, as Taeauna's shapely behind started to draw farther and farther away from right in front of him.

Crazier writer.

What am I doing here?

"So," GARFIST RUMBLED, "Dark Helms and lorn are all over these cellars. Do we dare try for the kitchens again, with most of the cooks dead and gone, mind, and see if we can get something cooked, and some wine to wash it down with, and a lantern to call our own? Or are we as likely to meet with Bowrock blades, rushing down here to sword everyone they don't recognize as one of their own?"

"Meeting with Bowrock blades is the more likely," Iskarra murmured. "Yet something cooked sounds good about now, and the wine, and I can see that look in your eye, Gar."

"I don't doubt it," the onetime procurer replied. "The kitchens it is, then. Which means we turn—"

Something large and dark came hurtling out of the darkness, flying along the ceiling with its claws outstretched, and smashed into Garfist hard enough to knock him back on his well-padded behind with a startled "Woof!"

Whatever it was struck the passage floor a good way beyond Garfist, and rolled a good way farther before coming to a stop. By which time two more flying things had pounced on Garfist, pinioning his arms.

"Lorn!" Iskarra screamed, drawing her hairpin again and her dagger and knowing they were useless as she did it. The first lorn was loping back to join the two Garfist was now struggling against, and three more were swooping at her.

"Get gone, gel!" Garfist snarled. "Run, Viper! Run!"

Iskarra dodged against the passage wall, hoping to keep the swooping lorn from striking her. And failing.

As the nearest lorn smashed into her and flung her along the wall, winded and draped over its arm, Iskarra fought against its clutching claws and her own gaspings to drive her hairpin repeatedly into one of its eyes. It squalled, splashing her with dark, sticky wetness as it died, and Iskarra fell free of it, bruising her bony elbows and wondering how long it would take the other two lorn to rend her.

Then she groaned. The passage was full of Dark Helms, running toward them.

"Flee, Viper!" Garfist roared, his bellow muffled under several struggling lorn bodies. Iskarra stared at him, or the heap of writhing lorn that he was under, and then could see it no more, as the foremost Dark Helms reached it and surrounded it in a ring.

And the rest of the Dark Helms came running for her.

Weeping, Iskarra turned and ran straight into the only lorn that had been behind her. It staggered, but she fell. Out of sheer backalley habit she kicked her legs as she did so, tripping it, and got her hairpin and dagger up into position while it was still falling. The knife skittered across lorn hide harmlessly, but her well-used hairpin sank up to her knuckles in a lorn eyeball, drenching her again and causing the dying lorn to shriek and spasm right up into the air off her.

Iskarra twisted, rolled, and came up running. Sobbing, she put her head down and ran as she'd never run before, seeking the Galathan border or the far end of the passage ahead, she cared not which.

As long as she could get there before any lorn or Dark Helm caught up to her.

JUST AHEAD OF them, the velduke slowed sharply, and then started to curse.

"What is it, Darendarr?" Taeauna asked, hurrying to join him.

"We're too late," Deldragon snapped, his ice-blue eyes blazing. "Too glorming late."

Right in front of his boots, the blood and bodies began. Dark Helms, here and huddled in a heap far down the passage. Between them, unarmored men in aprons and homespun: cooks and scullions.

Rod peered down at them and winced, feeling more than a little queasy. "If they've found your kitchens…" he said warningly, feeling even more queasy at the thought of food.

"Exactly," the velduke said grimly, stroking his mustache. "Amandur! Belros! Turn you around and go get as many men as you can and lead them to the kitchens. We'll be heading for the well. Again. Once you hold the kitchens, send most of your blades on to the well to join us. We'll be there. Alive or dead."

"But, lord!" Amandur protested. "Leave you, now? Alone down here?"

"I'm not alone. I stand with an Aumrarr and a man of mysteries. I need both of you to go, in case you encounter invaders; one man, alone, as you have just hinted, stands less chance of making it."

"Lord," Belros rumbled. "We hear and obey. Keep yourself alive, and so will we, and you'll have your blades right soon. Soon, I said; if I were you, I'd dawdle on my way to the well."

"And have them poison it, and doom us all?"

"Oh. Glorming bloody *shit*. Uh, lord."

ISKARRA'S BOOTS FELT like rocks clamped around her ankles, and her bony chest burned. Live or die, she'd not be running much farther. The thunder of Dark Helm boots was like a cruel roaring of waves crashing on rocks behind her. Not far enough behind her.

They'd catch up to her, soon. Even sooner, if a lorn came winging out of the darkness again. She could barely hold her hairpin now, let alone stab anything with it. Not that it mattered.

Not that anything mattered, without her Gar.

Let a Falconfar without Garfist Gulkoon in it be also a Falconfar without old Iskarra. Not that it would remember either of them, a day and a night from now.

Except for one Arlsakran, glorm him. And his poor daughters, all fourteen of them, if he hadn't worn any of them out and into early graves yet. He'd remember them. Much comfort would it do him.

No, she didn't much care now...

Hold! What was that, there?

Iskarra peered, stumbled, slowed hastily to keep from falling, and peered again. A grating! The first she'd seen, along all these passages, and it was askew. She looked back. No, too dark for them to see her. She bent and tugged at it and it came up in her hand.

There was a shaft down there, more than big enough for her. Right. If all she had to worry about was dozens of Dark Helms pissing on her head, so be it. She dropped her dagger into it and heard it *plink* off stone immediately. Ten feet down, not more.

She followed it, feet first, holding the grating above her like a hat.

And landed hard; the shaft was five feet deep, if that, but at least she had room to gently place the grating back into place above her, without any clangs or clanks. She found her dagger, and thrust it point-first into the deep darkness around her, hoping to stab anything that was lurking there before it did worse to her.

Nothing came at her out of the darkness, and she was able to snatch her breath back at last.

She was in some sort of dusty, disused basin that had once gathered some sort of liquid from overhead. Hmm, might still gather rainwater, down pipes from above. It didn't smell like a privy-sluice.

And it was large enough for her to get right in under the passage floor, out of view. So she did, lying down and keeping quiet.

Just in time.

"Glork! Glorm and bloody glork! There's a way-moot here! Anybody see which way she went?"

"No," a deeper voice said gloomily. "Why the lorn aren't flying ahead of us, I don't know."

The first voice chuckled nastily. "She killed two of 'em, in less time as it takes me to say it, that's why. All of a sudden like, they decided hunting that little lass wasn't in their orders. Well, I'm not wasting time on her, either. Our orders were to bring the fat one back alive, and we've got him. She'll never be fat."

"Ah. Good idea," the deeper voice said, as two pairs of boots scraped stone right above Iskarra's head. A moment later, two streams of urine came hissing and spattering down through the grating, wetting the wall not far from her.

"I thought they'd never get him tied. Fought like a stabtentacles, he did."

"He's only half-tied now! What they did in the end was tie the three lorn wrapped around his arms to each other, with his arms somewhere inside the bundle, so to speak. I wonder if he'll manage to strangle any of them before we get back to the wizard."

"Ho, now there's something worth betting on," the nasty-voiced Dark Helm observed as he started back the way he'd come.

Iskarra lay there in the darkness, wondering how long she should wait before getting back up into the passage again. If Garfist was alive, she had to find where they were taking him.

To a wizard. He was probably doomed anyway.

"But we doomed must stick together," she whispered to herself in the darkness, and got to her feet again.

The smell of what the Dark Helms had done reminded her that it was high time she relieved herself, too. She squatted right next to their wet, to keep the rest of the basin dry.

If the Falcon flew high, she and Garfist might soon need it again.

Chapter Seventeen

"WE TURN ASIDE here," Deldragon murmured, absently stroking his flaxen mustache, his eyes very blue in the glow of his sword. "I'm going to open a door, and I need you both to be very, very quiet. Step carefully, and put out a hand to touch my back as we move forward. Things are going to be dark."

The velduke quelled the faint magical sword-glow that had been giving them light enough to see by, and Rod and Taeauna heard the faintest of metallic scrapings as he lifted a metal rod out of a hasp, and swung wide a door they could barely see.

Beyond it, light was streaming up out of a stout iron grating in the stone floor of a room. The velduke approached cautiously; the radiance below was growing stronger, moving in the cellar level below them, to the sound of boots tramping from Rod's right toward his left, the light of a lantern moving with them. Taeauna reached her hand back for Rod, took hold of his arm, and towed him gently in a wide circle around the grating, keeping well back from it, so they were looking down through it at an angle, rather than standing at its edge peering down.

Rod looked, and saw.

A long, narrow cellar passage stretched straight as an arrow below, passing beneath the grating. There were doors in its walls here and there, and striding along it, right underneath him and heading steadily on down the passage, were twenty or thirty Dark Helms, carrying a large, securely tied bundle in their midst.

The bundle looked like a large, burly-limbed human with three or four lorn wrapped around him that had been lashed together into one helpless mass. Helpless, but squirming. Rod was sure he'd seen something straining to move within all those bindings. The light was coming from lanterns carried by the Dark Helms, and was already lessening, moving away from the grating.

"Toward the well," the velduke murmured. His voice was barely more than a whisper, and every bit as grim as an old gravedigger Rod had once talked to, who'd been burying his old wartime buddies, one after another, as their times ran out.

"So is there a way down, hereabouts?" Taeauna asked just as quietly, her slender but strong arms reaching out to tow Rod and Deldragon close together, so they could whisper and clearly be heard. "Or do we rush along on this level, try to get ahead of them, and descend somewhere closer to the well?"

"We can either go about three chambers that way, and down a staircase that'll let us travel parallel to the Helms," Deldragon replied, "or, yes, we…"

He stiffened, broke off, and stared down through the grating. Rod and Taeauna turned, did the same, and found themselves looking down at a lone woman; skeleton-thin and not young, yet somehow alluring. She was skulking along as silently as possible, staring ahead as if she knew full well she was following the now-vanished Dark Helms.

She was looking all around as she came, too, peering alertly everywhere. She didn't miss noticing the grating, and gave it a long, steady stare, just as if she could see the three people standing motionless in the dark room above her, their heads close together.

Then she moved on, out of their view, and Deldragon was shaking his head in amazement and towing Rod and Taeauna on across the room to a door on its far wall.

When they were through it and he'd closed it behind them, the velduke caused his sword to glow again, and over its faint, ghostly light told them, "That woman; I met her years ago, in a Stormar port, and never thought to see her here. She'll be up to no good, however she came to be inside my walls. I'm going to follow her."

"This is your home, Darendarr, and your fight," Taeauna murmured. "We're with you. Yet tell us more of yon woman. 'Years ago,' you said; you're sure this is the same person?"

"That face is not one I could mistake, and she has the same bag-of-bones build, the same gait; that lilt of the hips that tells you you're seeing a woman and not a young and thin lad. No, I'm sure. That's Rosera, or so she called herself then."

"Then?" Rod asked eagerly, more than intrigued.

Deldragon gave him a wry smile. "Once upon a time, I was a young rake, wandering around the Stormar ports and farther afield, in part because my father told me in no uncertain terms, with the aid of a bull whip, what he'd do to me if I drank and wenched my way across Galath. I was in Hrathlar, I think it was, when I saw this Rosera."

Taeauna grinned. "Saw her how, Darendarr? Come, we're not of Bowrock; there's no need to be coy before our ears."

The velduke sighed as he opened a door into the next chamber, this one full of barrels, and led the way across it to another door. "Well, let's just say she was dancing on tables in a dockfront tavern then, and so slender and supple a pleasure-lass was she that she could travel around a bed full of half-drunken men so swiftly and with such ease that I thought she must be using magic. She was agile enough a little later to squeeze out a tiny window with all their purses while they slept, avoiding the bedchamber's barred and guarded door."

"This 'they' included you, didn't it?" Taeauna teased.

"Of course," Deldragon sighed, "but there's no need at all to spread this tale about. I heard much more about her in Hrathlar, after that, back in those days. Suffice it to say that she's the sort that's always up to something, making a living by sly means. So if she's here, now, it bodes ill for Bowrock. Not to mention that I dislike my cellars being full of unwanted guests I did not greet, nor welcomed, nor had even saw entering my home. Come!"

He opened the door into another dark room, threaded his way down it through a maze of stacked pots and tables of dust-covered carvings and tools, and down a stair, his blade glowing faintly and eerily in the gloom.

"I don't want to shout and chase her, mind," he warned. "I want to follow her and see where she leads us. And I doubt not but that means we'll have to be exceedingly, glorkingly quiet, unless she's gone deaf down the years since I saw her."

"She left quite an impression," the Aumrarr purred. "Was she that good?"

The velduke turned to regard her, held up his blade so its glow shone on his face and she could see him rolling his eyes, and sighed heavily. Then, without a word, he turned away to thrust open the door at the bottom of the stairs, and led them out into another passage.

"How blasted big is this keep?" Rod whispered to Taeauna, who gave him a wide, understanding grin by way of reply.

Then they were stepping out into one of the largest rooms he'd ever seen in his life. Not high-ceilinged, like a cathedral or one of those towering hotels with a central atrium that elevators slid up and down the many-balconied sides of, but more like some basements he'd been in, with rough pillars here and there in odd places. Except that those basements had been cluttered and small. This room seemed to be empty of everything except pillars and echoes, and was very, very big.

"Jesus," he muttered, not quite under his breath. "What would something this big ever be used for?"

"Living," Deldragon replied, striding off along one wall. Rod had to trot to keep up with him and hear the rest of his reply: "Every jack, lass, and child in Bowrock. If dragons come mating."

"Dragons come mating? What, they cast lustful eyes on humans and tear us apart trying to, uh... you know?"

The velduke sighed. "You are from a far country, aren't you? Not often, but often enough that everyone remembers it all, at least in cradle-tales; every two or three centuries, I suppose, dragons get the urge to mate. She-dragons fly around seeking suitable lairs, always stone cities or fortresses men have built, and take possession of them. Usually that means shattering many of the interior buildings to form a bed of stone she can lie on, and it always means slaying or driving out any humans in the place."

"Oh."

"There's more than that, man. The drakes then get into the act; the male dragons. They roam the skies seeking likely-looking females lying waiting in their lairs, and try to conquer them in playful battles. If other males show up, the males end their wooing-frays and fight each other to the death, often wrecking much of the lair in the struggle, or crushing other buildings nearby when the vanquished dragon crashes to earth, dying, and often rolling around in its agonies. Those broken lairs don't seem to bother the she-dragons; they proceed to mate, then ferociously guard the area against all intrusion, including humans who've been there all along, but come to the notice of the wyrms, until the wyrmlings hatch, grow strong enough to fly, and depart with their mother. As I said, this doesn't happen often, but when it does…" The velduke stopped and swept his hand out in a slow flourish, to indicate the vast, echoing darkness before them.

"I'm a writer," Rod whispered. "Words aren't supposed to fail me. And 'holy shit' hardly seems appropriate, somehow."

"Oh, I don't know," Taeauna murmured, from just behind him. "They cover the matter pretty well, I'd say."

Deldragon turned with his hand on the ring of another door. "We go through a narrow spot, here. Stay close to me." He tugged, the door groaned open, and the ghostly glow of his blade moved into deep darkness.

THE TALONS OF the lorn were sharp, and embedded deeply, agonizingly, in his shoulders and nigh his elbows just below, on his left arm, and just above on his right. They were obviously trying to prevent him bending his arms.

Fair enough. He was obviously trying to kill them, by thrusting something strong, like his fingers, or sharp, like the little stabbing knife normally sheathed at the inside of his wrist deep into their eyes. The ropes so tightly wound around them all prevented either side getting away from the other, and with their wings bound so tightly against them, the lorn were unable to properly call upon their strong shoulder muscles to overpower the large and well-muscled human in their midst.

Wherefore one lorn was dead already, and dripping forth brains and life-blood in a slow trail of gore from one eyesocket, and another was frantically trying to drive its claws right through the fat arm they were embedded in, in an attempt to stop the arm's owner from slowly sawing off the talons of its other claw, to clear a path to its eyes.

A vain attempt. Talon after talon was dropping off, leaking blood in the wake of the bundle, and not only were the Dark Helms not helping (a few simple blows about the human's head would have ended its attacks, surely), they were chuckling and talking of placing bets on what would happen next!

This left the most helpless lorn—the one hanging downwards, its face seeing only stone floor sliding endlessly past—seething, and the other one hissing and voiding itself in fear, as it lost talons amid much pain.

Those talons were iron-hard, but the fingers above them could be cut as readily as Garfist sliced meat on a fireside platter. And being as it didn't seem likely he'd ever see a fireside meal again, he went on carving, and remembering those sizzling juices, the spiced sauces Isk prepared so superbly, the mouth-watering taste of the best roast boar they'd fire-spitted together...

His gut rumbled loudly in sudden hunger, suddenly filling both lorn with terror and causing them to sob involuntarily. Humans ate lorn? Had they but known!

The Dark Helms guffawed anew.

* * *

IF GARFIST DIED...

Iskarra winced at the thought, ran her fingers over the bony knuckles of the hand she was clutching her dagger with, and shook her head.

She'd go on, if she weren't dying herself by then. She'd not greet certain death by fighting hopeless odds, but she'd not abandon her old ox either, not while there was still a shred of hope, and if fighting for him landed her in a hopeless fray, then so be it.

Glorking, glorking wizards.

It had to be a wizard; who else could make Dark Helms and lorn work together? Or bring lorn down into dark cellars, where they'd never venture on their own, so hating the likelihood of not being able to fly; they even hated flying through windows into the largest rooms. So if she could hurl a dagger through a wizard's eye and then shout to the Dark Helms that the lorn had been promised them as meals, and start the Helms fighting the lorn...

It was a very slim chance for her, and less than that for Garfist, but at least they might not be the only ones who died this day.

"THERE'S THE WIZARD," Deldragon muttered, stroking his mustache. His voice was barely more than a whisper, and was almost lost to Rod and Taeauna in the humming of the gate.

Like the others, Rod knew what it was without anyone saying a word. A magical doorway linking the cellar of Deldragon's keep to somewhere else. It dominated the room, an arch of writhing, humming purple flame as high as three men. It burned without consuming anything, rooted in two small braziers at both ends but obviously not fueled by them. Two metal spheres were part of its flamings on one side of its curve, and a withered, shriveled, nigh-skeletal human dangled from them, his armor hanging loose or dropping off, piece by no-longer-fitting piece.

The cellar room was big, and many passages met in it, but the other room, the room that was somewhere else, that could be seen only through the arch, and not by looking around or past it, looked larger, and better lit. The line of Dark Helms marching out of it and into Deldragon's keep seemed to stretch a long way, and the velduke cursed softly at the sight of it.

Standing beside the gate was a young, coldly smiling man in dark thigh-length robes over darker breeches and boots. He looked as unkempt as a tavern-lounging sailor, with curly, dirty-gold hair, bristling brows and a ragged fringe of a beard along his jaw, but something about him—the arrogant way he carried himself, or his large and dark eyes, or their purple hue—shouted "Wizard!"

For a thrilling moment Rod felt like shouting, "Wizard!" himself, and striding into the room to flick his finger and cause the sneering man to fly apart in a flood of black tatters of robe, tumbling bones, and unpleasant wetness. But of course, here that wouldn't happen. Here in Falconfar he seemed to have no power at all, and would only be inviting his own swift death. "Swift" as in: before Rod Everlar, the Shaper, the Creator, the founder of this crazy feast, could do anything else at all.

Beside him in the darkness of their disused passage, lying chin-on-the-floor just as he was, Deldragon and Taeauna were keeping very still, and very quiet. The velduke had done something swift and magical to make his sword as black as pitch, and about as shiny.

They were no longer watching the line of marching Dark Helms. Instead, they were seeing a small knot of Helms marching up to the wizard, carrying a securely bound bundle between them. It was dripping blood, and there seemed to be frantic struggling going on, inside those bonds.

The wizard gestured that the bundle be lowered to the ground, and the lashings around it cut apart.

The bundle was duly lowered, and two Dark Helms went to their knees on either side of it, daggers in hand. The others all drew their swords and held them so the points hovered above the thickest central part of the bundle. The wizard watched, smiling. And Velduke Deldragon aimed his sword with slow and silent care.

The bonds parted, springing back. Freed lorn wings flapped and writhed, there was a frantic wriggling, an arm darted out of the opening bundle with a dagger flashing in its hand, Dark Helms shouted commands—and Deldragon's sword spat fire across the room straight into the wizard's face, hurling him backwards.

The mage's shoulder touched the purple fire of the gate for a moment and simply vanished.

Face staring in disbelieving pain, the wizard shrieked and frantically flung himself away from the gate; he ended up greeting the floor, face-first. Dark Helms by the dozens turned to glare at the source of the flame, and the velduke triggered his blade again, waving it back and forth to lash many of those menacingly staring Helms with flame.

Fire rushing and flickering around their helms, Dark Helms surged across the room at Rod and Taeauna and Deldragon, and beyond them, a thin female figure sprinted across the room as swiftly as an arrow in flight, and smashed right into a lorn that was flapping its way free of the bundle.

A dagger flashed twice, quickly, and the lorn sagged.

The figure leaned past it to slash at the golden-haired wizard as he scrambled to his feet to try to get out of reach, but brief threads of lightning crackled from the mage to the dagger blade, driving the woman with the knife back in obvious pain. Between them, the dying lorn fell to the floor.

At the same moment, the bundle heaved up into a large, fat, reeling man shedding two dead, limp lorn. He reached out for the wizard with his dagger.

The wizard stepped hastily back, shouting, "Take him! Take him and put his hands on the globes!"

Dark Helms turned their heads to the mage who pointed impatiently at the fat man. "Take him!" Then his pointing arm swept up to indicate the nigh-skeletal man hanging like an empty sack from the two spheres that were floating in the humming purple fire of the gate-arch. "And put his hands there! On those!" The wizard's pointing finger stabbed at the air impatiently, indicating the globes. "Hurry!"

Over the helms of the Dark Helm warriors advancing cautiously toward them, Rod, Taeauna, and Deldragon could see the Helms closest to the wizard hesitate for a moment, and then close in on the fat man.

"No swords!" the wizard shouted at them. "I want him unharmed. The man who cuts him, dies!"

The Helms lurched to untidy stops, swords flashing and singing as they were hastily sheathed. The fat man used that time to rush at the wizard, who backed away and tried to duck behind some Dark Helms. As the Helms vainly tried to grapple with the fat man and avoid hosting deep thrusts of his dagger, with much shoving and groaning and reeling, the wizard crouched and tried to cast a spell.

Deldragon unleashed his sword again, but the mage ducked lower and the flames meant for him raged around the shoulders of two cursing, writhing Dark Helms instead.

Taeauna, Rod, and the velduke were on their feet now, awaiting the menacing line of Dark Helms closing in on them, barely able to see the wizard and the fat man over looming armored shoulders. They saw Rosera darting past them both.

Then the Dark Helms were upon them, and there was no time to watch anything, anymore. Swords rang as the velduke and Taeauna parried and struck aside three blades each, in a whirlwind of steel that Rod winced at the very thought of, as he backed away from the Dark Helms stalking after him, and then started to back in behind his companions as he realized his retreat was baring Taeauna's side to any Helm who cared to stick a sword in it.

Deldragon snatched out his dagger in his other hand, and tried to parry with it so he could aim his sword again and unleash more sword-fire. Before he could, they heard the wizard shout in rage and pain. A spell like a wall of writhing lightnings crashed into the backsides of the Dark Helms facing Rod, Taeauna, and the velduke, and they roared and writhed wildly in agony and scattered, staggering weakly.

Taeauna was upon them like a flash, her slender sword thrusting up under the edge of one helm and then another, dead men slumping in her wake as their blood spattered the floor in front of them and they sank down to join it. Rod's stomach heaved, and he trotted desperately away from a Dark Helm intent on disembowelment, but he caught a glimpse of what had made the wizard strike at his own warriors.

The Rosera woman had caught his wrist in some sort of thin black cord—well, damn! She'd lassooed him, just like in the movies!—and dragged it around to spoil his aim. He was trying to tug free now, shrieking curses at her and fending off her dagger with his own; he didn't dare try to slice the cord because he needed his metal fang to parry hers.

Right beside the golden-haired wizard, a Dark Helm toppled over as the fat man tore a bloody dagger out of his throat, still wrestling with other Dark Helms, and from across the room, more Dark Helms were rushing to the wizard's aid.

The Rosera woman screamed a curse of her own as she was forced to turn and deal with them, the wizard whirled triumphantly away from her to slice her cord away from his wrist, the fat man bellowed in triumph as another pair of Dark Helms went down before him, and…

Rod was suddenly falling, his boots slipping helplessly in something wet and sticky. Much nearer Helms were looming up over him, swords reaching down—

And Taeauna crashed into those warriors from one side, hurling herself against them to make them lurch and jostle, their swords waving everywhere except at Rod.

Deldragon fired his sword again, sending fire howling just over Taeauna's wingless back. Rod saw the stump of one of her severed wings blacken and start to sizzle, as the sword-fire streamed around it, and the wizard screamed as that fire found his newly freed hand and blasted it, fingers smashed limp and blackened.

Then the Dark Helms closed in over Rod again, and were toppling over on him with wet sobs, Taeauna's blade darting back out of their throats dark and wet and glistening, blood spraying all over Rod as they came down, huge and dark and—

WHAM. Heavy!

Rod groaned and twisted as the armored hulks slammed into him and bounced him hard up off the stone floor and down again. All his wind had been driven out of him, he couldn't—

Couldn't—

Something boomed, the floor shuddered under Rod, and he was bouncing again, wincing and gasping for breath enough to moan, fighting to...

The dead men atop him were suddenly gone, plucked and torn away. All over the room Rod could hear a strange thudding: body after body being driven against stone, or against other bodies already against that stone...

Panting, shoulders settling against the trembling, calming floor, he could see the room around him again now.

The golden-haired wizard stood alone, staring down at his mangled hand. There was no one left around him at all except the ragged flesh-and-bones thing hanging from the gate. He must have managed some magic that hurled people away from him, probably to keep the big man or the Rosera woman from knifing him.

Behind him, the gate was noticeably darker, the hum of its flames lower and quieter. As Rod stared at it, it flickered.

That momentary darkening seemed to enrage the wizard. "Warriors of Arlaghaun, obey me!" he bellowed. "Seize him, and him, and *him*, and her, and bring them all here, disarmed, to the gate!"

His pointing hand had indicated the fat man, the velduke, Taeauna, and Rod. Great.

So, was this Arlaghaun? One of the Dooms? He looked rather young to have terrorized Falconfar, but then, if something Rod wrote could change everything, overnight...

But wait. How could this wizard be so powerful in Falconfar, yet a complete stranger? He'd glanced at all the Holdoncorp stuff, he was sure he had. Oh. Right. He wasn't the only Shaper, and perhaps their designers changed Falconfar whenever they typed stuff into their computers, not just when it got published.

And perhaps they weren't the only other Shapers. Shit.

"Wound them not!" the wizard called.

Right. Thanks for the reminder. He had no time just now for thinking about how things worked in Falconfar; he had to worry about staying alive. Again.

Rod had his breath back now. The floor cold and hard under him, he turned his head to look the other way, away from the humming purple fire of the gate.

Dark Helms were coming for him, of course, trotting across the room from where the wizard's spell had driven them. Swords sheathed, but hands outstretched to grab.

As Rod watched, one of them stiffened, staggered, and then fell. Taeauna was trotting behind him, bloody blade in hand, with her own hulking escort of dark-armored warriors closing in behind her. Which meant that the other flurry of Dark Helms, yonder, must be centered around the velduke.

"I threw a party," he murmured, rolling over to get up and run, "and men with swords came."

There were sudden grunts and sounds of struggling from the direction of the wizard; Rod looked that way as he gained his feet again, and saw the big man, bloody dagger in hand, straining in the grip of more than a dozen Dark Helms, fighting to stay where he was as they tugged and shoved, trying to drag him closer to the gate.

Fourteen—no, sixteen—to one…

The big man might be a mountain to each of them, but together they were hauling him inexorably toward the gate.

Rod ran for the darkness, away from the gate but also away from the Dark Helms, as they started running, too. Taeauna was surrounded by a swarm of them, now, just like Deldragon and the fat man. The Rosera woman, where was she?

Dark Helms were coming at him from this direction too, now; with every stride he was running to meet them. Rod breathed a bitter curse and turned in the only direction that wasn't full of Dark Helms.

Toward the gate. They were herding him; they're herding us all.

"Bastards," he hissed aloud. "Goddamned bloody bastards."

He saw the Rosera woman leaping out of the darkness again, racing past the wizard to pounce from behind on the Dark Helms struggling with the fat man. The wizard staggered hastily back with a shout: she'd thrown something, probably a small knife, into the mage's face on her way past.

Well, why shouldn't he throw something at the wizard, too?

Because I have nothing to throw, and I'm afraid of what he'll do to me, after...

The Rosera woman had a dagger in her hand, and was plunging it up under helm after helm from behind, darting and racing along the line of struggling warriors, letting them sag and fall in her wake. The fat man was still roaring and grunting in their midst, shouting something that sounded like, "Isk! Keep back! Back, hraul you!"

More Dark Helms were rushing at the fat man, now, slamming into the knot already around him and driving it a few staggering steps closer to the gate. Others rushed around it, trying to get at the woman who half-climbed a Dark Helm from behind to lean desperately in and get a hand on the fat man or something he was wearing.

What looked like a grotesquely long pink tongue—the tongue of a giant, as wide as the woman's head—shot out from where her reaching hand was, over her shoulder, stretching like bubble gum Rod had once seen a kid pull and snap, thinner and longer and thinner and longer...

The golden-haired wizard ducked aside, batting at it with his mangled hand, but it swooped around him in the air, and slapped across his face like a wet pink mask. And tightened, and pulled.

The wizard came staggering blindly toward the battling fat man and his Dark Helms.

"Smother him," Rod distinctly heard the Rosera woman gasp, before Dark Helms grabbed her and dragged her down. He saw daggers reach up for the long pink tongue, to slash and pierce.

And the pink tongue came away from the fat man with a wet, sticky sucking sound and snapped through the air to join itself, whipping around the wizard's head with a loud crack that might have been the man's neck breaking, so suddenly did he spin around and fall limply to the floor—right in the mouth of the gate.

Which flickered again.

And again, darker this time.

It was answered with a bright flash, a line of flame racing through the air from behind Rod to claw at the knot of Dark Helms. Some of them turned, breaking free, to see where this sudden torment was coming from.

The velduke was using his sword-fire again.

Well, why not? Save it for when, exactly? Death could come right now, and—

More Dark Helms turned, and Rod caught a glimpse of the fat man again, still struggling against dozens of gripping hands.

It seemed Deldragon had seen the man, too. The next bolt of flame was lower, racing at warriors' ankles.

Rod glanced at the Dark Helms closing in on him, and risked a look toward where the velduke must be. Dark Helms were heaped there; Deldragon must have unleashed some sort of magic on them, to free himself. Off to one side was another struggling mass of warriors, like the one gathered around the fat man. That must be Taeauna.

He should do something, should—

Do what? He couldn't even *get* to her, across the beams of sword-fire, and—

Dark Helms started shrieking, back by the gate. Rod turned his head in time to watch the warriors around the fat man start to fall over, still in one huge, struggling clump. They were falling because many of them seemed to have no feet anymore, just blackened stumps.

Rod's stomach heaved again, urgently this time.

As cruel fingers caught hold of his arms and shoulders, and what felt like a speeding truck—a truck that had lots of hard knees, and bad breath, and clanking armor—slammed into his back.

Chapter Eighteen

THE CHIMING OF chains came closer and closer, until it stopped in front of him.

Arlaghaun did not let his sigh show as he looked up from reading the last page of some forty that detailed the crafting of a failed magic, an account written centuries ago by a wizard who'd ended up as a dragon without knowing quite how. He put a hand over the brightest glowing runes to shield his eyes from their dazzle and looked up at his apprentice who was standing in the appropriately subservient pose he'd taught her. Whippings had their uses, it seemed.

They would have another one if she'd interrupted him for no good reason. That was, of course, unlikely; she was his best apprentice, not a fool. He kept his face expressionless, merely raising his eyebrows in a silent question.

"Yardryk, master. The expected debacle. But he has Deldragon and the wingless Aumrarr, too. At least, they're all fighting nigh his gate." Her lip curled. "Which is about to collapse."

Arlaghaun smiled. "Ah, Yardryk. Always so confident as he rushes headlong into his next pratfall. Still, he's too useful to be sacrificed; we should rescue him, I suppose. And the good velduke will have some magic about his person I can seize. If we take him now, he won't have chances enough to waste it all blasting my warriors. Moreover, if we keep Master Mage Brightrising alive, we can send him back to the keep to snatch magic later, with a Darendarr Deldragon *I* control striding at his side."

Amalrys nodded in her chains, returning his smile, ice-blue eyes dancing.

"Right. Let's have them all." Arlaghaun stood up from his book, turned and then stepped away from it to quell any spillover of magic, stretched his gray-clad limbs, and started to cast an intricate spell.

His apprentice watched him avidly, as always.

He smiled, his brown eyes flashing their usual fire at her, and seeing it returned.

Yes. Strong magic, elegantly unleashed, was the greatest aphrodisiac.

THE LITTLE POOL of water in the dark, wet forest glade glowed with sudden, silent fire that lit the faces of the four Aumrarr bent over it.

"You can farscry like a Doom?" Dark-armored Lorlarra's voice was rough with awe. "Sister, what are you?"

Dauntra gave her a look that seemed to add years to her young and impish beauty. "Just another Aumrarr, sister; no more. But I happen to be a sister who caught the eye of Lord Darendarr Deldragon seven summers back."

"Aha," said Juskra, her scars twisting her knowing smile. "You came to him in the moonlight, hmm? And he could not resist lovemaking in the air, and you starflew him to sleep."

Dauntra's smile was gentler than her scarred sister's. "Yes. Asleep I delivered him back to his bed. He slept as I drew his sword, and shed some of my blood and his, and mingled them together. Ambrelle, you know the spell."

"I do," the oldest Aumrarr said quietly, holding back her long purple-black hair so as to better behold the images moving in the little forest pool Dauntra had let a drop of her blood fall into. "So when you do this, and he happens to be unleashing the magics of that sword at the same time, you can watch his doings and surroundings. For a time."

"Is that what I think it is?" Juskra asked sharply. "That purple fire?"

"If you're thinking it's a gate some wizard created, that's now on the verge of collapsing," Ambrelle replied, with just a hint of a smile, "then yes, it is what you think it is."

"A gate cast by one of the Dooms?"

"Very likely."

"Almost certainly," Lorlarra corrected, an instant before the scene of struggling people in the maw of a flickering purple arc of flames exploded into a bright flash of many vivid hues, clashing and roiling like violently grappling mists.

The four watching Aumrarr cursed.

The pool went dark.

* * *

Everyone screamed, falling through the blinding brightness. Eyes wide but seeing nothing, nothing but light so stabbing that it made him sob, Rod Everlar fell endlessly, vaguely aware that others were tumbling with him yet unable to see them, falling...

Falling...

To find smooth stone underfoot, as gently yet as firmly as if he'd always been standing there.

Abruptly, the brightness all around him was gone, fled away to leave behind a few fading, gentle glows that left him blinking.

Eyes watering, shaking his head to try to clear his vision, Rod stared around. He was in some sort of large stone room, with a high, vaulted ceiling. There were many tall archways in the walls, all of them leading into passages stretching away into various glooms. Set on one wall close at hand, on a stretch that led out to a jutting corner of wall, was a tall, ornate oval mirror, stretching up from the floor taller than a person.

Taeauna was standing right beside him, and she was turning toward Rod, as if to check that he was there.

He saw her eyes measure him, and move on; she was glancing swiftly in this direction and that.

Rod went on doing the same thing. Deldragon stood beyond Tay, glaring around at everything with sharp concern in his ice-blue eyes, and the fat man and Rosera stood beyond him, shoulder to shoulder and looking wary. Over there, in the other direction, was the wounded, golden-haired young wizard, and on the floor, crawling mindlessly away from him like a worm Rod had once watched wriggling up out of a bait-bucket when fishing, was the pink tongue-thing that had enshrouded the wizard's head. To Rod's left stood a tattered handful of lorn and Dark Helms, staring around the hall in as much bewilderment as Rod was.

This place was huge, and solidly built, yet some-how—with its smooth walls, shaped ledges and ridges that framed the archways—far more elegant than the stark stone castle feasting halls he was getting so used to seeing. And it felt old, an age older than they did, despite their crumblings. What was this place?

As Rod turned to look behind him, Taeauna stepped protectively between him and the Dark Helms with her sword ready, murmuring, "Is this the place, lord?"

"What? Oh. No." Rod shook his head sadly. Then he frowned and whispered, "So what place is this?"

"Ult Tower," she said grimly.

Ult Tower; this?

Rod gaped at her. The abode of the wizard Ult?

He stared at the ceiling and then around the room again. Really? The black stone keep in the heart of Galath that the wizard Ult had built and linked to himself magically, stone by stone, so the tower was like his skin, and he could feel what was done to it and see out of it?

Hell, yes, that had been a tale! Vivid, seemed to flow into existence under his fingers as he typed, just as fast as his racing thoughts had taken him; that story, that he'd created Ult Tower for, had been one of his favorites. Still was.

Yes, this could be Ult Tower. He couldn't see any "black" stone, but any room could be sheathed in smoother, lighter stone. Or be covered in stucco or paint, if it came to that. So if this was Ult Tower, where was Ult?

Across a stretch of empty tiles, facing them, a man was suddenly standing in the room, watching them alertly.

Rod blinked again; that stretch of stone floor had been bare a moment ago.

The man held no sword, nor anything else. He was clad in gray, wore rings that winked with lights of their own, and there were more lights playing along a high collar or curving horn-like thing that swept up from one gray shoulder, the one that didn't have a cloak draped over it. It looked as if the man had grown one leathery, featherless Aumrarr wing that he'd curved toward the way he was facing, and that it had then been cut off, leaving only its fan-shaped root, permanently curved forward. Into something that looked very much like some sort of science fiction-ish weapon; the curve was topped with a row of winking openings that looked like the maws of a fighter plane's wing-cannons.

Obviously a wizard, but not Ult, surely? Rod supposed wizards could make themselves look like anything they wanted to, or perhaps not, because if they could, surely some of them would choose more handsome appearances, to lure the eyes and open the arms of passing lovely ladies. But Rod had always pictured, and written about, Ult as old and short and chubby-cheeked, looking out at the world in a kindly manner over spectacles. A little like a Rockwell Santa Claus without the beard and the overly red nose and cheeks.

This man was taller, rather younger, and well, *meaner*. Or at least looked to be, by the fire in his dark brown eyes and the twist of his thin lips. He had sharp features, the nose especially, but would have been termed "handsome" in a leather jacket and jeans, swaggering and posing outside a bar. Aside from that firing-horn thing sweeping up from behind his shoulder, he wore dark breeches and a matching tunic, with a half-cloak over them that drooped to cover his behind on their low side, and reached his belt at the highest point in its raked edge. Dark gray, all of it. Shaped eyebrows, razored sideburns running down the curve of his chin, close-cropped hair but dipping to his shoulders at the back. The Dark Helms and lorn were all hastily and silently kneeling to him, and he had an air of command. He looked more like some sort of stylish secret agent than anything else.

And Rod hated him on sight.

He was staring right at Rod, their eyes meeting like swords crossing.

"And just who are you?" he asked, his voice gloating, sparing not an instant of attention for Taeauna or Deldragon.

Rod knew he was reddening. "Who are you?" he snapped back. "And what have you done with Ult?"

His words seemed to strike the man like a blow across the face, and the name "Ult" echoed and rolled thunderously around the room, as if he'd shouted it in a voice as deep as stone.

Behind Rod, Taeauna made a sound that was not quite a gasp, and not quite a sob, and the velduke whispered something that was probably an amazed curse.

The gray wizard staggered back, the skin of his face rippling and twisting, and his eyes turned blue, staring pleadingly at Rod and the others. His face twisted and stretched as he shrank away from Rod, spreading into chubby cheeks... for all the world as if Ult was inside him, straining to break free. Then the wizard's jawline returned, wavered, slid away again...

Deldragon aimed his sword and sent a crackling bolt of fire racing at the wizard; it struck empty yet unyielding air just in front of the gray-clad mage, clawed along it, and then surrounded him, rushing tongues of flame that could not touch him.

The force of the flames bent the wizard's body back from the waist and made it shudder at first, but as they watched his face slid back into the semblance they had first seen, he straightened, and his lips twisted into a sneer.

Deldragon cursed, swung his sword so that its flames slashed across the breasts of the Dark Helms and lorn who'd begun drifting toward him, and thrust out his other hand at the wizard, a ring on his forefinger winking brightly.

Nothing seemed to race or fire from it, but the wizard acquired a look of horror, backed away swiftly, and then started to scream.

They saw his gray garments darken and then swiftly start to melt away, and the flesh beneath them receded almost as fast, the mage's shrieks rising with terror as he turned and ran.

Rod thought he got a glimpse of the man's face slipping again, but before the fleeing wizard ducked out an archway and vanished, everyone in the chamber clearly saw bared bones down his fleeing back, as flesh and all melted away. The Dark Helms and lorn, looking rather scorched, fled after him.

So much for that wizard, for the moment at least; what about the other one?

Rod turned sharply to look, and was in time to see the golden-haired young wizard who'd demanded their capture in the cellars stiffen and stop trying to cast a spell with his remaining hand as Rosera sliced into it viciously with her dagger. Severed fingers flew.

Over that mage's screams, Deldragon snarled, "Friends, I must get back to Bowrock!"

"There are gates all over this tower, to places all over Falconfar, if the wizard you just started turning to bone hasn't changed them," Rod said, remembering his tales of Ult, "but how we'll find the one for Bowrock, I don't know."

Taeauna stepped between them. "By recognizing what we can see through the gate. So let's hunt out the gates and start looking through them—quickly! If we see the wizard again just get through whatever gate you're standing in front of at that moment!"

"We're with you," Rosera said quickly. The velduke rounded on her.

"Not until you tell me what that is, Rosera," he snapped, pointing at the flesh-pink, ambulatory thing that now looked less like a gigantic tongue and more like a huge inchworm, as it arched and slithered, arched and slithered up her leg. "And what you were up to in my keep!"

The fat man behind Rosera started forward, his face hardening and arms spreading wide.

Deldragon shrugged and raised his sword meaningfully.

"Stand back and belt up, ox," the bone-thin woman said quickly. "Leave this to me."

The dagger spun from her hands like flashing lightning.

Past the velduke's ear it went, before he could so much as start to swing his sword her way.

Taeauna raised a pointing hand, and Deldragon spun around instead.

Rosera's dagger was standing forth from the throat of the golden-haired wizard. His dark purple eyes stared back at them in helpless horror, a wand falling from his maimed and bleeding hands.

Then he gurgled, his knees gave way, and he sank toward the floor. Halfway there, magical glows occurred in the air around him, brightening and swirling. As they watched, the dying wizard's body seemed to fade, and the glows claimed it and the wand, before the body could strike the floor, leaving only the dagger to clatter on the tiles.

The velduke whirled back to face the woman who'd thrown it. She was standing just as before, but had just put a wide, falsely merry smile on her face. "Well, y'see, Lord Deldragon," she said brightly, "my name is Iskarra, and 'tis like this..."

"I'll bet," the velduke said dryly.

"How much?" the fat man asked quickly.

Deldragon rolled his eyes, stroked his mustache, and then waved to them beckoningly as he started to stride across the chamber. "Let us walk as we talk. That wizard won't be gone forever, and if we haven't found one of his precious gates and got ourselves through it before he gets back, there'll be no more time for talking, for any of us."

Iskarra smiled crookedly. "But plenty of 'forever.'"

* * *

ARLAGHAUN SOBBED AS he lurched against a wall for perhaps the fortieth time. He didn't slow down. He didn't dare slow down.

The fragments of a shattered mirror showed him his own sharp nose and blazing brown eyes at the next wall he fetched up against. He snarled at his own reflection, and staggered on.

He was almost there, now... almost...

Rings flared unbidden on his fingers as he reached the blank wall that their magic would make yield, and fell thankfully through it. Ravaged flesh screamed agony anew as he staggered helplessly sideways, into yet another wall, and tried to curse but could not. The nauseating worm-like squirming in his chest was rising again, choking Arlaghaun with nausea; it meant Ult was fighting him again.

Falcon *damn* that man, whoever he was!

To name Ult, and goad Ult into rising again, after all these years! Years!

And where was Amalrys, to aid him? Where was she?

The Doom of Galath started running again, sliding his shoulder along the wall, too weak and dizzy to thrust himself away from the stone and not quite daring to, anyway, in case he fell and bared joints failed him. He was close, now, deep in the heart of the tower... Just a few more doors, just a few more...

Two more, now, as his rings flared again and seemingly solid stone melted away before him. Arlaghaun dared to let himself hope again, dared to let out his rage. How by the glorking Falcon could one stranger with two questions—no spells, not even a dagger in his hand; *two glorking questions!*—reduce him from ruling Galath to fleeing for his life, just like that? And where had Deldragon gotten such a ring? Shards and stars, what else in the way of magic did he have hidden away in Bowrock?

Arlaghaun tugged open a door that no magic he knew of would make open or shift into shadows, raised a hand that flared warningly as a trap-rune blazed up and then faded away again before one of his rings, tore open the last door, flung it shut behind him, rocked in the resulting slam, that must have shaken all Ult Tower—and fell thankfully over the stone lip into waiting relief.

The waters of the pool were warm and heavy, as always, like oil. As he surfaced, already soothed and numbed, Arlaghaun saw the weird lights converging on him, as the pool awakened to his need.

From the dark and distant corners they came, rushing to him, and he groaned in relief as the pain left him, holding his fingers clear of the water so his enchanted rings would do nothing to harm or twist awry the healings of the pool. What was left of his clothes were dissolving; he dragged the wandwing in its harness off his back and slung it over the low rampart, onto the tiles around the pool, and then started plucking off rings and gently tossing them after it.

The pool was sliding into him with a warmth that brought an almost sexual rapture, healing and soothing and banishing taints and aging and poisons... If it wasn't for the memories this most precious of Galathan magics stole, every time, he'd bathe here every night.

Come to think of it, this time there was something he wanted to forget: Ult. Let the pool go on sinking through him. He, Arlaghaun, was going to sink down into himself, too, and rout and shatter all that had once been Ult, once and for all.

He felt the lurking node of thoughts not his own, thoughts racing with renewed hope, with schemes against him. Taking care not to focus on it, and so alert it to his approach, Arlaghaun grinned a savage grin.

Ducking down, he surged closer in his mind, sharpening his will to a sword-keen edge…

Then he burst into the heart of Ult's buzzing thoughts with a savage roar, slashing, burning, rending: pouncing on the shrieking, fleeing light that was Ult.

Claw, slice, sear; ruthlessly lessening Ult here and then there, vanquishing his foe as he should have done years ago, tearing free memory after memory and thrusting them apart in his own mind, so that nothing of the lurking sentience of Ult could cling to them.

It took a long time, but every moment was worth it.

When at last Arlaghaun knew peace of mind and body, he floated in the gentle, shifting glows, immersed and warm, staring at the ceiling overhead. Not for the first time, the thought occurred to him that this most hidden of rooms was of bare, rough stone, as unfinished as a tomb. Now why was that?

Well, he'd just slain the last remnants of the only being who could have given him an answer. He shrugged. Let not curiosity ever become obsession.

"So who is that man?" he whispered to the dark and silent stone. "I'd never seen him before I first glimpsed him at the Aumrarr's side, I know I haven't, yet he looks so familiar."

"SO THAT'S JUST how it was, lord," Iskarra said warmly, concluding a long and fanciful tale as to why she and Garfist Gulkoon were in the cellars of Deldragon's keep in the heart of Bowrock.

As they all strode together down yet another long and many-doored passage in this seemingly endless tower, Deldragon regarded her thoughtfully, something impish or merry dancing in the depths of his ice-blue eyes. "I don't believe a word of it," he said, firmly but politely, as he stroked his flaxen mustache. "So tell me something else, instead: what are your intentions now?"

"To take every last bit of magic we can carry from these rooms all around us," Garfist growled, "and get ourselves far away from here. Somewhere in Falconfar, I care not where, that the mage whose tower we're standing in can't find us."

"There is no such place," Taeauna snapped. "Nor can you escape his scrutiny for longer than it takes him to mumble a rather simple spell, if you carry off even one of his things of magic. Your schemes doom you."

Iskarra sighed. "They always have."

"Yet we're still here!" Garfist rumbled triumphantly. "So I think we'll just keep right on scheming, and not listening to folk who have their own reasons for saying us nay for this and that."

Taeauna didn't bother to shrug; she was too busy pointing ahead. "Gates! A row of them!"

As if her words had been some sort of cue, the air brightened into a bright silver-gold shimmer and the passage around them rocked. From out of that shimmering, something small, strange, glowing and golden fell into Rod Everlar's hand. It resembled a miniature coach-horn, only with valves like a trumpet, and three misshapen eyes that winked and glowed with moving, vary-hued radiances.

It was soft, rather than as hard as any other metal object he'd ever touched, and warm, too, and…

That was all the staring at it he was able to manage, as something more sinister caught his eye. Down the passage ahead of him, just this side of the row of distant glows that Taeauna had just pointed out as the way out they were seeking, a warrior's helm—close-faced and menacing, for all that it was empty—was floating slowly down out of the ceiling.

Literally out of the ceiling. Rod saw it emerge from apparently solid stone, sliding down to hang in the air. As if it were watching him, and worn by a man whose stomach was on a level with the tousled top of Rod's head.

Shit. It certainly didn't look friendly; Taeauna and Deldragon were already stepping forward, swords rising.

At least it was just a helm, without arms and shoulders to swing some great big sword.

Something else was emerging out of the solid stone walls on either side of the passage, drifting forth in eerie silence. Arms, or rather hollow assemblies of armor plate to cloak the arms of an absent body, from flaring shoulder-plates to elaborate gauntleted fingertips. A giant's body, by the size of them. They were converging below the helm, where they would probably mate with…

A breastplate and chain-linked assembly of overlapping back plates, now rising in stately silence up out of the floor, to—

"Falcon!" Iskarra spat. "Are we just going to stand and watch it? Hack it to ribbons, or let's run!"

"Now," Taeauna said calmly to the velduke a moment later, as the drifting pieces came to smooth halts, and the air between them seemed to brighten. "Right where they're meeting."

Deldragon didn't bother to nod. Sword-fire streaking from the point of his blade was already lashing the armor where it was drawing together, snarling and clawing at the plates, curling around and between them.

And seeming to harm them not at all.

Leg armor was rising up out of the floor, and a sword as long as a lance was sliding out of the wall, wisps of smoke curling along its deadly-looking blade. Deldragon aimed his sword to blast its hilt with his sword-fire, trying to halt it and prevent it from joining the assembling armor.

He might have been shining a flashlight on the sword, for all the effect it had, and Rod and Taeauna gasped in unison as the sword-fire darkened, faded, seemed to cough and fade... snarled and spat, faded away completely... spat again, and then faded...

"That sounds not good," Garfist growled. Is it...?"

He fell silent. The sword-fire was gone again, and the blade of the velduke's sword was crumbling to rust-red dust, a collapse into nothingness that raced down the steel in a silent haste so swift and menacing that Deldragon barely had time to fling down the hilt before it reached his hand.

The hilt burst into dust as it hit the floor, and was gone just like that, and all in velvet silence.

Beyond it, a crackling arose in the air, a singing tension that rose in pitch as the armored guardian, wholly bonded together and with sword in hand, took its first tentative step toward them.

Its second stride caused a squeal of metal against metal, yet was smoother, more confident, with none of the swaying of the first. Its third brought it smoothly into the crouch of a veteran warrior, hefting that huge blade from side to side, its reach blocking the passage, walling off any way to the gates beyond.

Everyone cursed.

"What's that thing of magic in your hand?" Deldragon snapped at Rod. "Something we can use?"

Rod and everyone else stared at Rod's palm where the golden-valved horn was sinking into his flesh, apparently dissolving into him. He shook his head slightly in disbelief; he couldn't feel a thing, not even weight. If he closed his eyes, it felt like his hand was simply… empty.

Empty…

DARED SHE?

Amalrys stopped in front of the closed, featureless stone door, her eyes like two small but bright blue lamps, shivering in her chains not from being otherwise bare in the cold darkness, but from excitement.

And fear.

Dared she, really? To raise her hand against the man who'd put these chains on her, claimed her so cruelly, lorded it over her daily because he could destroy her at his pleasure?

Dared she lash out at him at last?

Yes, a voice whispered exultingly, deep within her. She laid her hand on the door, trembled as the glow grew around it, and then scraped her bare skin on its opening edge as she slid past a trifle too soon, in her eagerness to get inside.

FAR FROM A woman in chains forcing her way past a door in Ult Tower, a short, slender, and darkly handsome wizard rose from his claw-footed chair in one lithe movement to clench his fists, the better to hurl his will at her.

"Yes," Malraun breathed, putting all of his fierce will behind that word, feeling the distant Amalrys yield to it and embrace it as her own. "Yes, little unwitting slave," he murmured, "strike down your tormentor at last. Let there be one fewer Arlaghaun in the world."

As agile as any dancer, still thrusting his way deeper into the mind of Amalrys, he spun around and sprang back onto his chair, bouncing several times until his body was at rest again, his concentration never wavering.

"And if his slaying is beyond you this day," he remarked almost pleasantly, "let him taste torment, and be afraid, and be lessened. Aye, see that you humble Arlaghaun the Mighty."

He smiled, and told the ornately painted ceiling above, "For increasingly, his swaggering truly bothers me."

* * *

IN A DARK chamber of slowly dripping water, where every solitary drop plummeting the height of a castle into a patiently waiting pool awakened its own uncaring echo, the tall, blue-skinned wizard Narmarkoun sat alone, as always, and at ease.

Nearby stood the staff he'd been augmenting, upright in the air though there was no hand to hold it there. The cold fires of his spells still flickered up and down its length betimes, reflecting back off his scaled hands.

He smiled.

"Goad her indeed, Malraun, and think yourself her master," he told the darkness. "Succeed or not, survive or not. I care not. Her mind is an open door into yours, and you are mine as surely as she is, whenever I care to reach out and take you.

"And then squeeze."

THE WATCHERS SAW the gold-hued bauble disappear entirely into Rod Everlar's palm, sinking out of sight beneath his unbroken, unblemished flesh.

With a squeal of grinding metal, the armored guardian took another step forward, blade reaching out menacingly.

Rod Everlar reeled, raised a hand to his head, and fell, toppling onto his face without a sound, to lie in an unmoving heap right in front of the lumbering guardian.

Taeauna rushed to stand over him, sword raised against the reach of the looming guardian. Garfist and Iskarra looked at each other and with one accord spun around and fled back along the passage, leaving Deldragon standing alone where he was, stroking his mustache as he watched the guardian take another ponderous step, and then another.

The velduke seemed to reach a decision. He drew his dagger and snapped at the Aumrarr, "Get back! Yon guardian will kill you."

"If it does," Taeauna told him, her voice trembling on the edge of tears, "it does. Nothing in all Falconfar matters more than keeping this man alive right now."

Deldragon stared at her as the guardian took another slow step, and swung its sword that was longer than either of them stood tall, up and back, ready to sweep down and shear through anything less solid than an ox or a stone pillar. Then it paused again, waiting, motionless and expressionless.

The velduke stared up at it, then drew another dagger from his boot and hurried to Taeauna. "He's a Shaper, isn't he?" he asked quietly, his eyes very blue.

The Aumrarr drew in a deep breath and then let it out slowly, shuddering like a terrified child. Her face was white.

"He's *the* Shaper," she whispered. "Until he dies, and most of Falconfar with him."

Chapter Nineteen

"**W**HOLE ONCE MORE," Arlaghaun murmured contentedly, striding naked across the room with water dripping from him in a racing flood.

He had to walk briskly away, he knew, and firmly quell what he wanted to do now: take a longing look back at the pool. Its glows would be beckoning, he knew, and that was when it was at its most dangerous. If he slid back into its warm embrace, that was when memories would leave him, unregarded until he later needed them, reached for them, and found them utterly gone.

Which could well be fatal to the friendless, much-feared wizard Arlaghaun, most feared of the Dooms of Falconfar, and rightly so.

He allowed himself a tight little smile as he took down his least favorite cloak to dry himself with, wasting no time in toweling but simply donning it as if he were dry and clad, and wearing it close-clasped around him as he walked on in search of what he really wanted.

His rings and the wandwing, yes, but here on the shelf nearby, his best sword of spells, its blade winking a welcome of sparkling stars to him as he half drew it and then slid it firmly into its sheath again. The pendant that would turn aside blades, and the gorget that would blunt most spells. An unseen dagger that only his questing fingers could confirm still rode in its sheath, to wear up one sleeve, and an archer's bracer that was anything but what it appeared to be, to wear up the other. The slumbering spells it stored flickered into life at his touch.

Yes, *these* were happy to see him, these familiar magics, loyal and worthy of his trust, his closest friends in Falconfar.

Not that they had many rivals for such a title. Arlaghaun shrugged. When he wanted loving arms about him, he could compel such company; the rest of the time he was spared all of the life-wasting fripperies of pleasing friends, doing things for friends, entertaining friends… Bah! Friends! What use were such leeches, but to drain his wealth and time and power from him, stealing his freedom as surely as they stole a coin-worth here and a coin there?

He needed to gird himself with his strongest things of magic in as much haste as he could manage now, to go hunting the familiar stranger, Deldragon, and the rest.

None of them must be allowed to live, to flee this place and tell their stories of his weakness to others. For if they could draw blood so easily, and others heard of it, half the wolves in Falconfar would rush in to try their luck.

He caught up breeches and a tunic impatiently, tugging them on over his still-damp body. Swiftly, before they found one of his gates, or managed mischief... The sword, kick his feet into boots, the rings now... Haste haste haste!

Like a vengeful whirlwind he strode past the mirror that showed him his own blazing brown eyes, sharp nose, and thin lips—thinner than usual right now, by the Falcon!—and rounded a corner. Flinging the right door wide, he strode—

Almost into a pit that should not have opened in the floor at all! What the Falcon?

Arlaghaun sprang over it, took another step, and swayed back as arms folded out of the walls, propelling scything blades. Their deadly arcs shrieked sparks from his shielding-spells as he ducked his head down and went on, skidding to a stop and... Yes, the floor was opening up under his boots again!

He was under attack from all the tricks, traps, and creatures of his tower!

"But..." he spat in vain protest, as the seemingly solid stone of a nearby pillar faded away to reveal a tall, thin creature that unfolded into something that looked like a grounded bat, or a flesh-covered spider; all long, grotesque limbs ending in talons or large-fanged jaws instead of hands.

Several of those jaws grinned unpleasantly as it stalked forward to greet him, great arms stretching to clutch and rend.

* * *

AMALRYS SMILED INTO the glowing crystal with eyes that were very, very blue. "Dance, master," she murmured. "Dance as you force me to, and taste the whips, for once!"

Arlaghaun was raging silently in the depths of the crystal, loath to ruin automatons he'd created and beasts he'd captured and trained. He was beset on all sides, his brown eyes two flames of fury. His sharp-nosed face was bleeding copiously, laid open by the barbs of the krauglaur towering over him. Amalrys awakened bone scorpions and freed them from their hidden lairs, to join the fun.

At the very least, Arlaghaun was going to have to destroy a third of the tower guardians, spend most of his spells, and exhaust a good many of his enchanted items. Not to mention feeling just a touch of the pain and fear he so often and so glee-fully visited on others. There was still a chance that he might forget just where all of his traps and spell-traps were, in the frantic heart of the fray, and she had no intention of giving him any time to think or catch his breath. It was time, and far beyond time, for the oh-so-ruthless wizard Arlaghaun to sweat a little.

"Bleed, master," she purred, watching the krauglaur lurch sideways in pain and thrust its dag-gerlike tail into the heart of Arlaghaun's failing shieldings, sending him staggering and wincing in a shower of sparks. "Bleed for me."

The crystal flared so brightly she turned her head away, honey-blonde hair swirling. When she looked back, the krauglaur and one of the bone scorpions had become no more than blackened legs and smoke, and Arlaghaun was stalking angrily past them, brown eyes afire, a black wand as long as a sword in his hand.

Amalrys whistled at the sight of it. "Master has left his temper behind him," she murmured. "Time to plant some doubts, by making some of the automatons attack him in the name of Ult."

A rune flared on the wand that Amalrys recognized; she passed a hand over the crystal to make it convey sound in time to hear her master's roar.

Yet she needn't have bothered; the air itself bellowed with Arlaghaun's voice, echoing around her in the small room.

"Klammert!" he was shouting, waving his wand to carry his voice from end to end of the tower. "Klammert! To me!"

Amalrys sneered. "Such a capable master! Yes, when things turn rough, just call on another apprentice. We're all so expendable."

"SISTER," DAUNTRA SNAPPED, as Juskra started to dive again, "*must* you? We'll never reach the Doom of Galath at all if you stop to slay every last Dark Helm you see on the way!"

The fiercest of the four Aumrarr turned to deliver her reply with a glare. "I haven't slain a wizard in years, Dauntra. I'm out of practice. I judge a Doom to be worth about a thousand Dark Helms, so I'd better start killing them right now. I only see a dozen down there."

Dauntra grinned, shook her head helplessly, and waved her hand to signal Juskra to resume her dive.

When she did, her three sisters were right behind her.

* * *

THE COACH-HORN, OR whatever it was, loomed up before his eyes, revolving, fading through other, impossibly large images of itself, and washed over Rod, leaving everything golden.

A deep, rich, darkening gold that swallowed him as he plunged into it, the sound and noise of Ult Tower fading somewhere above him as he sank down, down toward… a darkness, a black speck in the distance.

That grew as he raced toward it, or it rushed up to meet him, becoming a tall black castle, a fortress with a needle-spired tower at one corner, standing in a great forest, with the trees closest around it bare-branched and dead.

He was racing through those branches now, blurringly fast, whipping past their stark dead spikes and across an open sward before reaching the dark, waiting opening of the arched front door. Then into that swallowing gloom, not slowing, but flashing across a cavernous hall full of emptiness and dust to soar up a staircase, whirling through more archways and darkness, a bewildering succession of many silent rooms, and—

To a sudden halt.

In midair, in one dark inner room, frozen, staring at the back of a tall stone seat in this heart of Yintaerghast, able to see only the arm of the aged man sitting in it.

The chair that did not turn, as an old and cultured voice from its depths said without greeting, "As you have come to suspect, Rod Everlar, the splendid forest kingdoms you dreamed of and wrote about now stand alone, embattled holds menaced by prowling beasts grown both numerous and bold, and by the creatures who serve the three Dooms."

Rod tried to speak, and found that he could not. His mouth, too, was frozen. He wished he could see the face of the old man in the chair.

"Each of these three evil, warring wizards," that dry and gently sardonic voice continued calmly, "seeks to gather the most powerful spells and enchanted items from the ruined castles of long-fallen mages and kings, and so rise to rule all Falconfar. The Dooms have grown powerful, but more than that, they have grown impatient."

Rod tried to struggle, willing himself to move, clenching his teeth and trying to buck and twist and... nothing. He could do nothing at all.

The room seemed to slowly grow darker, until he could no longer see the walls, or the chair with that arm resting along it. The voice, though it spoke gently, continued as loud and clear as ever. "Most of what is left of Falconfar is ruled by hard-bitten warriors who want to be rid of all magic and wizards. They are fighting men, to whom every problem is a reason for war. These days, in Falconfar, the holds are never far from boiling out into open bloodshed. You can prevent the slaughter, Rod Everlar."

Me?

"Falconfar needs a Lord Archwizard again. Yintaerghast calls to you for a reason. Go there, and go within, and claim your destiny."

Shit. I have a destiny. There goes my life.

"Seek not to resist it, Rod Everlar. A world depends on you, the blood of thousands upon thousands will be on your hands, if you come not to Yintaer—"

Seething, Rod found that he could suddenly speak, so he snarled angrily, "Shut up and go away! Get out of my head!"

Darkness whirled around him, swift and bitter-howling, and with it came brightness, and deafening noise... and then Rod found himself on a hard stone floor in Ult Tower, blinking up at Taeauna and Deldragon above him, as a sword as big as both of them swept down at them all.

"HO-HEY! LOOKEE HERE, Viper!" Garfist strained to reach over the width of a curved and fluted wooden chair and pluck up what had been slung over the ornately carved arm on its far side from him, almost entirely hidden in shadow. "A little beauty, by the Falcon!"

He held up a finely chased sheath with its own triple-stranded belt of fine leather. When he drew the dagger forth, its blade glowed like that of a lantern, and darkened as he slid it back home.

"Ho ho," he chuckled in delighted appreciation. "There's a fine little prize!"

"Indeed," Iskarra agreed politely, displaying a broad belt that gleamed with jewels that she'd wound twice around her tiny waist before buckling it above bony hips. "Not that I've been idle, mind you."

Garfist whistled in appreciation, and then said briskly, "Well, we'd best be on. The more we snatch, the more we'll have if we run into some apprentice or servant, and have to duel magic with magic, hey?"

"Hey," Iskarra agreed calmly. "Any such dueling will be yours to perform; I'll be fleeing into the next kingdom. For now, let us pass into the next chamber. This is a wizard's tower, remember; we're not going to get the chance to wander around here unregarded and unopposed forever, look you!"

They ducked through a curtained archway into a dimly lit room that seemed to be partly given over to storage, the rest dominated by some sort of work desk whose top was scarred with burned-in rings. "Alchemy," Iskarra judged. "Be careful what flasks you snatch, Gar; some of them may flame or burst if shaken overly much."

"If it doesn't look drinkable, I'll not be touching it."

"Gar, to you everything looks drinkable."

The fat man grinned broadly. "And I'm still here and flourishing, and larger than ever to prove it!"

Iskarra rolled her eyes and started looking along the shelves. Garfist gave her backside a friendly swat and sprang hastily back out of range, but received only a half-amused glare in return.

Still grinning, the onetime pirate turned the other way to peer around and behind the desk.

"Aha!" he cried, almost immediately. In a crock on the floor down beside the desk were a cluster of canes and scabbarded blades, leaning back against the wall and nigh-invisible in the shadow of an untidy heap of parchments. A long, slender blade caught Gar's eye, and in an instant it was in his hand. He hefted it approvingly, drew it, and whistled softly in appreciation.

"Now this," he said, turning toward Iskarra, "is a beautiful blade! Might suit you, actually…"

There was a strange wriggling under his hand, a *hiss*, and Garfist found himself holding a serpent.

As the fanged head turned in his direction, jaws spread wide, he darted his other hand at it desperately, seeking to catch hold of it behind the jaws to keep it from striking. The rest of it was coiling angrily around his arm, and there was nothing he could do about it.

Something metal flashed through the air right in front of his fingertips, severing and carrying away the snake's forked tongue and causing it to rear back in writhing pain. Garfist got the hold he wanted, and squeezed as hard as he could as he lumbered forward so he could smash the snake's head against the wall. Repeatedly, hammering it until it was bloody mush all over his knuckles, and the wildly whipping body and tail were jerking in listless, dying spasms.

"Th-thanks," he gasped to Iskarra, as she marched past him to retrieve her hurled dagger from where it had embedded itself in the wall. She let the fragment of tongue fall away from it, unheeded, as she wiped it clean on a handy tapestry.

"Employ Vipers to slay vipers," she replied, giving his backside a friendly swat with precisely the same force and aim as he'd dealt her.

Whatever response Garfist might have intended to make was lost in a sudden, loud shout that seemed to come from the very air around them, resounding through the chamber they were in and those behind it that they'd just traversed: "Klammert! Klammert! To me!"

The echoes of those words were thunderous.

Iskarra frowned. "Sounds like that wizard."

Garfist grinned. "And he sounds a little upset, no?"

"Yes." Iskarra looked swiftly about. "Gar, I'm not staying in here; this is a dead end. I want to be somewhere that has doors, or a passage, or somewhere else I can see to flee into. If he unleashes an army of guardians…"

"Then through there!" Gar suggested, pointing back through the arch and across the room they'd been in earlier. "We didn't open that door."

"Which was probably wisest," Iskarra muttered, following in his wake as the fat man lumbered across the room, hurling a chair aside.

The door swung open under his fist in silky, well-oiled silence, to reveal some sort of studying area with tomes on tables, and a staircase ascending between those tables, up into unseen levels above.

Somewhere above them, a door crashed open. In unspoken accord Iskarra and Garfist each ducked under a table on either side of the stairs.

They were still scrambling in and under when the lofty stairwell echoed with an excited, husky shout, "I come, master! I come!"

That cry was approaching rapidly, gaining volume as it grew closer, and they could hear hurrying, fast-approaching footfalls on the stairs. "My chance!" their rough-voiced owner gasped, as he came clattering down the last flight of steps. "My chance at last. Shine, Klammert, shine!"

Iskarra rolled her eyes, drew her sword, and moved to just the right place. She was hearing only one pair of hurrying boots; this Klammert dolt was alone. Whatever Gar did, she was going to…

Wait until just the right moment, and then bob up and thrust out her sword to trip this Klammert's racing feet, so that he—

Crashed face-first down the rest of the stairs at full rush, her blade clashing against Garfist's as he grinningly rose in perfect unison to do the same thing from the other side of the stairs.

With one accord they turned and watched the fat, young scraggle-bearded wizard slide heavily to a stop, his head and neck driven hard sideways by an unyielding wall.

Neither winced; they were too busy rushing forward to pluck wands and other useful-looking things from the sprawled apprentice.

Trading wide grins, their arms full of loot, Iskarra and Garfist rose to take themselves swiftly elsewhere in this gift-filled tower.

TAEAUNA AND DELDRAGON stood their ground, setting their teeth and angling their blades—for the velduke, two puny daggers—just so. They were doing so, Rod realized, as he rolled to fetch up against a pair of shapely Aumrarr ankles, to protect him.

The great sword swept down. Deldragon and Taeauna met its force and thrust desperately forward to deflect it from Rod on the floor beneath it, but the sheer force of the guardian's swing drove them both to their knees.

The sword shuddered and squealed against the tiled stone of Ult Tower's floor, right in front of them.

Rod groaned as they ended up kneeling on him. "Roll under me!" Taeauna gasped, "and get out behind us!"

The great sword came crashing in again, backhanded, and this time it drove Taeauna and the velduke before it, sweeping them away from Rod so he could roll wherever he wanted.

The great metal automaton strode right after him. It took a slow step forward and swung its sword again; if Rod hadn't kept rolling frantically back down the passage the way they'd come, that gigantic sword would have bitten into him.

With a battle-shout, Velduke Deldragon leaped into the air and crashed into the thing from behind, slashing wildly with his daggers at the places where the metal plates met, and only enchanted air was holding the lumbering construct together. White lightnings crackled briefly along both blades and then died as the nobleman fell past, and Taeauna launched herself at it in his wake, high and hard.

The guardian staggered, swayed, and then started to turn, sword preceding its arms. Deldragon trotted around to keep himself behind it, and sprang again. This time, when he landed, his dagger blade was burning with a white fire, and the armored titan seemed to be limping. Taeauna hit it again, as Rod rolled to his feet, glanced swiftly over his shoulder to make sure nothing was coming down the passage at him, and then started running uncertainly toward the fight. He couldn't just stand and watch his friends get...

The great sword sliced empty air again, the guardian turning now as fast as it could, spinning endlessly around as the velduke and the Aumrarr kept running to keep to its rearside, springing to attack it repeatedly from behind.

The helm started to turn around on the shoulders now, the better to keep them under scrutiny; Rod saw that and shouted, pointing, as he ran forward.

The velduke struck again, awakening more lightning, stabbing at the thing's left armpit. This time, when he fell away, lightnings remained, playing and crackling in the air at that joint. Taeauna darted in to hack and slice at the guardian's left knee.

The very tip of its sword caught her and hurled her away, blood spraying, but she waved Rod away and ran in at the thing again, calling to the velduke, "Wonder how many more of these the wizard has?"

"I was never good at counting," Deldragon bellowed back, slicing it again. "One... two... many!"

Rod groaned at that pun, whether it had been meant or not, as Taeauna ducked in again to hack and hew at that knee, the guardian's metal shrieking and squealing with every step now.

Deldragon crashed feet-first into the thing, causing it to sway as it tried to turn. It grounded the tip of its sword for balance and managed the turn, slicing back along its own leg as cunningly as any street fighter, and caught Taeauna tarrying at its knee just an instant too long.

This time, the great blade caught her squarely. She folded up around it with a sob as it bit deep into her and hurled her away. Deldragon shouted in anger and dared to spring at the thing's chest, kicking it high when it was half-turned one way, and leaning back to slice in another.

A metal fist dashed him brutally to the floor for his daring, but with a slow, inexorable, grinding groan of metal sliding uneasily down metal, the titan toppled over, crashing onto its side on the tiled floor and bouncing.

Staggering and moaning in pain, his face a mask of streaming blood, the velduke shuffled in beside it, slicing under the helm and then one arm as they bounced up, seeking to sever them from the body.

The blades of his daggers burned like torches. Gasping, he was forced to fling them away as the white fire reached the hilts, but the helm and that arm bounced and clanged free of the construct's body, and the guardian rose no more, its legs and remaining arm thrashing in slow, metal-shrieking futility.

Deldragon stared at Rod over the thing for a moment. Then they hissed at each other in horrified unison, "Taeauna!"

Rod could run much faster than the wounded velduke; he got to her crumpled body first.

There was blood everywhere, in a spreading pool around her, and more of it bubbled from her lips as she tried to speak, pointing up at him with a trembling, dripping finger.

Rod flung himself to his knees beside her, fumbling for his dagger, sliding in her blood and not caring. He had to—had to—

A hand that trembled almost as much as his own, but had a grip like a school workbench vise he'd once foolishly challenged, was suddenly around his wrist.

"Slaying her is hardly the mercy I was intending, man," Darendarr Deldragon snarled in Rod's ear, his hoarse voice managing to sting with both fire and ice at once.

"I'm not... Let go of me!" Rod snapped. "I'm saving her! I hope."

His voice broke on the last words, and he fought not to choke on his own tears, but something— perhaps that—made the velduke let go of him. Rod winced and sliced down, hard, then roared in pain as fire blossomed across his palm.

"Mmm, mmm," Taeauna managed to say, in her need, and together Rod and Deldragon got his bleeding hand to her lips. Rod had cut himself deeply, and there was plenty for her to drink, even if she couldn't manage to suck all that well.

Rod put his other arm around her and held his hand against her tongue; she was like the horses he'd ridden at camp, nuzzling him for sugar cubes. He nodded his thanks to Deldragon and was shocked to see clear awe on the velduke's face.

"Who..." he managed to ask, "Who's the wizard we saw? If this is his tower, what did he do to Ult?"

"That was Arlaghaun," the nobleman gasped, swiping blood off his face with one arm. "Considered by most the real ruler of Galath, and the most powerful of the Dooms."

Taeauna sat back into Rod's arm with a sigh. "My thanks, lord. I'll live. I need more, but let Darr drink of you first."

Rod nodded, but saw that his palm was almost healed. He held it out to the velduke and said, "Cut me. My knife arm is a little occupied."

"With a nice armful of Aumrarr, yes," the noble agreed, reaching to take Rod's dagger gingerly. "This is... Well, I can scarce believe it."

"He's a Shaper, Darr," Taeauna reminded the velduke, as fresh fire sliced across Rod's palm.

Then she turned her head against Rod's chest and added, "Years ago, Arlaghaun managed something magical that allowed him to conquer Ult's mind, and add it to his own. He gained this tower and all of Ult's magic and knowledge. That face we saw for a moment, when his twisted awry, was Ult."

Rod nodded. "I recognized it. So he subsumed Ult..."

He stopped at the expression he saw in Deldragon's ice-blue eyes. No one had ever regarded him with naked, deepening awe before.

Fearfully, Velduke Darendarr Deldragon started to lap at Rod's bleeding palm.

THE RING THAT let him fly over the pit traps was flickering and faltering by the time Arlaghaun reached the high hall where his spell had brought Yardryk and all the rest into the tower. He glared around, almost feeling the two brown flames of his own gaze.

The velduke, the familiar stranger, and the rest were long gone, of course, just as he would be, if he got across this room unscathed. He had spell-tomes and other magics aplenty hidden in a score of places across Falconfar. When he'd had time enough with them, whoever was turning Ult Tower against him would pay for doing so, painfully and in the end fatally. No one must defy a Doom and live.

He spent a shielding spell to shape a huge invisible cylinder of force across this last room, and sped along it.

Halfway across the hall lightnings burst from the mouth of a carved ceiling-boss, bolts crackling as they raked and then curled angrily around the cylinder of force, illuminating and clawing at it, their onslaught making it flicker and darken. They could destroy it, given long enough, but they would not be given that long enough.

Above his sharp nose, Arlaghaun's eyes narrowed; not all of his apprentices knew of that particular magic. There would be time to think on that later. Just now, he could see hidden doors swinging open in the walls of the great hall, and armored figures striding forth. Puny foes, but swift enough to reach the far end of his cylinder, deadly enough to an unprotected man, and numerous enough to overwhelm a lone foe.

Yet they were going to be too late. He was at the end of the cylinder, and willing it to swing away from himself, turning to serve as a great room-spanning ram, to thrust back those running armored automatons. That would win him time to do *thus*.

The Doom of Falconfar strode up to the tall, ornate oval mirror that adorned one wall, turned it with his fingers, just a little, until he heard the hidden catches *click*, then slid it aside to reveal the dark, narrow opening behind it. The glass had taken a long time to enchant, so he left it standing open behind him, hoping none of his guardians would shatter it while pursuing him.

Then he was hurrying down the short, curving, narrow way it had hidden, to touch the little glow on the rough stone wall at its end, and leave Ult Tower behind, through one of its most hidden gates.

"Fear my return," he murmured, the metallic shrieks of his armored sentinels shouldering against stone after him, fading as the glowing mists took him, "for I shall be exacting payment for this. And the price will be high."

* * *

"HE'S GONE!" AMALRYS spat, slamming her hand down on a defenseless crystal in a rattle of protesting chain. "Gone! Falcon take him and break him!"

She glared wildly around at the array of glowing crystals, seeing striding chaos in a dozen chambers of the tower as aroused guardians hastened to do whatever she'd goaded them to. She should calm them and return them to their resting-places, for Arlaghaun had destroyed many of them, and their own misadventures damaged more. Fires were raging in two rooms, and there was wrack and shattered ruin everywhere.

One scene caught her attention; blue eyes blazing, she thrust forward her manacled hands as if to throttle that crystal, the better to stare into its glowing depths.

She was seeing the row of gates out of the tower that all the apprentices knew of, and used often at the master's bidding, and the wide passage before them. Three intruders were sitting there together, in the lee of a riven, still-struggling armored guardian: the Galathan noble, the wingless Aumrarr, and the mysterious man who traveled with her.

As Amalrys watched, they rose, blood-spattered but seemingly unhurt, and looked to the gates.

Stop them, a voice thundered in her head, sending her reeling. *Send the guardians against them*! *Let them not escape*!

Mind whirling, drooling blood across glowing crystals—Falcon, she'd bitten her own lip, and no wonder, at that mind-thunder!—Amarlys sprang to do just as she was told, hissing commands and slapping crystals and...

Arching back and away from it all in a sudden spasm, control of her own limbs torn rudely from her, as a stronger voice than the first roared, *"LET THEM GO. HARM THEM NOT!"*

And so it was that the wizard Malraun became directly aware of the wizard Narmarkoun, in the torn and tortured depths of Amalrys's mind. Two furious mind-bolts lashed out as one, each seeking the death of the other... and each fading into futility as the ravaged mind around them exploded.

Amalrys collapsed across the array of scrying-spheres, her eyes two burnt and empty holes.

Smoke curled forth from her ears, mouth, and nostrils as her lips gasped the last thought she'd clung to: "Arlaghaun, I love you."

IN THE PASSAGE of Ult Tower where the row of gates hummed and glowed, Rod, Taeauna, and Deldragon turned at sudden rising sounds of thundering haste, to behold a host of clawed, bladed, armored things racing toward them from one end of the passage, and another, similar host hurrying from the other.

Great jaws, closing...

"Falcon!" the velduke cursed in a slow whisper, aghast, as they saw death coming for them.

Chapter Twenty

"I CAN'T BELIEVE this!" Garfist Gulkoon said delightedly, launching himself into a slide.

Shining gold coins parted in two waves before his ample chest as he came slithering down the highest of the bright, golden hills that filled the little room, in a cascade of gleaming wealth, to fetch up against the back wall beside Iskarra in a prolonged and hissing crash. "Bright fancy-tales often talk of rooms full of gold, but this is real!"

"Nice it is, to know your wits still work, Gar, if slowly," his longtime partner replied bitingly, parting the little belly and striking breasts her reunited crawlskin had given her, and raking handfuls of coins inside. "Everyone has to keep their coins somewhere, and this wizard obviously has too many to fit them all into boot heels and moneybelts. I presume you've refilled yours?"

"Uh, well… no," the fat man frowned, settling himself beside her.

"Why not? I don't recall you strolling nonchalantly out of a home you'd just plundered all that often. I *do* recall you running for your life, many a time, with breath running short and swords slicing at your backside. Not much time for picking up coins then, aye?"

"All right, aye, right ye are," Garfist growled, scooping up coins and starting to kick his boots off. Iskarra wrinkled her nose at the smell.

"Right as ye always are, Isk," he added grudgingly, scooping out a leather insole to get at the hollow heel from within. "But can ye believe this? I mean, all this gold, and he just leaves it in an unlocked, unguarded room!"

"Shows you how much gold matters to him, aye? Gar, he rules Galath, even if he doesn't wear the crown. Where the rest of us have to pay for everything, he just takes what he wants. So what's gold to him? And, look you, I'm not so sure 'tis as unguarded as all that; we walked in easily enough, but we haven't tried to get out yet."

Garfist frowned. "This is a trap, ye mean?"

"This is a wizard's tower, I mean. So 'tis full of magic, see? So every second stone in the wall could hurl itself at us or turn into a stabbing sword or fall away to let out some sort of guardian like that armor we watched come together. If you can work that with spells, it seems to me it'd be simple enough for you to make a spell that unleashes a guard like that when a gold coin from this room goes past you, except in the wizard's purse! Or just 'past you,' and he uses some secret way in and out we haven't found yet. There still seems to be fighting going on, so let's bide here a little while. Mayhap someone'll kill the wizard for us!"

"Ye really think so?"

"No, but I'm tired, Gar. Tired of running about. I wouldn't mind a little lounging around on heaps of gold. A little while, only." Iskarra stirred the coins beside her with a bony fingertip. "Something to tell your children about."

"Viper," Garfist growled, "I'm hardly likely to have any brats now, after all the years of—*hem*—dalliance afore I paired with thee, when I fathered none."

Iskarra gave him a look.

"What? I fathered no brats!"

Iskarra's look didn't change.

Garfist stared at her. "I did?"

Her nod was slow but definite. "Your panderlasses grew not round with child from the herbs they ate, not from any failing of your seed. Those merchants in Torond, and Srelkar? Their daughters didn't know about those herbs."

"So that's why they've tried to have me downed so many times, for so long," Garfist muttered. "Fart of the Falcon!"

He shook his head and added softly, "Glorking world. So I've sons and daughters, hey?"

"Daughters only, that I know of. Quite a number. They're who I send those clay jugs I make to, with all the fictitious births scratched on them. Handy custom, birthing jugs; make the bases thick enough, and you can hide a dozen-some coins in the clay, with no one the wiser."

Garfist was starting to look aghast.

"Oh, aye," Iskarra told him. "I send them all coins on your behalf, when we have any to spare."

Garfist snorted. "As if we ever do! Why, Viper mine, if we'd coins to spare, we'd not have to still be running about thieving and swindling and hacking at folk. We could be—"

"Sitting on our backsides drinking ourselves into graves, in some fine keep in the forest? Lord and lady of a handful of muddy farms? Would you really sit still for that, Gar? Longer than, say, six nights, or however long it took you to bed all the good-looking lasses, and all the rest of us females who gave you sharp words and scorn? Tell truth, now!"

"Truth?" Garfist turned a face to her that was both earnest and solemn, and said, "Isk, there was a time as I'd not have stopped running or fighting for anyone or anything. But my bones ache, now, and my wind comes hard, and betimes I dream of a Falconfar where no one spends their time stealing or swinging swords as a profession, and there's food enough for all. Wouldn't that be a world, now!"

They stared into each other's eyes for a long, silent time before his face changed, and he burst out laughing. "Nah! Never happen! Never happen!"

A sudden thunder arose all around them, the clamour and din of many large and heavy creatures moving in haste. From rooms all around them it came, a rushing in one direction that went on and on.

Looking over the heaped coins and out the door of the room, they could just see, in the passage beyond, a motley army of flying lorn, running Dark Helms, and all manner of lumbering monsters, strange metal automatons with blades or pincers for hands and wheels as well as feet. All rushing past as Iskarra and Garfist cowered down together, slowly going pale at the thought of trying to fight past so many guardians.

Coins slid noisily as they trembled, and a metal helm as large as Garfist's middle thrust through the doorway, peering.

Garfist and Iskarra closed their eyes and stayed as still as they could, barely daring to breathe. No man was ever so tall and broad, and no man snuffled so loudly and wetly as it sniffed the air for the scent of humans, but whatever sort of beast it was wore oversized armor of the same design as the Dark Helms.

It seemed like a heavy-booted, hastening eternity to the cowering pair before it snorted in disgust and was gone, joining the headlong hurry.

"Falcon spew!" Garfist hissed. "'Tis coming back, after, to seek us out. I know 'tis! It snorted just as night-wolves do, when they do that. What're we going to do?"

"Stop mewling and dig," Iskarra snapped. "Down right here, down the wall, and see if this room has a door in it like the last three did; the row of empty ones, remember? Then see where it leads."

Nodding like a fool, the panicked ex-pirate elbowed her aside and started scrabbling in the coins, clawing them aside with his hands like a child in a frenzy to recover a favorite lost and buried toy. Almost immediately he let out a shout of triumph, and dug even faster.

"Careful, idiot!" Iskarra snapped. "Bury yourself headfirst and the coins will kill you, never mind about monsters coming back for us. They slide, look you. And if that door opens into this room, forget it! We'll never thrust it open against the weight of all of these."

"Doesn't," Garfist panted, disappearing rapidly deeper amid all the sliding wealth. His ample behind and two well-worn boots were all she could still see of him now; her warnings might just as well have been given to a stone wall.

Garfist managed to do something, and the half-revealed door burst open, away from them, shoved by an enthusiastic flood of coins. With a wordless roar of triumph Gar rode them through the doorway and into—

A sudden, raging glow of magic, roiling up bright and purple.

"Oh, Falcon!" Iskarra cursed wearily. "Where now?"

The gate-magic had already swallowed Garfist, so she shrugged, raked a huge armful of coins down her bodice and grabbed two fistfuls more, kicked off, and slid after him.

Into softly falling mists of blinding brightness, through which she tumbled, so gently that not a coin strayed out past her throat, to...

A hard stone floor somewhere, where she bounced, coins bounding in all directions, some already rolling or *clink*-slithering, with Garfist rolling over ahead of her with a frown on his face, feeling for his handiest weapon.

They were in a turret room, high in a castle, with disbelieving warriors frowning at them and dropping jaws at all the gold coins that had accompanied them. Grim warriors with crossbows in their arms, standing at windows ready to use them.

A face or two among them looked a little familiar. As another handful of gold coins bounced and rolled out of the front of her ragged garb, Iskarra struggled to her feet, heart sinking, and gasped, "We come in peace! What castle is this?"

"Bowrock," one warrior snarled, bringing his bow around to aim at her breast, so close that the point of its quarrel almost grazed her slight bosom. "Are you wizards?"

"Do we look like wizards?" Garfist demanded sourly from the floor, where he'd paused, quite suddenly, at the appearance of two crossbows thrust right into his face.

"Bowrock," Iskarra groaned. "Is the siege—?"

"Well underway," a warrior told them sourly. "'Raging,' as the minstrels like to say. Look out this window, and you'll see the massed armies of Galath ranged around our walls."

Garfist and Iskarra didn't wait to do that before they began to really curse.

"WE CANNOT PREVAIL against so many!" Taeauna shouted. "Run!"

She caught hold of Rod's arm and raced to the nearest gate, moving so swiftly that even at a dead run, he found himself being dragged the last few strides.

And then shoved into the glowing mists, without pause or word; the tumult of roaring monsters, Taeauna's cry of alarm, and Deldragon's snarled defiance all chopped off abruptly.

* * *

"DIE, WITLESS WARRIOR!" Lorlarra snarled, twisting a helm in a brutal, ruthless jerk. She felt the man's neck break more than she heard it, and let go, to bat aside a slicing sword and snatch at the next Helm, her dark armor trailing a tangle of slashed straps and plates.

"Slay them, sisters!" scarred Juskra cried, from the other side of the dell. "Slay them all!"

Ambrelle soared into view, large and severe, purple-black hair streaming.

The dozen-some Dark Helms in the dell were crying out in real fear, now. As they turned to offer her raised swords and brandished spears, the youngest of the four Aumrarr swooped in from behind them. As she passed over the warriors, Dauntra rang her mace off a row of Helms as if she were at an anvil, in a great hurry to hammer a shield back into shape.

Seven Dark Helms fell as one, and Juskra whooped in delight.

LORN WERE SWOOPING, talons out. Taeauna's back was unprotected, all her will and effort bent on shoving the Shaper through the gate, so Deldragon stroked his flaxen mustache, set his jaw, and stepped in front of her, daggers raised.

"I never wanted to be a hero," he told the lorn calmly through the din of racing monsters and automatons. "I just wanted to do the right thing. For Galath, and for Falconfar. And if that makes me a hero, that's a sad thing, for it means most Falconaar don't want to do the right th—"

His words ended in a grunt of pain, as two lorn smashed aside his daggers and the arms that held them, his bones shattering, to drive their talons deep into his chest. They'd been aiming for his throat, but—Falcon, the pain!—it didn't matter much, did it? Throat or chest, he'd protected the Shaper and the Aumrarr, and now he was dying.

He hadn't expected to fall so swiftly, though. His heart seemed to thunder in his ears as Taeauna turned and saw him. Anguish twisted her face as she reached for him.

"Come!" she cried. "Lord Rod can heal you again! Come!"

But something bat-winged and long-jawed was hurtling right at her, and Deldragon fought his way to his feet, arms flailing, stumbling, and thrust her away, back into the grip of the mists. The glow belled out, reaching for her, and he managed to hiss hoarsely, instead of the gallant farewell he'd intended, "Go! Go and save Falconfar!"

Then the bat-winged monster slammed into the velduke and he was gone, one open and reaching hand the last she saw of him as she stared in horror—and the gate-magic whirled her away.

"WELL," THE HARD-FACED commander snapped, "that glorking well looked like magic to me! Empty air one moment, then the pair of you whom I've never seen before, in Bowrock, standing here the next!"

He waved his hand around the small turret room, with its cots and lanterns and chests of smoked fish and cheese. "Look you; do you see a door anywhere here, that we somehow haven't noticed yet? Or figured out a clever enough lie as to what it could possibly open into, the other side of yon wall, that isn't empty air and a long, killing fall down onto the butcher Ulkorth's back shed? Hmm? And if there's no hidden door, only one thing brought the two of you here: magic."

Iskarra put her foot down on Garfist's, hard, to quell the angry rumble that meant he was about to say something imprudent.

"Of course it was magic, lord," she said soothingly. "We deny that not. Yet not our magic. We were prisoners in Ult Tower, and managed to get free when some wizard or other attacked the Doom of Galath, and they started fighting with spells. Blowing the place apart! That's where all these coins came from; we scooped them as we ran."

"So every last one of them could have a spell on it, just waiting to go off, or could turn into a Dark Helm the moment our backs are turned," the commander snarled. The warriors crowded behind him, blocking the turret room's only door, muttered in grim agreement.

"Hold on, now!" Garfist growled, waving one hairy hand. "You—"

His words ended in an "eeep!" as Iskarra's fingers thrust daggerlike into his breeches, driving his unlaced codpiece, beneath, sharply sideways into something tender. More than one warrior of Bowrock chuckled, and a few winced.

"Lord," Iskarra said firmly, "I will be happy, if it wins us both a safe place among you—a place to die fighting here on the walls beside you, if things go darkly—to yield up all our coins into your keeping. If you put them in yonder fish-chest, and set the chest out on the walls where we can all watch it, surely if it bursts apart when the coins turn into scores of Dark Helms, they'll be hurled right off the walls, down onto the heads of those besieging you, yes?"

The commander stared at her in silent thoughtfulness, and Iskarra added firmly, "If we live through this, we can all share the gold. I promise this. Hear me, everyone? Yet, lord, heed me: if I were one of the warriors standing behind you, and I heard my commander say something about there being magic on my pay-coins, and then try to take them, I'd wonder just what else he was going to try. If you take my meaning."

She fell silent to give the warriors time to mutter. They obliged.

"So," Iskarra asked, "do we all share? Or will you try to sword us, and discover just what other magic we may have picked up in that tower?"

The man's eyes narrowed, and she added quickly, "Magic that guards us as we sleep, that will be unleashed in an instant if you harm us, and that you'll never find."

"You're pretty rauthgulling clever, aren't you?" the commander asked darkly.

"That she is," Garfist growled mournfully. "That she is."

His long-suffering tone roused more chuckles from behind the commander. Who scowled, feeling the weight of his men's regard, then lifted his jaw toward Iskarra as if it were a weapon, and snapped, "You've just told me you both carry magic that can harm us. So I'll need you both down on your backs on the floor, arms and legs spread wide. Bared swords will be held across your throats, and two men with ready bows will stand over each of you, until one of Lord Deldragon's hired wizards inspects you. You agree to this, now, or I'll have my men empty their bows into you both, and all the gold will be ours regardless."

"Inspect us for what?"

"What magic you're carrying, and if you're wizards yourselves."

"And if we're not? Is my offer then acceptable? Your men are listening."

The commander stared into her eyes, and she stared right back into his, as silence fell and deepened. Not a man spoke, or even coughed.

"Your offer is acceptable," the commander snapped, at last, and there was a brief, hastily stifled cheer from behind him.

"Then," Iskarra said sharply, her voice snatching all eyes and attention back onto her, "we shall do as you say."

She calmly unlaced her bodice and pulled her clothing down, baring herself to her waist as a shower of gold coins bounced around her feet, and warriors of Bowrock stared and swallowed.

Her arms and hands were bony, wrinkled, and age-spotted, but her torso and breasts were smooth, unblemished, and magnificent. And aside from an assortment of daggers sheathed here and there on her arms which she slowly and almost contemptuously drew and flung to the floor out of reach, one by one, it was clear she wasn't hiding more coins, or any visible magic, anywhere above her waist.

Iskarra gave the watching warriors a pleasant smile, and said, "Give them the gold, Gar. All of it. Yes, what's in your boots, too."

He stared at her, and then started emptying. More gold cascaded. Then more.

And then, as the watching warriors started to chuckle, even more. By the time he tipped out his codpiece, they were roaring with laughter.

Iskarra watched as her stout partner hopped about, emptying one boot and then the other. He managed to wink in the midst of it all, so briefly she was sure only she saw, to signal to her that he remembered the huge weight of coins still hidden inside her false, crawlskin-endowed belly and breasts. She smiled, and when he was done looked at the commander, hands on hips.

"If you'd like to blindfold us both, so we can't see anyone to cast spells," she said sweetly, "I'll lie down here and taste that swordblade, unless you'd like to examine me further for coins and magic?" She started to undo the belt of her breeches.

Face flaming, the commander said quickly, "That won't be necessary. None of it. Get dressed, woman."

"My name," Iskarra said softly, "is Iskarra. Lord Deldragon, who knows me personally, can vouch for that."

It was the commander's turn to wince.

ONLY A HANDFUL of Dark Helms were still standing; the dell was strewn with the sprawled dead and the downed, faintly groaning wounded. The four Aumrarr were flying around them in a gleeful ring, as they stood huddled back-to-back, swords raised grimly, knowing they were about to die.

"You!" one of them spat at Dauntra, as she swooped close. "Without your wings, you little minx, you'd be on your back in my bed, moaning for my loving! And I'd have my hands around those magnificent—"

"These?" the stunningly beautiful Aumrarr asked eagerly, yielding promise in her large, dancing brown eyes. Striking his sword aside with her own, Dauntra rammed her bosom into his helm, slamming him back against his fellows and sending their reaching blades wild as they fought for balance.

"Well, why don't you?" She caught hold of his helm, planted her boots on two adjacent shoulders, and beat her wings once, good and hard, soaring up into the air with the terrified man shrieking as his own weight slowly tore hair and then an ear off his head, as the helm came off. He caught hold of it with desperately clawing fingers an instant before he would have fallen back atop all the waving swords of his fellows.

"All talk and swagger," Dauntra sneered, flying higher. "Just like all the rest of—"

Something struck her, then. Something silent, that came racing through the air like a vast, invisible wave. Magic, a great unleashing, from... she turned toward where that wave had come from, catching the eyes of Lorlarra, Juskra, and Ambrelle, as they all flew up from the Dark Helms they'd been slaughtering. They, too, turned in the direction of... What lay in just that direction from here?

Ult Tower. Arlaghaun's, now; that lone, distant elder fortress.

"Something's happening, sisters," Dauntra said unnecessarily.

"Something big," Juskra agreed, scratching at her bandages. "I wonder if Oh-So-High-And-Mighty Arlaghaun's grip on Galath is slipping, at last?"

"Come on, sisters mine," Ambrelle said severely, tossing back her purple-black hair as she beat her powerful wings, soaring upwards.

The three younger Aumrarr mounted up into the sky in her wake, the Dark Helm in Dauntra's grip yelling in fear as he saw how high up he was being taken.

"Oh," she said to him, gently and courteously, "I am sorry."

And she let go.

His dying scream hadn't a chance even to get properly going before it ended in a heavy *thud*. On rocks. Ah, well. It was high time Dark Helms in Galath had a bad day. Or six.

Grinning ruthlessly, the four Aumrarr shook out their wings, put their faces into the wind, and streaked off across the sky.

As SHE FELL out of bright mists, there came a joyful cry from near at hand.

"Tay!" Rod greeted her joyfully, embracing her. "Where's Deldragon?"

Arms tightening around him, Taeauna burst into tears.

"Oh," Rod said, feeling suddenly sick. "Oh, God."

Awkwardly, he tried to comfort her, to stroke her back, only to bump his hands against the stumps of her wings and abruptly abandon the attempt in confusion.

Taeauna's grip was so tight he could barely breathe, and when she rocked back and forth in her sobbings, she took him off his feet on the "back" and slammed him back down on the "forth" as effortlessly as if he'd been one of those cardboard cutouts of people set up in a video rental store. Jesus. Jesus shitting Christ. Or, glorking, wasn't that what Falconaar said? Jesus glorking Christ?

Glorking, indeed. There was a tall black castle right behind Taeauna. Rod lifted his head to look. In a forest, with the nearest trees all dead and bare.

Oh, shit.

A huge, square, massive fortress of stone, with four bulging turrets at its corners, one of them soaring above the rest like a huge black rocket ship. It ended in a needle-pointed spire high, high above them, looking from down here as if it were scratching the tattered white clouds.

"Yintaerghast," he said quietly, and felt Taeauna stiffen in his arms and then turn in his grasp like an angry whirlwind, to stare and then start to curse.

Which was when the air around them glowed, sang, and formed a lattice-work of what looked like massive prison bars, or some sort of large cage for elephants or dragons or the like, and...

Was gone again, the singing dwindling into wild, high shrieking, like someone slashing harp strings with a sword.

Not too far away, someone else spat out an astonished curse.

Rod and Taeauna turned to see who, in time to see the wizard Arlaghaun finish a second spell with a triumphant flourish, his brown eyes blazing, and point at both of them.

Aside from a brief crackling in the air around those two pointing fingers, nothing happened.

"So..." Arlaghaun hissed slowly, glaring at Rod. "You must be the Dark Lord! Well, there's another way..."

The brown flames of his eyes seemed to glow brighter and grow larger. Taeauna's mouth tightened and she drew back her sword to hurl, but Rod grabbed at her wrist. "We'll be needing that. What if he turns it back at us like some sort of arrow?"

The crackling seemed to be inside Rod's head this time, those two angry brown eyes hanging in the middle of his head like glaring dagger-points. Infuriating, violating, but... fading now, into futility.

"Lord Rod?" Taeauna murmured, still clinging to him.

"Yes?"

"Ah. You're still 'you.' Another spell fails."

The anger on Arlaghaun's sharp-nosed face was open and ugly, now.

"So much for ruling your mind," Taeauna said in Rod's ear. "It seems, in Falconfar, you are immune to most—perhaps all—magic."

"So it seems, indeed," the wizard sneered, and waved his hand.

Behind him, lorn by the hundreds rose from the trees. Without pause, all of them swooped at Rod and Taeauna.

The Aumrarr spun around, tugging Rod with her. "Into the castle!" she cried. "It's our only escape!"

Rod needed no convincing. He put down his head and sprinted across the open sward, managing to run almost as fast as Taeauna.

A shadow fell across them, her shapely behind in front of his right arm turned and flexed, her sword swept up, and he swerved and slowed, to give her room to twist around and hack lorn.

"Keep running!" she shouted into his face, then grunted fiercely as her blade cut deep into a swooping lorn.

Rod heard them crash to the ground together and roll. He kept running.

Behind him Taeauna sobbed for breath, amid the wet and meaty sounds of her sword hacking flesh. When she cursed, a breath later, she sounded closer. Then, abruptly, Rod was plunging through the open castle door into cold gloom beyond.

His racing feet slipped on debris, leaving Rod gliding helplessly across a slick marble floor. Was it gravel? Fallen plaster? Did they have plaster in Falconfar? He slid for a long way before his right foot went out from under him and he crashed down on his backside, coming to a slow and groaning stop amid much dust.

"Tay?" he coughed, wincing, as he rolled over and up to his knees. "Taeauna?"

He was kneeling in the dimness of a huge, high hall, the open door a window of bright sunlight, and he was alone.

"Taeauna?" he fought his way to his feet and into a slipping, arm-flailing run, back across the great open expanse of rubble-strewn marble to the door.

To blink at the sunlight, and no sign of Taeauna at all, only the wizard Arlaghaun standing triumphantly, arms folded across his chest, with a sky full of wheeling lorn behind him.

Lorn that came rushing down at Rod, diving with talons spread, six—no, seven—no, nine—converging on him.

In sudden terror he tugged at the half-open door, trying to get it closed before they plunged through.

It was thrice his height, as thick as he was, and looked as if it hadn't moved in centuries. It moved not for him, feeling as firm as fused stone against his struggles.

Lorn loomed, sunlight blotted out behind them, and Rod turned and fled, tears stinging his eyes.

Tay was gone, taken or torn apart, and he was alone.

Alone in Falconfar, its so-called Dark Lord... Powerless, knowing nothing, and fleeing alone into a haunted castle.

He was not going up the stairs, not going to meet that faceless old man in the chair. He refused to be herded, or to be slain, or to wind up in some chamber with a scepter in a stone that he was supposed to draw forth and hear angelic choirs singing that he was the new Lord Archwizard; or worse yet, the old, old one returned! No, he would not allow any of this to happen!

Rod ran past the stairs going up, and another flight that went down into utter darkness, and through archways into a labyrinth of crumbling, once-grand chambers beyond.

He wasn't quite sure why castles always had these high, echoing rooms, big and cold and seemingly used for nothing more than rushing through like some airport or train station, but they always did.

This wasn't his castle, not something he'd created or written about, but it had been in one of the first Holdoncorp games, back when he eagerly read and reviewed everything they sent him. In the early days, when they'd still bothered to send him things for review. Before he'd realized they ignored his comments and criticisms, despite the contract. Back then, the Dark Helms had been skeletons in black armor, commanded by animated empty suits of black plate armor that had a few showy, menacing magical powers.

In that early game, Yintaerghast had been a vast ruin for players to send their characters into, exploring. They were supposed to kill a few monsters, find a little treasure, and... Oh, yes, try to find a way back out again.

Well, that wouldn't be a problem for him; there was always the front door just a few rooms back that way, standing stuck open, so... Wait a bit, though, there'd been something more.

Something that would explain why no lorn were clawing at him right now, or flying all around these rooms like great bats, and why Arlaghaun wasn't standing gloating over him right now, too.

Rod stopped in a hall where ornate, high-backed loungers had collapsed into heaps of gilded half-wreckage and dust. He had to think, and try to stop panting, and try very hard not to cry.

If Taeauna was gone, she was gone, and there was nothing he could do about it. There was nothing left for him to care about.

There was nothing left for him at all.

He might just as well draw the dagger at his belt and kill himself. If he could, that is, since he was in a world where he healed in mere moments.

Rod shrugged. He'd never liked pain, and lying there enduring it seemed pointless. Not to mention something that Taeauna would have been openly contemptuous of. God, he missed her tart comments and angry snaps at him!

He tried to laugh at that, but it came out as sobs. His hand went to his dagger.

THE WIZARD WITH the blazing brown eyes pointed his sharp nose up into the sky and raised his voice, just a little. "You will stay. If he seeks to come out, keep hidden and let him get a little way from the castle, so he can't run back in time. Then pounce and capture him. If he gets away, all of you—mark me well: every last lorn now here—will pay for it with your lives, and your deaths will not be swift."

Arlaghaun waited for the lorn encircling him to bow their heads in assent. When all of them had, including the oldest and largest, who commanded the rest, he turned, took a step, and vanished.

Lorn hissed in hatred and distaste, and glared at the spot where he'd stood.

"Patience," the oldest, most battered one—the one whose hide was going purple and not just mottled brown—said to the others, as he turned away. "There will come a day. Oh, yes, there will come a day…"

WHEN HE BECAME aware of the dark, chill room around him again, Rod Everlar knew a lot of time had passed.

He felt… empty. Cried out. He lifted his head to look around, and was instantly aware of two things: something had moved, somewhere in the room, and he remembered something else about Yintaerghast; some Holdoncorp designer who wanted a test of brawn and wits had come up with a story for the castle that made it a prison and robbed those inside of magic.

It was shrouded, or shielded, in some mighty spell laid by a long-dead wizard that twisted the minds of all living creatures who entered the castle. That'd be this Lorontar mage Tay had mentioned; was he the man in the chair, upstairs?

It stripped away all their knowledge of magic: forever? Or just while they were inside? Well, either way, that'd be why Arlaghaun, and all wizards, would dare not enter...

Yes! It took away any magic at work on anyone, so wizards couldn't magically force some poor servant critter inside and expect it to go on obeying them the moment it was through the door.

Then there was that last bit, the prison bit. Well, he could test that himself, right now. All he had to do was find a window.

Apparently, the spell would make all the castle's empty windows look out into a swirling void that didn't allow anyone to leap, fall, fly, or climb out; those who tried just got thrust right back in. Or would that work on him, the immune Dark Lord?

If it did, he might be able to kill himself here, after all.

He'd been turning on his heel, hand on dagger and peering hard, all the time he'd been thinking these thoughts. Seeking any sign of whatever it was that had moved. He was still looking.

He'd looked up, too—twice—in case something was lurking overhead, but the lofty stone ceiling offered nothing more than a peeled, ruined painting and inky black tatters of cobwebs. Motionless tatters.

Rod drew his dagger and started to prowl the room, walking behind the heaps of ruined furniture. Whatever he'd seen, or thought he'd seen, it had been higher than floor level, but of course someone could crouch down.

Or some *thing*…

Something moved again, in the corner of his eye. Rod whirled around to peer at the shadows there. Nothing.

Angrily he strode in that direction, then abruptly spun all the way around again, hoping to catch something, even if only fleetingly, at the edge of his vision, again.

Again, nothing. There was nothing but the darkness.

Yet he didn't feel alone in the room. He looked around again, walking into the two darkest corners, one after the other, and finding… nothing.

So, was he keeping company with something invisible? Either a monster or some ghost of the castle or… Well, who'd just gone missing?

"Taeauna?" he asked, trying to make his voice sound calm, as if he were just casually interested. And certainly not afraid.

There was, of course, no reply.

Shit, he could stand here forever! Enough of this foolishness. Stride out of the room, then turn to see if anything followed. If it didn't, all the better, and if it did, he'd at least be facing it and could get this over with. Now, there was the arch he'd come in through, so wide it took up almost one entire side of the room. There was a smaller arch in yonder wall, and a closed door in the center of that wall; the first normal-sized door he'd seen in Yintaerghast thus far.

So, which?

Back out the way he'd come, for now, Rod decided instantly. He'd best look around all the large, open rooms on the ground floor first, before he started going through any doors, and ended up lost.

There was no hurry, after all. He wasn't going anywhere fast, because he didn't dare step out into the forest at night, and by day, well, there were no doubt lots of lorn perched in the trees all around, ordered to stay and wait for him to emerge.

Rod cast a last look all around the room and made for the door, dagger held ready. If there was one thing he had left to do, it was to find that wizard and kill him for what he'd done to Taeauna. It wasn't as if somehow he could find his way back home, to the real world, since he hadn't the faintest flipping idea of how to even begin doing that.

It had to be him, this Arlaghaun the Doom of Galath, who'd done something to Tay.

Rod got to the door, whirled around one last time to look at the usual nothing, and froze.

There was something, all right. About a dozen feet away from him, and drifting silently closer.

A black cloak, with a cowl, hanging in the air in the shape it would have if someone were wearing it, the cloak on their shoulders and their head looking right at him as they wore that hood up over it.

Rod swallowed. Icy fear? Oh, yeah...

He knew the dagger in his hand was trembling as he raised it, point thrust right at the thing.

Its slow, steady drift toward him didn't slow.

"W–who are you?" Rod asked, trying to sound calm but firm. Even in his own ears, his voice came out like a young child's high, shrill squeak.

There was no reply from the empty cowl, as the silent thing moved menacingly forward, rising a little as if to engulf him.

Chapter Twenty-One

IT WAS TALLER than he was, now, and as dark as deep night, looming over him, and flowing soundlessly forward. Swift-rising fear took Rod a step back from it, and then another, before he swallowed and deliberately stepped forward again. Right into it.

He felt a moment of intense chill. Then there was a sort of sigh, all around him, and he was blinking around at the gloom of the chamber again. The cloak was... gone.

Rod whirled around to see if it had just passed through him, like the sort of ghost that lurked in older movies. In doing so—to find that it hadn't—his gaze dropped down long enough to see the last of its darkness fading away into nothingness, in a ring around his legs.

He shivered again. Gods, he felt cold.

Had it… gone into him? Infused him, somehow, with its essence, to poison him or eat him away, or control or just wreck his mind?

Dared he even think such thoughts, if he was the Shaper of Falconfar? Did his thinking of something make it real, or at least more likely?

"Oh, shit," he snapped, exasperated. No Taeauna was standing nigh his shoulder to answer him.

And suddenly he was in tears all over again.

ULT TOWER LOOMED up, vast and tall. Though they were heading for its upper windows, they did not expect to find it unguarded.

They were not disappointed.

The lorn burst out of the window at them, talons reaching for Dauntra's head. The Aumrarr caught hold of one of its feet, then folded her wings upwards and together, becoming in an instant a teardrop plunging to earth. The lorn was jerked helplessly after her. Then Juskra caught hold of its other foot as she swooped past, folding the creature over onto its back. Lorlarra and Ambrelle's boots struck the lorn in this awkward position, diving as fast as they could.

The lorn's spine shattered even before its body was broken around the lip of another, lower window. Dauntra flung it aside so her sisters could streak past, into Ult Tower.

"Ah, sisters," Juskra cried, "it feels good to abandon skulking and running for a bit! 'Tis time to let the wizards worry!"

"Let us hope, sisters mine," Ambrelle called back, as the four Aumrarr burst through the deserted room and out into a passage beyond, "that they worry for more than a fleeting moment or two, this time. I want to be more than a mere annoyance, casually slain."

"Now that's an epitaph," Lorlarra commented, as they parted to swoop past a stiffly striding titan of spell-animated armor on either side. Its arms ended in bristling fists of bared swords affixed at all angles, but it was too slow to harm them.

The Aumrarr ducked under the arms of another lurching automaton to glide past a grisly assemblage of undead human parts; two naked and rotting men joined together by a long metal frame from which sprouted many waving human arms that were far too short to clutch at the passing sisters.

They ascended to the ceiling again in a flurry of beating wings, slowing as they came out into one of the cavernous halls and found it full of restless guardians and tower creatures.

"Ult had a far-viewing glass in one of the halls," Juskra mused, peering down at some wildly lurching constructions of mismatched limbs and heads that were probably abandoned experiments. "Do you think it's still there?"

"Worth looking for," Ambrelle replied, brushing back an errant lock of her long purple-black hair. "Finding it will save us having to go through room after room, which will take forever, by the Falcon, if all Arlaghaun's creatures are out and active, like these."

A group of lorn came streaking out of a high gallery to pounce on the four Aumrarr and were met with laughter, ready swords, and hard-swung maces.

The first lorn to taste that greeting tumbled toward the floor with a shredded wing, and was diced bloodily by a reaching automaton before it could strike the tiles.

Another two lorn were wounded only slightly, but flapped hastily away, freeing Dauntra and Juskra to strike from behind at the lorn fighting their sisters. Aumrarr blades promptly met in writhing lorn bodies; what fell into the clutches of the waiting automatons this time was dying or dead.

Triumphantly the Aumrarr flew on, ducking around the tallest guardians, until they came out into a hall where Dauntra pointed and said, "There, sisters!"

The mirror, taller than a man, was affixed to a wall on some sort of frame in which it had been slid sideways, to reveal a dark and narrow opening it obviously concealed much of the time.

Scenes were moving in the depths of the glass. The Aumrarr circled, swooped, hacked, and soared aloft again, not tarrying to fight, but wounding and rushing back up out of reach, until they'd sworded guardians enough to clear one end of the hall and win themselves some time to look into the mirror.

They beheld armies massed in front of soaring fortress walls, stones and fiery trees soaring into the air.

"Bowrock! Under siege!" Ambrelle snapped.

"Galath goes on tearing itself apart," Lorlarra said bitterly, trailing the straps and shards of most of her once-magnificent dark armor. "Let's look at other places and things, sisters, before we go racing off to join any frays."

"You look first," Dauntra told her, turning to face the rest of the hall, and the guardians creeping back toward them. "Juskra and I will buy you the time. Cry us out the best entertainments."

"Doom slaying Doom, kingdoms swept away by devouring dragons, that sort of thing?"

"That sort of thing," Juskra agreed, burying her sword-hilt deep in the face of a menacingly hissing darkjaws. "I trust your judgement, sisters. In Falconfar, these days, I trust nothing more."

THERE WERE, ROD Everlar thought, no tears left in him.

Shivering, for he could not seem to shake this bone-deep cold, he wandered through the deserted castle. Or rather, not quite deserted castle. Phantoms glided silently in dark and distant places, but tarried not to confront him. Fear rose in him from time to time at what he saw, like fingers of bone at his throat, but somehow it didn't seem to matter as much, with Deldragon and Taeauna both gone. Nothing mattered as much.

He kept walking, even into the darkest places where bones crunched into dust underfoot.

If there were stairs that still led down, he could not find them. The stairs by the entry hall went down, turning at a landing, but three steps below it ended in a great fall of stone that had human skulls in it.

Rod suspected there was a narrower down bound staircase at the back of the kitchens, but the ceilings of three rooms had fallen in there, and he could not fit between the precariously jammed fallen stone arches to clamber farther in.

Besides, something was waiting for him in the second room, beyond the tangle of interlocked stone: two eyeballs that floated in the air above a skeletal jawbone and two hands. He could see no skull, nor any other bones, but the floating remains watched him, turning to keep him in view as he struggled through the rubble.

So at last he went where he'd always known he would go: up the grand stairs to the upper floors of the castle. The light grew as he ascended, and he found nothing more sinister on the steps than a line of rusted flakes that had once been a sword; a sword that had not been there in the vision the golden horn had brought upon him, of the old man in the chair whose face he'd never managed to see.

In that vision, Rod's travel up the stairs and through the rooms had been a lightning-swift, flying whirlwind. This time he trudged, but found every room just where and how it had been in the vision.

Instead of turning into the darker rooms that would lead to where the old man had been sitting, Rod turned the other way, into a large chamber whose windows opened onto a view of not the forest outside or waiting lorn, but a bright void of milky white mists. The room was empty except for something dark—a discarded cloak, perhaps—lying on the floor in a distant corner.

There were doors farther along the wall he'd come in through. He headed for them and halfway there, became aware that the thing in the corner was stirring.

He stopped and watched it come for him, flowing over the floor. It didn't seem to be moving fast enough that he couldn't outrun it, but then, he had no idea just how swiftly it could travel. It looked pinkish-white, where it wasn't covered in dark green blotches of what looked like mold. There was something familiar about its shape…

It was about three of his strides away when he saw hairs bristling in it, and knew what it was: a boneless, empty human skin.

Face down, arms trailing behind, rippling as it crept along the stone floor. Somehow he thought it might be female, but how could one be sure?

Rod knew one thing, though, as he stepped sharply to one side and it veered to follow. He didn't like the look of it at all.

His dagger might shred it, but what then? To cut it he'd have to almost touch it, and what sort of horrid life-drinking, poisoning, flesh-melting things could it do to him, if it sprang up his wrist and touched him?

Rod broke into a sudden run, around behind it and toward that row of doors. Would it turn to follow, or just reverse its flow, or fold over on top of itself to come after him—and how fast?

It half-turned, and then folded over, quickly. Not so quickly that it caught up to him, though. Rod hauled open the first door, saw nothing perilous in the little chamber beyond, and that at least two more, larger rooms opened out beyond the little chamber, and was through the door with it slammed behind him in a few lightning-swift instants.

He was panting a little as he stood in the sudden silence, listening and peering. Nothing moved, and he could hear nothing, certainly nothing slithering on the other side of the door.

So he walked carefully around the walls of the little chamber, to the open archway in its far wall, where it gave into a much larger chamber, and stopped to listen and look again.

Several closed doors and an archway opening into a smaller, darker room could be seen. A gallery or balcony stood to his left, looking down into an open area to his right that held only a throne. A throne with a cloak draped over it.

Rod approached it very cautiously. This looked very much like a waiting trap, and what better place to put a trap for fools, but a throne?

There was no way he was going to sit on that stone seat, but he wanted to get a look at it. Was anything written on it? To look properly, he'd have to move the cloak, and *was* it a cloak? Or was it another shed "seeking skin," like the thing that was lurking just a closed door away?

Rod looked up, in search of ropes or wires or seams in the stone that looked like they might herald a stone block that would crash down. Nothing that looked suspicious, beyond a few cobwebs in the corners. Then he peered around at the walls, looking for holes that might spit darts. None that he could see.

Then he shivered again. Jesus glorking Falconfar on a stick, he was cold! There was something about this place that made the chill creep into your very bones… Or was this something done by that ghostly cloak, melting into him, somehow lurking inside him now?

And what did it matter now, anyway, without Taeauna?

In sudden brisk impatience, Rod strode to the throne, and from behind the seat used his dagger to pluck up the cloak and whisk it away.

Nothing happened. Nothing tumbled out of the cloak as it fell onto the floor, and there didn't seem to be anything unusual about the garment itself; just heavy wool, dyed dark red and lined with dark brown linen of some sort. It was just a cloak, with no hood nor pockets or armholes or even a stitched yoke; just a rectangle of thick, warm fabric with lacings joining two corners to bind them together across the breast of a wearer.

Warm. Oh, how he wanted to be warm. Rod dug his fingers into the fabric, pinching and flexing it with cruel force. It seemed to be mere cloth, not any sort of lurking creature; not that he cared much if it were.

He shrugged, swung the cloak over his shoulders, and laced it up, settling it around himself. It swished around his legs, and he couldn't resist striking a pose.

It didn't smell of mold or feel like it was about to crumble or tear; it felt solid and trustworthy and warm.

Reassuring, even. Rod took a few strides and nodded. Somehow, with the cloak swirling around him, he felt capable. Confident. Right.

Yes, and he should be heading this way, to the blank and empty back wall a good four paces behind the throne. The chill was gone, and he could feel himself relaxing, the tightness in his fingers and shoulders and back, from hunching against the cold, now slipping away...

Yes, here. Why hadn't he known it or felt it before? The wall cracked soundlessly at his approach, parting in a hitherto completely hidden door, that opened inward into darkness beyond, with a strange, brief sound like a jangle of strummed harp strings.

A stray thought told him he shouldn't stride quite so boldly forward into such proverbial pitch darkness, and reminded him that he had in fact been exploring Yintaerghast far more cautiously just a few rooms ago, but somehow, now, it didn't matter. This was the right thing to be doing, the fitting thing, he was where he belonged, expected...

That brought him up short, blinking in the impenetrable darkness. Expected? By whom?

As if that thought had been a cue, the darkness rolled back as if it was a curtain, to leave him staring at... a stool and beyond it a slope-topped writing desk of some glossy-polished wood. There was a huge book open on the desk, a row of glowing inks of various hues in dark metal florette holders set into the top edge of the desk in a row, and... three magnificent quill pens, hovering in a silent, immobile line in midair.

His pens, something was telling him. So this must be his place to be a Shaper. At last, here in front of him.

With no Taeauna to tell, anymore.

His throat closed again, tears rose in him... And in a sudden fury of madly-swirling cloak he was seated at the desk and impatiently plucking one of the quills out of the air, stabbing it into ink, and drawing.

He tried to draw Taeauna's face, tried to capture her staring up at him out of the page, but somehow the faces—he drew dozens across the two blank facing pages, in mad haste, exasperation rising in him—were all real, and vivid, and even seemed to move slightly, whenever he looked away from them. But they were other people's faces. People he'd never seen before. Beautiful women, even Aumrarr, but not Taeauna.

In baffled rage he threw up his hands, drew a big-nosed, bearded dwarf with Norse-like sword and helm and armor, and then put a stone arch behind him, with tentacles reaching through it. Now, his dwarf would need a mace, a dagger or three, and so Rod swiftly drew sheaths belted here, there, and everywhere, straps crisscrossing, and added a shield. With a blazon on it, of course. Hmm, two crossed hammers...

God, he was a lousy artist. What was he trying to do, entertain himself with bad cartoons? Writing was what he did, and writing was what he was good at. Wherefore...

"Korgrath Foehammer was an even surlier dwarf than most," he scribbled, "and this day was not a good day. But then, days for Korgrath seldom were..."

THE FRESH SENTINEL trudging forward to begin the next watch nodded to the gruff old dwarf he was replacing. "Anything?"

"Naught."

"Korgrath in a temper?"

"No more'n usual," came the very dry reply, delivered with a knowing look as Auld Orvran lurched on his way. "He might not gnaw your nose off, if you keep to yerself an' far enough away."

Baurgar grinned and went on out through the arch, to join Korgrath Foehammer on the high ledge. It would have been astonishing news if

Korgrath wasn't snarly and surly. Korgrath lived his life out in a standing bad temper.

"I'm here," he said in polite greeting, coming around to where Korgrath could see him.

"Get out of my watch-view, dolt," the Foehammer snarled, eyes still fixed on the endless, unchanging vista of brown, needle-sharp mountains thrusting up into the sky. Not even greatfangs were witless enough to come near Stonebold, anymore. "Hard to watch for foes with you standing in the way like a brainless heap of meat."

Baurgar had already started moving aside, silently mouthing Korgrath's all-too-familiar words as they were uttered, until his gaze happened to fall on the Foehammer's shield.

"New blazon, Foehammer?" he asked, startled. This was a change, and Korgrath never changed. The shield looked the same as it had yestereve; the same dents, the same scratches. The arms painted on it were neither new nor bright, yet they were different: a pick shattering a stone in two had become two crossed hammers.

"What foolishness speak you?" Korgrath snapped, glaring at Baurgar and then down at the shield. "I've not..."

He fell silent, staring open-mouthed at the crossed hammers.

Then he looked up at Baurgar again, an unfriendly glare that became something far more dangerous as his eyes narrowed under bristling brows. "Have you dared to work magic here? On watch, before the very gates of Stonebold?"

Baurgar stared steadily back at him. "As if I can afford any magic, let alone wield it! No doing of mine, Foehammer. On the name of my house I swear this."

Korgrath stared into his face for a long and silent time, and then nodded, slowly.

Then he looked down at his shield again. "I believe you. Which means a thing more: I have to say I know not at all how these crossed hammers came to be here."

Then he went pale, and Baurgar went pale with him, as the same thought came to them.

What came out of Korgrath's jaws was a stream of low, fierce, and biting oaths.

What came out of Baurgar's mouth was the murmur, "There's a Shaper at work in Falconfar."

KLAMMERT CLAWED HIS way up a wall that seemed to be leaning this way and then that, and allowed himself a groan. "Master?" he mumbled. Arlaghaun had been summoning him...

There was a splitting agony in his head, and sharp stabbing pains in his neck. He groaned again, and clung to the wall. There were some healing magics hidden in a room down *that* hall, if he was remembering rightly.

Into every life, a little pain must fall. Why, by the Falcon, did it fall into his so abundantly?

ROD'S STOMACH GROWLED suddenly, reminding him of its emptiness. Hmm. How long had he been sitting here?

He looked down at the quill in his hand, and the words he'd just written: "The storm that swept now across the Sea of Storms was a lightning bolt-hurling chaos of flashing, glowing skies and a roiling of waves like so many uncounted storms before it…"

He sat back from the book and blinked. Where was he, anyway? How had he come here?"

He blinked again, and when he next became aware of himself, he was writing something else: "There was a beast that hunted lorn, a great black leathery thing of bat-wings and ripping jaws and three-taloned feet, but for centuries it had slept in its own shape, one more ornamental gargoyle among the rest, on the battlements of Dorn Keep. Now it was awake, and great was its hunger…"

THE CLOUD OF lorn streaked toward Bowrock, eager to rage along its battlements plucking off heads and disembowelling knights and armsmen. They hissed jests and sneering comments about the oh-so-proud, yet oh-so-feeble warriors who served Deldragon, and taunted that they wouldn't still be alive to do so by sunset. None of them bothered to fly rearguard or watch with any care; dragons were so rare as to be nigh-mythical, these days, and besides were far too large to approach unseen, and nothing else in all Fal-confar was left to defy lorn this high in the skies.

Wherefore the grotesque dark, sinuous thing of many jaws, many pairs of bat-wings, and many claws, all joined together in a disorderly string of bobbing limbs and muscled bulk, rose unregarded from among the dark and endless trees to ascend and follow the lorn. It looked too ungainly to stay aloft, let alone manage any speed through the skies, but its wings carried it with uncanny speed up above the cloud of lorn and into their bright-blinded spot, where looking back would mean gazing into the sun.

And then it really started to fly.

The dozen or so lorn at the rear vanished into those jaws without fuss or outcry. By the time the rest noticed something was amiss, and wheeled to see what it was and give battle, a second dozen had been devoured.

Learning what little they could do against this strange nightmare of a foe cost the lorn a score of their remaining strength.

Learning that they couldn't flee from it by outflying it cost the rest of the lorn their lives.

But then, truly wise lorn have always been a rarity.

So THIS WASN'T godhood, this being a Shaper. Rod Everlar didn't sit down and deliberately decide to write that Arlaghaun's hands, manhood, and head all abruptly fell off, and then sit and watch some great magic instantly make that happen. Whatever he wrote seemed to pour out of him without his having any conscious control over it at all.

So what would happen when he dreamed? Did he reshape Falconfar, or did it whisper instructions to him?

Glorking bloody sh…

Rod shook his head in exasperation, and flipped back through the book. There were all his sketches—heads of beautiful women he didn't even know, though he supposed they were now walking around Falconfar or perhaps even rising from tombs they'd been sadly put in—and the dwarf by the archway, and then page after page of scribbled text. Eight pages in all, so little of the blank book that it scarcely showed as a page-thickness, around the edges.

Rod shook his head and yawned. Whoa, did he feel tired, suddenly. No longer cold, not at all, but bone-weary. So was it all the running and fighting? The grieving? Or was Shaping inherently exhausting?

Or had he just been sitting here for a long, long time, and didn't know it? The moment he'd sat down, a faint, warm glow had started to occur in the air, like lantern light, and it was still there above him, the air amber to golden, as he glanced at it.

He caught himself yawning again, and shook his head. This would never do; if he was going to fall asleep, he needed someplace to lie down that was safe from… creeping shed human skins and… and…

Huh. This room was the safest, most comfortable place he'd found yet in Yintaerghast, and he suspected that if he got off the stool, he'd be wobbling-legged weary, far too tired to even safely walk around the castle, let alone face monsters and traps and Falconfar knew what else…

Rod moved the quill back into position in the line in midair, and let go of it. It floated in the air, rather than falling. Cool.

He took hold of it, waved it around, and put it back in the air again. It floated serenely, as before.

He smiled at it… and that was the last thing he remembered doing…

Dust drifted across a dark floor in Yintaerghast, gathering into a serpentine line whose drifting *hiss* was so soft that an awake and warily alert warrior would not have heard it, let alone someone cozened by enchantment, who was now slumped over an open book at a writing desk, snoring gently.

The dust went on gathering unhurriedly, until it had built into a heap about the height of a large man's fist. Then it stirred, swirling into the air in a slow and silent spiral that outlined the ghostly figure of a tall, thin, bearded man who towered over the sleeping Rod Everlar, growing slowly more solid.

The face that watched the sleeping writer was at first just an oval with hints of two eyesockets, then something that had a nose, a long, strong nose, with bristling black brows above, and a bald pate above that...

A soft smile was clear upon that face long before it had features enough to tell an observer who'd been alive for centuries—had there been any such entity present—that the dust had taken on the semblance of the long-dead Lord Archwizard of Falconfar.

Red eyes, burning with power. The eyes of Lorontar, the builder of Yintaerghast, called by some the Smiling Tyrant.

Then the dust slowly sank down again, for undead shadows skulk best when they keep hidden from those they stalk. The dust scattered and faded, still smiling.

THE GUARDIANS WERE gathering in such numbers— striding, rattling, and flying down every passage to the hall, and coming yet—that Dauntra and Juskra were now panting as they fought. The beautiful Aumrarr and her fierce, scarred sister were almost too winded from their hewing to gasp, "Lorlarra! Aid! We grow weary, and they tire not! Still they come!"

Dark-armored Lorlarra had just turned from the mirror to fly up and answer their plea, hefting her mace in one hand and her bright blade in the other, when Ambrelle, who was still staring into the depths of the glass, cried out, "Sisters mine! Let us tarry here no longer. I've found something far more desirable to slay than nigh-mindless enchanted minions. Come! To the gates!"

She soared up on high, but each of the younger Aumrarr swooped down and past the mirror to see for themselves before they rose to join her in a flapping, excited cloud, taking up the cry, "To the gates! To the gates!"

Through guardians large and small, seeking battle or lying defeated, the four winged women raced, seeking a good gate to plunge through.

Rod Everlar found himself abruptly back in front of the writing desk, blinking. He'd been striding through the castle like a conqueror, parting walls at a touch and causing pillars to swing open by his very approach, to yield up to him glowing swords and gauntlets, wristlets and scepters, and—and something he didn't know the name of, that he'd been holding up and staring at a moment ago...

Dreaming. He must have been dreaming. So none of those beautiful glowing things were real. He was sure the items were magical. He sighed sadly; beautiful glowing things never were real, were they?

Or were they? Were the dreams this castle's way of telling him where its treasures were hidden?

Magic had been at work on him from the moment he'd first stepped inside Yintaerghast.

Excitedly Rod slid off the stool—finding himself just a little stiff—and strode out of that hidden chamber, pausing apprehensively only for a moment when its walls closed up again behind him. In the dreams, he'd walked past the throne and across its room, and a pillar had yawned open to offer him a scepter floating above a sword.

In front of him, a pillar opened to do just that. Shaking his head in bemusement, Rod took hold of both floating items without hesitation, feeling tinglings crawling up his arm from their power.

He hefted the sword, and the tingling rose into almost a song.

"Wow," he murmured, feeling power course through his arms. "Rod Everlar, dragon slayer."

A wall across the room opened, and something yellow-eyed and baleful slunk in. It looked something like a crocodile, and it was big. As it waddled purposefully toward him, Rod backed uncertainly away.

This certainly hadn't been in the dream.

In a room in Ult Tower far from battling guardians, a tall and handsome man stood before a glowing mirror, sound asleep. Far away across Falconfar, on the other side of that glow, a Doom was watching approvingly. A scaly, blue-skinned Doom.

"Whole again, entirely healed," the wizard Narmarkoun murmured. "And my pawn, though you'll know it not until the right time comes, and I force you to do my bidding. You may thank me."

"My... deepest... thanks," the sleeping man mumbled, his words evoking gentle chiming that told Narmarkoun the spell was done, and the mind-link sealed.

Still asleep, the healed man turned from the mirror and lurched stiffly across the room, awakening just as the gate that would take him to Bowrock claimed him.

After all, it wouldn't do for Velduke Darendarr Deldragon to march into his own besieged home fast asleep and snoring.

Chapter Twenty-Two

THE SWORD SPAT purple lightning that was mightier than Deldragon's blade. Rod turned away from the cooked, smoking hulk of the crocodile, smiling and shaking his head. He hadn't even tried the scepter yet.

His stomach rumbled again. Hmm. It wasn't likely that an abandoned, half-ruined castle would have pleasant edibles lying around for the taking, and he'd certainly seen none. Nor had he ever heard of or written about any sort of magic sword or wand or anything in Falconfar that conjured up food. It was just one of the things enchanted items didn't do. Blast things, yes, change their shapes, all of that, but not serve forth steaming, filling food.

There were all those half-remembered fairy stories about mud and weeds being turned into mouth-watering food that got eaten, and then the magic wore off and the diners got very, very sick as, inside them, the transformed viands turned back to what they'd been before the magic got at them. That was probably why he'd never written about such things in Falconfar.

The Holdoncorp designers had put little glowing tankards into their games; you touched one (usually at full run, fleeing or charging at monsters), it flashed and vanished, and you were instantly healed and made bright with fresh energy. But somehow, in their games you never actually sat down and ate.

All of which meant that he could wander around this castle collecting these glowing, humming, monster-blasting goodies until he collapsed from lack of food and water. Fairly soon.

He had to get out of Yintaerghast. And find someone who'd feed him instead of killing him, without Taeauna at his side to know what to do, how to pay and speak and all of that. Without her beauty to lower bows and open doors. Taeauna…

No! Rod turned and slammed his fist against the wall, not caring how much it hurt. He was not going to slide back into tears now; he was not!

She was gone, and that was it. Nothing was going to bring her back.

"But I," he promised the silent gloom in a fierce whisper, "am now at war with the wizard Arlaghaun. And every last lorn in Falconfar. I will blast them all. In her name, I will blast them all."

And for that, he would have to give in to the whisperings in his head. The ones that had started the moment he'd touched the sword floating inside the pillar. The ones that were urging him on, right now, to cross this room and pass through the hidden door he could not yet see, and in a chamber beyond do thus and so, to gain an enchanted, hidden circlet and gorget.

Even a Lord Archwizard could never have too many gewgaws that blasted this and set fire to that. Magic wasn't limitless, and there were a lot of lorn.

Not to mention three Dooms who might take a lot of blasting.

Rod gave in to the whisperings. It seemed to him that he trudged around Yintaerghast for a long time, growing increasingly light-headed, dry-throated, and afflicted with rumbling of the innards; and increasingly weighed down with items that glowed and tingled with power, a belt and a baldric bristling with them, plus all the things he was wearing.

There came a time when at last the whispering told him to go back to the castle door he'd first come in by.

He obeyed, and came down the great stair just itching to raise a little scepter of twisted silver metal set with sky-blue gems. The moment it came into his hand, and glowed as if pleased to be selected, the swirling milk-white void outside the door melted away, to reveal…

The starlit darkness of a night lit by a low moon. Rod Everlar stepped out onto the sward half-expecting to find Arlaghaun standing like a statue waiting for him, wearing a cruel smile as lorn rose in clouds from the trees to rend him. Lorn that might well have perched up in those boughs to tear Taeauna's dangling body apart. He felt sick.

Something stirred in him, then. Something colder and firmer than the whisperings, but in the same place. Something that ran up his spine and forced him upright, abandoning his grieving shudderings, to lurch away across the grass until Yintaerghast loomed well behind him.

Then he found himself turning, to face northeast, and running a hand along his belt until his fingers were resting on the carved ivory head of a dagger. It glowed, and Rod was abruptly… elsewhere.

On a bare, high hill above rolling farmland, with the mountains much closer and woods mere dark and distant smudges under the moon.

He tried to gaze all around since this view of Falconfar was beautiful, serene under the stars, but that cold firmness within him was making him turn slightly, to look at a particular height on the horizon, and reach for the dagger again.

The moonlit hill suddenly held a standing, staring Rod Everlar no longer. He was now two long, teleportational journeys away from Yintaerghast, where a dark, taloned creature flapped bat-like wings to rise off a branch and streak off toward Ult Tower, to warn Arlaghaun.

THE WIZARD WITH the sharp nose and the blazing brown eyes was halfway up the long hall before he mastered his temper, and turned abruptly aside to thrust two fingers into the eyes of a statue, to cause the wall behind it to roll back.

"By the Falcon," he whispered softly, seeking to let out a little of the rage still towering in him.

His own guardians had been roused against him. He hated to blast and mangle his own work, but he would hate even more to be injured and then slain by his own hacking, punching automatons. The lorn and Dark Helms would gleefully swarm him if they saw him struggling along, wounded.

Arlaghaun drew on a pair of gauntlets he'd hoped he'd never to have to use, donned a cloak that would enable him to fly as deftly as any lorn, and caught up a staff from behind the door that was taller than he was.

Cloak swirling, he left the hidden room, drew its door closed, whispered a word to the door, and kissed it, to seal it to all creatures save himself.

Then he turned hastily to face the dozen or so marching metal giants that were already headed toward him.

Arlaghaun hefted the staff, smiled a grim smile, and blasted the foremost striding titan to shrieking, tinkling shards. The other guardians kept coming, mindlessly.

He raised the staff and fired again. The largest metal automaton plunged face-first to the floor, its slow topple ending in a thunderous *crash*.

Arlaghaun used his cloak to leap and then hover aloft, that he not be hurled off his feet. All around him rang out lesser crashes, as just that fate befell the other guardians.

He let his thin lips form a warmer smile. He would rule in Ult Tower again. Very shortly. Even if it had no guardians left.

Except him.

"IT'S ANOTHER OF those nights," one knight in magnificent armor said to another, who'd just arrived to relieve him.

"Where he just sits, staring at nothing and breathing? Like he's empty?"

The first knight nodded sourly, stepped around the new arrival, and strode off down the dark passage that led out of Galathgard.

Across the moonlit courtyard was the gatehouse, and in the gatehouse there was a fire, and smoked meat hanging over the table in front of it, and a great wheel of cheese, and casks and casks of wine, and a bed.

So he hurried. Until he came out into the moonlight, when he couldn't help but stop and stare in amazement at what was blocking his way onwards. And shouldn't have been there.

Barefoot in the ruins, stunningly beautiful in the moonlight, a nude woman was standing waiting for him.

Aye, for *him*. She was looking right into his eyes, and smiling provocatively, her arms spread welcomingly. Pert and saucy, impish...

Beautiful... Falcon, what a beauty! Those breasts, large and night-dark smiling brown eyes, and... He'd just started to notice the wings soaring up behind her shoulders when strong fingers caught hold of his helm from above and jerked it around sideways with brutal force. All the way around.

And then he was beyond noticing anything at all, ever.

"Dauntra," the owner of those strong, scarred hands commented, letting the knight fall into a lolling, lifeless heap. "I get to do the preening and posing next time. You look about as alluring as a carthorse."

"Spare us your preferences, dear," Dauntra replied serenely. "And there isn't going to be a 'next time.' That's the last bodyguard, save for the three who are in there with him until morning."

"Well, I'll be the one who strips down and minces in to distract them, then. You've had your fun."

"How so? You killed him before I could! And before you come up with a jest about my loving the dead, Juskra, just leave off trying, hmm? I've heard them all before, anyway."

"I'm not surprised, sister," Juskra said sweetly. "Here, hold this."

"Am I your dressing-maid, now?"

"Oooh, now there's a calling that suits you. I—"

"Juskra," Ambrelle interrupted severely, "will you shut up? Just get your clothes off and get in there. Lorlarra should be in place by now, and I'll be right behind you." The oldest of the four Aumrarr hefted her sword meaningfully, tossing her magnificent purple-black mane. "And if you stoop to any more such sauce when we're in there, I'll feed this up your backside!"

"Sister!" Bared, the fiercest of the four Aumrarr was a mass of crisscrossing sword-scars; her forearms looked like white snakes were tangled tightly around them. Which made her mock-scandalized pose, fingertips at her throat and eyes wide, all the more ridiculous.

The three Aumrarr chuckled together, and Dauntra held out her arms to receive the last of Juskra's war-harness.

Giving her a look, the scarred Aumrarr filled those waiting arms, and then defiantly peeled off her yellowed and stained bandage, and laid that on top of the heap, too.

"Juskra," Dauntra growled softly.

The scarred Aumrarr elegantly put out her tongue in reply.

THE KING OF Galath muttered something darkly, under his breath, and stirred in his great chair, booted feet sliding along the polished tabletop. The fire crackled unregarded in the hearth.

"Pardon, your majesty?"

King Devaer lifted his eyes to give the knight standing over him an unfriendly look. "I said: I want a woman."

"But majesty…"

"I know, Glaroskur, I know. Not a wench within a day's ride of this crumbling ruin, and I don't fancy the backsides of any of you. But what's the good of being glorking King of Galath, and Lord of the rutting Falcons, too, if I can't have a woman? Go and get me a woman!"

"Majesty?"

"Go to the stables, get on a horse, take Joss and Rakaer with you, find some suitably beautiful woman, bring her back here without taking her yourselves, and bring her to me!"

"But your highn—"

"That was a royal command, Glaroskur!"

The knight regarded him unhappily, then bowed deeply, turned, and marched out.

Devaer sighed in bored exasperation, listening to his bodyguard's boots tramping into the echoing stone distances of cold and empty Galathgard. He hated and feared the touch of Arlaghaun's mind on his, that cold and utter tyranny, yet somehow it thrilled him, too.

And when the wizard who really ruled Galath needed him not, he felt so empty. Bored, listless, lying here in idleness, ready to scream and claw the walls...

The sounds of Glaroskur's boots stopped, and there came a strange but very brief wet, startled, choked-off sound.

The King of Galath frowned. "Glaroskur?"

Silence. He swung his feet down off the table, stood up sharply, shook out his silken sleeves, and bellowed, "Glaroskur?"

"Your majesty," a soft woman's voice said from behind him, "may I serve you, instead?"

Devaer whirled around, clapping his hand to his sword, and felt his jaw drop open. He couldn't help it; couldn't help staring, either.

The nude figure who stood barefoot in the doorway was one of the most beautiful women he'd ever seen, and by the Falcon, she was an Aumrarr! Not a soft, yielding beauty; but a hard-muscled, sharp-jawed warrior, by her looks, her shapely body covered with sword-scars, a fierceness about her face... but a look of yearning, too, of yielding to him. She was kneeling to him, too, going to her knees more gracefully than any servant lass or high-born lady.

Devaer found his mouth was very dry, and his manhood was stirring urgently. He managed to swallow, and peered wildly around, thrusting a hand up into his lank black hair to adjust his crown without even realizing he was doing so. "Y-you're alone?"

"Quite alone," came the soft answer. "Summoned here by magic. Not meaning to, or even knowing what he did, your knight just blundered through a gate that took him to my bedchamber, far from Galath, and in the same stroke, brought me here. So it seems, as you are deprived of his vigilance, I should... guard your body."

Someone sniggered from the doorway behind him.

King Devaer whirled around again, sword flashing out, but was far too slow to block the two blades flying toward his throat.

Almost severed, his head lolled limply on his shoulders as his life-blood fountained in all directions, and he emptied his bowels and started the slow stagger that would end up on the floor.

Juskra got up off her knees without waiting to see if the body and the head stayed together when they hit the floor. She was too busy scowling. "Is that all the fun you wanted me to have? He wasn't half bad looking, and I was just warming to the task."

"I'll say. 'Guard your body,' she gasped breathlessly. Falcon, Jusk, I almost spewed!" Lorlarra jeered, clutching at her throat in mock nausea and striking a pose in the dark tatters of her armor.

"Oh, your majesty," Ambrelle twittered in mimicry, "just let me kneel here in my bared skin and worship you! Urrrkh!"

As the mock-vomiting of the oldest Aumrarr rang out loudly, Devaer's body fell heavily to the floor, sword clattering, and his head rolled free.

"Behold the King of Galath," Lorlarra said grandly, as it came to a stop near her boot.

"And Lord of Falcons," Ambrelle agreed gravely, tossing her long purple-black hair. "Don't forget that. Fetch me that crown, Lorl; I think Arlaghaun has controlled it long enough."

"Wait!" Juskra threw up her hand, frowning. "What if he traces us through it?"

"Let him," Dauntra said softly from the doorway behind her, murder in her usually impish brown eyes. "If he comes after us, we'll be ready for him. So let him try his worst, and come within reach." She hefted her sword. "I believe I'll welcome that."

ROD EVERLAR FOUND himself standing on yet another grassy hilltop, turning to face a distant peak he did not recognize.

Turning because he was forced to do so. Something that dwelt in Yintaerghast—that old man in the chair?—was in his head, riding his mind. Something he might have unknowingly invited in, when picking up the first few enchanted items; it had definitely been in his mind, whispering instructions and urging him on, for his acquirings of the later ones.

And now, teleport by teleport, from hill to hill, he was being forced across Falconfar toward a definite though unknown destination.

What had that television character roared? "I am a free man!" Well, damn it!

"I am!"

Screw this destiny shit.

"Screw it!"

Rod Everlar's shout echoed back to him off dark standing stones all around him on that particular hilltop, but they neither moved nor answered.

DAWN CAME SLOWLY to Galath, and found four Aumrarr flying high and fast out of the heart of the kingdom.

Out of the dark trees below, lorn took to the air, spiraling up to meet them.

The four never slowed.

As rose-red dawn gave way to the bright sun of the morning, Juskra looked back. "I'm glad you kept crown and head together," the scarred Aumrarr called to Ambrelle. "They'll come in far more useful than just the crown."

In reply, the oldest Aumrarr smiled and held up the sack in her fist, purple-black hair streaming out behind her as she flew.

Then her face changed to its usual severe expression, and she pointed down with her other hand at the swiftly climbing lorn. "Sisters mine, we have visitors."

"Six-and-twenty," young and beautiful Dauntra called, having just finished counting them. "Let us see what they decide to do if we ignore them, and just fly on."

Lorlarra nodded. "Well said," she called back. The ongoing disintegration of her armor had left her almost bare, but trailing a tangle of dark straps and armor plates.

So the four Aumrarr did just that, turning not a handspan aside from their chosen path. The lorn circled uncertainly in front of them, trying to catch their eyes.

All four Aumrarr met their gazes, gave them polite, pleasant smiles, and flew straight on.

The lorn traded puzzled frowns with each other, flapped hastily aside to meet and confer in harsh whispers, and then turned to look again at the four Aumrarr, now past them and streaking steadily away across the sky, as straight as four speeding arrows.

The winged women did not look back.

After several brief and uncertain hissed exchanges that decided nothing, the lorn dropped away, seeking their forest perches again.

THE DOOR BLEW inward, shards and dust swirling and bouncing in the short passage that led to his main scrying-room.

"Amalrys?" Arlaghaun spat out her name, his thin lips even tighter than usual, letting her hear all of his anger in that icy query, letting his magic carry his quiet voice the length of the ruined hall.

There came no answer. But then, he hadn't intended to wait for one.

His many shieldings—even the strongest one, that could hold up Ult Tower if it was hurled down on his head—were up and flaring in front of him as he strode down the hall, brown eyes afire and sharp nose twitching, his hands flexing in his hunger to throttle his disloyal apprentice.

He stopped dead. Many of the scrying-crystals had shattered, their magic now but sparkling dust and ash on the floor, and draped across the frame that held the surviving stones, smoke smudged around her gaping mouth and empty eyesockets, her bare body covered with ash, lay Amalrys.

She was very still. The Doom of Galath stared hard at her for a long moment, and then peered swiftly all around the room. Then he sent forth his shieldings in a questing cloud.

There were no sudden flarings to mark lingering spell-traps on her or between him and where she lay; Arlaghaun strode to her and took her in his arms.

She was lighter than he remembered. Chains chimed softly as limp limbs sagged; her body was cold.

Arlaghaun held her across one arm, as if she weighed nothing, and with his other hand stroked her honey-blonde hair. His thin lips quivered, just once, but his burning eyes remained dry and hard.

Taking her by the chin and turning the ruin of her face away, the Doom of Galath idly entertained thoughts of making love to what was left of his Amalrys one last time.

She was beautiful still, but where would the thrill of surrender come from? His memories would outshine all, and they would serve him until he captured someone better. And that would be soon.

He let her body fall and turned away, somewhat wearily telling the still air around him, "Behold. Arlaghaun is master in his own castle again."

The still air declined to answer, of course.

Arlaghaun walked back down the passage, dismissing for now thoughts of just how many guardians he'd had to blast and maim to make that claim, and put his hand on a particular stone.

It glowed obediently, and took him in an instant to another room, where a blank, solid wall stood in front of his nose.

"One more thing to do before I compel Klammert," he murmured. "Somehow, there's always one more thing to do."

Arlaghaun thrust a hand at the wall, and it melted away at his touch; he stepped through the wall as if it wasn't there, into a large hall choked with the broken, heaped bodies of guardians.

Picking his way around them, he reached the mirror and slid it back into place, to once more conceal the passage that led to his escape gate.

Scenes were moving in the mirror. Folding his arms across his chest, Arlaghaun stepped back to watch.

THE LOAD OF stone plunged down out of the sky and slammed into the mud like a giant's fist, bursting apart in all directions. Hurtling stones sent men and horses screaming alike as they were tumbled, crushed by thudding stones, and then buried.

"Glorking Deldragon!" Baron Chainamund snarled through his bristling straw-yellow mustache, retreating hastily for all his great bulk. "Where's he getting all this stone from?"

"The houses of Bowrock that we're smashing down with our catapults, Chainamund," Klarl Snowlance replied wearily, in his reedy voice. "Ondurs, could you judge just where that was fired from?"

Marquel Mountblade was busy wiping dust from his everpresent monocle; he paused just long enough to shake his head. "Somewhere near the northeast tower," he replied sourly. "Which is about as much as we already knew. We're going to be here a long time, lords."

"Right," Arduke Stormserpent said briskly, a rare smile on his usually stern, dark face. "I'll have my playpretties brought in by coach, then. And the uppermost racks of my wine cellar."

Those words brought Velduke Brorsavar's head around, huge in its gleaming helm. Thankfully, it, too, was wearing a smile. "Will you be sharing, Laskrar?"

"But of course, lord. For the greater glory of Galath," Stormserpent replied with a low, sweeping bow.

"Ah, now, that's the best news I've heard these last five days!" Arduke Windtalon put in, turning from the maps of Bowrock he'd been peering at. He'd used his helm to hold one corner of their curling edges down, freeing his shoulder-length mane of copper-colored hair. There was a certain eagerness in his almond-hued eyes. "As Mountblade says, these fortress walls aren't going away anytime soon."

Several of the Lords of Galath tried to peer up through all the drifting smoke, past the chaos of dead horses and heaped rubble and tents, at the battlements looming somewhere near, but the smoke was too heavy, just now, to see anything properly.

Arduke Lionhelm stiffened, and pointed right up into the sky overhead. His handsome, hawk-eyed face wore a look of astonishment. "Look! Aumrarr!"

"Aumrarr? Here?"

"They're either spying, or running missives for Deldragon," Baron Chainamund snarled, sweat running down his florid face. "Shoot them down!"

Smoke promptly hid the winged women from view, even as a bowman came crashing through the rubble, calling, "Lord? Your will?"

"Ignore him," Velduke Brorsavar snapped, his gleaming-armored shoulders as broad as the two nobles standing beside him put together, "and get back to your post. Shoot at nothing until I give such an order, or Velduke Bloodhunt, yonder, does."

"Aye," Arduke Lionhelm agreed. "Barons tend to slay too swiftly, and then storm about raging that they can't question corpses, after."

"Lords," the bowman said gravely, bowing low. Then he rose, turned, and fled back through the rubble even as Chainamund roared, "How dare you, Lionhelm?"

"Very easily," the arduke replied with a shrug, his hawk-eyes hard. "I grow weary of foolishness, Chainamund. Dispense with it, and we'll get along fine. Spew more of it, and I'll begin to consider how well Galath will get along with one less blustering idiot of a baron in it."

The florid baron's mustache quivered, like a bush disturbed by men fighting in it, and his face went from angry red to roiling purple. "Veldukes," he yelped, "d-did you hear that? Did you?"

The broad shoulders of Velduke Brorsavar turned, a mountain of metal moving, and their owner said coldly, "I certainly did, Glusk Chainamund. And your blusterings, too. I have time for neither. Still your tongue, or I'll find myself agreeing with Lionhelm."

Four Aumrarr came swooping out of the smoke just above his head, then, gave him wide smiles, and let go of something that fell through the air to bounce wetly on the cracked slab of stone the two veldukes had been using as a table.

The object was round; it rolled and hopped the length of the table before wobbling off one edge to thump to the ground below. And stare endlessly, bulging-eyed, up at the sky.

A noble who'd been humming to himself stopped doing so, abruptly.

"Falcon!" Marquel Blackraven swore, his emerald eyes hard as he stared at it. Behind him, Lords of Galath glanced over, stared hard, then crowded forward to stare some more.

Even if the glint of the crown hadn't still been about its brows, they all knew what it was.

The severed head of the King of Galath stared up at them, unseeing.

By the time Arduke Stormserpent and fat, florid Baron Chainamund had stopped swearing and peered into the skies again, there was no sign of the winged women. After a moment, they looked down at the head again.

"Bloodhunt!" Velduke Brorsavar bellowed into the smoke, his deep voice as strident as any warhorn. "Come quickly! I need you here!"

"So that's it, then," Arduke Windtalon said flatly, clapping his helm down over his shoulder-length copper hair. "End of siege."

"Certainly not!" Marquel Duthcrown snapped, striding forward to stand over the severed head with his sword drawn, and hastily settling his own helm back into place, wisps of stray white hair thrusting out in all directions under its edge. "Certainly not! We have a royal command to follow; a sworn duty to perform!"

"That writ ended with the severing of that royal neck," Arduke Lionhelm said firmly, "and I for one was not witness to your coronation, Duthcrown. Presume not to speak for the throne."

Duthcrown glared at him, mustachioed lip drawn back to expose his teeth, and barked, "You speak open treason! Chainamund! Murlstag!

Dunshar! To me! Stand with me, here, and guard the crown against all such traitors!"

"Before we speak of such guardianship," Arduke Stormserpent said sharply, his dark face even sterner than usual, "suppose we hew a little closer to common agreement on just who's a traitor, and why. Nobles who presume to stand in judgement over the rest of us tend to annoy me. I'm annoyed right now."

"And isn't that just too bad?" Baron Chainamund sneered, face reddening anew as he bent, snatched up the crown, and clapped it on his own head. "Stormserpent is annoyed. Pity." Twirling his great straw-yellow mustache with one fat finger, he roared, "Hear ye, all: I hereby proclaim myself King of All Galath! King Glusk, the first of that name! And I now decree that Stormserp—"

His words ended in a great gout of vomited blood that drenched the point of the swordblade that had suddenly burst forth from his ample stomach.

Arduke Lionhelm let him spew his way down to a last throat-gurgling choking before he put a boot on Chainamund's back and kicked the dying baron off his steel.

"Enough," he said, his voice ringing as cold and hard as iron. "We will have order, or there will be war here, at the very gates we're besieging. Lords, Galath will survive only—"

"How dare you?" Marquel Duthcrown cried, waving his sword. "You murder a crowned king, in front of all of us—"

"Duthcrown, be still!" came a deep roar. "Speak such foolishness to your mistresses, not to us!"

Velduke Aumon Bloodhunt, with his knights behind him, was standing atop a nearby heap of rubble, glaring down, more white than gray in his hair now, but angry blue eyes snapping as bright as ever. "I am the ranking noble here, as it happens," he added, his deep voice only a trifle quieter, "and I say Chainamund was no more king than a stable-boy who happens to lay hand on a crown and prance about with it! Let us draw off from the walls, beyond the reach of Deldragon's catapults, and hold council."

"Bah!" Duthcrown spat, striding to meet him. "For years you and the other toothless old lions have farted and swaggered and paraded before us, whenever you're not fawning and simpering before this wizard and that! Well, I'll stomach no more of it!"

Waving his sword, he charged up the slope, losing his helm in his haste, his white hair wild in the wake of its tumbling. Bloodhunt's knights rushed to meet him, swords singing out, and—

Another fall of stone crashed down from the sky, shattering and burying the men on the slope; one moment their swords were flashing in the dust, and the next, dust was drifting above a new heap of rubble, where all those men had been.

"The crown!" Klarl Snowlance shouted, his reedy voice rising as shrill as a war-horn. "Where is the crown?"

"The crown," Lionhelm bellowed, "is here!" The hawk-eyed arduke grounded his sword on a stone in front of him, and all of the converging nobles saw that its point was encircled by the Crown of Galath.

"I am not claiming it," the handsome arduke added, just as loudly. "I propose to take it into my hand and go away from the walls, as Velduke Bloodhunt has so wisely suggested. Then let us parley in peace, lords, and—"

With a great roar, burly Klarl Dunshar and two of his knights who were even larger men than their master, with their three breastplates gleaming like oversized shields, abreast, charged at Lionhelm, swords out. Baron Murlstag joined in the rush, yellow eyes flashing, and Ardukes Stormserpent and Windtalon spat curses and hastened, tall and swift, to defend Lionhelm. Swords flashed out, all around the heaps of rubble, and as the nobles who wielded them started shouting, some of their heralds and equerries sounded war-horns to spread word.

Even as stone-faced Baron Lothondos Pethmur commenced to sternly lecture the unheeding air, "I for one have no interest in continuing a siege when the man who ordered it lies dead!" the sounds of sword on sword, war-cries, and the screams of the dying arose, sudden, loud, and enthusiastic, on all sides.

To the astonishment of Deldragon's defenders on the walls above, bloody war had suddenly erupted among the besiegers below. Everywhere they could see, the Lords of Galath and their armies were killing each other.

Rod Everlar sighed as he found himself on yet another hilltop in the brightening morning.

This time, he was facing a crumbling stone door, set into a grassy hump of earth. There had been words graven into the stone, once, but they had largely crumbled away. Not that Rod needed to read them, to know that he was staring at a tomb.

He wasn't surprised in the slightest when the dweller in his mind forced him to take a scepter from his belt that he'd never used before, aim at the door, and whisper a word he did not know.

Nothing seemed to erupt from the scepter, but the door shattered as if a titan had dealt it a mighty blow.

Its stone shards bounced and rolled past Rod Everlar's feet as he lifted them to begin the short walk into waiting darkness.

In Ult Tower, a sharp-nosed wizard stiffened, his brown eyes blazing fresh fire. "Lorontar! I knew it!" he spat.

Whirling around, Arlaghaun snarled into his apprentice's face, "The shade of the undead wizard Lorontar is riding yon Shaper, controlling him, and that control comes through Lorontar's command over the enchanted items the man bears!"

Fat, scraggle-bearded Klammert had already gone pale; now he was leaning back and away, as if Arlaghaun's sharp nose was a dagger. "Aye, master," he said huskily, "but why? Why send yon man to open a tomb?"

Arlaghaun sighed in exasperation, and then explained as if to a simpleton, "He is sending Everlar to the tomb-caches of other dead wizards, to fetch and gather magics that will enable the undead Lorontar—an utterly evil and extremely powerful archwizard, even in ghostly undeath—to rise to life again!"

Klammert pointed at the mirror. "Master, he's gone in."

"Work with me!" Arlaghaun snapped. "We'll raise a gate and bury him in Dark Helms!"

"LORN!" AN ARCHER shouted, turning to aim. The older warrior standing beside him on the battlements of Bowrock struck his bow aside, and wasn't gentle about it.

"Those are Aumrarr, fool! If you can't tell lorn from women with wings, you shouldn't be up on these walls!"

He ducked aside as a young and achingly beautiful winged woman swooped in low over the ramparts, and winked at him. Hastily he gave her back a wave and a smile.

Lorlarra, flying in Dauntra's wake in a welter of disintegrating dark armor, blew him a kiss. That raised a ragged shout of laughter from the men on the battlements.

One of them called, "Looking for someone handsome?" He struck a pose.

It wasn't hard to tell that the four Aumrarr were peering at every face as they glided along above the walls. Soon fierce and scarred Juskra made a sudden, wordless sound and pointed, and the four winged women converged.

"Friggin' Falcon!" Garfist swore, as dark wings loomed. He grabbed a sword from the man beside him as he turned to Iskarra. "They're coming for us!"

"Of course they are," she said bitterly. "Who else would they be after, in all besieged Bowrock? I know not what we did to anger the Falcon, but I wish most fervently that…"

The man whose blade Garfist had borrowed tried to snatch it back. Garfist hung on to it, offering the man a hard elbow and a harder knee instead. They struggled together as Dauntra and Juskra sped past, plucked up Iskarra by clamping firm hands around each of her bony wrists, her drawn daggers waving vainly, and flapped up into the morning sky.

Lorlarra and Ambrelle slammed right into Garfist, knocking him free of the other warrior and the other warrior's blade, and caught him by the ankles as he rolled helplessly, the men of Bowrock scattering.

A moment later, Garfist was hanging head downward in the air, high over the heart of Bowrock, with two pairs of wings beating hard above him, their owners puffing and panting, and straps and dangling plates of dark armor flailing him across the face. He roared in anger and tried to squirm free, snaring the nearest armor-strap in one hairy fist and tugging, hard.

A wing slammed into the side of his head as his captors lurched, dipping alarmingly.

"Stop fighting us! You'll die if you fall!" Lorlarra gasped, from the other end of that strap.

"Yes!" Ambrelle added severely, through her own tangle of purple-black hair. "Stop struggling; we're rescuing you from all this!"

Garfist let go of the strap, and twisted his neck around until he could glare up at her. "Why?"

"We need hands that can act where we dare not go."

"Go to do what?" Iskarra called, as her pair of Aumrarr brought her near.

"Slay Dooms, rescue Falconfar... that sort of thing."

"I see," Iskarra said weakly.

Chapter Twenty-Three

PUT THEM ON. *Quickly.*

The voice in his head was strong and firm, now; whispering and suggesting no longer.

Rod drew on the gauntlets, halting in alarm for a moment as sudden lightning arced between them, crackling and spitting.

Now get out of the tomb. Hurry.

Rod hurried out of the chill, earthy darkness, out into a vivid purple glow that was already disgorging black-armored warriors. They trotted toward him, raising shields and hefting swords.

Point your fingers and blast them. A vivid image unfolded in his mind of how to unleash the powers of the gauntlets. *Kill them all. Do NOT let the finger-beams touch the gate.*

Rod pointed his fingers and blasted, hastily moving from one warrior to another. The gauntlets seemed able to spit one pencil-thin crimson beam per finger, if he concentrated on maintaining all the beams he willed into existence, but those beams shot out arrow-straight from his fingertips, and had to be aimed precisely. They melted through armor and flesh alike without pause, slaying almost as fast as he could aim them.

But the Dark Helms were fast, too. They came rushing at him in such desperate haste that Rod was almost forced back into the tomb, and they died so swiftly that they fell in heaps, forming a wall. He hurried along the slope, trying to keep from being literally buried in foes, foes who had plenty of swords and daggers to stab with.

Keep moving. Circle out and around the gate. Don't let any Dark Helms get where you can't see them. You must kill them all.

The finger-beams soon started to fade, reaching shorter and shorter distances, until there came a time when one of them sputtered and failed completely. The face of the foremost onrushing Dark Helm changed from terror to triumph.

Shake the gauntlets off, jump sideways at the last minute, and grab the horn-headed scepter!

Rod hesitated for an instant, and felt sickening surges in his arms and legs, forcing him to shake the gauntlets off—sickening because they were being done to him. He was as much a slave as any shackled, flogged unfortunate, but his master was sitting in his head!

The horn-headed scepter proved to unleash cones of ravening fire that could reduce several armored warriors to blackened, tumbling bones in the space of a deeply drawn breath. It was just a little slower at slaying than the gauntlets had been, which would have doomed him if there'd been many Dark Helms left.

However, only a few came trotting through the glowing purple arch now, sporadically, and perhaps twenty were left on the hill, skulking behind the bodies of their dead fellows, trying to get close enough to Rod to rush and hack at him before he could burn them down.

Rod felt sick. The stink of cooked Dark Helms was like burned roadkill, a reek so strong that it was almost choking. Part of him wanted to burn down every last Dark Helm, in Taeauna's name, and part of him was screaming that he was a writer, not any sort of fighter, and certainly not any sort of killer.

Yet here he was, dodging and ducking among the heaped dead, peering at wherever he thought a warrior or two was hiding.

Behind you, fool.

Rod spun around, scepter spewing flame even before he got properly turned. That was what saved him; the ribs beneath the arm that was swinging a sword at his head were boiling away before the blade could get to him, robbing its swing of strength and height so that it was falling free by the time it bounced off his shoulder and tumbled past. Rod crisped that warrior and the three right behind him in frenzied haste, as their sprint carried their collapsing bones almost into him.

And then there were no more Dark Helms, and the gate was pulsing bright purple, flickering and dancing.

Don't even look at the gate; for you, it's a trap. Get back to the tomb door, looking all around as you go.

Rod stumbled over bones and corpses, wondering how it was that flies discovered the dead so quickly, and where they all came from. He looked this way and that, but…

Keep looking around, idiot, the sharp voice snarled in his mind. A moment later, it added: *There!*

Someone was standing atop the tomb-hill, where there had been no one a moment earlier. Someone with burning brown eyes.

Arlaghaun.

That was all Rod had time to see before a spell burst in the air all around him, washing over him and setting the trampled grass aflame.

He felt heat on his face, heat that should have blistered and then blinded him, that should have scorched his hair off, consumed his flesh, and sent his ashen bones tumbling, but instead washed over him and was gone, leaving him tingling in three places along his belts, where enchanted items had suddenly faded away.

Sacrificed to save him, Rod thought blearily, as the mind-voice shouted at him, *Aim the scepter! BLAST HIM!*

He obeyed, but Arlaghaun was suddenly—not there. The hilltop was empty again.

Run to the tomb, and in, the mind-voice commanded. *Look toward the gate as you go.*

As if those words had been a stage cue, Arlaghaun appeared out of nowhere, standing just in front of his gate, his hands weaving the empty air in the intricate gestures of a powerful spell.

I THOUGHT so. The mind-voice sounded very satisfied. *Fire the scepter at the gate. NOT at the wizard. At the gate.*

Clenching his teeth, Rod did as he was told, knowing he had no choice anyway.

Close your eyes!

Rod wasn't quite fast enough. The gate's explosion not only shook the hill and flung him to his knees atop some very hard armor, to say nothing of the dead man inside it, but it also seared his eyes with a white flash that snatched all Falconfar away. A flash that showed Rod a glimpse of Arlaghaun, arms windmilling wildly, being hurled forward onto his face.

Get into the tomb!

Eyes running, barely able to get up and keep from falling, Rod stumbled and swayed his way around heaps of cooked warriors, seeking the front slope of the hill he'd fled along just moments earlier.

Hurry!

He couldn't see properly through the streaming tears, couldn't—

He stumbled over a dead Dark Helm, his arm slamming down onto rising grass. He had reached the front slope of the tomb. Rod clawed his way along it, trying to hurry, until he found the doorway and fell through it.

Get well in, then turn around. Don't stop hurrying.

Had the voice in his mind sounded sarcastic?

Rod obeyed, swiping at his eyes with his sleeve, the horned scepter warm in his hand.

When he got his vision clear enough to be able to see more than watery light and dark, he found himself staring at a rectangle of sunlight. In the distance, that sunlight was falling on a great heap of dead Dark Helms. A gray-robed man was climbing the far side of that heap, rising higher and higher as he gained its top.

It was Arlaghaun. He was looking right at Rod, and smiling.

Rod aimed the scepter, but the voice in his mind said sharply, *No. Waste it not. Put it back in your belt, and draw forth the draeuth.*

"The what?"

An image was thrust impatiently open in Rod's mind.

Oh. That strange metal thing he'd been guided to, back in the castle, that looked like a knuckleduster welded to a set of panpipes. Rod slid his fingers through its loop, and drew it out of his belt.

Now the arlaunkh.

"The—?"

A metal rod about the length of his forearm, this one, that curved gently to form a pleasant-to-the-hand grip. He'd been thinking of it as "the big scepter," but—

Right. Point the big scepter straight overhead, and the draeuth down the passage at the doorway outside. You fire them both like THIS. Do so.

Rod obeyed, feeling something that sounded and looked like the beige, many-popping-bubbled foam of a fire extinguisher spraying forth from one, and a cone of similar but white foam from the other.

An instant later, Arlaghaun shouted something triumphant, roiling flame came roaring into the tomb, and its stone-lined ceiling shuddered, cracked, and fell in on top of Rod Everlar.

The flames met the brown ray and wrestled with it, snarling; only a few tongues streamed past to lick at his arms and shoulders. The white ray melted away stones as they fell, burning a circle to the sunlight. So nothing crushed Rod's skull or broke his neck. Stones slammed down around him, though, bruising and wedging him, shattering bones with sudden, sharp pains that made him gasp and then shout.

Keep hold of them both, and keep firing, or you are doomed.

Arlaghaun's flame died away, but Rod could hear him chanting something that sounded like a spell.

Melt away any stone that could fall or slide sideways onto your head, then start blasting them down all around you, to free yourself. Hurry. You MUST free enough space for your arms to reach everything on your belts.

Rod obeyed, watching tons of stone melt away. Whatever Arlaghaun had cast came streaming down the passage again, and again fought the brown ray, beating it back this time almost to Rod's hand.

Aim the arlaunkh—the big scepter—at the ceiling of the passage into the tomb. Bring it down, just as the wizard collapsed the tomb atop you.

Rod obeyed again, and with a slow, thunderous roar, the passage disappeared.

Keep on freeing yourself. Down to your legs, now. Haste matters more than care. If you burn yourself, you'll heal. HURRY.

Arlaghaun was clambering over stones at the front of the tomb now, trying to get closer; Rod could hear them shifting and clattering as the wizard sought to climb up on top of the ruined hill.

To get at Rod Everlar.

Stones were slumping like butter around his ankles now, then just melting away. He could move, though lifting his left leg brought stabbing agony that left him panting and leaning against the stones that were still there.

Fuse those stones together, so they can't shift and trap you. Arlaghaun comes.

The arlaunkh failed quite suddenly, crumbling to dust in his hand.

The black scepter, now, the one with the eye. The eye is its tip, not its handle; the eye should face away from you. The mind-voice was noticeably fainter.

Rod grabbed at the black scepter, almost dropped it, then straightened up, and found himself staring into Arlaghaun's burning brown eyes and soft, thin-lipped smile.

"So, Shaper, we meet at last."

Rod winced. Couldn't someone write better dialogue than that?

He aimed both the draeuth and the eye scepter at the wizard and intoned, "With the fate of all Falconfar hanging in the balance!"

It was Arlaghaun's turn to wince. "Did Lorontar actually say that?"

"Does it bother you, not knowing?" Rod asked, as sweetly and carefully politely as any unhelpful civil servant, and triggered both enchanted items.

Their raging onslaught battered something unseen in front of Arlaghaun's nose so fiercely that the wizard was forced to arch over backwards, away from the magic trying to slam into him.

Arlaghaun took a step back and lost his footing, to be hurled away over the rocks like a rag doll, out of sight down off the hill.

Rod laughed aloud. He hadn't really hurt the wizard, he knew, but it was nice to land a blow on that sneering face. For once.

Move not. Give your leg time to heal; shift your weight onto the other one.

The voice in his mind was back to being a whisper, now.

"Who are you?" Rod dared to ask it. Was it Lorontar, the long-dead Archwizard? Or—

"Lord!" The soft, urgent call was coming from behind him, accompanied by a high, chiming rattle of chain.

Rod whirled, so quickly his leg burned like fire.

"Tay?" he managed to cry, through the pain.

"Lord Rod!" Taeauna was crawling forward over rocks, bare except for metal collars about her throat, ankles, and high on her thighs; collars that were joined with dangling lines of fine chain. "Come quickly! You've wounded Arlaghaun sorely, and so given us time to escape! Come with me!"

No! The whisper in Rod's head was frantic and fierce. *It's a lie! A trick! She's Arlaghaun's creature; believe not a word she says!*

Rod shook his head as he clawed his way up over the rocks, bruising his knuckles in his haste, still clutching the draeuth and the scepter.

"Taeauna!" he hissed. "Are you… all right?"

"I have been Arlaghaun's thrall," she replied, waving one hand to indicate her bared self, and flick the nearest length of chain. "But if we hurry, now, and you free me…"

No! Whatever you do, don't go with her! The whisper-thin voice in his head was shrieking now. *Arlaghaun controls every word that comes out of her mouth! Cleave to her, and you embrace your doom!*

"Fuck *off*," Rod told the voice in his head firmly, and hurried over the rocks to Taeauna.

MISTGATES WAS A strong castle, soaring up like a great lone fang from a hard cliff of purple-gray rock that had stared into winter storms for centuries upon centuries, as defiantly as the face of any grim dwarf. High were its walls, so lofty that it had not one set of battlements, but two: a third of the way up its flanks, a crenelated balcony had been carved out, like the lower jaw of a gigantic dragon, for the use of bowmen seeking to feather targets on the narrow overland road that snaked up through rising rocks to skirt the front gates of the castle.

These days, with the master of Mistgates heeding not the Mad King in Galathgard, and so being shunned by most nobles of the realm and by fearful traders alike, few folk came along that road.

Yet there were travelers on it now, many of them. They wore the best of gleaming armor, mounted knight after mounted knight, their lances like a forest, but a forest bare of leaves for they bore no banners.

At first sight of them from the high battlements of Mistgates, galloping hard along the road that would bring them into the very lap of Velduke Mardrammur Mistryn, horns were winded over the castle, to sound an alarm.

Mistryn was one of the veldukes who did not ride to Galathgard upon the whim and pleasure of King Devaer, and most of Galath had heard by now, with Bowrock under siege, just how much the King of

Galath loved veldukes who did not bend their knees to him often.

Wherefore the great doors of the castle were firmly closed and barred, after the best-armed and armored Mistryn knights and armsmen—enough to match the approaching knights, and to spare—had issued forth in full battle array, prepared with pikes and caltrops. On the walls above, a long line of archers stood ready.

The knights slowed their mounts as they came up to Mistgates, and drew no swords, but held up empty hands to wave "peace" and then "parley."

A tall man in armor whose painted breast-blazon proclaimed him the personal champion of Mardrammur stood forth to meet them, and called, "You ride in Mistryn lands, and are come to the gates of the House of Mard, and you are many and well armed. Yield unto me your names and purpose!"

The foremost rider doffed his helm, patted the neck of his snorting mount to calm it, and replied, "You know me, Roeglar. I am Samryn, loyal knight of Velduke Bloodhunt, and we before your gates are all now also knights of the King of Galath, His Majesty Melander Brorsavar, who rides with us!"

Roeglar gave him a hard look. "Brorsavar is king, now?"

"Brorsavar is king. Things change in Falconfar, sword-brother."

"That they do. And all too swiftly, these days. That they do."

"Well, have we leave to pass within?" Samryn clapped his hand meaningfully to his sword-hilt.

"I'm thinking, sword-brother. I'm thinking."

* * *

"THIS WAY," TAEAUNA gasped, and was gone down behind some rocks with a rattle of chain. "Hurry!"

"Hurrying is all I seem to do, these days," Rod chuckled to himself, following her just as fast as he could.

Don't follow her! the ignored mind-whisper shouted.

Rod found himself plunging face-first down into a cleft among the rocks, where Taeauna waited to catch him.

His weight bore her over on her back, of course, his face cushioned against the softness of her breasts.

"Oh, Lord Rod," she murmured, chains rattling around him as they bounced together, and he tried to mutter apologies. "I have worried about you so!"

"I... I love you!" she added, as he wallowed his way hastily up off her body. He'd been on the verge of daring to kiss her, but those words made Rod blink, hesitate, and then smile.

Which is when she leaned forward and kissed him.

No! Don't do this!

Her lips were warm and sweet and hungry, her tongue thrusting deep into his mouth, rolling and thrusting something that tasted spicy-sweet... Had some Holdoncorp idiot put chewing gum into Falconfar when he wasn't looking?

It tasted pleasant, though...

And it was even nicer to have Taeauna thrusting herself against him, her bare body like silk against him, her mouth making little moaning noises of want and need...

476

Jeez, this was like a bad sex scene in a film, some sort of porn feature with the woman in chains and... and...

...And why was everything getting so dark?

Dark around the edges... He stared through the dwindling, deepening hole that was left, at Taeauna's eyes... So sad as he stared into them, her mouth still so soft and sweet... Were those tears?

Can't see... Everything going as gloomy as nightfall... That spicy-sweet taste rising again in his mouth...

No! Told you! Doomed! She's Arlaghaun's creature! DOOMED!

Fade to black.

THE HAND THAT came down on his wrist was slender and shapely and as strong as unyielding iron.

The stout onetime pirate struggled to free his hand, grunting and sweating and suddenly throwing all his weight behind a shove, followed by a titanic pull.

The delicate-looking hand remained right where it was, but its strikingly beautiful owner put her face very close to his.

Which meant her bosom thrust against him, somewhere just under his chin, soft and yet shockingly firm.

"Garfist Gulkoon," Dauntra of the Aumrarr said pleasantly, "or to use the name you were born with: Norbryn, if you try to steal from me, or any of my sisters, ever again, we shall remove a surplus part of your anatomy. Your right thumb, I think. If you try again, the left one. Then your male member, which I doubt you've been able to properly see for years, without the aid of a mirror, and then your nose. A man looks somewhat strange without a nose. Then we'll start on your fingers. This may perhaps have a detrimental effect upon your future endeavors, but frankly I care not. Now, do we understand each other?"

"Y-yes," Garfist managed to squeak, letting go of the little dagger he'd tried to draw out of her elbow-sheath. Without seeming to hurry in the slightest, she caught it in midair, her large and impish brown eyes never leaving his.

"Sorry," he muttered. "Uh... ah... how is it you know my... cradle name?"

"Old Ox, we know all about you," Dauntra said, and kissed him.

A moment later she drew back her warm lips from his, smiled again into his incredulous face, and added sweetly, "That's why I'm being so gentle with you. I could have just bitten off your nose and some fingers, and started chewing."

THE STONE FLOOR was cold and hard and uneven; Rod came awake shivering in the dark.

He was naked, and in some sort of room underground, probably a dungeon cell. He wasn't chained, and there didn't seem to be anyone else sharing the room with him. Or at least, he couldn't hear anyone else breathing but himself.

No Taeauna, no enchanted items, not even the little whispering voice.

There you're wrong, came the faintest of whispers. *Fool of fools.*

"Lorontar?" Rod asked.

Silence.

"Lorontar?" he asked again, raising his voice. It echoed back to him, and from a great distance away there came a faint, short grating sound.

Then silence again.

"Damn," Rod murmured, sagging back down.

I was right, the tiny voice deep in his head said, so faint he had to strain to hear it at all. *Next time, listen to me, and believe. IF you get a next time, Rod Everlar.*

"Damn," Rod said, more loudly.

There came no reply, so he lay still in the darkness, and let it swallow him. It was dark enough to suit his mood, at least.

After what seemed like a long time he sighed, got up to his knees, and started crawling forward, gingerly feeling in front of him with outstretched hands. It wasn't long before he came to a wall; he turned left and felt along it, finding the seams of what was probably a door. A little way beyond that was a corner, and it didn't seem to take all that long a time before he'd found his way all the way around the walls of his smallish rectangular room.

He laid back down again and tried to think of the real world, tried to recall things in all their vivid colors, smells, and... and...

Taeauna. Always her face intruded, smiling, lips parting to meet his... Or falling into his bed, that first time he saw her, bleeding and crying out for him, the Dark Helms bursting in on them...

Taeauna, who'd betrayed him. In the grip of Arlaghaun's spells, though, and she'd fought to show him that, at the end, when it was too late. She'd felt sad at his fate.

Where was she now?

For that matter, where was he now?

Well, trapped in Falconfar, that much was certain. Try as he might, he couldn't think strongly enough of the real world, the world of Rod Everlar the writer, to leave this dark, cold place.

He was stuck here, presumably in Arlaghaun's clutches, for who knew how long? Until he died, perhaps, of thirst or the cold. A Shaper made powerless to shape...

Hmm. Perhaps...

He sat up against the wall, and started to sing, moving his hands through the air as if he was drawing some sort of intricate picture.

"Oh, I'm Shaping... shapes to change the world... shapes to make the Falcon fly where the Falcon has never flown before... just Shaping..."

If he could goad the wizard into sending someone to stop him...

He went on singing random nonsense about Shaping until he ran out of words, and then just hummed the notes of his "I'm just Shaping" refrain, over and over again. Waiting.

There came a metallic crash in the distance, and then footfalls, and a light! A torch, glimmering and bobbing in the distance, showing Rod the door was just there, and had a tiny slot window in it, up high. Too high for him to peer through. No lock or handle or keyhole, no hinges that he could see.

The light grew, moving steadily nearer and nearer. Rod looked quickly around, to see if he'd missed anything in the cell, and to judge its size better. It was just a bare room—no water, no toilet hole, no manacles, nothing—and it was about twenty feet across by about a dozen deep. Just the one door, nothing of interest on the walls, floor, or ceiling...

The torch flared right outside the window, blinding-bright.

Rod hissed in pain and turned his head away. Too late, of course. He heard something scraping momentarily against a stone wall. The torch was being slid into some sort of holder, he guessed.

Then a bar was lifted, wrestled, and set down; a heavy timber, by the sounds of it. The door grated open.

If this had been the climax of a movie, or a crucial scene in some heroic novel, he'd leap to his feet, brain his jailer, and flee to freedom.

Rod sat right where he was, still blinded.

Someone with heavy feet came ponderously into the cell and took him by the throat.

The hand around his throat was huge and horribly strong, and it smelled. Of swamp-water and some sort of rank, underlying musk. Rod blinked, trying to see, and then decided against it.

Whatever this was, it probably wasn't human.

Rod felt himself being lifted off his feet and carried, strangling in that grip. Out of the cell, he thought, smelling the torch now, very near.

And then the torch moved, was thrust against him, and held there searingly.

Rod screamed, as loud and as hard as he could and then tried to stop, in horror, as he felt flames being thrust against his mouth.

God, the pain!

Every breath was an agony, every...

He barely noticed when the torch was returned to its wall-holder and he was carried a step back, into the doorway.

He certainly noticed when the creature's other hand slammed one of his forearms against the door-frame.

And then drew away, only to slam back hard, breaking his arm across that stone edge.

Rod screamed again, or tried to.

He went on with that raw sobbing as he was flung to the cell floor, kicked in the ribs until he was over on his back, and then fresh agony, like ice, took the hand on his other arm with him.

Moaning, rocking, Rod tried to see through streaming eyes. One arm was broken, and his other hand was—gone.

It had been chopped off, with one hard and heavy blow from a dripping axe.

A hand that was slimy, olive green, and with fingers the shape of fat carrots took up his severed hand from the floor.

Rod fell back, still trying to scream. The door slammed, the bar was dropped back into place, and the torch was taken away.

His mouth was a cooked ruin, his chest burned deep and raw, and...

Not a word had been spoken to him.

That I can remedy. Heed me henceforth. After all, I told you so.

The tiny voice, so deep in his mind and sounding now so weary and feeble, was scant consolation.

"Keep me sane," Rod told it, or tried to; the words came out more as bubblings than anything else.

Sane? Ha! YEARS too late for that!

Whatever reply Rod's pain-mazed wits might have come up with was lost in a sudden voice purring nigh his ear.

"We'll just see how swiftly you heal, Shaper." It was Arlaghaun, gloating openly. "Of course, just one trial won't suffice. I'll be sending quite a procession of visitors to you. Perhaps even your little chained Aumrarr."

Rod struggled to utter suitable obscenities in reply, but couldn't. So he settled for fainting, instead.

WHEN HE AWAKENED, a little later, all the pain was gone. He seemed to have his hand back, and his broken arm felt whole. He was tingling, though, all over.

Then he heard a whooshing sound, as if something was approaching him very rapidly. The air seemed to crackle, with a very high-pitched singing sound, and rose-red radiance surrounded him.

When Rod opened his gummy, encrusted eyes, and turned his head to look at where the magic had come from, he found himself staring through the open cell doorway at a distant robed figure, standing well down a stone passage beyond. It wasn't Arlaghaun, but someone younger. Younger and broader of shoulders and belly, with an unkempt, curly beard like a fringe all around his jaw.

The mage was glaring at him, a little fearfully, and raising his hands to warily cast another spell.

Another trial. Well, magic he could ignore, as it seemed to ignore him. Rod closed his eyes again.

Briefly he entertained the idea of rolling to his feet and racing out of the cell, kicking the young wizard where it would hurt most and then running like hell... but no. Arlaghaun would be watching, and that brutal, slimy thing with the green hands was probably the least of the horrors that wizard could send to disembowel or acid-melt or sting or even lay eggs into him, his latest helpless captive.

Yes, Arlaghaun was watching right now.

Rod smiled, just to give the wizard something to think about.

"Wizard," he added, as another spell washed over him, "your doom is now inevitable. I was going to spare you, but now, I think not."

Mere empty words, but perhaps they would worry Arlaghaun, and give him something to try to unearth. Or something else to waste his time on.

Another spell cracked and crackled over him. Rod yawned, and went to sleep again.

"WHAT WOULD YOU say to me," Velduke Mistryn asked, over their third pouring of wine, "if I said I was seriously debating whether or not to kill you, here and now, and take the crown of Galath for my own?"

"I'm not sure, Mard," King Brorsavar replied quietly, his broad shoulders shifting not at all, neither of his hands heading for a weapon-hilt. "Is it something you feel it's likely you'll say to me?"

Mardrammur Mistryn smiled. "No. No, I don't think so. Not anymore."

After a moment, he added, "I can tell by your face that you're protected against the mranth."

"That and the fact I haven't fallen dead on that face just yet," the king said dryly. "Pity to taint good wine with it, though."

"For Galath, one must make sacrifices."

"Indeed."

Chapter Twenty-Four

ROD WAS GETTING used to the pain. Arlaghaun didn't send his apprentices to the cell often, just to try casting spells on his wounds or severed stumps from time to time.

Yet the Doom of Galath seemed to have a small army of cruel, malicious monsters that delighted in breaking limbs, raking open skin, and even eating hands and feet right off Rod Everlar's living body.

Seeking to learn the secrets or limits of a Shaper's healing and magic-immunity powers, my left testicle.

And it had been the right one, too, from time to time.

It still hurt like sin when he was violated or had something torn out or chopped off, but he was getting used to it.

It was true. One really could get used to anything.

He was getting weaker, yes; he had no idea how long he'd been here, but there'd been no food. No water, either, but the various monsters often forced open his mouth—or broke his jaw, if he resisted—and relieved themselves down his throat. Most of their urine was like liquid fire, or worse, but some was nearly water. Close enough, it seemed.

He was tired now; he was always tired. He ached, too, in every waking moment. So much for being a Shaper, or a Lord High Archwizard…

Rod was lying on his back, on the patch of cell floor that had just enough of a hump to serve him as a sort of pillow. There wasn't much left of his right leg below the knee since it had been crushed to bloody pulp by a laughing, cursing monster with a face like crawling eels, but it was slowly healing, and there were, as he'd already reminded himself, no pressing social engagements that he had to hurry and be on his feet for.

He didn't bother to open his eyes at the sounds of lightly trudging footfalls, but couldn't help being mildly interested. Whoever was struggling with the door-bar was weaker than the monsters.

His soon-to-be-visitor was breathing heavily, now, and setting down a lantern on the floor. Rod heard an uncertain, wary male voice murmur a brief incantation, and then a face seemed to form in his mind, like patches of frost spreading across a winter-lashed window.

It was the fat young scraggle-bearded apprentice who'd once hurled spells at him.

Yes, said the whispering voice deep in Rod's mind. *YES.*

And Lorontar the Archwizard reared up like a snake inside Rod and struck, lashing without warning through Rod's thoughts right into the fearful mind of the apprentice Klammert.

In a few terrified instants Rod became aware of the apprentice's name, that Arlaghaun had sent him to attempt the dangerous task of spell-probing Rod's mind because the Doom preferred not to risk his own wits, and that Lorontar had been biding his time down deep in Rod's memories for just such a chance as this.

And had now seized it.

Lorontar had ridden Klammert's probe right back into the apprentice's mind, overwhelmed him, and taken control of his body.

Rod opened his eyes in time to see Klammert turn and rush off down the passage. His contact with Lorontar faded with every running step, but he'd "heard" enough to know the thralled Klammert was hurrying to try to slay Arlaghaun.

Leaving the cell door open.

Rod Everlar rolled over, found his right foot coming back to what it should be, got up awkwardly on that shifting clubfoot, and staggered out into the passage.

He had no idea where he was, or what was the way out, but he could hear the faint din of Klammert's headlong rush out of the dungeon, up ahead; it was easy enough to follow it.

"Even a fool like Rod Everlar can manage that," he told the stone walls around him.

Politely, they declined to reply.

* * *

THE GATE OF spikes would have slain Klammert in an instant, if the running wizard had merely been Arlaghaun's apprentice. Lorontar, however, knew secrets of Ult Tower that the Doom of Galath had never learned, and had chosen this route well.

He flung his fat, borrowed body under the first portcullis, and then drew back before the second with perfect timing, hearing Arlaghaun's gloating laughter peal out of the empty air at so easily trapping him.

Wasting no time on a response, he touched the second portcullis and murmured the command that would make it melt away and trigger the backlash.

When Ult Tower shook and Arlaghaun's chuckles became a sudden, raw scream, Lorontar did allow his borrowed body to shape a small smile.

In the instant before he vanished, taking himself magically to where he could blast the Doom of Galath personally.

After all, traps and trigger-spells were expensive things; there was no sense damaging them when they might well belong to him very shortly.

Ruling Galath seemed to involve a lot of traps, these days.

ROD CLIMBED TWO sets of worn, bloodstained stone stairs before he was free of the dungeon and stumbled onto a floor of interlinked, furnished chambers. My, but there seemed to be a lot of other prisoners, he thought to himself, many of them things with hairy claws or tentacles protruding from their tiny cell windows.

By then, his foot was whole again, and the architecture of the smooth stone walls, the ledges and trim around the archways, and the lofty vaulted halls, was starting to look familiar. This was probably Ult Tower.

He started to move cautiously, recalling all the guardians. He had no idea where he should go, but if he found that row of glowing gates, almost anywhere in Falconfar would be better than here.

The great fortress seemed deserted, and no wonder. Every servant and guardian who had any wits to think was probably hiding and cowering right now. Anything that could make the whole place shudder and rock, as it was doing quite often, as he walked, was something to be avoided. A few stone shards and a lot of dust came raining down from time to time, but Rod could only shrug. If Ult Tower was going to come crashing down on him, there was nothing he could do about it. And after all the agonies of his imprisonment, he found that he didn't much care.

He turned a corner and saw a beaded curtain in an archway ahead. It was the first "filled" archway he'd seen thus far, so he went over to take a look. When Rod parted it with his hand, lightning bolts stabbed through him.

Doing nothing, of course, though they'd probably have slain anyone else. He peered into the room beyond, and whistled.

A glowing sword was floating horizontally above a huge, magnificently carved table. Plinths ranged around the walls were topped with carved heads that sported superbly made war helms, and as Rod stared at them, Ult Tower rocked under the fury of another unleashed spell, and the helms either acquired momentary glows, or lightnings crawled across their curves. One plinth was fashioned into the shape of two upthrust hands, and the rings on those carved fingers were winking and shining.

Rod shouldered through the curtain, and became aware of movement to his right. A half-suit of armor was floating silently off its plinth and drifting menacingly toward him, reaching out an arm to pluck a sword from the wall.

He ran forward and snatched the big sword out of the air over the table; the power in it ran numbingly down his arm and left all his hair standing on end. Without pause, the advancing guardian rose a little to clear the table, and drew back its blade to hack at him two-handed.

Rod rolled off the table and fell into a crouch underneath its lip. When the guardian drifted over the edge, a moment later, and started to turn, to descend and slice at him, he waited for his chance to strike at its open bottom. The moment he saw the emptiness inside the armor, he thrust his new-found sword up through it, hard.

Blinding lightnings blazed, and the armor flew apart violently, toppling plinths and splintering legs off the table which thankfully seemed to have about a dozen legs left and therefore refrained from collapsing.

Rod's glowing blade was flung back past him into the far corners of the room, and in its wake he discovered his sword-arm was as limp as a rag because it was shattered.

Really shattered; almost boneless.

Recalling the procession of enchanted items sent by Lorontar that had so mysteriously appeared and had sunk into him, Rod dragged himself out from under the table, plucked rings off the plinth's fingers, and worked them onto his own fingers; both the good hand and the shattered one. Some of them started to fade away almost immediately.

Smiling wryly, Rod crossed the room to select a suitable helm.

THE BOLTS OF writhing lightning were emerald green, and tore through stone as readily as wood and flesh. "Die, Lorontar!" Arlaghaun roared triumphantly, brown eyes blazing like an eager fire.

"I did," the deep, dry, unfamiliar voice coming from the lips of his apprentice drawled, sidestepping the ravening destruction. "You should try it sometime. Now, for instance."

The lances of silver-blue magic that raced from his fingertips then were so many and so swift that the Doom of Galath barely had time to curse.

BEHOLD ROD EVERLAR, writer of fantasies. Strolling around this vast citadel fashionably dressed in... a helmet. *Ave Caesar, morituri te salutant.*

Rod grinned wryly at the mirror he'd found. It was probably magical, but it was much too small to step through as some sort of gate, and he didn't know what it was for or how to call on its powers, whatever they were, so he continued on with looking for swords and daggers. And if he couldn't find pants of some sort, at least a goddamn belt would do to carry them all with!

He probably needed every combat-useful shard of magic he could find. After all, if he might have to fight all of Arlaghaun's beasts and magical suits of armor or other toys, lorn, Dark Helms and apprentices—to say nothing of the Doom of Galath himself—he needed all the help he could get.

That he could carry, at least. There were a dozen helms back in that first room with the curtain, and a chair that glowed interestingly, too, but he couldn't carry everything.

Shaking his head at the appearance he'd presented in the mirror, Rod went to the next room, and peered in.

A whimpering woman stared fearfully back at him. She wore only chains, and manacles at her wrists and ankles secured her upright in a huge "X" in midair.

It was Taeauna.

THE SECOND STONE from the left-hand end of the row of tell-stones flared into sudden, starry light.

The slender, darkly handsome wizard turned to regard it, and calmly watched it shatter, hiss, and melt away.

"Well, now," Malraun murmured. "Something is very amiss at Ult Tower."

He spun gracefully around to ready his most powerful scrying-crystal, and added mockingly, "That's so sad."

The crystal started to glow and then burst with a shriek, hurling shards in all directions. If his personal wardings hadn't been up and active, one of them would almost certainly have beheaded him.

As it was, still in possession of his head, Malraun smiled, shook his head, and strolled into another room with a calmer demeanor than he truly felt, to awaken three lesser scrying-crystals.

It seemed like the Falcon itself was breaking loose at Ult Tower, and he intended to watch every moment of it.

"L-LORD ROD?" TEARS were already streaming down Taeauna's face, but they seemed to flood forth even faster, dripping off her chin, thence to her breasts, and on to the floor.

"Tay!" Rod said eagerly, going to her. He raised a hand to her cheek, and tried to kiss her, but she shook her head and wept.

"Lord, I'm so s-sorry! I—"

"Taeauna, it wasn't you who threw me in a cell and tortured me. Now, let's get you free of these; do you know if any of these magical gewgaws I'm carrying can cut through chain? Without frying you, too?"

Taeauna shook her head again, as Ult Tower shook again, around them, in a thunderous rolling booming that numbed Rod's bare feet.

Rod tried to put a comforting arm around her, but his shoulder came to just under her armpit, so he went on tiptoe to kiss her, and say urgently, "Taeauna of the Aumrarr, I blame you for nothing. Nothing. But help me now. Tell me how to free you."

Her tears stopped suddenly and her head jerked up, eyes glowing like two lamps. She turned her head, as if startled and seeing him for the first time, and said softly, "Shaper of Falconfar, only the tears of Arlaghaun can part these chains. His tears, freely given. I need you to—"

"Swallow your lies, creature of Arlaghaun," said a mocking voice from behind Rod. "Listen to her not, Dark Lord. The real Taeauna is imprisoned inside her, somewhere; see those glowing eyes? That's Arlaghaun trying to lure you within reach."

Rod turned, selected the most powerful-looking sword from the bundle in his hands, hefted it, and said to the short, sleek, darkly handsome man he found himself facing, "And who are you?"

"I am Malraun. Also a wizard of Falconfar, but nothing at all to do with the Doom of Galath or his cruelties. I mean you no harm, nor this Aumrarr. Put your sword down; I have no quarrel with you."

"And if I do step aside, what do you plan to do?"

"Cut those chains and free her. You don't need anyone's tears—"

"Listen to him not, lord! This man is evil; he will carry me off and turn me into a monster!"

Malraun rolled his eyes, and said to Rod, "That's not your Taeauna talking. That's Arlaghaun, and he's desperate."

"He hasn't seemed all that desperate to me, thus far," Rod replied, keeping his sword up and in Malraun's way.

"He wasn't fighting just to keep hold of his life, then," Malraun replied. "He is now. He's awakened Lorontar from beyond the grave, as minstrels like to say, and much of yonder end of Ult Tower is vanishing as we speak, as they hurl spells at each other and Arlaghaun rapidly comes to the grim realization that he's far more of an overconfident idiot than he thought he was."

"I don't trust you," Rod muttered.

"Very wise of you, Dark Lord. I don't trust any wizard, and neither should any sane person. Yet consider: I translocated myself here, right behind you, and could very easily have blasted you to dust, and yet I attacked you not. I could have just melted the chains of your Taeauna with a spell, without any warning, but have not. I'm perfectly willing to melt her chains right now, with you holding that impressive sword to my throat. What say you?"

Rod looked at Taeauna, who hissed, "No! Lord Rod, listen to him not!"

"Watch her eyes, Rod," Malraun said calmly. "See that glow? That's Arlaghaun, inside her head, working her lips."

"No! Rod, don't let him!"

Malraun looked at Rod, shrugged and spread his hands. "I can free her; do you think the real Taeauna wants to be chained here, nude and helpless? And remember who put her there."

Rod swallowed, looking from Taeauna's pleading face to Malraun's, and back. Then he said roughly, "Do it. Free her."

The wizard nodded and started forward.

The air in front of him cracked apart, purple fire leaking around the edges of a great night-black slash that sent the air in the room into a whistling, rushing roiling—and Arlaghaun was suddenly standing in Malraun's way.

"Oh, no, you don't," he snarled, "hedge-wizard!"

Malraun merely rolled his eyes and unleashed lightning from his hands. Four bolts streaked past the Doom of Galath on either side, parting Taeauna's chains in a welter of sparks.

As she fell to the floor, Rod made a dash for her, sword up to ward off anything Arlaghaun might do.

The Doom of Galath sneered, raised a hand that was suddenly ablaze like a bonfire, and hurled flame at Malraun.

Who stood, smile unchanged, as the burst of flame washed over nothingness just in front of him, and slid away, fading as it writhed and lashed the floor.

Rod ducked away from Arlaghaun to prevent the mage making a grab for him on his way to Taeauna, who was rolling around and sobbing, but Arlaghaun turned and spat, "You should have stayed where you belonged, Shaper!"

And the ceiling opened up in a shower of falling fangs.

Rod shouted and hurled himself forward, knowing it was in vain. He and Taeauna were both going to be impaled on the scores of plunging blades...

The air sang bright and blue, Rod was nearly deafened by the sudden sound of hundreds of blades clanging and clashing—and Arlaghaun disappeared into a bloody pulp amid a column of edged steel slamming down deep into the floor, so thickly clustered that they were almost edge to edge.

"Who—?" Malraun snapped, staring at Rod as he skidded into a dazed and suddenly silent Taeauna. "Did you...?"

"No," said a deep, dry, slightly husky voice from behind the wizard. "It wasn't the poor Shaper. It was me."

Malraun whirled around. "Klammert?" he asked incredulously.

"This was Klammert, and will be again, very shortly."

"Lorontar!"

"Indeed. Not quite as dead beyond dead as Arlaghaun thought he'd just made me. Overconfidence seems to run rampant among wizards, these days. You, for instance, thought you'd just stroll in, seize the Aumrarr, and thereby lure the revealed Dark Lord to willingly follow you, into your clutches. Narmarkoun, who's watching us all right now, is just as convinced that you'll be walking right into his little trap."

"Oh?" Malraun's voice was soft, his eyes glittering. "And what is oh-so-wise Lorontar convinced of, just now?"

"That all the spells Arlaghaun cast and held in abeyance, to take effect at the time of his death, will come down on the head of this poor wretch I've possessed. Such a waste of apprentices."

And that was when the room exploded.

A TALL AND blue-scaled Doom of Falconfar absently caressed the smooth skulls of his dead wenches, as they pressed in ardently around him, and settled himself deeper into their icy embraces. Their companionship would have to suffice; aside from Narmarkoun himself, there were no living men or women for many days of travel from this room.

"And about now," he murmured into their endless grins, expecting no reply and receiving none, "ah, yes, there, unnoticed in all the tumult of unleashed magic, the shadowy wraith of Lorontar races from the burning body of the unfortunate Klammert into the Aumrarr. Whom Malraun will now carry off, little knowing that by doing so he dooms himself. Lorontar knows the Dark Lord will try to come to Malraun, who knows not that Lorontar wants Malraun. Neatly done."

He turned away from his spell-spun scene of the sobbing, reeling Taeauna, as it showed Malraun snatching her and opening a ring of purple fire in the midst of all the roiling fire and lightnings.

"Yet a mistake, Lorontar. You may gain control over Malraun's magic and servitors, yet in doing so you have forewarned me, and Narmarkoun is *not* an overconfident fool. Though I look forward to the luxury of becoming one, when I am Lord Archwizard of Falconfar."

Behind him, unregarded in his fading scrying, Malraun and the Aumrarr vanished through a swirling, dwindling iris of purple fire, leaving a despairing Rod Everlar reaching vainly for them.

ROD STOPPED GRIMLY in front of the magic mirror. Thankfully, Arlaghaun and Lorontar hadn't destroyed it in their spell-battle, though the far end of the hall, behind him, was twisted and blackened.

He clanked at every step, clad in ill-fitting but hummingly magical armor, and staggered under the weight of all the magic he was carrying.

He might need it all to rescue Taeauna.

He didn't even know where this Malraun laired, but the mirror should show him where Taeauna was, and if the orb in his left gauntlet did what Klammert's notes said it was supposed to do, he could use it to control one of the gates of Ult Tower to go to whichever place he was thinking of.

"Taeauna!" he snarled at the mirror, picturing her face. "Show me Taeauna!"

The scene of a castle against racing white clouds obediently dissolved into a darker scene of a torch-lit chamber full of Dark Helms.

They stood in a ring, laughing, no swords drawn. In their midst, in the center of the ring, was a woman clad only in manacles, who swung a sword at them all desperately; a sword that harmed them not, as it sprang back from spells that were protecting the warriors.

Rod clenched his teeth as their laughter rose higher, and looked again at Taeauna.

She was crying as she swung the sword.

Here ends Book One of the Falconfar Saga. The adventures of Rod Everlar, Taeauna, and the other folk of Falconfar will continue in **ARCHWIZARD**

DRAMATIS PERSONAE
[named characters only]

"See" references occur where only partial character names appear in the novel text (such as when a surname is omitted). Not all folk in Falconfar have family names; Aumrarr, for example, never have surnames.

Some lore has been omitted here so as not to spoil readers' enjoyment of later books in the Falconfar saga. These entries do contain some "spoilers" for DARK LORD, and for maximum enjoyment of that book, should be referred to when three-quarters or more of the text has been read.

A note on the nobility of Galath: from lowest to highest, their ranks are: knight, baron, klarl, marquel, arduke, velduke, lordrake, prince, king. A knight is a "sir," but barons and up are addressed as "lord" (it is acceptable to call the reigning monarch "Lord of All Galath," but "the Lords of Galath" are the collective nobility). Outside Galath, the "Lord" of a place is usually its ruler.

Amalrys ("Ah-MAUL-rees"): Apprentice to Arlaghaun, who keeps her in Ult Tower, nude and manacled in enchanted, chiming chains, as his fetch-and-carry assistant.

Ambrelle: Aumrarr, the eldest and most severe of "the Four Aumrarr" who fly together, seeking to avenge the slaughter at Highcrag.

Ammurt, Tauntyn: Baron of Galath (noble), formerly a border knight (his keep, like those of most border knights, was in impoverished northwest Galath) by the name of Tauntyn Lhorrance, ennobled as Baron Ammurt by King Devaer (in Chapter Eleven of DARK LORD), to replace Baron Gustras Ammurt, who was slain (with all his kin and household) by the wizard Arlaghaun for ignoring the summons of the king to Galathgard.

Arlaghaun: "The Doom of Galath," widely considered the most powerful of the three Dooms (wizards of peerless power), and the true ruler of Galath. Arlaghaun inhabits Ult Tower, the black stone keep of the long-dead wizard Ult, in Galath, and with his spells commands many lorn and Dark Helms and controls the every utterance of King Devaer of Galath. Some judge his power so great that they even call him "the Doom of Falconfar."

Aumrarr, the: A race of winged warrior-women who fight for "good." They seem human except for their large, snow-white wings, and fly about taking messages from one hold to another, battling wolves and monsters, and working against oppressive rulers. They are dedicated to making the lives of common folk (farmers, woodcutters, and crafters, not the wealthy or rulers) better, and laws and law-enforcement just. Their home, in the hills north of Arvale, is the fortress of Highcrag.

Authren, Beln: Seneschal of Morngard and loyal retainer of Baron Mrantos Murlstag. A burly, no-nonsense warrior who hates disorder and intrigue, preferring strict discipline, adherence to laws and rules, and open dealing.

Barrowbar, Kandron: Velduke of Galath (noble), dead of "old age" Before the events of DARK LORD, unbeknownst to Galath, he was the first of several nobles murdered by the wizard Arlaghaun to gain their wealth and magic and lose their fierce opposition. Barrowbar was the last of his line, so his title died with him.

Belrikoun, Urleth: Ruling Scepter of Sholdoon, an independent, rather lawless wealthy port of feuding merchants on the shores of Ommaun the Wyrmsea (far southeast from Galath, across the Falconspires mountain range). A fat former pirate and daily glutton who is also shrewd, just, and occasionally kind.

Blackraven, Larren: Marquel of Galath (noble), a young noble newly ascended to his title upon the death of his father, Orlarryn (murdered by Arlaghaun, whom he discovered forcing himself on his wife, Lady Mraetha Blackraven, and attacked). Larren has no inkling his parents' death was magical, truly believing the lightning bolt that split their turret in a fierce storm to be a "misfortune of the gods."

Blaurin, Marlax: Aging veteran armsman, wise and opinionated; a guard for Lord Tharlark at Tabbrar Castle.

Bloodhunt, Aumon: Velduke of Galath (noble), an elderly, plain-spoken, "embrace the old ways" Lord of Galath, with a haughty streak but a love of justice. His failing body gives him constant pain, which in turn keeps him constantly angry.

Braelyn ("BRAY-linn"): Aumrarr, who often visited Hollowtree. In Chapter One of DARK LORD, Warsword Lhauntur momentarily mistakes Taeauna for her. Braelyn was killed at Highcrag.

Brorsavar, Melander: Velduke of Galath (noble), a stern, just, "steady" and therefore popular Lord of Galath, well-respected by most of his fellow nobles. He is a large, impressive-looking man, with shoulders as broad as two slender men, standing side by side, and at the end of DARK LORD gains status.

Carandrur, Iglun: Small, sly cobbler of Arbridge, and member of the Vengeful.

Chainamund, Glusk: Baron of Galath (noble), a fat, unhappy man widely disliked among his fellow Galathan nobles for his unpleasant, haughty, and aggressive manner, and his dishonesty (more than a few of them refer to him as a "weasel").

Chulcemar, Baereth: Armsman of Tarmoral, part of the castle guard of Wrathgard.

Darfest, Markoun: Loyal armsman of Bowrock, holding the rank of Swordguard, and stationed in Deldragon's keep.

Dark Helms: Warriors, described as "ruthless slayers in black armor." Living men and (increasingly, as their losses mount over time) undead warriors, these enspelled-to-loyalty soldiers are the creations of Holdoncorp.

Dauntra: Aumrarr, youngest, most beautiful, and most saucy of "the Four Aumrarr" who fly together, seeking to avenge the slaughter at Highcrag.

Deldragon, Darendarr: Velduke of Galath (noble), independent of King Devaer and prepared (with hired Stormar wizards and loyal warriors) to defy Arlaghaun's influence. Deldragon dwells in the fortified town of Bowrock on the southern edge of Galath, which surrounds his soaring castle, Bowrock Keep. A handsome, dashing battle hero, of a family considered "great" in Galath, whom foes of the Doom of Galath rally to, but who is increasingly embattled within his realm.

Dhaerar, Vorl: Satrap (regional ruler) of Scarlorn. His palace is haunted by the ghosts of his aunts; these phantoms strangle spies and foes of Dhaerar.

Dombur, Kundrae: Traveling merchant (his coffee-hued skin marks him as visibly from Marraudro, in the Spellshunned Lands), and member of the Vengeful.

Dooms, the: Wizards so much more powerful than most wizards that they are feared all across Falconfar as nigh-unstoppable forces. For decades there were three Dooms: Arlaghaun (widely considered the most powerful of the three); Malraun; and Narmarkoun. Rod Everlar comes to be considered the fourth Doom.

Dunshar, Annusk: Klarl of Galath (noble), a cruel, burly warrior of much experience, a willing servant of (and spy for, upon his fellow nobles) the wizard Arlaghaun. Disliked by most of his fellow Lords of Galath.

Durraran, Imgrul: Vintner of Hollowtree, of Lord Eldalar's household in Hollowtree Keep.

Duthcrown, Oedlam: Marquel of Galath (noble), a young but prematurely white-haired noble of sour, sneering disposition but much wealth—hence his many mistresses.

Eldalar, Baerlun: Lord of Hollowtree, a stiff, gruff old warrior displeased and more than a little afraid at "the way things are unfolding" in Falconfar (Galath in particular). He's more than just displeased after he hears of the slaughter at Highcrag.

Eldenstone, Korgrath: "Foehammer," locally famous dwarf warrior, a guardian at the gates of the mountain fortress of Stonebold.

Everlar, Rod: Hack writer of novels, who believes himself the creator of Falconfar. In Falconfar, a "Shaper" (one whose writings can change reality), believed to be one of the Dooms (powerful wizards). Referred to as "the Dark Lord" (the most evil and most powerful of all wizards, a bogeyman of legend) by the other Dooms, to blame him for their misdeeds. Publicly called "Rodrell" by Taeauna, to avoid using his true name. Considered the Lord Archwizard of Falconfar by the Aumrarr (the first Lord Archwizard since Lorontar).

Fandrel, Dursra: Wandering peddler; a fat but tough old woman known to babble "words of the gods" when drunk.

Feskeldarr, Glaroskur: Knight of the personal bodyguard of King Devaer Rothryn of Galath.

Forarr, Korryk: Armsman in the service of the wizard Arlaghaun, who holds a low opinion of most of Arlaghaun's apprentices.

Galzyn, Roeglar ("ROW-glar GALL-zinn"): Loyal knight of Velduke Mardrammur Mistryn, duty captain of the gateguard of the castle of Mistgates.

Glaethyn, Lemral: Elderly armsman of Tarmoral; a veteran warrior.

Gulkoun, Garfist: Often referred to as "Old Ox" or "Old Blundering Ox" by his partner Iskarra Taeravund, this coarse, burly and aging onetime pirate, former forger, and then panderer later became a hiresword (mercenary warrior), and these days wanders Falconfar with Iskarra, making a living as a thief and swindler. "Garfist" is actually a childhood nickname that he adopted as his name, vastly preferring it to Norbryn, the name his parents gave him.

Hammerhand, Burrim: Lord of Ironthorn, a large prosperous, military strong-hold in the forests north of Tauren and northeast of Sardray, that for years has had three rival lords, ruling from three separate keeps. Gruff and shrewd, Hammerhand is the strongest of the three, a large, hardy, capable warrior and battle-leader.

Haremmon, Marl: Satrap (regional ruler) of Scarlorn. A stern, just warrior, tall and imposing of appearance.

Holdoncorp: A large computer gaming company that licenses the electronic media games rights to the world of Falconfar from Rod Everlar, and develops a series of computer games that increasingly diverge from Everlar's own vision of his world. Despite what some readers may think, Holdoncorp is *not* based on any real-world corporation or group of people. *Dark Lord* is a fantasy story, not a satire of anything real.

Hornsar, Beldros: Velduke of Galath (noble), independent of King Devaer, an aging recluse, last of one of the realm's "great families," who keeps to his strongly fortified and defended castle of The Horn, atop a mountain in the north of Galath.

Hraskur, Arl: Waveking of Harfleet, an independent port on the shores of Ommaun the Wyrmsea (far southeast from Galath, across the Falconspires mountain range). Enamoured of feminine beauty, Hraskur is a wise, worldly ruler who is increasingly wary of threats to his rule.

Imlaun, Jarth ("Imm-LON"): The youngest body-guard of Baron Darl Tindror; a scarred, laconic young warrior.

Imbrar, Orvran: "Auld Orvran," elderly dwarf warrior, guardian at the gates of the mountain fortress of Stonebold.

Jorduth, Klel: Cynical armsman, a guard for Lord Tharlark at Tabbrar Castle.

Juskra: Aumrarr, the most battle-scarred, hot-tempered, and aggressive of the "Four Aumrarr" who fly together, seeking to avenge the slaughter at Highcrag.

Klammert: A wizard, one of the youngest and least accomplished apprentices of the wizard Arlaghaun; a pudgy, less than brave man.

Korlyn, Torl: Armsman of Tarmoral, part of the castle guard of Wrathgard.

Kylmar, Parl ("KYE-ul-mar"): Knight of Bowrock, trusted bodyguard of Velduke Darendarr Deldragon.

Lhauntur, Duskos: Warsword of Hollowtree (master of defenses; a knight of Hollowtree who commands the other knights of Hollowtree), a small hill-hold that is Rod Everlar's favorite place when he thinks of Falconfar. Lhauntur is a dry, cynical, wary man.

Lionhelm, Halath: Arduke of Galath (noble), a handsome man who sees loyalty to King Devaer as his only way of surviving, but has his own ideas about true justice and proper rule, and is quietly seeking a means of destroying the wizard Arlaghaun. Somehow.

Lorlarra: Aumrarr, one of the "Four Aumrarr" who fly together, seeking to avenge the slaughter at Highcrag.

lorn, the: Race of winged, flying horned and taloned predatory creatures that dwell in rocky heights such as castle towers and the Falconspires mountain range. Often described as mouthless by humans because their skull-like faces have no visible jaws, they typically swarm prey, raking with their talons and even tearing limbs, bodies, or heads off or apart. They have bat-like, featherless wings, barbed tails, and slate-gray skin. Arlaghaun, Malraun, and many lesser wizards have discovered or developed spells for compelling lorn into servitude.

Lorontar: The still-feared-in-legend first Lord Archwizard of Falconfar, once the fell and tyrannical ruler of all Falconfar, and the first spell-tamer of the lorn. Long believed dead but secretly surviving in spectral unlife, seeking a living body to mind-guide, "ride," and ultimately possess. So greatly is his memory feared that no one, not even a powerful wizard, has dared to try to dwell in his great black tower, Yintaerghast, since his presumed death.

Malraeana: Aumrarr, put into spellsleep to heal by Ambrelle of "the Four Aumrarr," after being sorely wounded in battle.

Malraun: "The Matchless," wizard, one of the Dooms of Falconfar. A short, sleek, darkly handsome man who dwells in a tower in Harlhoh, a hold in the green depths of Raurklor, the Great Forest. Malraun spies on the doings of Arlaghaun, his spells penetrating even into the heart of Ult Tower, but largely keeps the lorn and spell-subverted traders who serve him out of Galath (though to stop Arlaghaun from expanding that realm, he has increasingly caused outlaws from it, and poor or disaffected Stormar, to raid the western borders of Galath and "keep Arlaghaun busy" directing the nobles of Galath in fighting them off).

Marintra: Aumrarr, one of Taeauna's closest friends, and onetime lover. Slain at Highcrag.

Mistryn, Mardrammur: Velduke of Galath (noble), a well-respected, senior noble of Galath (his family is considered "great"), but increasingly isolated due to his opposition to what he calls "the wizard-dancing rule of Devaer the Dangerous." Known as "Mard" to his friends, Velduke Mistryn has in recent years kept to his castle of Mistgates, in mountainous central southwestern Galath.

Mountblade, Ondurs: Marquel of Galath (noble), a young nobleman who wears unnecessary monacles for "style" and dwells in the castle of Mountgard, a stone mansion surrounded by magnificent gardens, in south-central Galath.

Murlstag, Mrantos: Baron of Galath (noble), a cruel, bullying man who obeys Arlaghaun eagerly, out of sheer terror of magic. The barony of Murlstag is in the southeastern reaches of Galath, south of the barony of Tindror; Murlstag and Tindror are longtime foes who hate each other passionately. Murlstag is cold and cutting of speech, and possessed of strange yellow eyes. His baronial castle is the small fortress of Morngard, now infested by lorn sent by Arlaghaun to serve Murlstag—and spy on him (just as Murlstag spies on his fellow nobles for Arlaghaun).

Narmarkoun: Wizard, one of the Dooms of Falconfar; a tall, blue-skinned, scaly man who dwells alone in a hidden subterranean wilderland stronghold, Darthoun, a long-abandoned city of the dwarves—alone, that is, except for dead, skull-headed wenches animated by his spells, and breeds greatfangs (huge dragon-like scaly flying jawed lizards he uses as steeds). Most mysterious and considered the least in power of the Dooms, Narmarkoun is an accomplished, patient magical spy.

Nornil, Samryn: Loyal knight of Velduke Aumon Bloodhunt.

Nyghtshield, Margral: Baron of Galath (noble), a one-eyed veteran of much monster-hunting in the forests of the realm, nominally loyal to King Devaer but increasingly displeased by Arlaghaun's cruelties and the decline of Galath into a land of suspicions and harsh authority.

Ohmront, Belros ("AH-mm-ron-t"): trusted arms-man of Bowrock, stationed in Deldragon's keep.

Olnar, Raruskyn: Smith of Arbridge, a terrifically strong man who is a spy and sympathizer for the Vengeful.

Orstras, Hondemur: Innkeeper, master of The Two Drowned Knights in Arbridge. A spy and sympathizer for the Vengeful, and a spy for Lord Tharlark.

(Parl: see Kylmar, Parl.)

Pethmur, Lothondos: Baron of Galath (noble), a stone-faced veteran warrior who likes stability, obedience to authority, and plain dealing; he hates sly folk and intrigues, preferring the sword, bended knees, and clear decrees.

Phandele: Aumrarr, put into spellsleep to heal by Ambrelle of "the Four Aumrarr," after being sorely wounded in battle.

Pheldur, Iyrimmon: Traveling merchant (his almost black-hued skin marks him as born in Inrysk, in the Spellshunned Lands) and member of the Vengeful.

Qelhand, Daern: Veteran armsman of Murlstag, trusted by Baron Murlstag for important (often covert) tasks.

Quevve, Natharra ("Kuh-WEV"): "Natha," a dusky-skinned Stormar native who works as a "castle courtesan" (hostess) for Velduke Darendarr Deldragon, in his keep in Bowrock.

Reskrul, Naunath: Traveling merchant from Scarlorn, a fat and cheerful trader who leads a mule-train of small goods (tools, buttons, and the like) to small holds like Hollowtree every year.

Rosera: Name used in the past by Iskarra "Viper" Taeravund.

Rothryn, Arbrand: King of Galath and father of Devaer. A stern, just man, widely respected, and covertly slain by the wizard Arlaghaun, in a "hunting accident" in Terth Forest. The king was torn apart and devoured by seven monsters, all spell-commanded by the hidden wizard.

Rothryn, Bellomir: Lordrake of Galath, half-brother to King Arbrand Rothryn. A shrewd strategist and counter-of-coins, who was openly slain by the wizard Arlaghaun.

Rothryn, Devaer: King of Galath, a young, handsome, and haughty wastrel youngest prince who became the puppet of the wizard Arlaghaun, after the Doom of Galath slew the rest of Devaer's kin, to put him on the throne of Galath. Now widely known as "the Mad King" because of his apparently nonsensical decrees. As monarch, he has many other official titles, including "Lord of Falcons."

Rothryn, Keldur: Prince of Galath, the eldest son and heir of King Arbrand Rothryn.

Rothryn, Rarcel: Lordrake of Galath, half-brother to King Arbrand Rothryn. A "merry mountain" of a jovial warrior, openly challenged and slain by the wizard Arlaghaun.

Saeredarr, Taerith: A young and secretly ambitious wizard, loyal apprentice of Arlaghaun, the Doom of Galath, who taught him tantlar magic.

Sahrlor, Dyrak: Knight and sometime ruler of Arbridge, who drowned in the stream that bisects Arvale some years before the events chronicled in DARK LORD, while fighting Sir Eldrel Tabbrar. The death of the two knights is commemorated in the name of Arbridge's inn, *The Two Drowned Knights*.

Snowlance, Broryn: Klarl of Galath (noble), a reedy-voiced, sickly successor to a brawling, roaring, hard-drinking legend of a father, Urlos Snowlance. Loyal to King Devaer, but with increasing misgivings (kept to himself).

Stormserpent, Laskrar: Arduke of Galath (noble), a tall, muscular, darkly handsome accomplished warrior of a nobleman often found hunting (or fighting, in battle) alongside his friend, Arduke Yars Windtalon.

Tabbrar, Eldrel: Knight and sometime ruler of southern Arvale, who drowned in the stream that bisects Arvale some years before the events chronicled in DARK LORD, while fighting Sir Dyrak Sahrlor. The death of the two knights is commemorated in the name of Arbridge's inn, *The Two Drowned Knights*.

The current Lord of Arbridge, Lord Qreskos Tharlark, who actually rules all Arvale, now dwells in Tabbrar Castle, the keep Tabbrar built out of the rising rock of the Falconspire Mountains at the south end of Arvale.

Taeauna ("TAY-awna"): Aumrarr, who in desperation "calls on" Rod Everlar, seeking to bring him to Falconfar so he can use his powers as a Shaper to deliver her world from the depredations of the Dark Helms (especially those commanded by the wizard Arlaghaun). A determined, worldly, experienced Aumrarr who harbors secrets yet to be revealed.

Taeravund, Iskarra: Best-known as "Viper" from her thieving days in the southern port of Hrathlar (her longtime partner-in-crime, Garfist Gulkoun, prefers to call her "Vipersides"), this profane, homely woman has been a swindler all her life, and has used many false names (including "Rosera"). Possessed of driving determination and very swift wits, she is as "skinny as a lance" (in the words of Garfist Gulkoun), but usually wears a false magical "crawlskin" (the magically-preserved, semi-alive skin of a long-dead sorceress), that she stole from a wizard in far eastern Sarmandar, and can by will can mold over herself to make herself look fat, lush, or spectacularly bosomed (and cover leather bladders in which she can hide stolen items). She now makes her living as a thief and swindler, wandering Falconfar with Gulkoun.

Teltusk, Tethgar: Arduke of Galath (noble), a young, well-intentioned Lord of Galath who wants to be loyal and do good—and fears that Arlaghaun will slay him soon, no matter what he (or any other Lord of Galath who cares about the realm) tries to do.

Tharlark, Qreskos: Lord of Arbridge; former arms-master of Sir Sahrlor of Arbridge, who now rules all Arvale from Tabbrar Castle. A cruel, ruthless hard-bitten warrior who wants Falconfar swept clean of all magic and wizards. He encourages the Vengeful without officially acknowledging or working with them.

Thrayl, Arlak: Shopkeeper of Arbridge (sundries), and a member of the Vengeful.

Three, the: See "Dooms, the." Specifically, the three paramount wizards of Falconfar before the arrival of Rod Everlar.

Tindror, Darl: Baron of Galath (noble), a gruff, decent, lawful man who opposes King Devaer's rule because of what he calls its "lawlessness by whim." From his castle, Wrathgard, he governs his small farming barony of Tarmoral on the eastern edge of Galath, where the realm meets the Falconspires mountain range, and a trade-road leads up out of Galath into Arvale. Tindror's neighbor and longtime foe is Baron Mrantos Murlstag.

Trar, Imb: Satrap (regional ruler) of Scarlorn. A master actor and diplomat, who sees intrigue and manipulation of local wealthy merchants as the key to his own strong rule and the lasting contentment of his people.

Ulkrar, Gelzund: Armsmaster (weapons trainer and captain-of-the-guard) to Lord Tharlark of Arbridge. A cruel, capable man, and an accomplished warrior.

Ult: Wizard of Galath, who built Ult Tower, a black stone keep in the heart of the realm that he magically linked to himself, stone by stone, so the tower was like his skin; he could feel what was done to it and see out of it. The wizard Arlaghaun took over his body and conquered his mind, inhabiting both, and so gained control of Ult Tower.

Umbaerim, Belgard: Armsman of Tarmoral and trusted bodyguard of Baron Darl Tindror.

Vargrym, Narjak: "Trusty" (fetch-and-carry worker) at The Gauntlet and Feather tavern in Bowrock.

Vengeful, the: Secret society of Falconfar, male-dominated, who meet masked in upper rooms of nights, to plot how to find and slay wizards—for they deem all use of magic a "dangerous affront to the gods" that "twists and stains" those who dare to try it. The Vengeful have a strong chapter in Arvale, and (as fear of Arlaghaun grows) are gaining strength in all places that border Galath. All three of the Dooms have encouraged the Vengeful; their scouring the lands of hidden and lesser wizards eliminates potential rivals by slaying wizards or forcing them to seek refuge and apprenticeship with the Dooms.

Waerlyn, Laranna: A beautiful, graceful woman who works as a "castle courtesan" (hostess) for Velduke Darendarr Deldragon, in his keep in Bowrock.

Windtalon, Yars: Arduke of Galath (noble), a tall, debonair, exotic-looking (almond-colored eyes, wears his copper-hued hair in a shoulder-length, free-flowing mane) nobleman who often hunts (or fights) alongside his friend, Arduke Laskrar Storm-serpent.

Wundaxe, Baurgar: Dwarf warrior, guardian at the gates of the mountain fortress of Stonebold.

Xlanglar, Gethkur: Armsman of Tarmoral and trusted bodyguard of Baron Darl Tindror.

Xeldrar, Raeth: A veteran knight of Hollowtree, on duty at the gates of Hollowtree Keep, who with his fellow duty-guard Samdlor Zarzel saw Rod Everlar first appear in Falconfar.

Xzemros, Amandur ("ZEM-rose"): Trusted arms-man of Bowrock, stationed in Deldragon's keep.

Yarandur, Tarsil: Trusted and loyal knight of Bowrock, stationed in Deldragon's keep.

Yardryk: Wizard, apprentice to Arlaghaun; young, supremely arrogant and ambitious. More capable at magic than his master the Doom of Galath believes him to be, but not capable enough to openly rebel or depart Arlaghaun's service and hope to survive. "Brightrising" is a general nickname given to the successfully ambitious, not part of Yardryk's name.

Zael, Mrauker: Satrap (regional ruler) of Scarlorn. Darkly handsome, popular, and glib.

Zaer, Taraun: High Lord of Zancrast, a bustling independent port city on Ommaun the Wyrmsea (far southeast from Galath, across the Falconspires mountain range). A vain, jaded man who is swift-witted but believes himself to be a genius, and personally irresistable.

Zarzel, Samdlor: A veteran knight of Hollowtree, on duty at the gates of Hollowtree Keep, who with his fellow duty-guard Raeth Xeldrar saw Rod Everlar first appear in Falconfar.

ABOUT THE AUTHOR

Ed Greenwood is known for his role in creating the Forgotten Realms setting, part of the world-famous Dungeons & Dragons® franchise. His writings have sold millions of copies worldwide, in more than a dozen languages. Greenwood resides in the Canadian province of Ontario.

www.solarisbooks.com   UK ISBN: 978-1-84416-651-0   US ISBN: 978-1-84416-588-9

Arch Wizard is the second thrilling adventure in The Falconfar Saga.
Having been drawn into a fantasy world of his own creation, Rod Everlar
continues his quest to defeat the corruption he has discovered within. He
sets off in pursuit of the dark wizard Malraun, only to find that he has
raised an army of monsters and mercenaries in order to conquer the
world...

 SOLARIS FANTASY

"Attractive characters and an imaginative setting combine in an excellent, fast-moving quest novel."
— David Drake, author of the Lord of the Isles series

GAIL Z. MARTIN
THE SUMMONER

Book One of the
CHRONICLES OF THE NECROMANCER

www.solarisbooks.com   ISBN: 978-1-84416-468-4

The world of Prince Martris Drayke is thrown into sudden chaos and disorder when his brother murders their father and seizes the throne. Cast out, Martris and a small band of trusted friends are forced to flee to a neighbouring kingdom to plot their retaliation. But if the living are arrayed against him, Martris must call on a different set of allies: the ranks of the dead...

SOLARIS FANTASY

"A rich, evocative story with vivid, believable characters moving through a beautifully realized world with all the quirks, depths and levels of a real place. A terrific read!"
—A.J. Hartley, author, *The Mask of Atreus*

GAIL Z. MARTIN

THE BLOOD KING

Book Two of the
CHRONICLES OF THE NECROMANCER

www.solarisbooks.com   IISBN: 978-1-84416-531-5

Having narrowly escaped being murdered by his evil brother, Jared, Prince Martris Drayke must take control of his magical abilities to summon the dead, and gather an army big enough to claim back the throne of his dead father. But it isn't merely Jared that Tris must combat. The dark mage, Foor Arontala, has schemes to cause an inbalance in the currents of magic and raise the Obsidian King...

SOLARIS FANTASY

JAMES MAXEY

BITTERWOOD

"For the sake of humanity, join in Bitterwood's revolt." – Kirkus Reviews

www.solarisbooks.com ISBN: 978-1-84416-487-5

It is a time when powerful dragons reign supreme and humans are forced to work as slaves, to support the tyrannical ruler King Albekizan. However, there is one name whispered amongst the dragons that strikes fear into their very hearts and minds: Bitterwood.

◖ SOLARIS FANTASY

JAMES MAXEY

DRAGONFORGE

A NOVEL OF THE DRAGON AGE

"Maxey's world is stunningly imaginative." – Publishers Weekly

www.solarisbooks.com   UK ISBN: 978-1-84416-644-2   US ISBN: 978-1-84416-581-0

After the death of King Albekizan, Shandrazel and his allies struggle to keep the kingdom intact as the radical human prophet, Ragnar, gathers forces to launch a full-scale rebellion against the dragons. When all-out war erupts, legendary dragon hunter, Bitterwood, must face his own personal daemons and choose where his loyalty really lies.

SOLARIS FANTASY

ALL-NEW STORIES BY
JANNY WURTS
HAL DUNCAN
JULIET E McKENNA
CHRIS ROBERSON
AND MORE...

THE SOLARIS BOOK OF NEW

FANTASY

EDITED BY GEORGE MANN

www.solarisbooks.com ISBN: 978-1-84416-523-0

The Solaris Book of New Fantasy is a short story anthology of the highest order showcasing the talents of some of the best loved names and hottest new writers in the fantasy genre. Stories range from classic high fantasy to contemporary dark fantasy and include new works by Janny Wurts, Hal Duncan, Juliet E. McKenna, Steven Erikson, Lucius Shepard, Mike Resnick, Mark Chadbourn, Chris Roberson and many others.

Ⓠ SOLARIS FANTASY